MW01611313

The Reluctant Debutante

Ladies of Mayfair
~ Book Four ~

WENDY MAY ANDREWS

CB&O

Sparrow Ink
www.sparrowdeck.com

Dedication

To everyone in my life who has stood by me through this amazing journey, especially this particular project when I had to second guess everything.

Mum & Dad, you have supported me through thick and thin since birth. Thank you so much!

To my hubby, you are the very best! Your support means the world to me and makes all this possible. I love you forever.

Angelika and Monika, thanks for listening to everything over and over. I couldn't do it without your friendship xoxo

Acknowledgements

Jahleen Turnbull-Sousa, this was the best edit ever. Thank you for taking on this project and helping it become even better. I look forward to this new adventure together.

German Creative, I am in love with my cover. You were so easy to work with and so kind despite my insistence when something wasn't quite right and my not really knowing what I was doing. Thank you for your patience and the final beautiful product.

Clean Indie Reads, my online tribe, thank you for kindly answering all my newbie questions. The online world can be a very scary place so it's wonderful to find such a large group of supportive, knowledgeable writers who are willing to lend a helping hand or a listening ear.

Chapter One

"Who is that ravishing creature entering the devil's lair?" Bryghton Alcott, the fifth Duke of Wychwood, asked his friend, his gaze arrested by the slender figure climbing the stairs to a midsize townhouse as they rode past.

Turning in his saddle to gape at the young woman, Lord Lynster grinned, thrilled to know something his powerful friend did not. He turned back to face the duke. "You don't know who that is?"

"Would I be asking you if I knew?" Bryghton said, with a wry twist to his lips.

His left eyebrow tilted at a somewhat haughty angle, the young baron finally answered with a touch of dramatic flair, "That, my good fellow, is the devil's niece, Lady Victoria Bartley."

"Really?" the duke asked, incredulity now echoed in his voice. "How did I not know that the devil had a niece? Surely this information could be used to my advantage."

"I have no idea how you could have researched your enemy so thoroughly and yet not know that he is living in his niece's house. I never thought to mention it since it seemed to be a matter of common knowledge. Of course, the lady was a child when the devil inherited her father's title, so I suppose you took no note of her existence."

Alcott's face held a far-away expression for a few moments before his gaze sharpened on his friend's face. "You said the devil is living in her house. What do you mean?"

"The earl only inherited what was entailed. The previous earl doted on his only child and left everything that was unentailed to his daughter, including the London townhouse we just rode past. The new earl, the young lady's uncle, is her guardian until she gains control of her own fortune. As such, he and his family live with Lady Victoria when they are in Town. She lives with them in her former home when they are in the country." Alfred, Lord Lynster, "Fred" to his friends, looked at Bryghton with a touch of anxiety, unsure of how his friend would use this information to his advantage. "The young woman faced much tragedy at a tender age, losing both her parents in that terrible carriage accident that made the devil the earl."

"Yes, and no doubt she could use a friend, being stuck in the same house with Bartley and his family as she is," concurred the duke, his handsome face darkened by a sinister cast.

"What are you about, your grace?" asked the baron with sharp suspicion.

"Oh don't 'your grace' me, Fred. Despite my vendetta against her uncle, I am not about to begin preying upon an innocent young woman. She is perfectly safe from me. If I were to manage an acquaintance with her it would merely be a fact-finding mission, I assure you." Bryghton mustered an almost convincing look of innocence despite his strong desire to grin over his friend's evidently mixed feelings.

"I fully understand your desire to seek your revenge from the earl, but you really should leave his female relatives out of it."

"Of course, of course," the duke soothed, without full sincerity. "Now where were we riding to? I declare your chatter has completely discomfited me."

Alfred, placated, answered with a low chuckle, sarcasm dripping from each syllable. "I am sure it was my chatter which distracted you. You are just trying to avoid seeing your mother."

"How could you say such a hurtful thing to a peer of the realm?" Wychwood mocked.

"Well then, lead on. Our tea is no doubt growing cold as we speak."

"You just want to witness another one of my mother's scenes where she tries ever not so subtly to persuade me that I am ready to be leg shackled."

"She merely wishes to secure the succession. Wychwood is a fine old name and it would never do to allow it to die out, my friend."

"With Drake still hale and hearty it is in little danger of dying out," the duke declared with a roll of his eyes.

"Well, according to your mother one of you needs to produce an heir before she leaves this world."

"And there you have hit the problem right on the nose. Ever since I had the nerve of doing something so déclassé as entering my thirtieth year, my mother has been taking on the airs of one who is on her deathbed. Never mind that she is only fifty and is as healthy as a work horse."

With a twinkle in his eye, Alfred struggled for seriousness. "Never allow your mother to hear you comparing her to a beast of burden, nor revealing her age. I am quite sure she is still trying to convince her suitors that she is barely a day over forty."

"Well, she will catch cold at that, since she is forever harping upon my thirty years. She may have been a young bride, but I am quite sure my father did not invade the schoolroom in order to marry her."

Having the final say as always, Alfred said the only thing that his friend could not argue with. "At least you have a mother to harp at you."

Bryghton glanced at his friend uncomfortably. Loving his mother fiercely despite her meddling in his affairs, Bryghton could not imagine how his friend had endured the loss of his own the previous year. Alfred's words won him the argument, and for the first time in several months the duke was relieved to see his mother's house come into view, having been struck by a sudden urge to see her.

Riding around to the mews, the two gentlemen threw their reins to the waiting grooms and dismounted. As the head groom came out to greet them, the duke addressed him.

"We shall be a while with the duchess, Gerrard. Be so kind as to ensure they are properly watered while they wait."

"Very good, your grace," answered the servant deferentially before continuing in more familiar accents. "Enjoy your visit with your mum."

Grinning, the duke answered with a wink, "I shall try."

Striding towards the front of the elegant townhouse, Bryghton called over his shoulder to his shorter friend, "Hurry along Fred, you did say you do not wish to drink cold tea."

He struggled to maintain a straight face as he heard a snort coming from behind.

Chapter Two

"The Duke of Wychwood and Baron of Fielding to see you, your grace," intoned the faithful butler.

"Thank you, Walter. Please have the tea brought in shortly," answered the duchess as she rose gracefully to greet her guests.

"Hello, Mother. You are looking lovely as ever." The duke bent over her hand and gave her a quick kiss on the cheek.

"I am so pleased that you have finally graced me with your presence, you naughty boy. And you brought your friend Alfred, how lovely. Come give me a kiss, Alfred, and tell me all that is new with you. How is my dear friend, your Aunt Sybil? It has been some time since I have heard from her. I hope she has not fallen into ill health."

"No, no, your grace. Thank you for asking after her. She is quite well. Aunt Sybil has been staying with my little sister since my mother passed. Now my sister is getting ready to come up for her first Season, so you can just imagine what an uproar the household is in."

"Is little Eloise really coming to make her debut? How delightful! Yes, poor Sybil must be nearly beside herself. I remember what a time we had with Alanna's first Season. Well, I look forward to seeing them about Town when they come up. I must remember to write to her and make some arrangements. Will they be on your estate for a while yet?"

"Oh, yes, your grace. I would not think they would leave home for at least a se'nnight. If you post a note in the next couple of days they shall certainly receive it before they get under way. I am sure

Aunt Sybil and Eloise will be delighted to hear from you. It is kind of you to remember them."

"Not at all, Alfred," dismissed the duchess with graceful kindness before turning to her son. "Now you, my boy, are another thing all together. Why has it taken you so long to get around to visiting your mother?"

Surprised by the urge to blush and stammer out an excuse, the duke managed to maintain his composure and answer in a voice tinged with ennui, "But surely it has not been that long since my last visit, has it, your grace?"

"Oh, don't get all starchy with me, Alcott. I was merely jesting. You know a fond mama would be very happy if her children visited her every day. Or better yet, if they did not have to visit at all because they still lived under the same roof."

Alcott suppressed a sigh. His mother had never gotten over his desire to have his own home, but lately this conversation had turned into a routine. He vaguely wondered if it was his milestone birthday this year, or her upcoming turn of the half-century that had brought this about. With a thinning smile, he decided to ignore her statements and tried to turn the conversation to something innocuous.

"It is quite lovely outside today, Mother. Have you had an opportunity to take the air?"

"Not yet. I shall be making some visits later this afternoon. I wanted to stop in and welcome that wonderful diplomat's family that has just returned from some assignment or other. You know, they have a charming daughter who will be making a rather late debut into London Society this year. Perhaps you should escort me so that you could meet her," the duchess said with a hopeful lift as her sentence trailed off.

Alcott made every effort not to glower at his mother, turning his glare instead onto his unfaithful friend, who could not quite suppress his snicker at the anticipated direction the conversation had taken. Turning back to his mother after withering Fred with his glare, Bryghton managed to politely decline the invitation. "I must make my excuses, mother, and decline your enticing invitation. Lynster and I are promised elsewhere. Perhaps another time."

"That would be quite lovely," she said, beaming with joy.

Bryghton felt like biting off his tongue at his mother's reaction to his final polite statement. She lived in constant hope of arranging an advantageous match for her children. Thus far she had focused mainly on her oldest son and only daughter, leaving his brother to his own devices for the time being, and much to the duke's disgust. Misery did love company, he thought with sarcastic humour. Thinking of Drake seemed to conjure him from thin air, and the young man strolled into the room with graceful nonchalance.

"Alcott and Lynster! Walter just told me you were here to visit the duchess. How pleasant to see you." The younger gentleman belied his air of disregard by gripping his brother's hand in an affectionate shake and allowing his eyes to twinkle with glee at seeing their mutual friend.

Fred, used to the young lord's pretence of indolence, greeted him with enthusiastic good cheer. "Drake, my boy, it is a delight to set eyes on you. Where have you been? It has been an age since I have seen you about Town."

Seating himself in an elegant sprawl, much to his mother's disgust, Drake shrugged and answered his friend in a voice of studied boredom. "I was rusticating on the family estate, old chap."

His fond mama could not abide by this and interjected. "Do not mind him, Alfred. He wants everyone to think he is the laziest young man in all the king's realm, but he was really doing a round of all our estates checking on our stewards and overseeing the spring breeding programs."

"Mother, must you interfere with my image?" the young man protested, fighting a blush rising up his cheeks.

Happy to have his mother's attention elsewhere, the duke felt his mood lightening and allowed himself to relax and enjoy the moment. He could not resist a pleasant chuckle at his brother's expense. Despite his own discomfort, the young man grinned at his older brother in perfect harmony.

Drake's grin turned devious and he questioned his mother in an innocent tone. "Who did you say you were going to visit this afternoon?"

The duchess grinned in delight over her son's question. Drake's plan to tease his brother fell flat, however, when his mother kept her attention on him. "Would you like to join me, dear? Your brother is busy this afternoon but I would dearly love your escort."

Keeping his smile fixed in place, Drake managed to excuse himself. "I believe I too am occupied this afternoon. But thank you for the invitation. Where are you going?"

The duchess was not overly disappointed, but sighed slightly and said, "Next time then," not bothering to go into detail.

She turned from her sons and focused her attention on Lord Lynster. Although he was merely a baron, his title was an old one and he was reputed to be very wealthy.

"My dear Alfred, you have not yet responded to my invitation to the supper I shall be hosting when the Season gets under way in two weeks. You really must attend in order to ensure my darling Alanna has a successful night. This is her third Season, and I am hoping it will be her last."

Poor Fred, suddenly looking quite uncomfortable, replied, "Of course, your grace, I apologize profusely for my negligence in not responding sooner. I would not dream of missing your event." He quickly sought to steer the conversation elsewhere. "Your grace, on the ride over here we saw someone we thought we should ask you about. Are you familiar with Lady Bartley?"

Bryghton was surprised at his friend's choice of conversational gambit, but delighted that he had brought it up. It was actually a brilliant idea on Fred's part, since it would keep the duchess from getting her hopes up about a Fred-Alanna alliance, and it helped the duke get the information without needing to ask himself. He would never in a million years ask his mother about any female, since she would instantly be set on arranging a match, even one as ineligible as this—Bryghton would never have a romantic interest in the devil's niece.

"Lady Bartley? The Earl of Pickering's wife? She is a rather mousey woman who has nothing of interest to say if her husband is anywhere around, but on her own she can be a pleasant enough companion, I suppose." The duchess paused and wrinkled her nose as she gave the matter more thought. "She almost never goes about in Society. She has a somewhat bourgeois background and is no doubt not completely comfortable in highborn company. Why would you be curious about her?"

Looking embarrassed, Fred explained himself. "I apologize, your grace. I was unclear. I actually meant Lady Victoria Bartley."

The confused furrow on the duchess' face instantly disappeared. "Of course! I fully understand any interest you might have in her! She is rather ridiculously beautiful, is she not? Poor little soul. Her father was the proper Earl of Pickering but he and his wife died when she was about twelve years old. She was an only child, so upon the earl's death his title and estate went to his younger brother. Lady Victoria's parents were a kind, lovely couple, well liked by everyone. Her mama comes from a nice family. I was friends with one of her sisters when I was a girl. The earl and his wife doted on their daughter and left her very well provided for financially but rather carelessly left her to the guardianship of the new earl."

The duchess warmed to her subject and carried on her tirade of gossip. "While I do not believe the girl is being ill-treated, you cannot say she is getting proper care either. She must be at least twenty and has yet to make her curtsy to the Queen or Society. She should be getting married and setting up her own home by now instead of looking after all her little cousins, which is what I have heard she is doing. Her aunt and uncle are using her as little more than a governess!" The duchess seemed genuinely distressed over this, and a lull fell over the conversation while everyone digested this information.

Drake and Bryghton both looked uncomfortable at the mention of the Earl of Pickering. Their mother had been kept blissfully ignorant of any details of their feud with the vulgar little man and they wished to keep it that way.

The Duchess of Wychwood looked at her firstborn with shrewdly narrowed eyes for a moment. "Lady Victoria might make a good duchess," she mused. "Perhaps I should invite her to my party."

This was a bit more than Bryghton could stomach. "She might make a good duchess for someone else, but not for me. I cannot understand you, mother. One would think you should never wish to become a dowager. Why are you so anxious to see me wed?"

Taken aback by the fierceness of her son's words, the duchess merely blinked at him for a moment while forming her reply. "I know it will no doubt be quite dreadful to become the dowager duchess, but if it is the price I must pay, I am willing to do so. We owe it to the House of Wychwood to ensure that our name does not die out. I would rather be the dowager and be around to meet your babies and help guide your wife than keep my position as the duchess and mistress of your homes and risk the end of all that your father and grandfather held so dear." At this point she grew misty-eyed, and her sons became truly uncomfortable.

Drake shot his brother an ugly look as he shifted closer to his mother to pat her on the back rather awkwardly. "Do not worry, mama. Bryght knows what he owes to our name. You just have to give him a bit more time. And you are far too young to be a grandmama any time soon anyway."

It was the perfectly correct thing to say at that moment and their mother brightened considerably. "Well, those are very true words you have uttered there, Drakey. I am too young to be a grandmother. But I do think I should like to become a mother-in-law sometime in the not-too-distant future."

After that heavy-handed hint, the duchess delicately wiped her eyes with a kerchief and stood gracefully. The three gentlemen quickly rose as well. "Thank you so much for coming for a visit, but I must bid you farewell for now. I must make my preparations for making my morning calls."

Accepting their dismissal, the three gentlemen bade their farewells and watched the duchess depart from the room. After the sound of her footsteps disappeared up the stairs, they burst into raucous laughter.

"These visits are getting worse each time!" said Fred. "I usually find them highly diverting, since she never turns her matchmaking attentions my way, but this time she went over the top! Do you really think she was serious about matching me up with your sister?"

"Well, you could do much worse!" answered the duke.

"That is not the point!" declared the harried young baron. "Alanna is a lovely girl, but I am far from ready to become leg shackled."

"Welcome to my life," Bryghton said with a grin, restored to good humour. "Now that our duty is done here, shall we be off?"

"What are you two up to this afternoon?" asked Drake with mild curiosity.

"We were debating between going a couple rounds at Gentleman Jack's or taking a ride in the park. I am leaning more towards the boxing studio, since going to the park will only lead to the ladies getting their hopes up."

Fred rolled his eyes at this arrogant statement before turning to his friend's brother. "Why do you ask? Did you wish to accompany us?"

Drake made an effort to maintain his air of disregard but it was nearly impossible to hide his eagerness for the promise of sport. He gave a negligent shrug, belying the gleam in his eye. "I could probably bring myself to take one of you on in the ring."

Bryghton laughed at the understatement. "You are welcome to join us, cub. Hurry up and tell the footman to have our mounts readied."

Drake gave a mocking salute to his brother before striding from the room with a jaunty step.

Turning to his friend, the duke enquired, "You do not mind having him tag along, do you, Fred? He can be a bit of a pest at times, but he's not a bad fellow."

Fred laughed good-naturedly. "I don't mind at all. You do realize he is much older than the twelve years you seem to make him out to be?"

"In years, perhaps," was all Bryghton would admit to as they strode from the room in fine humour.

Chapter Three

"Gwennie, please be careful. Please don't get too close to the edge of the water. You can see the pretty ducks from over here." Victoria watched with anxiety as her young cousins threw bread crumbs to the greedy birds along the edge of the Serpentine.

Seeing that the children were ignoring her, she shared a look of exasperation with their nursemaid, Pansy, and the two of them went to grab the children before disaster struck.

"Come along, Gwen, Felicia, Vanessa, and Daniel. That is enough time spent with the ducks. We ought to be heading home shortly. Did you not want to play ball for a few minutes before we get on our way?" Victoria was hoping her distraction tactic would work so she would not have to move on to threats to get the single-minded children to listen to her.

Victoria was thrilled when her ploy seemed to have success. The three girls finally responded to her coaxing and turned reluctantly towards her. Vanessa grabbed her brother's hand as she turned to go. Daniel, just turned three and stubborn as a goat, as Pansy would say, was not ready to go. He yanked hard on his hand, breaking his sister's hold. He regained control of his arm but lost his balance in the process. Looking on in horror, Victoria watched her youngest cousin topple over the bank into the Serpentine.

Victoria's heart seemed to stop, then resume beating at triple its speed. Her surroundings disappeared from her senses as she picked up her skirts and ran to the banks of the river. Seeing, with relief, that the water at this particular spot was neither too deep nor very swift, Victoria did not even pause to remove her boots, but plunged into the water to retrieve the little boy.

Poor little Daniel had not yet learned how to swim, so in his fear he merely thrashed about. His small fist connected sturdily with Victoria's jaw as she reached to scoop him up. This momentarily paused her rescue effort, and she called sharply to him in an attempt to settle him down.

"Daniel, my sweetheart, you must stop flailing about! You are going to drown us both."

Her voice got through to him and he turned his wild eyes to meet hers and reached frantically towards her. Relieved, Victoria grasped him and pulled him towards her. He wrapped his arms and legs tightly around her while she stood in the chest-deep water and contemplated their precarious situation. She looked at the bank and wondered how they could possibly scale it without ending up back in the water. Despair tapped at the back of her mind as she saw the three girls and Pansy standing on the edge crying and wringing their hands.

Victoria called up to them in an attempt to reassure. "Do not worry, girls. I have him and we will get out very soon."

Anything more she might have said was drowned out, as Daniel picked that moment to put an end to his silent terror and began to wail.

"Hush, Daniel. That is not a very manly way to handle this situation. What would Everett say if he saw you at this moment?" Victoria realized she must be truly desperate if she was trying to calm Daniel by mentioning her oldest cousin. He was the firstborn of her uncle's children, the cherished heir, and he delighted to lord his position over his younger siblings. Daniel adored him. But even this could not motivate the terrified toddler to silence.

All she could do was try to cuddle the small child until he began to calm. She hugged him to her and spoke soft, comforting words into his ear. As his wails began to slowly subside, she again glanced up to the bank of the river. She almost dropped Daniel in surprise, as on the bank staring down at her were three handsome men.

A fierce blush stole over her entire body, which served to momentarily warm her against the chill of the water swirling around her. One of the men was particularly striking, and, despite herself, Victoria had trouble tearing her eyes away from his. The man did not seem to care how rude he was being in staring at her, and seemed mesmerized by her nonsensical mutterings to her young charge. Finally, he caught himself from his reverie and sprang into action.

Stripping his perfectly tailored coat from his shoulders was a momentary effort. Disregarding the hard work of his tailor and valet, the duke shrugged out of it and tossed it to his brother as he called over his shoulder to Fred. "Bring our horses closer. If I cannot leverage her up the bank on my own, they can be of assistance."

Keeping his voice as low and calm as possible, Bryghton reached down towards the frightened child. "Hand him over to me. We shall get him on shore first, and then we can more easily pull you up."

Despite having calmed down, at these words Daniel tightened his grip on his only means of survival and let out another frightened wail.

"Daniel, my darling, it is going to be all right. This kind man is going to pull you up and give you to Pansy. Pansy will have a lovely warm blanket to wrap you in and I am quite sure she still has a couple of those delicious cookies you loved so much. If you are very brave and let go of me, I promise you can have the biggest piece of dessert that Cook has prepared for us tonight."

These were magical words, and Daniel pulled back and looked his cousin in the eye with a serious expression. He thought the matter over for half a minute, looking between his cousin and the stranger. Just behind the stranger he could see Pansy and his sisters. The deciding factor was the other man holding the halter of three large, magnificent horses. Daniel reached his arms towards the stranger.

"That's a good boy," Bryghton called his encouragement as he reached for the sopping child. With no visible effort he pulled the boy up and handed him over to the maid, somehow managing to remain perfectly dry himself.

Victoria was beginning to feel quite miserable. She was soaked from head to toe, most of her body immersed in the water. Her heavy skirts were feeling like lead weights as they pulled her towards the current. Her boots were slowly sinking into the sludge on the river bottom. And the gorgeous stranger was now looking at her appraisingly.

"Can you reach my hand?"

Victoria felt a shiver slither up her back at the sound of his deep voice as he leaned down for her.

Wishing there were some other way, Victoria looked at him then up and down the river once more. Unfortunately, the riverbanks had not changed in the last few minutes and there was still no way to get up the bank on her own. Turning back to the stranger, she gritted her teeth and stretched out her hand.

Bryghton was struck by the young woman's beauty. Her remarkable eyes held so much expressive emotion. He could tell she was scared and embarrassed but she had the wit to realize she had little choice if she wished to be rescued from her precarious position. The duke knew that not too much farther downstream the river deepened considerably.

The feel of her cold little hand in his large, warm one sent a strange sensation through him, but he knew this was not the time to be distracted. Despite her slight frame, her soaking clothes were weighing her down considerably, and effort would be required to get her out. In a similar gesture to hers, he too gritted his teeth and yanked on her arm.

With a plop, and after a swift scrabble up the bank, Victoria landed on the edge of the river next to the impeccably dressed, handsome stranger. Blushing again, she offered a shy, hesitant smile as she pushed herself to a seated position.

"Thank you so much for your help, sir. You showed up in the nick of time."

Adrenaline was dissipating, leaving strong emotions in its wake. "It was a ridiculously foolish thing to do, jumping into the water fully clothed without a plan as to how you were going to get out," Bryghton declared with vehemence.

Blinking rapidly in shock over his words, Victoria gaped at the stranger.

"I appreciate your help, sir, but you have no place censoring me in this way. What do you suggest would have been a better response to my cousin falling in the river? Would you rather I had stood on the banks wringing my hands as he drifted away and drowned?"

By this point Victoria had risen to her feet and her words brought them both up short. Bryghton realized he was being a beast as her eyes welled up with tears in reaction to the very real danger her little charge had been in. Struggling to maintain her composure and her footing as she swayed in her dripping, heavy clothes, Victoria took a deep breath to calm herself and continued in much more sedate tones.

"Perhaps you are right, sir. Thank you for pointing out the error of my ways. Should I ever be in the unenviable position of witnessing a loved one falling into a body of water, I will do my best to find a better solution to the dilemma than throwing myself in after them."

Impressed by her lack of deference and the recovery of her composure, Bryghton forced an unusual apology past his lips.

"No, I was wrong. What else could you have done, really? How were you to know we were coming along and could have helped you? You did the best you could in a terrible situation. I am just glad we happened along to lend a hand. It was very brave of you to jump in after him rather than wringing your hands, as you said."

At this point the others began to chime in. "Oh, m'lady, that was the grandest thing you did! I wouldn't have known what to do if you weren't with us!" cried Pansy, weeping indelicately into her sleeve.

Embarrassed by all the commotion, Victoria patted the maid lightly on the back as she bracingly said, "I have every faith that you would have thought of something if I had not been here, Pansy. Everything turned out fine, so please do not carry on so. These fine gentlemen were here to lend us a hand just at the right time. Was that not lucky?"

Victoria continued patting Pansy's back while all the children crowded around needing their own reassurances. Looking on, the men could not help but admire the young lady's composure despite her frightening experience.

"Thank you once again, sir. We must not hold you and your companions up any longer. Daniel and I really must be getting home since the poor little dear will no doubt catch a chill if we do not get him out of his wet things as soon as possible."

"You should probably get out of your wet things as soon as possible too," said Drake quickly before turning bright red with embarrassment over his inappropriate comment.

Taking pity on the poor young man, Victoria smiled as benignly as possible through her own discomfort. "Come along children, we must not take any more of these nice gentlemen's time."

Exchanging an uncomfortable glance, the three men each launched into speech.

"Do not leave on our account," Fred beseeched.

"Could we at least escort you home?" asked Drake.

Overriding them all, the duke, ever in charge, stepped forward, picked up Daniel and said with finality, "We will see that you all safely arrive home."

Unused to anyone taking over her control, Victoria blinked in confusion before hastening to catch up, as the duke had walked away without even a by your leave.

Her brow knitted in frustration, Victoria reached out to take Daniel from him. "I do not even know your name—you cannot just walk away with my cousin," she said, anger colouring her tones.

Overhearing, Fred and Drake both began to laugh. "That should put him in his place, do you not think, Fred?"

"I must say, I have never known of a pretty young woman not knowing who the Duke of Wychwood is. We must make note of this date—an Alcott of Wychwood was anonymous for once."

Bryghton threw a withering look in their direction before turning back to face Victoria. "I apologize, m'lady. Please forgive my rudeness." With a flourishing bow, he presented himself. "I am Bryghton Alcott, the fifth Duke of Wychwood."

A hot flush stained Victoria's cheeks as she realized the social faux pas she had just committed. "Your grace, I apologize. My only excuse is that I do not go about in Society."

"Please, no apology is necessary. I do not know who you are either, so let us call it even. Allow me to present my brother Drake and my good friend Lord Alfred Lynster. You may call him Fred if you wish to be friends with him."

Victoria bobbed a polite curtsy to the gentlemen before again reaching for Daniel. After settling the tired little boy in her arms she introduced herself and the children. "I am Lady Victoria Bartley. My uncle is the Earl of Pickering. These lovely young people are his youngest children. This is Gwendolyn, Felicia, Vanessa, and Daniel."

While making the introductions, Victoria had been looking at the children and had thus missed the significant looks being exchanged between the three men. When she glanced back at them she saw awkward discomfort displayed on Drake's face, but she mistakenly thought he was still embarrassed over his earlier comment, so she chose to ignore it.

"We do not live far from the park, so you need not escort us home. We shall be fine on our own. But thank you so much for all you have done."

Victoria hoisted Daniel into a more comfortable position, and then grabbed Vanessa's hand. Just before turning away she remembered her manners. "It was a pleasure to meet the three of you. Goodbye."

Bryghton found that he did not want to see her leave. "May I call on you some time?"

Drake and Alfred looked at him in shock. The duke tried to ignore them but could not suppress a wry grin over the absurdity of him asking a lady if he could call on her.

Victoria surprised them all. "Thank you, your grace. Please do not think I am unaware of the great honour you have paid me, but I do not think that would be wise. I do not receive guests." With another curtsy, Victoria turned and walked away, Pansy and the other girls hurrying after her.

Chapter Four

The three men stood watching the small group walk away, with varying degrees of disbelief imprinted on their features. Bryghton, trained from birth to reveal as little of his feelings as possible, had a nearly impassive face despite being the most shocked.

"What just happened?" asked Drake.

"Your brother was turned down for the first time in his life," said Fred with exaggerated, sarcastic politeness.

The duke turned to his companions with a sardonic grin. "You two could be at court as jesters, you are just that funny."

Drake looked at his brother in inquiry. "Why would you ask her if you could call on her? While she seemed to be a perfectly lovely young woman, you would never go to the devil's house, no matter how wonderful she might be."

Fred draped his arm around the young man. "Do not trouble yourself, your all-knowing brother no doubt has some plan to use this encounter to our advantage in some way." Then, turning to the duke, he asked, "So, what is your plan? How are you going to use the earl's niece to exact revenge?"

Loath to admit that the thought never even crossed his mind while he had been speaking with her, the duke put them off for the time being. "The plan has not yet been fully formulated." Not wanting to pursue the topic, Bryghton looked down at himself. "What do you think? Am I still passable, or must I return home and change before we continue on with our outing?"

Ever accommodating, Fred reassured his friend, "Never fear, Bryght. You look perfectly fine. Just brush off your knee there a little bit and no one will ever know you had been crawling along the bank of the Serpentine this afternoon."

Despite his discomfiture over the mention of Pickering, Drake hastened forward to act as valet and assist his brother back into his tightly fitted jacket.

"Even though it was strange to have run into her, I suppose it is good that we decided to cut through the park on the way to Jackson's. I must admit to being uncomfortable over any mention of the earl, but as a gentleman one must always be ready to come to a lady's aid no matter who her relatives may be." Drake admitted this almost reluctantly, and his brother laughed at his expense.

"You are quite correct, young cub. Now let us be off—I shall need to go a couple rounds to work off the energy generated from that wee bit of a scare."

Alfred turned a look of surprise upon the duke. "Were you actually scared, Alcott?"

"I am man enough to admit that when I saw the little boy tip over the edge and the lady jump in after him, I had a terrible feeling in the pit of my stomach. I cannot say if it was fear, but it was undoubtedly uncomfortable."

The duke's companions had to admit they had felt the same, so they merely nodded. The three men climbed back onto their now restless mounts and continued on their way.

Despite his expertise in the ring that day, it was clear the duke's attention was elsewhere. Drake was ecstatic to come so close to besting his older brother, and he gloated over his near win.

"I have never in all my life come so close to beating you, Bryght. I must be getting better at boxing." The young man was almost giddy with glee.

Not wanting to burst the youngster's bubble, the duke smiled indulgently. Fred was not nearly so circumspect. "Surely you realize it was merely the duke's inattention that allowed you to actually plant him a facer."

"Be that as it may, you cannot dispute the fact that I did draw some claret. That split in his lip does not lie," declared the young man with pride. "It does not matter how it happened, as long as I did not blindside him."

"Let him be, Fred. The cub displayed to advantage. I was distracted, but he is correct. I should never have allowed my thoughts to get in the way. It was a fair fight, Drake, and you did well. I would say you are improving. We shall have to go a couple rounds again soon."

Grinning with delight at his older brother, Drake left the sporting club with his two companions, the three gentlemen setting off towards St. James Street to enjoy a brief repast at White's before going their separate ways for the evening.

"You have been rather quiet," Bryghton commented to his brother after they had waved off Lord Lynster.

Drake's shrug demonstrated his lack of interest in discussing the matter, but the duke persisted. "Come on young cub, 'fess up to your big brother. What is troubling your mind?"

"I have been thinking about Lady Victoria," Drake admitted with reluctant slowness.

"Might I ask why?"

"She was so brave jumping in to save the little boy like that, without any concern for her own well-being."

He paused for so long that Bryghton thought he was finished with his statement, but then Drake continued. "I was thinking about the fact that she is no doubt innocent from any involvement in her uncle's schemes, and we should not involve her in any revenge we might be seeking. In fact," he warmed to his topic, turning bright eyes to regard his brother closely, "I think you should leave any revenge solely to me. It was my mess from the beginning. You should not be involved with pursuing the earl. And if you wish to seek a closer acquaintance with Lady Victoria you should not consider my feelings on the matter."

Bryghton was shocked into silence momentarily. Recovering himself, he kept a tight rein on his feelings as he answered. "But Drake, of course it involves me! What the earl did to you was despicable. And I feel very responsible. Not only because you are my little brother and I am the head of our house—as such I would feel as though I were involved anyway, but also because I should have ensured you were better occupied. If I had realized how bored you were, I would have satisfied your need for occupation within the dukedom. You would not have then felt the need to try to earn your own blunt through the earl's questionable investment prospects."

Drake shook his head in denial. "I wanted to prove to you that I did not need your patronage, that I could do it on my own."

"You always were ridiculously independent," chided Bryghton, fondly.

Drake again offered a negligent shrug. "If I failed to mention my appreciation for how little recrimination you have offered, I apologize. It was a foolish decision to spend all my money buying into Pickering's scheme. And then when I made myself a laughing stock by going after him at his club! You curtailed any lectures you so obviously wanted to offer, and instead sent me on the rounds of your estates to oversee the stewards. Not only did that teach me so much—things that I will need to know to run my own estate after it recovers from the mortgage I placed on it—but it also got me out of Town to wait for the scandal to die down."

"Drake, my boy, I do not think there was a scandal. Yes, it was a touch irregular to try to challenge the earl to a duel over a business deal gone wrong, which is how many think of it, but there are far more shocking affairs going on regularly, so no one is overly concerned with your little scene."

"Be that as it may, I was mortified by the entire ordeal and I appreciate how you handled it. Despite how you occasionally speak to me as though I were still at Eton, you did not ring a peel over me, nor did you attempt to thrash me."

"How could I have thrashed you when Viscount Dalton had already done a rather thorough job of it for the insult he felt you had offered to his uncle?"

Drake's face took on a thunderous cast, but he forbore to comment on that. "As I was saying, you need not pursue vengeance against the earl. It is my affair, and you need not avoid contact with his niece in order to spare my feelings. She seemed lovely, and I am certain I would soon get over my discomfort at any mention of her uncle."

"My boy, I am not certain what you think took place today, but while Lady Victoria is uncommonly good looking I cannot overlook her connection with the Earl of Pickering. I appreciate your generous offer of absolution from the feud, but I do not want it. I did not care for the earl before he fleeced you, I despise him now, and cannot stomach the thought of pursuing any sort of connection with him."

"Well, then, why did you ask her if you could call on her?"

"That, young cub, is a mystery."

Giving his brother a dubious look, Drake finally allowed the subject to drop, and bade the duke a fond farewell. Bryghton remained behind at the club for a few moments longer, staring into his glass of brandy as he contemplated their conversation and the events of the day. Shaking his head to rid himself of the doldrums, the duke realized there were no answers to be had in his glass, so he tossed back the rest of his drink and strode with purpose from the club.

Chapter Five

Victoria huddled in her room near the nursery, wishing there was a fire going. She was rarely allotted the luxury of having a fire during the day unless she had fallen ill. The shiver deep in her bones made her think that might not be far from the truth, but she hesitated to make more work for the servants since they were constantly kept so busy by her aunt and uncle. Her uncle was such a pinchpenny he kept the barest minimum of staff, so all the help were terribly overworked. She was still debating with herself whether or not to disturb any of the servants when Pansy scratched on her door.

Catching sight of the young lady huddled under the quilt, the young maid bounded into the room. "Oh, m'lady, don't say you've gone and catched the cold! What should I do, m'lady? Should I fetch Mrs. Marks?"

"Do not trouble the housekeeper, Pansy. I am finally starting to feel warm. I was just so worried about little Daniel that I waited too long to get my own wet clothes off," Victoria replied in an attempt to soothe the distraught nursemaid.

"I think you should ring for someone to fetch you something," Pansy insisted.

"Well, a cup of tea would be quite lovely, I must admit."

"I'll tell Mary to fetch it right off, m'lady," said the young maid, her tone earnest.

"Thank you, Pansy. Are the children settled in comfortably after their scare?"

"Oh, m'lady, do not worrit your head over them, they are playing as though nothin' out of ordinary happened a'tall."

"Well, that is good, so they will not miss me if I wait here a few moments longer." She sighed with relief.

"You just go and take all the time you want, m'lady." Pansy bustled around the small room, dragging another blanket from the wardrobe to drape it over her young mistress. "You need to warm up quick like and not catch your death. I don't think I can handle those children on my own, m'lady."

Victoria could not prevent the dry chuckle at this self-serving statement. "I will do my best to survive in order to accommodate you and the children."

Realizing how her words had sounded, Pansy had a good laugh at her own expense. "So sorry, m'lady. I promise I didn't mean it that way."

Victoria smiled warmly. "Never fear, Pansy. I took no offense. But if you would not mind leaving me be for a few minutes, I would dearly love to close my eyes and rest."

"Oh m'lady, say no more. Of course I'll leave you be. You jest close yer eyes and get a wee rest." The young nursemaid bustled around a bit more, but then finally left Victoria in blessed silence.

Victoria tried to get a short nap, but when she closed her eyes all she could see was the handsome face of the Duke of Wychwood peering down at her from the bank of the Serpentine. His warm green eyes had twinkled at her, even though he had considered her foolish beyond belief. Despite his haughtiness, which she usually found to be most off-putting, she had been drawn to him in some way she could not comprehend.

Leery of men in general, as she had spent most of her life at finishing school where the only male figure was the aging dancing instructor who had been brought in once a week, Victoria had been struck almost mute in the company of the three noblemen. It was only her concern for the children that had forced speech from her lips.

When the duke had asked if he could call on her she had very nearly swallowed her own tongue in shock. She asked herself yet again, Why would the handsome man want to visit me? And a duke, at that? Not that it mattered why. There was no chance of her ever entertaining a visitor. She could never imagine asking her uncle or aunt for permission. Her position in the household felt tenuous enough without her asking such a request. Victoria shivered at the thought of the scene that would no doubt ensue.

Sitting up in her bed, Victoria flung off the covers and forced herself to climb out. Nothing would be accomplished by wool-gathering, she admonished herself. Daydreaming about handsome dukes was a pointless activity. She would probably never see the man again. The children were no doubt wondering what had become of her. With a final sigh, Victoria slipped her shoes back on and left her room, making haste to return to the nursery.

"Aunt Victoria!" Gwendolyn announced with delight as Victoria stepped into the room. All the children stopped their activities and ran to embrace their favourite relative. "We were so worried when Pansy said we were not to disturb you." The serious young girl looked truly troubled over the thought of something being amiss with her beloved "aunt."

Returning the girl's warm embrace, Victoria soothed, "Have no fear, I am here," before winking exaggeratedly at her young cousins, causing them to laugh uproariously. Not wanting the youngsters to be troubled on her behalf, she quickly turned the subject.

"What have you all been up to since returning home?"

This may not have been the best choice of conversational gambits, as Daniel hastened to pout. "Pansy and Mary made me have a bath, Aunt 'Toria. I hate having a bath."

Swooping in to hug him, Victoria laughed. "I know you do, darling, but you were probably stinky from our adventure in the park." She took a deep breath. "Now you smell delicious."

The little boy giggled. "Good enough to eat?"

"I think so. Definitely good enough to tickle." She promptly suited her actions to her words. The rest of the children joined in as they all gave way to giggles and squeals of delight.

Into this scene walked Everett. As the oldest, he had a terribly inflated opinion of his own importance. Being only eleven, he still hovered between the nursery and young manhood.

"What is going on in here?" he demanded with hauteur.

Looking up from the heap they were in on the floor, the other children blinked at him while they struggled to control their giggles. Victoria was the first to find speech.

"Hello, Everett. We were just playing. Did you enjoy your time with your tutor?" she asked kindly, despite the urge to roll her eyes at his superciliousness.

"Of course, Aunt Victoria. It is very important that I complete my studies if I am to succeed at Eton."

"Of course it is. Which is why the rest of us try our very best to not disturb you while you are busy with your schoolwork. But now you seem to be done. Would you care to join us in some games?"

Trying to remain aloof, Everett struggled to suppress the little boy side of himself that could not help asking, "What kind of games did you have in mind?"

The younger children longed for the attention of their big brother, so Felicia, the middle child who was forever trying to broker peace, generously offered, "If you would like to play with us, you could pick the game."

Everett could not resist this offer. He put his haughtiness aside for a time and fell in with his siblings. "I say we play spillikins," he declared with glee. Felicia ran to the cupboard to grab the sticks as the other children cleared a space on the floor.

Victoria watched happily as the children played together in temporary peace, taking turns trying to pick up each one, giggling at each other as other sticks were jiggled and a turn forfeited. The doting guardian smiled proudly as the older siblings made allowances for little Daniel's lack of skill, voting to allow him two turns to their one because, as Everett said somewhat condescendingly, "he's just a baby."

There was almost a scene over this comment, as Daniel wanted to belligerently deny such a declaration. Peacemaker Felicia stepped in once more with reason. "But Daniel, don't be upset. If Everett says being a baby means you get two chances, you should be happy."

There was no argument for this, even for a three-year-old, so the game continued in harmony. Everyone was amazed at the end when five-year-old Vanessa was found to be the winner. Her small but steady hands had managed to pick up the most sticks from the haphazard pile.

"All right, children, it is almost time for us to go have a visit with your parents, so you should tidy up, comb your hair, and wash your hands. We will be having our supper when we come back to the nursery." Victoria bustled about helping the children ready themselves for the daily ritual of visiting briefly with the earl and countess. It was her least favourite time of day, but she never revealed this to the children.

Gwendolyn quickly arranged herself and, always such a little helper, made herself useful by combing Daniel's hair and retying Vanessa's sash.

"Thank you, Gwennie. You tie the best bows." Victoria grinned at the young girl while she finished straightening Felicia's bow.

After examining all five children, Victoria glanced in the mirror to ensure her hair was sufficiently tidy, and then they all marched down the stairs to be briefly examined by the Bartley parents.

The earl was not always present, but the children's mother made sure she was there every day. Victoria knew her uncle's wife thought it made her an attentive mother to have these brief visits each day with her children, but Victoria could not help contrasting it with how much time her own parents had spent with her when she was a child. They had spent most of her life on their country estate, rarely coming up to the city even when the House was in session. Although she had had a governess, both of her parents had participated in her studies, making sure they knew exactly what she was learning.

Victoria suppressed her sigh, giving her head a firm shake to dispel the bittersweet thoughts as they stood in the foyer waiting for the butler to announce their presence to the countess. This pretension was the earl's idea of formality. It made Victoria and the children feel like visitors in their own home.

Daniel and Vanessa held tightly to Victoria's hands while Felicia and Gwen chewed their lips nervously. Only Everett was able to hide his agitation but Victoria could still detect his fidgets. She tried to distract them with a pleasant thought.

"Mrs. Marks told me Cook has prepared your favourite dessert today, children." Her effort succeeded, as all five of them turned to her with excited grins.

"Truly, Aunty?" asked Felicia, while Everett declared, "All right, custard!" with glee.

All six of them had happy smiles when the butler finally returned to escort them to see Lady Bartley.

"Hello, my children," greeted the mousey woman as the youngsters entered the room and gathered around her. "I am sorry to have to tell you your father could not make it home from his Session in time to see you today."

Daniel pulled his thumb out of his mouth long enough to answer, "That's all right, mama," as he patted her leg before wandering away to stare at a table covered in knickknacks he was not supposed to touch.

Eyeing her son with apprehension, the countess said, "Remember Daniel, you can look but you cannot touch."

"I know, mama." He replied before sticking his thumb back into his mouth.

Turning back to her older children, she asked the same question she asked every day, "So, what have you been up to today?"

The three girls looked at each other before glancing nervously at their cousin, unsure if they should tell their mother about their adventures in the park. Victoria had not told them to keep it a secret; she would never ask them to hide anything from their parents. But the girls still wondered if it was best to keep it to themselves. They were saved momentarily by Everett launching into speech.

"I completed my level of mathematics with my tutor this afternoon, Mother," he announced importantly.

Victoria was happy to see the countess respond with suitable excitement. "Oh, Everett, that is marvellous. I do wish your father were here to congratulate you himself. That is a remarkable accomplishment. You must be proud of yourself. John had mentioned that you were struggling with some of the lessons."

Everett flushed with embarrassment, angry that his tutor had been telling tales behind his back. Victoria winced in sympathy but held back from commenting.

"I may have struggled, but I got through it," he said almost sullenly. "What else did John tell you?"

Realizing her misstep, the countess stammered out an answer. "Not much, Everett, dear. Your father just wants John to keep us apprised of your progress. You know how important it is to the earl that you do well at Eton."

Not appeased, Everett shrugged in an effort to appear unaffected, turning his back on the ladies and joining his little brother in looking about his mother's parlour.

The countess turned to her daughters with upraised eyebrows. Felicia, the typical middle child, and always seeking to make peace, blurted out, "We went to the park today when our lessons were done. Victoria gave us crusts to feed to the ducks."

Lady Bartley smiled rather wanly at her niece over this statement before turning back to her daughters. "That must have been lovely. It was a nice day to be at the park, I am sure."

Gwendolyn, trying to learn grown-up ways, turned to her mother with a question of her own. "What did you do today, Mother?"

Surprised and strangely gratified, the countess' smile finally showed some genuine warmth. "Why thank you so much for asking, Gwendolyn. I had quite a lovely day myself. I spent some time on Bond Street visiting my dressmaker, since I will be attending some special functions with your father. Then I had a few calls to make on some of my friends. And just before you children came to see me I was meeting with Mrs. Marks about the menus for this coming week. Your father wants to host a dinner party for some of his associates, so I had to discuss all the preparations with the housekeeper to make sure everything will be just as he wants it. It is not for several days yet, but there are ever so many details that need to be sorted."

The girls were heartily bored by the time their mother got to the end of this speech. Victoria was torn between the urge to giggle or weep. If looked at dispassionately this scene would be terribly amusing. The countess had no idea how to interact with her own children. But Victoria could not be dispassionate about the situation since she loved the children so dearly. She quickly stepped in to ensure no misery would ensue.

Dropping a brief curtsy to her aunt, Victoria politely excused them. "It was lovely to see you, my lady. The footmen will be bringing the children's supper to the schoolroom momentarily, so we should be getting back. We wish you a good evening, do we not, children?"

Happy to be returning above stairs, the children quickly chorused their agreement.

"Goodnight, Mother."

"Have a lovely evening, Mother."

"Goodnight."

Impulsively, Vanessa ran to her mother and threw her chubby arms around her neck, giving her a warm hug. The countess, taken aback, was gratified at this childish display of affection, and returned the hug awkwardly before the little girl pulled away and ran to grab her cousin's hand.

"Thank you, Victoria," the countess called after them rather uncharacteristically. She usually hid it fairly well, but she resented her husband's niece's presence in their lives. She was particularly resentful of the young woman's close relationship with the children. Unable to generate closeness with them herself, she was deeply jealous of their attachment to their cousin whom they insisted on calling their aunt. So it was decidedly rare that she showed any gratitude for Victoria's role in the children's life.

Victoria acknowledged her aunt's words with a smile and an inclination of her head while she herded the children from the room. There was much less decorum amongst the group as they ascended the stairs. The volume rose the farther they got from the foyer as they all tried to speak at once.

"Did Mrs. Marks tell you what we are having for supper?" Perpetually in a growth spurt, some of the children seemed to be always hungry.

"I worked up quite an appetite walking to the park, Aunt 'Toria," said Vanessa endearingly.

"So did I," chimed in Felicia.

Victoria smiled warmly. "I must say, I think I did too."

"What are we going to do after we have our dinner?" Everett asked curiously.

"Some of us will have to go to bed straight away, as we have had quite a day. The rest of us will no doubt manage to keep each other amused until bedtime," Victoria answered.

"Aww, Aunty, how can you talk about bedtime?"

"I apologize, Everett, but I am truly looking forward to my own bedtime. I had some adventures today that I need to sleep off."

Everett looked unconvinced, but Victoria quickly turned his attention. "That was marvellous news about completing your mathematics, Everett. That is an impressive accomplishment. I am very proud of you. I think I should send a note to the kitchens declaring you ought to be served a double portion of dessert as a small reward."

The youngster grinned in delight, looking much more like a little boy than he would ever admit to being. "That would be grand!"

"But what about us?" the girls demanded.

"Everybody is getting custard, have no fear. But you must agree that Everett's accomplishment is deserving of something a little special, don't you? When you manage something similar, I promise I will ensure the cook provides you with a double portion of dessert too."

Gwendolyn thought about the matter seriously for a moment, fixing Victoria with a determined stare. "Be sure not to forget."

"I promise," vowed the doting cousin, managing to contain her amusement to a pleasant smile.

The rest of the evening passed uneventfully as the children ate their supper, played some games, and then retired for the night. Victoria was relieved to seek her own bed as soon as the last of her charges were tucked in. Tomorrow it would start all over again, she thought with a small sigh as she slipped into slumber.

Chapter Six

The duke was having a far different evening.

After leaving the club, Bryghton went home to his elegant townhouse on Charles Street. His butler greeted him as he stepped into the foyer.

"Welcome home, your grace. I trust you had a pleasant afternoon."

"I did. Thank you, Jeeves. Do you know if Henry is still at work in my office?"

"I believe so, your grace. I have not seen him all afternoon. I did see the housekeeper taking him a plate a few hours ago."

"That boy works too hard, doesn't he, Jeeves? I must say, it is a useful quality in one's secretary."

"I would imagine so. Would you like me to summon the housekeeper to provide you with some refreshments?" asked the butler, ever attentive.

"No, thank you, Jeeves. I have just now come from White's, so I am perfectly refreshed. I am to be dining somewhere in a couple of hours and ladies do tend to frown if I do not give proper attention to the meal that is set before me."

The usually stiff butler could not help grinning over this wry statement. With a slight nod, he said, "As you wish, your grace," while the duke strode purposefully down the hallway to his office.

The well-oiled door opened without a sound as he stepped in and took note of his diligent secretary hunched over an open ledger with a furrowed brow creasing his youthful forehead.

"What seems to be troubling you, Henry?"

With a start of surprise the young man bolted upright, and almost knocked over a bottle of ink in his haste to stand. "Your grace, I did not hear you enter. You fairly scared me witless, I must admit."

Chuckling, Bryghton walked further into the room, pausing next to Henry's desk to look at what had been occupying him. "Sorry for startling you, old chap. I could not resist surprising you since you seemed so absorbed. But tell me, why the worried frown?"

Flushing slightly, the hard-working young man explained. "I was not frowning, your grace, I was merely concentrating. I was trying to make sense of the report I was reading concerning the expenses involved in the running of one of your estates. I was simply calculating to ensure that everything adds up."

Bryghton, always aware of all that was going on with his various holdings, glanced down at the papers on Henry's desk. "I am confident you can work it out, but is there anything you would like me to take a look at?"

Henry hastened to reassure his employer. "Thank you, your grace, but I am quite certain I shall be able to work it out on my own." He smiled, and continued, "I did not expect to see you this afternoon. Was there anything you wished me to do for you?"

"It seems to me you might already have enough to do this afternoon, Henry."

"No, no, I assure you, I am quite capable of taking on any other assignments you might wish to give me."

The duke looked dubiously at the young man's eager face for a moment, but then conceded that despite Henry's furrowed brow earlier, he really was a most competent assistant. Bryghton asked a question of his own. "How are you coming along with your research into Pickering's background?"

"Lord Bartley?" Henry asked redundantly. "I have been digging around as much as possible, your grace. So far I have not found anything we did not already know. He is a despicable man who takes advantage of anyone who comes into his path. He has also made some mistakes with some of his investing in recent years and has nearly run through his fortune. From what I have been able to ascertain, he has begun to dip into his niece's funds."

"Lady Victoria? How could he touch her money?" Bryghton asked with disgust.

"The earl is her guardian and the trustee of her funds until she marries or turns twenty-five. It is a rather commonplace practice, is it not, your grace?" Henry seemed surprised at the duke's interruption.

"Yes, you are probably right, Henry. It is just that I happened to meet the young woman this afternoon. While I am sure I must have been aware at some point that Pickering had a niece, I had never had occasion to give her much thought. She seemed like a nice enough young woman. It is all the more proof of how despicable the earl is that he would be stealing money from his own niece."

"Quite true, but we really did not need any more reason to despise the earl, did we?"

"Excellent point, Henry. Carry on with what you were saying."

"I do not actually have much more to say, I am afraid. Despite everything we know about him, I have yet to come across anything we can use against him—not even his misuse of his niece's funds. While it is dishonourable and deplorable, it is arguably within his rights as her guardian to access her monies." Henry hesitated to go further, but took a deep breath and then continued. "Even what he did to Drake was not precisely illegal, or at least not provable."

Bryghton growled low in his throat, but could not deny Henry's words. "Keep digging anyway. And while you are looking into Bartley, please find out whatever there is to know about his niece."

Henry quirked a curious look at his master. "Lady Victoria? There is very little to know about the young lady. I thought you said you met her today."

"I did. And her three young cousins, the offspring of the devil himself. It made me wonder why she was with them rather than out with some other young ladies doing whatever it is young ladies do all day. It struck me as though she were acting as those children's governess."

"Perhaps she is close with her young relatives."

"Perhaps. But my mother said the lady has not yet made her curtsy to Society. She is the daughter of an earl. It is her right, and most young ladies would go to nearly any length to assert that right."

"Perhaps she is shy, and has no desire to traipse about London with other young ladies," Henry pointed out reasonably.

"Lady Victoria is far from shy. I might not know much about her, but that was fairly evident." The duke finally found something to smile about, as he reminisced about their encounter.

Shaking his head from the reverie, Bryghton continued in brisker tones. "Look into it, Henry. See if there is anything there that we can use against the earl. I have engagements this evening, so I must go if there is nothing else to discuss at the moment."

"No, I believe that is all for the time being. I shall keep working on what we have discussed. Enjoy your evening, your grace."

Bryghton eyed his secretary speculatively. "You should try to enjoy your evening, too, Henry. You know you could always join me as I make my rounds."

Henry flushed to his roots at the thought. "Thank you for the invitation, your grace," he replied, "but I do not think it would be an enjoyable way for me to spend my evening."

The duke raised one eyebrow in sardonic question. "What are you saying Henry? You do not think you would enjoy the Countess of Standish's hospitality?"

Henry gave the duke a look of exasperation. "I am quite certain you know that is not what I meant, your grace. While I am sure no one would give me the cut direct were I to accompany you, I certainly would not be welcomed with open arms as you are wherever you go. I would not be dressed appropriately, nor am I the font of social conversation that you seem capable of being. I would much rather stay here and work than stand about at some ton event listening to the aristocratic crowd gossip."

"You do have a point, Henry. I must admit, I too would much rather stay home. But much of my work is accomplished by listening to that gossip, so I must bid you adieu." Bryghton swept from the room, heading to his bedchamber to prepare. He had an impressive list of social engagements for the evening and he began to don his elegant clothes like an actor for a part in the theatre.

His valet cased him into his close-fitting coat, careful not to disturb his beautifully tied cravat or his artfully disarrayed hair. "You are looking particularly marvellous this evening, your grace."

Regarding himself critically in the mirror, the duke had to concede rather dispassionately. "I suppose I would have to agree with you, Timothy. Thank you." He continued with a lopsided grin. "No need to wait up. I will no doubt be quite late, and I should be able to manage to undress myself without assistance."

Timothy looked horrified at the idea. "Your grace," he gasped, "surely you jest. I just helped you put on that coat—I am quite certain you will not be able to get it off without me. Be sure to ring for me as soon as you return home, no matter the hour."

The duke grinned with amusement. "Yes, sir."

The valet knew he had overstepped, but he grinned back at the duke unrepentantly before sweeping from the room.

As Bryghton descended the grand staircase, his footsteps echoing rather hollowly from the high ceiling, he was delighted to see Alfred already waiting for him.

"Freddy, you are always so reliably punctual. How do you do that?"

Grinning good-naturedly, the baron shrugged dismissively. "I am not nearly so vain as you, nor am I so high up the aristocratic ladder that all eyes will be on me. So my toilette does not take nearly as long as yours."

"Well, that is excellent since it means I do not have to wait for you. I must admit I am actually looking forward to dinner with Lord and Lady Astley. I am becoming decidedly hungry."

"I have heard good reports about the skills of their kitchen staff, so your hunger should soon be appeased."

After enjoying a delectable repast with the Earl and Countess of Standish and twenty of their guests, Alfred and Bryghton continued on to the Melbourne ball. After being announced and descending into the assembled throng, the two men made their way to the side of the room to observe the crowd for a moment.

Keeping his eyes on the crowd and his voice low so as not to be overheard, Alfred teased the duke. "Are you sufficiently fed to survive the evening's rigours, Wychwood?"

"I must admit that I am, Freddy, my boy. The countess certainly knows how to spread a feast. But the chit she sat me next to was not the most entertaining dinner companion."

Alfred stopped looking around and turned a look of surprise upon his friend. "You did not enjoy Lady Isabelle's company? Why ever not? She is expected to be the toast of the ton."

"I have no idea why she would be," the duke drawled, pausing to sip from the glass a passing footman had just passed him. "I will admit she was pretty enough to look at, but she had nothing to say. Attempting to carry on a conversation with her was painful, Freddy. I have met my share of debutantes. I would take any of the silly ones who chatter about nothing over one who has absolutely nothing to say."

"Mayhap she was merely overcome by your exalted presence," offered the baron.

Bryghton merely snorted in derision over the suggestion, not bothering to comment further. The two men were silent for a moment before the duke changed the subject in a nonchalant voice.

"I wonder what Lady Victoria would think of this occasion."

Alfred lost all interest in gazing about at the other partygoers and turned a serious face to the duke. "Why are you wondering about her? What are you about, Alcott?"

The duke avoided his friend's eyes, keeping his own sweeping about the room, and acknowledging acquaintances with a nod or a wave. He finally answered, "I am not about anything, Fred. But I must admit the lovely lady has remained firmly entrenched at the back of my mind since we made her acquaintance."

"Well, dislodge her from there. Not only is she the niece of your sworn enemy, but she is also an innocent young woman. And she told you that you may not call on her. Nothing could possibly come of thinking about her."

"That is where I disagree with you. Plenty can come of thinking about her. For one thing, it can enliven this deadly dull fete."

Now the baron was truly concerned. "There is nothing dull about the Melbourne's ball. What is amiss with you this evening, your grace?"

Clearing his throat, the duke turned to his friend contritely. "Naught is amiss, my good man. You know I hate this type of thing. I am only here out of respect for Lady Melbourne's efforts to garner support in Parliament. But since I agreed to attend, I no doubt ought to put a good face on it." With a grin, he chided Alfred, "What are we doing standing about? There are ladies to be danced with, Freddy."

The orchestra struck up a new song, and with that the duke turned briskly and approached a nearby lady to invite her to the dance floor. Watching the duke with a worried look, the baron hesitated for a moment before he too found a partner and joined the dancers.

An hour and several dance partners later, Bryghton remembered that somehow his dinner companion had extracted a promise from him for a dance, so he went in search of the unconversational Lady Isabelle.

He bowed over her hand. "Dare I hope you have saved me a spot on your dance card, my lady?"

Blushing at the duke's attention, Lady Isabelle nodded mutely while Bryghton suppressed his sigh. He lead her out to the dance floor. "Are you enjoying your evening, my lady?" he asked politely but without much interest.

The very young lady again nodded, not taking her eyes off his waistcoat. Bryghton decided to give up on his efforts at conversation and for a moment merely enjoyed the music. He had to admit that although she had nothing to say, she was a gifted dancer. After a few moments, he was surprised to hear her voice.

"I am enjoying the evening, your grace," she insisted quietly, as if he had been trying to argue with her. "But I must admit I wish my parents had left me in the schoolroom."

Bryghton had to admit that he found this statement to be particularly intriguing. He tried not to laugh.

"I have to tell you Lady Isabelle, I do believe that is the first time I have ever heard that statement in all my life."

The young lady smiled ruefully without quite meeting his eyes. After another lengthy pause she blurted out, "I know it is not the usual sentiment amongst the debutantes, but I am sure I cannot be the first to think this way. The schoolroom is so much safer than the ballroom."

"I assure you, my lady, you are in no danger here."

She finally met his eyes for a brief second before turning back to look at the crowds as they swept along in the dance. "Surely I am, your grace. Well, I am fairly certain I am in no danger from you, but you cannot say there is no danger to an innocent young woman in this gathering of highborn Society. I am an heiress, your grace. There is a plethora of dangers."

The duke raised his eyebrows at her words, but had to admit there was some truth to them. Intrigued, he questioned her further. "What good would staying in the schoolroom have done you, my lady?"

There was another pause and Bryghton wished the poor young woman would hurry with her words, as they were nearing the end of the dance and he was actually interested in knowing what she would say. Finally, she said, "I would have an extra year to prepare."

He couldn't help himself; he threw back his head and laughed. At the sight of her stricken look and the force of the many eyes turned in their direction, Bryghton quickly suppressed his mirth and offered a sincere apology.

"I am so sorry, my lady. I was not making fun. Your statement merely caught me by surprise."

"It was not meant to be funny, your grace," she said, a touch indignantly.

"I am sure it was not," he soothed. "I have a perverse sense of humour."

He escorted her from the dance floor. Despite his previous abhorrence of talking to her, he found himself wishing to prolong the conversation. "Did you not mention your feelings to your parents?"

The pause was shorter this time, but she still barely raised her eyes above his buttons. "I did mention it, your grace, but they thought I was being missish. My mother claims that her debut was the best months of her life and insisted that I would soon agree with her."

"I take it you have yet to do so," he concluded in kind tones, unsurprised when she had no reply beyond a shake of her head.

"Well, my lady, I see there are others clamouring to claim your hand for the next dance. I do hope you come to see the benefits of the Season, but if you do not and if you are ever in need of a hand of help, please know you can turn to the Duke of Wychwood for assistance."

This surprised the young woman sufficiently to bring her eyes once more to his face for a searching moment. "Thank you, your grace," she whispered briefly before turning to the young gentleman impatiently waiting to claim her for the next dance.

Bryghton turned to his friend who had sidled up to him and was now eyeing him with amusement. "It would appear that was far less of a chore than you had anticipated," Alfred said.

The duke shrugged. "In a couple years she might be an interesting woman. While she is disconcertingly quiet, I can see that it isn't because she's dimwitted. In fact, she might be far more intelligent than I even realize." He paused for a moment and looked around the crowded room. "In fact, many of these ladies might have more going on in their upper works than they are letting on. It's going to take some getting used to." He smiled over Alfred's dubious expression. "What say you to moving on to our next engagement? I do believe we have spent sufficient time here."

And so it went. Alfred followed his friend through the crowds of a few more ballrooms before they finally decided to head home in the wee hours of the morning. As the baron was climbing out of the carriage he was interrupted by the duke's words.

"I do believe I will be spending some time in Hyde Park tomorrow. Do you care to go riding with me there in the afternoon?"

"I thought you had seen reason on the subject of Lady Victoria."

"I did not say anything about Lady Victoria. I just find myself wishing for some time spent in the out of doors," said the duke with a semblance of innocence.

Alfred eyed him askance, debating how to answer, and disliking the look upon his friend's face. He finally replied with an attempt at light humour. "Well, of course, I shall accompany you. Somebody has to keep you out of trouble."

"Good luck with that," said the duke, grinning at the look of chagrin upon the baron's face. "Good night, Freddy. I shall see you on the morrow."

Chapter Seven

Victoria had slept soundly all through the night. Blessedly, not a single one of the children had disturbed her in the wee hours and she woke up feeling fully refreshed from the adventures of the previous day. When she finally made her way out of her bedroom after brushing her hair and washing the sleep from her eyes, she was surprised to see the children quietly entertaining themselves.

"Good morning, children," she said as she made her way to the table being set for them by the attentive maids.

Looking up from the dolls she was helping her little sister play with, Gwendolyn smiled cheerfully. "Good morning, Aunt Victoria."

"Did you sleep well, Gwennie?" Victoria asked.

"I did, thank you."

"Me too, Aunt 'Toria," piped up Daniel from the corner in which he was playing.

"It smells delicious in here. Hurry and wash your hands children, it looks as though it is time for us to break our fast."

Victoria's words prompted a flurry of activity as the children hastened to obey. "It would seem everyone is as hungry as I am this morning," Victoria remarked as they hurriedly took their places.

There were a few minutes of relative quiet after the maids filled the children's plates and everyone tucked into the delectable-looking food. After they had assuaged some of their hunger, Victoria endeavoured to make a plan for the day's events.

"What do you think we should do today? Does anyone have any suggestions?"

"I have to do my lessons this morning, Aunty," said Everett importantly.

"Well, of course, everyone needs to do their school work. I was meaning later, perhaps this afternoon. Do you think you shall be working on your lessons all day?"

"Possibly." The boy gave a negligent shrug.

Victoria turned to look at the younger children. "What about you girls? Or Daniel? What would you like to do this afternoon?"

"I want to see the duckies," Daniel declared emphatically.

"Oh Daniel, my darling boy, I think that might not be the best idea," warned Victoria.

"Duckies," the little boy insisted.

The doting cousin gazed at the little boy in consternation, but his big sister stepped into the fray. "Why don't we go to the park and play ball? That would be really nice, wouldn't it Daniel?"

The little boy looked at his sister seriously for a moment before grudgingly agreeing that it would be.

Victoria beamed at the children. "Wonderful, we shall go to the park when our lessons are complete. When we are ready to go we shall let you know, Everett, and you can decide whether or not you can accompany us."

"That sounds like an acceptable plan," the young man said, as haughty as ever.

Victoria just barely managed not to roll her eyes at his silliness, but maintained her smile as she looked around the table at her very favourite people. "If you have eaten enough, we should all get on with our day."

There was a brief scramble as the children pushed back from the table. Victoria helped the maids clear the table while the children rushed to get their books.

Everett left to join his tutor and Victoria resumed the daunting task of teaching the four younger children, despite their vastly different ages and abilities.

The lessons always flew by and today was no exception. Victoria was startled when the footmen arrived with their midday meal, and she glanced at the clock on the mantle to verify that half the day was already gone.

"That was wonderful, children. I think that is enough for today. Let us put our books away and wash our hands. It is time to eat."

"Yay!" Daniel shouted with delight. "Are we going to go to the park now, Aunt 'Toria?"

"In a bit, Daniel dear. But you mustn't bellow so in the house. You would not want your father to come running up here thinking we are being accosted, would you?"

The little boy laughed at Victoria's words. "That's silly, Aunt 'Toria. Papa is at the House, he can't hear me."

"Perhaps he can, you were quite loud." She endeavoured to keep a straight face to impart the lesson despite the little boy's giggles.

"Sorry for being too loud, Aunty."

"Never mind, Daniel. Come and let me see if you scrubbed off all your dirt." The little boy came over for his cousin's inspection, and then the meal proceeded uneventfully.

After everyone had eaten to satisfaction, all the children were bundled up in jackets and boots to ward off any chill in the spring air, and they set off to enjoy themselves in the park. Pansy was loaded down with a basket of balls while Victoria ensured Vanessa and Daniel's hands were both tucked firmly in her own. The horrors of yesterday's adventure were still entrenched in her mind and she was determined not to have a repeat performance. Steering the small group in a direction opposite the Serpentine, they finally settled on a sunny open area where the four youngsters could dash about and their cousin and maid could sit on benches nearby.

"Pansy, I must say I do not know how you and Molly did it. I do hope my aunt and uncle manage to find another governess shortly. I do not know how much longer I can keep up with these four."

"Well, m'lady, you were always such a great help, especially whenever we were taking the children out of doors. But they sure are a handful. You're very good with them, m'lady," praised the nursemaid. "You might even be better with them than any governess they've ever had."

"That is so kind of you to say, Pansy, thank you. But I fear that it may not be perfectly accurate. I am just grateful that Everett has a tutor. Ensuring he is prepared to enter Eton is most definitely beyond my skill."

"But none of this should be fallin' upon you, m'lady. It still strikes me strange that you have been actin' as the children's governess for this long."

"I do not truly mind, Pansy, and I do owe my aunt and uncle for taking me in."

"Not to my way o' thinkin' if you don't mind me sayin' so, m'lady. Seein' as how his lordship got to be earl, don't he owe you?" reasoned the maid persistently.

"Hush, Pansy, it really is not an appropriate subject for us to discuss. I apologize for bringing it up. I was just wondering out loud for fear that I may be doing the children a disservice."

Pansy meant to allow the subject to be dropped at Victoria's bidding, but she suddenly thought of a bewildering idea. "Are you sure they're even lookin'?"

Victoria blinked at the maid as her stomach sank. Could it be true? What if her uncle and aunt were not actually looking for a governess? She resolved to push the thought away for the time being, and refused to dignify Pansy's question with a comment of her own. Looking off into the distance, she allowed her mind to wander for a moment to pleasanter things, relishing the brief interlude while the children were busy entertaining themselves and each other.

A few streets over, the duke was having an awkward conversation of his own.

"Come along, Freddy, or do not, it really makes little difference to me. I am going to Hyde Park. I would welcome your company, but only if you are not planning on bending my ears with your lectures. Need I remind you that I am a grown man, and a duke besides? I do not need you to censure my actions."

The duke's exasperation was causing him to be much higher in the instep than was his wont, which made his trusted friend gaze at him in surprised consternation.

"No, my lord duke, you do not need to remind me. However, need I remind you that the Alcotts just barely managed to control one scandal involving a Bartley. I would think you would not wish to court another."

"Come now, Alfred, surely you know I am clever enough to avoid a scandal."

The two men gazed at one another for a moment of belligerence. The kind-hearted duke was the first to concede. "Oh, come down off your high horse, Freddy. I am not courting a scandal. I admit to you freely that I am inexplicably drawn to the beautiful Lady Victoria. I am well aware of how ridiculous it is considering she is the devil's niece. Were it any other female you would be delighted that I seemed to be finally doing my mother's bidding. As it stands, I can assure you that I am not about to pursue any sort of relationship with the chit. I am merely curious about her. And I admit that I actually feel a sense of concern over her welfare. Do not ask me why, as I have no explanation. But I feel as though I really must see her again. She expressly forbade me from calling on her, which is a good thing, as the thought of calling at Pickering's door gives me the shudders. But that leaves me with little recourse than to frequent the park to see if we might run into her once more. So that is what I am going to do. If you are so concerned that I am heading for trouble, you might as well accompany me so as to prevent it if you can."

After this speech Alfred was not left with much choice but to swing up onto the back of his horse and set out towards Hyde Park with his friend. As they rode along, he cast the duke a wry glance. "I cannot say why I am accompanying you, as I have no idea how I shall keep you out of trouble when it presents itself."

The duke threw back his head and bellowed with laughter, causing his highly strung mount to prance skittishly. Bryghton regained his composure and control of his horse, and grinned in good humour at his loyal friend.

"I know you think this is a foolish errand, but I appreciate your company. It will be less obvious if we happen across her together rather than me searching her out on my own."

"Have you given any thought to what you intend to say to her if we do happen to find her?"

Bryghton shrugged dismissively. "I am certain it shall occur to me when the time comes."

Alfred shook his head but continued riding along at his friend's side. He really had nothing pressing he ought to be doing with his day. And despite his misgivings about the duke's interest in the young lady, he convinced himself that no harm would come from this day's activities.

It took them a fair amount of time to find their quarry, as it was a large park, and it took the men a while to realize the young lady would no doubt be averse to spending time in the same area where they had come so close to tragedy the previous day.

The duke was taken by surprise by the joy he felt when he finally set eyes upon the lovely Lady Victoria and her passel of cousins.

Victoria had been lost in thought when Daniel called out, "Isn't that our duke from the river?" She was startled from her reverie, wondering if she had conjured the Duke of Wychwood with her thoughts.

Heat stained her cheeks as he rode towards them on his huge beast of a horse, accompanied by his friend, the baron. Victoria stood up, feeling flustered, and wondering what to do about this turn of events.

"Good afternoon, your grace," she greeted, while executing a perfect curtsy. Watching her attentively, her three female cousins followed suit, with varying degrees of skill. Not to be outdone, Daniel looked seriously at his sisters before turning back to the duke and bowing respectfully.

Unaccustomed to the sight of children performing such niceties, Bryghton grinned with delight. "Thank you all, those were quite well done. Hello, Daniel, I see you have recovered from your harrowing ordeal from yesterday."

"What's a harrowing deal?" the young boy asked, causing the duke to grin again.

Bryghton's grin was a powerful thing, and Victoria's breath caught at the sight. Their eyes met, and for the briefest moment she actually thought she felt the earth tremble. She decided it must have been the footsteps of the powerful horse the duke was riding, and burst out laughing at her ridiculous notion. She was immediately embarrassed at her outburst, but grateful for the laughter, as it helped to break the spell he had seemed to cast over her.

The duke and baron swung down off their horses and strode forward to greet the small group properly.

"Fancy running into you a second time," the duke declared.

Alfred rolled his eyes and drawled, "Fancy that," rather faintly behind him, causing Bryghton to throw a quick glare over his shoulder.

Daniel, ever tenacious, approached the duke and repeated his question. "What's a harrowing deal, duke?"

Bryghton smiled at the little boy and crouched down in front of him. "A harrowing ordeal is a scary adventure, such as you had yesterday when you and your cousin were in the river."

Daniel grinned at the duke importantly. "I had a harrowing deal. Did you ever have one?"

Victoria quickly coughed delicately to catch his lordship's attention. It would decidedly not do to tell Daniel any stories of adventures the duke might have had as a youngster. It would be all she could do to handle whatever antics the little boy might get up to with his own imagination.

Bryghton looked up at the sound and caught sight of Victoria shaking her head vigorously. He grinned at her knowingly.

"I do believe your adventures have topped any I might have had, my boy." Bryghton stood back up. "I am just glad to see that none of you are any worse for the wear."

He took a moment to look around at the others. He was taken aback by the startlingly sweet sight of the three little girls holding hands and regarding him steadily. He bowed slightly to them and offered them a greeting of their own. "Good day, ladies."

Continuing to look at him with serious faces, the two youngest girls kept silent, but Gwendolyn managed to find her tongue. "Could we pat your horse, your grace? He is ever so beautiful, but so large we are a bit afraid."

Bryghton looked to their cousin for guidance but she merely looked back at him with curiosity, waiting to see what he would say.

He turned back to the little girls. "It is good that you are a little bit afraid. This particular horse is not all that gentle and he has never been around children before. But I am quite convinced he will not harm you as long as I am here, so yes, you may pat him if your cousin says it is all right."

Victoria had to suppress a sigh as all the children clamoured around her begging her to say yes.

"Only for a moment, children. And you must be very quiet so as not to distress the lovely horse. Like the duke said, that horse is not used to children, so he might be afraid of you if you make too much noise." The children gave her dubious looks, but they obediently tiptoed closer to the duke and whispered as he held the large animal's head so that they could pat it gently.

"He's so pretty, your grace," whispered Felicia shyly, which brought another smile to the duke's lips. "Thank you for letting us touch him."

Daniel was too short to reach the monstrously large horse's head, so Victoria had to help him. She grew more nervous as she approached the handsome duke and his beast, and she began to babble as she lifted up the little boy.

"We are not used to such large animals. The children and I do not ride very much. Of course, we have all been taught how to but we have not had much occasion to do so, you understand. And none of the horses in my uncle's stable are nearly so large as this one. He must be very fast." She could not quite make eye contact with the duke, but she noticed the amused twist to his lips and managed to rein in her own, pressing them together to stem the tide of words as she blushed with embarrassment.

The children, satisfied with their experience, now lost interest in the adults and the animal. Victoria put Daniel back down, and he ran off to play once more with his sisters. Watching the children play, Victoria struggled to think of what to say to the two gentlemen who showed no signs of leaving.

Mustering her courage, she turned back to them. "That was very kind of you, your grace. Thank you for your patience with the children."

"It was my pleasure, my lady. I will admit to you I do not recall speaking to any children since I left Eton, other than my brother and sister, but they seem to be exceptionally interesting youngsters."

Victoria laughed at this. "How could you know whether or not they are exceptional if you have nothing with which to compare them?"

Alfred had to laugh at this. As concerned as he was about his friend, it was obvious the young lady was not laying a trap for the duke. He allowed himself to relax and enjoy the interchange as the duke too laughed over her question.

"You have a good point, my lady, but all I will admit is that I find anyone who loves my horse to be exceptional."

Victoria tilted her head slightly. "That is a questionable manner with which to judge exceptionalness, your grace."

"Perhaps, but I stand by it," he replied, enjoying the interchange. It was obvious that she was inexperienced and nervous, but she was a far better conversationalist than the beauty he had danced with the previous night. He wondered what Lady Isabelle would make of Victoria. He rather thought the two would hit it off nicely.

Unsure of what else to say to the gentlemen, Victoria attempted to dismiss them. "It was kind of you to stop and inquire into our well-being, but I would not want to detain you from your important affairs, your grace."

Bryghton smiled, amused over her inexpert attempt, and quickly assured her, "Oh, Freddy and I have nothing of import to be accomplishing at the moment. In fact, he had just been saying how much he would enjoy playing ball, had you not, Freddy?"

Alfred, Lord Lynster, sixth baron of Fielding, looked incredulously at his dear friend the Duke of Wychwood. Did he really expect him to play ball with a passel of children? It would seem he did. Blinking with something bordering on bewilderment, Freddy found himself approaching the four youngsters and asking if he could join in their game. The little ones were delighted with the adult attention and welcomed him enthusiastically.

Lady Victoria might not be familiar with the ways of the ton, but she was quite certain it was out of the ordinary to the extreme for a baron to play ball in the park with even his own children, let alone ones he had just met. She turned to the duke with laughter dancing in her eyes.

"That was rather masterful, your grace. What do you have against your friend that you would toss him to the wolves like that?"

Bryghton smiled at her turn of phrase. "Do you truly consider your young charges to be wolves?"

Allowing a small sigh to escape, she quirked her lips into a slight smile. "At times, yes," she admitted.

"Why do you not have more help? This is the second time I am seeing you with them with only a nursemaid to accompany you." This was beyond the pale of polite conversation, but Bryghton could not resist the need to know.

Victoria was unnerved by the intensity of his question, but was blissfully unaware of his breach of etiquette. "My aunt and uncle have yet to replace the governess who quit," she answered simply, uncomfortable with how close this was to her and Pansy's earlier conversation.

"How long has she been gone?"

"Two months."

"Two months," he repeated. "And the care of the children has fallen on you?" Bryghton was aghast.

"Well, we have Pansy who is a marvellous help. And we also have a lovely young maid named Mary who does much of the work in the nursery." Seeing the duke's dubious expression, Victoria had to admit, "But yes, you are correct. It is a rather large responsibility." She chewed her lip with worry, not noticing how his eyes focused on that telling action.

"I worry that although I was well educated myself, I was not really trained how to teach others. I went to finishing school, your grace, not Eton." Perhaps regretting her confidences, she continued. "Of course, I am not expected to teach Everett. He has a tutor because he is preparing to enter Eton himself. He is very serious about his studies. And of course, little Daniel is quite young to be worrying about lessons. And the girls are doing well enough." Realizing she was babbling again, Victoria cut herself off and changed the subject.

"But of course, you do not wish to hear all about this. Were you on your way somewhere when you spotted us?"

Bryghton blinked and tried valiantly to keep a blush from staining his cheeks. "Fred and I were just out taking the air," he prevaricated. "Hyde Park is a lovely space to enjoy when we are so far from our country estates."

Alcott wished he could persist in questioning her about why she was being turned into a governess, but decided to try a different tack for his questions.

"Have you been to Almack's of late, my lady? I have heard there is a new conductor for the orchestra. I was wondering what you think of his skills."

Victoria looked at him questioningly. Thinking back to their conversation of the previous day, she could not recall whether or not she had mentioned that she did not go about in Society. But surely he must realize she did not. Of course, being a duke, he might not take note of all the ladies traipsing about Society during the Season, she mused. She wondered whether she could brazen it out or if she should be forthcoming. She decided on the bald truth, as she did not think she had the required skills to tell tales and would be quickly caught out in any lie.

"I have never been to Almack's, your grace. I am not out, nor have I made my curtsy to our queen," she admitted with quiet dignity.

Bryghton, much more experienced in the ways of the world, had no trouble hiding the fact that he had already known this, and he was pleased his ploy had worked, giving him the opening to question her further. "Why ever not?" he asked, allowing his indignation over her mistreatment to colour his tones.

Victoria eyed him nervously, unsure of why he would seem so upset. "You make me feel as though I ought to apologize, your grace, but I am quite certain I have no idea why."

"No, I apologize, my lady. You have nothing for which to be sorry. I am merely wondering why you have yet to be introduced to Society."

Victoria shrugged her helplessness. "It is a rather complicated situation."

"I do not see why. You are the daughter of an earl, are you not?"

At her nod he continued. "It would seem to me that it would be your aspiration to take your rightful place in our world. Do you not want to?"

Looking at him with honest, steady eyes, Victoria stated the truth. "I have given the matter little thought. My parents died when I was twelve, and I have been living with my uncle and his wife and children ever since. My parents had stipulated that I was to be sent to school for a time, and of course my friends there often spoke of their eagerness to make their come out, but it was never discussed in my home. If I ever brought it up, my aunt was extremely uncomfortable with the subject and it was continually postponed. My uncle says it is too expensive a venture for us to consider at this time. He has his own children's futures to consider and cannot be overly concerned with mine."

Bryghton felt a wave of anger crash over him at Pickering's despicableness but made every effort not to allow it to show.

"But do you not have any other relatives who could help you in this way? I can understand that Lady Bartley is perhaps overly busy with her children," he said, despite the fact that it did not appear to him that the lady was at all occupied with her offspring.

She shook her head in denial of his words. "I do not have many relatives that I am aware of, your grace. And it doesn't truly matter. I am too busy with the children to give it any serious thought. Besides, I do believe I would be terrified to go to a ball or any of the things my friends used to look forward to. Even if I had the appropriate gowns and such, I would not know how to go on."

Bryghton was drawn to the young woman's simple honesty and humility. He marvelled that she seemed so pure despite being under her uncle's influence for the past several years. He grew more determined to do something about her situation, but remained uncertain of what it could possibly be. He persisted in his questions.

"Did you not stay in touch with any of your friends from school? Could you not go about with some of them?"

Smiling sadly and pulling her eyes away from the handsome face of this man so intently questioning her, Victoria wondered absently why it seemed to matter to him. "I did stay in touch with a few of my friends, but no one has invited me, and I am not going to push myself upon them. They are all so busy with their own Seasons and some of them have married already, so…" She trailed off with a slight shrug, illustrating the impossibility of what he was suggesting.

Bryghton had to admit that no doubt jealousy would prevent any of her supposed friends from wanting to have her near when they were making their debut. Her beauty would cast all others into the shade. Even if any of her friends were kind enough to include her, their doting mamas would surely insist otherwise.

"Perhaps you could come with me and Fred to some parties. I am sure any of my friends would welcome you."

Victoria allowed herself to laugh at this preposterous suggestion. "I may be a green girl who has no experience with the ways of the ton, but even I know that would never do, your grace. You cannot escort me about without setting all the tongues wagging. Besides, I have nothing appropriate to wear."

"You look perfectly fine to me."

Victoria by now had had nearly enough of the duke's pestering. "Your grace, I must say, I believe you are being quite unkind to badger me about these things. You know it is an impossibility for me to go about in Society. It is prodigiously mean-spirited of you to suggest that it is not."

Bryghton was surprised at this turn of the conversation, and he hastened to assure her that his intentions were the complete opposite. "No, my lady, I assure you, I did not mean any unkindness. It is not an impossibility, I am certain of it. I know of just the thing. My sister shall shortly be arriving for the Season. I would think she is of a size with you. You could borrow some of her gowns and fripperies and go about a little with her. She would love to have a new friend to accompany her, as she does consider the Season to be a bit of a bore."

"I do not know your sister, but I do find it hard to believe she would fall in with a plan such as you are suggesting." Realizing that her words may give an indication that she might actually consider such a course of action, she hastened to add, "Not that I am at all interested in gadding about amongst Society. I can assure you, I am perfectly content with my life the way it is."

Alcott gazed at her speculatively for a moment, which caused the blush to rise in her cheeks. In deceptively soft tones he asked her, "Really, my lady? You are perfectly content to look after four or five children essentially by yourself? You are the daughter of an earl. You should be having your own children, not looking after your uncle's."

She could no longer hold his eye, as she could not fully deny his words. She finally admitted the complete truth in a soft voice. "I am not perfectly certain I would be permitted to enter Society, your grace." Tears glistened briefly as they gathered on her lashes but she refused to allow them to fall.

Bryghton hissed at the sight and hardened his resolve to somehow save the lovely young woman from her circumstances. "Why do you say that? Have you asked?"

"No, not precisely. It is just a feeling I have. I have been helping to care for the children ever since I came home from school. It was suggested at the time that I owed it to my family to do so, and that I needed something to occupy my time. Two months ago, when the governess quit, I was told to take over her responsibilities until she could be replaced. I have a hard time believing it could take two months to hire a governess. I am beginning to believe my uncle and aunt are not even trying. I do not think it would be possible to go about the Season and look after the children at the same time."

"But surely you see that it is not your responsibility to raise your little cousins, no matter how much you might care for them."

Gazing at the duke helplessly, her eyes beseeching, Victoria struggled for words. "I do not gain my majority until I am twenty-five. Until then I am dependent upon my uncle. That is another five years. I do not wish to anger him. It could make life difficult."

By the end of her speech Bryghton was straining to hear what she was saying, as her voice dwindled to a mere whisper. He kept his own voice low as he replied.

"You could always marry."

She gazed at the duke for a long moment with her eyes wide and luminous. Bryghton was taken aback when she burst into laughter.

"I was not jesting, my lady," he said with indignation.

"No, I am sure you were not. It is true—I could marry. But the truth of the matter is that it is a circle we are speaking in. If I do not

go about Town I will not meet anyone I could possibly marry. If I do
not marry, I do not have access to the funds that would allow me to
go about Town. "

Seeing the truth of her words but refusing to accept them,
Bryghton insisted, "I am certain we can find a way."

Smiling sweetly, Victoria turned back to watch the children. "I
appreciate your concern for my well-being, your grace. I recognize
you are displaying me a high degree of honour to do so and I thank
you for it. But I am perfectly fine. Now I do believe it is time that
you rescue your friend or the children shall have him worn quite
ragged."

The duke allowed himself to be dismissed, recognizing that no
more could be accomplished this day. He called out to Alfred that it
was time to be going.

The baron approached with a wide grin. "My lady, those children
are great good fun but they could run you to the ground if you let
them. I would never believe it if you had told me how much I would
enjoy playing ball with a passel of youngsters. Thank you."

Victoria was gratified at the baron's kind words. "I am sure they
were highly diverted by your attentions, my lord. Thank you for your
kindness. And I will admit that I appreciate the fact that they will
probably be easy to put to bed this evening since you wore off so
much of their fidgets with your brisk game. So I thank you."

As Alfred gathered up his reins from the duke, Bryghton turned
to say his own farewells to the lovely lady. He bent over her hand
but then turned it to place a warm kiss on her wrist. Her lips parted
with her indrawn breath and he gazed intently at her. Victoria felt as
though the air around them hummed with the excitement of it all
and she found she could hardly stand still with the commotion she
felt inside. Her churning feelings caused her to finally snatch her
hand back from his grasp.

Her action broke the spell binding them, and Bryghton grinned
with delight. "I do reserve the right to speak to you again if our paths
happen to cross some day."

"Very well, your grace. But I may reserve the right to run in the
opposite direction should I see you approaching my path," she

replied with a pert grin, knowing full well she would never run away from the handsome man despite whatever problems he may present.

She watched them ride away, shaking her head as she recalled their discussion. Victoria could hardly believe how personal their conversation had been. She would never have thought that she could have revealed such intimate thoughts to anyone. What had caused her to open up so, she wondered. Perhaps it was just the fact that an adult of her own social standing had taken the time to ask after her and her situation. Or perhaps she had truly lost her mind in the face of the man's handsomeness and apparent interest in her concerns. Whatever it was, while it had felt comforting to share her burden momentarily, it could not happen again. Thus resolved, she put the man from her mind and returned her attention to her young charges.

Chapter Eight

Grinning at his friend as they rode away, Bryghton could not resist commenting. "You look a little worse for the wear, Fred. I do not believe you are presentable for anything. We must return you home for a change of clothes."

The baron shot his friend a look of disgust. "It was you who sent me to play with the children."

"You did not need to do so with such a degree of enthusiasm, though, my dear boy," Bryghton answered with a mocking smile.

Fred could not resist returning the smile with a rueful one of his own. "Those children were actually great fun to play with. I can hardly credit it, but I had a good time with them. Have you ever spent time with youngsters?"

"Not since I was one myself," the duke laughed. "I dare say even any of our friends that have some of their own tend to leave them with their nursemaids. I must admit that it is a rarity that I so much as set eyes on a child, much less spend time with one."

Fred had a distant look on his face for a silent moment before he carried on the conversation. "It rather puts a whole new dimension on your mother's push for a grandchild. If you could be guaranteed your son would turn out like that little Daniel, it would not be such a terrible thing. I might even be willing to get leg shackled in exchange."

The duke threw back his head and shouted with laughter. "Do not let my mother catch wind of your change of heart, I beg of you.

She will have you matched up before you can catch your breath if you are not careful."

"I tell you, it might not be such a terrible thing after all, Alcott."

"Perhaps not, but do you not wish for it to be your choice, and not my mother's?"

"Well you do have a good point there, your grace."

"Exactly, so keep those thoughts to yourself. I can assure you, I have absolutely no intention of telling my mother I might have seen her point until I am positively certain, and have even made my choice."

Alfred gazed at his friend speculatively for a moment as they rode in silence. "I think it is going to be a prodigiously interesting Season this year, is it not, Alcott?"

"I think you are correct, Freddy, my boy," the duke agreed with a grin. "Now we are just about to your lodgings. Do you think your staff could rustle us up some sort of repast while you make yourself presentable?"

Freddy laughed. "I am quite certain they could manage."

As they turned onto Park Lane, the baron's address on the western edge of Mayfair, they were surprised to see the travelling coach pulled up in front of his house.

"I say, my dear Fred, I thought you were not expecting your aunt and sister until next week," commented the duke as they rode closer.

"I did not think I was either," said the baron, laughing. "But it would seem that I was mistaken. It is a lucky thing for me that my staff is always in readiness and that I also happen to adore my aunt and sister, so it is not such a hardship. I had not mentally prepared myself for the rigours I might face as the older brother to a debutante, but I shall manage, I am sure."

The duke grinned at his companion. "Rigours indeed, my friend. I have had a couple of years' experience on the subject. It is indeed a unique experience to watch your little sister make her curtsy to Society. But it is not nearly as bad as you might think. Let us go and greet your ladies."

The two handsome noblemen rode swiftly down the street, pulling up in front of the baron's elegant townhouse and throwing their reins to a hastily summoned footman. They were just swinging down as Sybil stepped out onto the steps to oversee the footmen bringing in the luggage.

"Freddy, my dear boy, how lovely to see you! And your grace, what a pleasure to see you as well."

"Aunt Sybil, welcome back to London." The baron dropped a kiss briefly to her thin cheek.

The duke bowed gallantly over the lady's hand. "My lady, it is a pleasure to see you. My mother was just the other day expressing a desire to see you. You must call on her once you are settled."

"How kind of her to remember me. Thank you, your grace, I will be sure to make a call soon."

The doting aunt turned her eyes back to her nephew and they sharpened on his appearance. "I say, Freddy, whatever happened to you? You look as though you have been roughhousing as you did when you were a boy."

"You would never believe me if I told you, Aunt Sybil. But you are quite right. I no doubt look a fright and must change my attire forthwith. Would you be so kind as to ring for some refreshments for the duke and me while I run up to my room and tidy myself?"

Sybil watched with a degree of disbelief as the baron dashed up the stairs before even finishing his sentence. She looked back at Bryghton with bewilderment. He merely grinned and shrugged in answer.

"Yes, well, come in Wychwood and get settled in the receiving room. I shall have the housekeeper see to a repast. No doubt Eloise would be glad of a small bite as well since we have just arrived ourselves."

"Please do not feel that you must entertain me, my lady," the duke allowed graciously. "I am sure you must have a myriad of things to do if you have just arrived."

"Are you trying to get rid of me, your grace?" she asked with feigned outrage.

"Never, my lady!" he said with aplomb. "I merely do not wish to impose."

Sybil laughed. "You are a duke, Wychwood. Is it not your birthright?"

Bryghton could not resist laughing with her despite shaking his head in denial. He was saved from a need to reply by the hasty arrival of the young lady of the house.

"Alcott!" Eloise declared with loud joy, dashing into the room. Just as she was about to throw herself at her big brother's dearest friend she caught her aunt's eye glaring at her and pulled herself up short while blushing fiercely.

Dropping a hasty curtsy, Eloise quickly apologized. "I am so sorry, your grace. I quite forgot myself for a moment. My hoydenish ways of the schoolroom are apparently harder to abandon than I thought."

Delighted by her honesty, Bryghton did not take umbrage with her behaviour. "Since I have known you forever, I am certain we are allowed to dispense with some of the formalities even though you are now a young lady."

Eloise's cheeks remained stained with colour, but she managed to overcome her discomfiture just as her brother entered the room. This time she did throw herself at the baron. "Alfred, I am so very happy to see you. Thank you for all the lovely dresses Aunt Sybil had made for me. Please do not lecture about any of the bills you may have received. It was ever so exciting to have the dressmaker come, and I am just thrilled about being here for my Season."

Alfred blinked rapidly as he set his little sister back on her feet after her energetic hug. He ruefully thought of the quiet he had been enjoying and shook his head over the hubbub that was to come.

"I am delighted to see you too, Eloise. How was your journey here?"

"It was prodigiously boring, I must say, Freddy. But never mind that, we are here now, that is all that matters. You have no idea how excited I am to finally get to make my come out."

"Yes, of course," Lord Lynster answered almost faintly as he contemplated just how drastically his household had changed that afternoon. He stepped towards the door. "Well, ladies, the duke and I should leave you to get settled in. We have some things we must be doing this afternoon." He was interrupted by the arrival of the housekeeper with a trolley of refreshments, as he had requested.

Alfred released a silent sigh of resignation as he smiled politely and resumed his seat. "We shall leave momentarily," he said wanly.

Bryghton took pity on his friend and quickly satisfied the worst of his hunger while listening politely and with at least a degree of attention as Eloise prattled on about all the things she planned to do as the Season got under way. The duke stood when Eloise paused to take a breath.

"Thank you, ladies, for your kind hospitality. That quite hit the spot. And now we must be off. No doubt we shall be seeing much more of one another over the coming weeks."

With relief, the two gentlemen bowed themselves from the room and strode from the house. They held their silence until they were at the mews retrieving their horses. Bryghton was the first to break the silence when he burst out with a chuckle.

"I must say, Fred, you shan't have to worry about awkward silences with your sister around."

The baron laughed, too. "That is true, Alcott, although silence was never one of my fears."

The two shared another chuckle before swinging up onto their restless horses and riding off in companionable silence as they continued on with their previously interrupted plans of making some morning calls and then stopping in to the duke's club. They listened to some of the current gossip, perused the latest bets being written into the books, and then went their separate ways to prepare for their evening's entertainments.

Chapter Nine

Victoria had struggled with the decision of whether or not to tell the children to keep their encounter with the duke and the baron a secret, but she had come to the conclusion that it would be an impossible task to expect them to do so. There was half a chance that they would forget all about the encounter anyway, and making it more important than it was by telling them it was a secret would ensure that they would remember. If the event did happen to come up, she could brazen it out much better if she placed no importance on it with the children. As a plan, it was the best she could come up with. She had never been told not to talk to her peers, but somehow she had a feeling her uncle in particular would not be happy about it were he to find out. With a mental shrug she resolved to put the matter from her mind, since worrying about it would do her no good.

The children had chattered cheerfully as they clamoured their way back to Victoria's townhouse. As they approached the front door it struck her as ironic that this was, in fact, her house. It certainly did not feel as though she had any control over it. She wondered vaguely whether or not she would feel differently when she turned twenty-five.

"Welcome home, m'lady," the butler welcomed as he opened the door with a respectful bow. "Did you and the young ones have a good time?"

"Thank you, Maxwell, we did," Victoria answered while the children noisily chimed in with their comments.

"It was grand!"

"We played ball for hours!" declared Daniel, with slight exaggeration.

"It was perfectly wonderful, Maxwell," Gwendolyn summed up all the others' opinions.

With proud appreciation, Maxwell stood aside and watched as Lady Victoria ushered the children up the stairs, listening attentively as they all vied for her attention. The housekeeper joined him at the bottom of the stairs.

"She does a lovely job with those youngsters, does she not," Maxwell asked rhetorically as they disappeared from view.

"She does that, there's no doubt," Mrs. Marks agreed. "But it sure don't seem right."

Maxwell's sigh was heartfelt. "I must agree with you there, Mrs. Marks, but there's naught we can do about it but do our best to support her."

The two aging, faithful servants stood in companionable silence. After a moment Mrs. Marks, always busy, cleared her throat. "I ought to be about my business, I s'pose."

"Take care, Mrs. Marks." Maxwell watched her bustle away before turning to his own to-do list.

Meanwhile, above stairs, Victoria was overseeing the children as they changed their clothes and washed their hands in preparation for their afternoon visit with their mother. *It always seems to come to this moment,* she thought with some trepidation. *Why does it seem that the rest of the day flies by and this moment drags with the slowest of speeds?*

Once the four youngest children were ready, Victoria sped through her own preparations and they slowly descended the stairs once more.

They were announced into the room just as Mrs. Marks was rolling in the tea trolley for Lady Bartley. Victoria's heart sank when she saw that the earl was also present, waiting with his wife to see the children.

Victoria dropped a brief but respectably deep curtsy to the earl and countess and explained briefly that Everett had remained with his tutor before moving to the side of the room and taking a seat, settling herself to observe as the children interacted briefly with their parents. She watched the awkward byplay for a moment but then soon lost herself in a reverie.

Allowing her mind to drift was a mistake Victoria soon realized as her uncle's sharp question brought her hastily back to reality.

"You were speaking to two gentlemen in the park?" he asked in a tone bordering on harsh.

Victoria realized the question was addressed to her but she was unsure what had preceded it. Since they had not told Lady Bartley about Daniel's fall into the Serpentine, Victoria was unsure how much detail to go into.

"Uh, yes, we did speak to them briefly," Victoria acknowledged.

"Daniel said one of them played ball with him," the earl prompted in the same hard tone.

"It was grand!" Daniel insisted with jubilance.

Victoria could not help smiling at her little cousin's joy. She turned to her uncle with an innocent look. "He really did seem to have more skill in the matter than I do, my lord. The children were delighted."

"No doubt," he replied coldly. "Who was this lord who had the nerve to play with my children?"

"Well, my lord, I do not know about nerve. I thought it was prodigiously kind of him to take a few moments with the children. His name is Lord Alfred Lynster, the Baron of Fielding. Do you know him? We do not really know him very well, of course, merely meeting him briefly, but he did seem to be a very nice young man." Victoria said all this with a soft, sweet voice and not an ounce of guilt showing on her face. In all reality, she had nothing for which to feel guilty, and she refused to accept that her uncle might feel otherwise.

"I have made his acquaintance. How do you come to know Lord Lynster?" he continued his questioning.

"The children and I met him in the park this week. By coincidence we seem to have been there at the same time on a few occasions of late." Victoria's efforts at making light of the matter were dashed to pieces by Daniel's addition.

"He and the duke saved me from my harrowing deal," Daniel said with importance.

"What duke?" Pickering demanded while his wife gasped.

"What harrowing ordeal are you speaking of, Daniel?" Lady Bartley asked somewhat shrilly.

"Fell in the river," Daniel answered hesitantly before shoving his thumb in his mouth, nervously realizing the adults were getting upset. He edged closer to his dear Victoria for comfort.

The earl and his wife gazed at Victoria with dismay. She had still not answered the earl's question, as the countess was peppering her with questions of her own.

"Daniel fell in the river? When did this happen?"

The three girls were now silently gazing at their parents with wide eyes. Vanessa's lower lip began to tremble and tears gathered in her eyes.

Seeing the children's distress filled Victoria with dismay and she gathered them to her, pulling Vanessa onto her lap and cuddling the others close for comfort. Keeping her voice as calm as possible she endeavoured to answer her aunt's questions.

"It was not such a big thing, which is why I did not mention it before. There was naught to be concerned about. Daniel did fall into the river and I jumped in after him. We then had the dilemma of how to get back out. These gentlemen had been passing along at the time, and stopped to help us with our predicament. That is how we met. Then today they saw us again and kindly stopped to ask how we were faring. Then Lord Lynster joined Daniel and the girls in a bit of a ball game."

"Thank you for saving my darling," Lady Pickering declared with uncharacteristic feeling while her husband interjected.

"The children and the baron played ball leaving you to talk with a duke?" he questioned harshly, seemingly unconcerned with his son and niece's frightening experience.

Victoria allowed herself a wry smile over the very different reactions of her uncle and aunt. Enjoying the countess' rare appreciation, Victoria smiled at her aunt. "Of course, my lady. I love Daniel. And truly it was not such an ordeal. We did appreciate the gentlemen's help, but we could have managed on our own."

Growing ever more frustrated by his niece's avoidance, the earl insisted, "Victoria, who was this duke who had the audacity to speak with you?"

"I assure you, my lord, no audacity was involved. He was the epitome of kindness. It was the Duke of Wychwood."

Unaware of the history between the duke and her uncle, Victoria was surprised to see him first grow pale and then his face flood with hot colour.

"How did you come to be speaking with the Duke of Wychwood?" he demanded angrily. "Was he following you?"

Confused, Victoria eyed her uncle questioningly while answering in all honesty. "I strongly doubt that, my lord. He had never made my acquaintance before that day. He and his brother and the baron just happened to be passing through the park on their way somewhere when they saw Daniel fall and me jump. Being the courteous gentlemen that they are, they felt duty bound to assist."

"And we shall be forever in their debt," declared Lady Pickering with uncharacteristic feeling. Her husband glared at her before turning back to Victoria.

"You are to have nothing to do with those men, Victoria."

Victoria was taken aback, and found herself questioning her uncle's decree. "Why not, my lord? As my lady pointed out, we are in their debt for helping Daniel and me. It would be churlish to rebuff them if our paths should cross in the future."

"If you cannot abide by my dictates, then you must keep the children home," her uncle countered, without explanation.

Staring at her uncle with a mixture of growing dread and determination, Victoria kept her voice steady, not allowing any belligerence to enter her tone. "That would be fine, except that you have not yet hired a governess and the children really must take the air. I would be happy to relinquish that responsibility to someone else."

There was a moment of strained silence while the earl and countess looked at each other almost guiltily. Seeing their exchange, Victoria realized her suspicions were correct. She was the children's governess. Bolstered by the sensation that there was nothing to lose, she launched into renewed speech.

"While we are on the subject, I realize this may not be the time for this discussion, but I feel I must bring this up now. It would be very helpful if you could hasten to find a replacement for the governess, as the Season is about to commence and I feel that it really is time that I take my place in Society."

Stunned silence followed this statement. The children were quietly watching the adult interaction with their eyes widened by curiosity, unaccustomed to seeing their father at a loss for words. The countess had dismay clearly painted on her face while the earl struggled to contain his anger at his niece's words. Striving to regain control of the conversation and his usually tractable niece, he demanded in cold tones, "To what do you refer when you speak of your place in Society?"

"My father was the Earl of Pickering before you took on that role. As his daughter, it is my duty to take my place in Society. I have already turned twenty. I should be searching for a husband in order to set up my own household."

Seeing the closed look upon her uncle's face, she tried a different tack. "I cannot presume upon your kindness forever. It was fine when I was a child, but no doubt you and my aunt would be happy to be free of my care."

The countess had no reply for this. She looked to her husband, who, rather than answering Victoria's question, demanded harshly, "Did the Duke put you up to this?"

"I do not know what you mean by asking if he put me up to this, my lord. I am not asking for anything out of the ordinary. Are you not expecting to present your daughters to Society when they come of age? Do you not think my father would have expected the same for me? I am well past the age at which most girls enter Society. If I do not do so soon it will be too late for me. The Duke of Wychwood has nothing to do with this. He did ask me why I do not go about in Society, and I was embarrassed to not have an answer to his question, but I have been pondering the situation for some time."

This was again followed by strained silence. As she had spoken, Victoria had felt her resolve harden. She did have a desire for a home and family of her own. While she loved her uncle's children dearly, they were not her children. And she did not wish to be her uncle's unpaid servant any longer, nor had she ever felt welcome in his home.

"You are not to speak to the Duke of Wychwood any more, Victoria," the earl said with conviction before continuing in an effort at a reasonable tone.

"As to your desire to enter Society, I am sorry to say that we cannot spare the funds. We are somewhat strapped financially at the moment. I am hoping to recover in time, but right now funding a Season is out of the question." He paused for a moment, making an effort to gauge her reaction. Victoria held herself stoically at his pronouncement. "We will also make an effort to get you some help in the nursery so you could have a little spare time for yourself in recompense. And if you truly wish to be married, perhaps I could look about amongst my acquaintances to see if there is anyone suitable so that you could marry without the expense and effort of a Season."

Moving Vanessa off her lap, Victoria stood gracefully and held herself with quiet dignity. "I would appreciate help in the nursery, my lord. I am not a governess, I am your niece, and I would like some time for myself. I would also prefer to choose my own husband were I to marry, so thank you for your offer, but I do not think I will take you up on it at this time. Now, I think it is time for the children to have their supper, so we will bid you adieu."

Without another word, Victoria watched as the children dutifully kissed their mother and father before joining her by the door. Victoria curtsied to the earl and countess before gliding from the room. The children were quieter than usual, but they still made enough noise to cover over the conversation that followed their departure.

Pickering got to his feet and began to pace about the room while his wife watched him anxiously. "The poor dear has a point, my lord. It really is her right to take her place in Society. While I do not enjoy the Season overmuch, should we not make an effort? It might be good for me to get some experience at it before I have to do the whole thing for our daughters." The countess quaked into silence at her husband's furious expression.

"Have you any idea how much a Season might cost?" he demanded angrily.

"Not really, my lord, but surely we are not in straightened circumstances," she answered meekly.

"Near enough."

"But what about the girl's funds?" asked the countess, appreciation for Victoria's saving of her youngest child causing Lady Pickering to persist. "Did she not inherit quite a large fortune from her parents? I would think this would be exactly what it should be used for, therefore making it unnecessary to worry about our finances in connection with launching her into Society."

"You know nothing about the matter," the earl insisted. "Her funds are not currently available for something so frivolous." He refused to say anything more on the matter and his wife finally subsided.

Mrs. Marks, though, had heard the entire exchange as she had neared the door to collect the tea trolley. She filed the conversation away to think on later and decide what ought to be done for the darling lady of the house. The entire household worried over the future of Lady Victoria. Most of the servants had been with the Bartley family since the previous earl had been alive. Much of the staff had been let go by the penny pinching current earl, but those that remained had a sense of loyalty towards Lady Victoria. Mrs. Marks was no exception, and she wondered how best to help her.

Chapter Ten

"Did we get you in trouble, Aunt Victoria?" asked Gwendolyn in a small voice once they had returned to the nursery. "Daniel did not realize he shouldn't mention about falling in the river."

Victoria gave her cousin a quick hug. "Do not worry your dear little head for a moment," she said. "I am not in any trouble. And you children should never keep secrets from your parents." Seeing the dubious look on the girls' faces, Victoria could not help but laugh, but then she hastened to change the subject.

"I don't know about you, but I find that I am quite famished. This has been an eventful day all around, and I am definitely looking forward to seeing what Cook has prepared for us."

Her statement did the trick; the children were distracted and the evening progressed as usual. They were joined by Everett for their evening meal and a few games before they all bundled into their nightclothes and were tucked into their beds.

Victoria heaved a sigh of relief once all five were finally asleep and she could make her way to her own room. Her thoughts were a tangle of frustration and longing. Unsure what to make of her uncle's promise to hire extra nursery help, Victoria allowed her mind to wander over the possibilities. Looking into the mirror as she took down her hair, she had a conversation with her own reflection.

"Why would the earl demand I not speak to the duke, I wonder. He seemed like a perfectly respectable member of Society to me, not that I know much about these matters. The earl's command did not strike me as being motivated by concern for me or even the children, but I have no idea what moved him. And do I still need to obey the earl now that I am twenty years of age? Do I need his permission to enter Society with or without any funds? What am I to make of the duke's offer to lend me some of his sister's gowns? Would it be scandalous to take him up on the offer?"

Victoria saw herself blush at the thought, which made her laugh lightly. "Yes, it would be a trifle irregular, I am sure, but probably not utterly beyond the pale. Perhaps, were I to run into him again and he brought it up we could manage to come up with some sort of scenario in which it could be managed. But only if the earl actually does get someone to be with the children," she concluded with another sigh. "While it should not be my responsibility to care for them, I do love them and could never live with myself if something were to happen to them because I was not here to watch over them."

Thus resolved, Victoria pushed the matter of the Season from her mind for the moment and took to her bed. She slept deeply while the duke's handsome face figured prominently in her dreams that night.

Over the next few days Victoria obeyed her uncle's edict that she not venture to the park despite her newly minted conviction that it was no longer his right to dictate her life to such an extent. She reasoned that he was well within his right to dictate his children's behaviour, and since they were currently still in her hands she felt duty bound not to take them where there was a chance that they would bump into the duke.

By the third day after the conversation with the earl, though, with no change in sight as to her getting any help with the children, she and the youngsters were climbing the walls with frustration over being cooped up inside. Victoria reasoned that the children really did need some fresh air and there were other places they could go besides Hyde Park.

After their morning lessons were concluded Victoria delighted the children with a proposal. "All right children, I think we have been inside this house for much too long. What say you to a walk around the block?"

The three girls stared at her unblinkingly for the space of a couple of heartbeats before bursting into noisy cheers. Daniel, not really receiving lessons, had been playing on his own in the corner, and quickly ran over to see what the noise was about.

"What's going on, Aunty?" he asked anxiously.

"We, my little man, are going for a walk. Put your toys away and we shall hurry and put our books aside, and then we will go out and see what is to be seen on our block."

The children were so excited that it was challenging to get them ready. Victoria regretted that she had not thought of it sooner, seeing how happy they were about the prospect of going outside. She determined to speak to her uncle about what parameters he considered appropriate, since it was obvious she could not keep them cooped up inside.

They managed to make it down the street to a small parkette without incident. The children made good use of the opportunity to run around playing a game of chase within the confines of the small space. They made no comment on how poorly it contrasted with Hyde Park, but Victoria felt sad for them nonetheless. After a short time she felt frazzled from continually glancing over her shoulder, unsure if she was looking forward to or dreading the possibility of seeing the duke. When she could no longer bear the tension she rounded up the children and shepherded them back to their house.

Responding mechanically and distractedly to their energetic chatter, Victoria was relieved when they reached their own front stairs. She was halfway up the stairs when a distinctive jingle caused the fine hairs on the back of her neck to rise. Turning her head sharply, she saw the Duke of Wychwood riding towards her on his beautiful large horse, its ornate harness jingling distinctively with each step.

Her breath froze in her throat as their eyes met and held. For a moment she could not even blink. He pulled up at the bottom of the steps and was about to swing down from his saddle when Daniel caught his attention.

"Aunt 'Toria, it's the Duke, what do we do?" Bryghton's smile of amusement quickly turned to puzzlement at the discomfort displayed on the children's faces.

Vanessa, who rarely had much to say, answered his unasked question.

"We aren't allowed to talk to you, m'lord."

"It's 'your grace,' noddy," hissed an older sibling.

Bryghton ignored the interruption. "Why not, my dear?" he asked calmly, bending to be at eye level with the bashful little girl.

She shrugged uninformatively, turning her eyes to the ground. Bryghton looked to the child's cousin for explanation.

Victoria, too, shrugged helplessly. "The earl was quite clear on the subject, although he did not provide an explanation."

"Is that why you have not been in the park for the past few days?" he asked quietly.

Victoria's eyes rounded in surprise. "How do you know we have not been there?"

Bryghton blushed at his admission. "I rode through the park every day hoping to see you there."

Victoria's face turned a bright red before all colour drained from it. "I am so sorry, your grace, but we must be going. Come along children."

The duke could only blink in surprise as the young woman who had seemed to have the steadiest of nerves appeared to be on the verge of panic. He could barely reconcile the lovely lady who had stood defiantly in the river just days ago with this skittish, wide-eyed maiden looking pale and distraught.

Quickly shaking himself out of his inertia, Bryghton jumped down from his horse and approached the stairs as she was hastily urging the four young children up to the door. "My lady, please, might I have a moment of your time?"

Casting an anxious glance back at him before quickly checking on the children's progress, Victoria took a step down the stairs in his direction. In a hushed undertone she pleaded. "Not in front of the children, please."

Realization dawned on him. The children would not be able to keep a secret, nor would their cousin ask them to. If she spoke to him in defiance of the earl's clear orders she could face a great deal of difficulty. Bryghton stopped in his tracks and watched with a crease of worry forming between his brows.

As the children reached the top of the stairs, Victoria again turned to him. "My uncle has promised to provide me with a little more freedom shortly. Perhaps I might run into you then." Her whisper was barely audible. She blushed fiercely at her own boldness, which the duke found quite charming.

Bryghton Alcott, fifth Duke of Wychwood, stood on his enemy's front steps for a long moment after the door had been firmly closed behind the young lady and her charges. It crossed his mind to hope the butler had not noticed him there, which caused him to realize he was running the risk of making a fool of himself, and so he quickly turned on his heel and regained his seat in the saddle. With a final quick glance at the closed door and unopened drapes, he dragged his attention away and set off on his own errands. But the lovely young Lady Victoria did not leave his thoughts despite all the other distractions he dealt with throughout his day.

Bryghton was relieved to meet up with Fred at his club late that afternoon and hailed him heartily as soon as he was free of the doorman.

"Alfred my boy, I am quite delighted to see you, you can have no idea!"

Surprised by this uncharacteristic outpouring of enthusiasm, Fred raised an inquisitive eyebrow at his friend and waited for him to continue.

Realizing he might be attracting the attention of the other patrons, the duke frowned to himself and bit his tongue, waiting silently while they were shown to a table and served with their usual drinks. As soon as the waiter departed, Bryghton again launched into speech.

"You know much more about the law than I do, do you not, old chap?"

Fred was gratified by his friend's words, but modestly replied, "Well, I did pay more attention in school than you did, so perhaps I know a bit more, but I cannot guarantee I know what you are looking for." The duke shot him a wondering look, and the baron capitulated. "But I would probably be able to find out whatever you would like to know. What particular part of the law might you be interested in, Alcott?"

"Women's rights," the duke declared, keeping his voice low, having the presence of mind to realize it was not a highly popular subject and would give rise to uncomfortable speculation were they to be overheard.

Fred barely contained his own tones as he repeated the duke's words incredulously. "Women's rights? Why ever would you be wondering about the rights of women? You take excellent care of your mother and sister—they certainly have no cause to complain that their rights are being infringed upon!"

The duke nodded in agreement, accepting his friend's words with pride, but then shook his head in quick denial. "It is not my mother or sister's rights I am concerned with. You are correct; they have little room for complaint." After a brief pause he continued in even lower tones, a hardened edge creeping into his voice.

"I am worried about the young Lady Victoria Bartley. She has already turned twenty and is being kept as a veritable indentured servant in her own home. Did you know that house where the earl is living is actually hers? Of course you do, you mentioned it that first day I laid eyes on her," Bryghton interrupted himself before continuing. "And she has been ordered not to associate with me by her cad of an uncle. I am wondering what her rights are as to her inheritance and entering Society."

Fred had been nodding thoughtfully as the duke vented his frustrations and concerns about the young woman. Now as Bryghton wound down to a conclusion, he had some questions of his own.

"What do you hope to accomplish by getting involved, Duke? When we first saw her I thought we could somehow use her to get to her uncle, but now that I have gotten to know her, I have no intention of being party to using her. It strikes me that she has absolutely no involvement in her uncle's schemes and as an innocent young lady she deserves our protection."

"Well, I agree with you, of course," Bryghton interjected with some puzzlement.

"That protection extends even to us, Bryght. As gentlemen of the ton, we cannot get involved in her situation without some sort of intentions to offer her our protection. You know how it works. If we draw attention to her, she will be exposed to the censure and criticism of all the biddies and busybodies of the ton. You could inadvertently put poor Lady Victoria into a rather uncomfortable situation. Or, on the other hand, you could raise her expectations as to your intentions."

Bryghton's mouth was left momentarily ajar, as his glass stalled midway towards it. After blinking rather owlishly at the baron, the duke threw back his head and laughed heartily. He lowered his volume when he noticed inquiring looks directed their way, but his eyes continued to dance with merriment.

"Thank you, Fred. I was so caught up in my concerns I needed a good chuckle. And your concerns are valid, if a bit unfounded. I have absolutely no intention of raising false hopes in her heart, or of exposing her to the claws of the cats of Society. But I am worried about her. As gentlemen," he placed gentle emphasis on the word, repeating what Fred had said, "we have an obligation to protect her from her predator of an uncle."

The duke waited for this statement to sink in before repeating his question. "So I still wonder what her rights are. Do you know how we could find out? And would the stipulations of her inheritance be a matter of public record that we could access without the earl knowing? I know you said that everything not entailed went to her but we need to find out when she gains control of it. Is it like most young ladies—that she can gain her independence at the age of 25— or is she to be under the cad's control all her days, or until she marries, whichever comes first?"

Alfred sat in quiet thought for a few moments before answering. "Either one of our secretaries would know how to find the information. I do believe the matter of inheritance is considered public information, but I do not think we can access specific details without that becoming public knowledge as well. You know how these things work, Alcott."

Now it was Bryghton's turn to sit in quiet speculation for a moment before he snapped his fingers. "Most everyone knows about my issues with the earl. We could start with our continued investigation into him. It would not be considered terribly odd to be looking into his guardianship as well. This should not bring any untoward attention on his niece if our interest is expressed in that context."

"You are ever a canny one, your grace. I do believe you have hit on just the right strategy."

Satisfied that he had the outline of a plan, the duke finished his drink and then rose to take his leave. "I am promised to my mother's dinner this evening. My sister is supposed to be arriving this afternoon. Would you care to join us?"

"Thank you, but I doubt she would appreciate her numbers being thrown out at this point." As the duke was about to protest he interjected, "Besides, my aunt is expecting me for a dinner of her own. Speak to your secretary and we shall come up with a plan of action on the morrow."

The duke accepted his friend's refusal with good grace, nodding his head in acquiescence. "Then I wish you good day." He strode from the rooms, his purposeful strides preventing much interference, and a footman hastened to open the door for him.

The major domo hastily gathered his composure to bow over his well-born customer. "Good day, your grace."

Ever polite, but clearly distracted, the duke nodded and smiled briefly in the servant's direction on his way out the opened door. He remained in a brown study until he swept into his mother's home some twenty minutes later.

"Bryghton!" shrieked his sister as she dashed hoydenishly down the stairs, hurling herself into his outstretched arms as she reached the bottom.

"Hello, brat," he greeted her affectionately, planting a kiss on her forehead.

"I am not a brat, I am a lady," she declared, laughter gleaming in her eyes even as she tried to look severe.

"It would be much easier to treat you like a lady if you acted like one," Bryghton said with a sarcastic quirk to his brow.

"Children, no squabbling." Drake entered and disarmed the potential scene as he enveloped his young sister in a warm hug. The two were close in age and had shared the nursery for much of their lives until Drake had gone away to school. "Have you been here long? Why did you stay on the estate for so long? Did you not know our mother would be pining for you?"

"She was not pining for me, you gabby head," replied his sister warmly. "You know she loves Town so much more than I do. I am quite certain she has been having the time of her life without me underfoot complaining."

"You might be right, sister dear. Clearly she has forgotten how you feel about these things or she would not have planned a large dinner party on the night of your arrival."

Alanna groaned audibly. "Must you remind me? I had barely gotten my foot in the door before she was hurrying me off to my room to get ready." She paused for a moment but then grinned at her brothers. "But if it means having both of you around I suppose I can tolerate all the rest. Tell me, duke, will I pass muster even though I am travel worn?"

Bryghton bowed over his sister's outstretched hand and flourished a courtly kiss to her wrist. "If I were not your brother I would say you look ravishing, my dear. I do believe you are more in your looks than even the last time I saw you. Is it possible that you are growing even lovelier as time passes?"

Alanna blinked at her brother in awe. "I now understand where your reputation comes from."

The Duke of Wychwood grinned rakishly at his sister but forbore to comment. It was just as well, because at that moment his mama the duchess arrived on the scene.

With an indulgent smile at her three children, she heaved a dramatic sigh. "There is nothing in the world as lovely as having all my children together at one time."

"Good evening, your grace," Bryghton greeted formally as he bent over her hand with another gallant flourish. "One would never believe that you could possibly be our mother. It could be argued that you could pass for our sister, to be sure."

"Well, I would hope so, you flatterer," she answered with delight before taking a more serious tone. "But I am your mother and as such you should listen to me. It is high time you all saw to finding mates. I know I do not look the part, but it is probably time for me to have grandchildren. You, Alcott, must be thinking about the line and what you owe to the family and all that. What would your father say if he were here to see how you are carrying on?"

Bryghton caught Drake's eye and both gentlemen burst into raucous laughter. The duke sobered first. "I apologize, Mother, but you must know he would no doubt pat me on the back and say good for me. I know the passage of time allows memories to fade, but surely you remember how he carried on."

The duchess coloured slightly at this reminder that all had not been as perfect as she would like to let on. "Well, be that as it may, you must still produce an heir. You are not getting any younger, Bryghton."

"But I am quite far from my dotage," he countered drily.

The duchess carried on as though he had not spoken, turning to chide her daughter, "And you Alanna, surely you should have been able to find someone to suit you by now. This is to be your third Season, you unnatural girl."

Alanna maintained a rather stony silence, familiar with this routine, and waited for their mother to conclude her tirade. Having said her piece, the duchess abruptly changed the subject.

"Now my darlings, are you ready for a lovely evening?"

Her three darlings looked at each other rather dubiously before shrugging almost helplessly. Drake finally gave voice to their thoughts. "I suppose we are as ready as we will ever be."

"Who are you expecting this evening?" Alanna asked.

"Ah, the guest list is sure to be pleasing." With that, the duchess launched into a descriptive list of all whom she was expecting.

Chapter Eleven

"Aunty 'Toria?" began the youngest of the girls, standing bashfully at Victoria's side.

"Yes, Vanessa, what can I do for you?" Victoria crouched down to give her shy young cousin her full attention.

"Do you s'pose we will get in trouble for talking to the duke?" she asked with a worried frown.

"No, my dear. We did not engage his lordship in conversation, nor did we spend any amount of time with him, so I should not think your father will find fault with us." Victoria made every effort to sound convincing, but she was herself unsure of the truth of her statement.

Victoria wondered if she should have made a greater effort to keep the children entertained indoors, but the poor darlings had been dreadfully bored of being shut up inside. She could not be blamed for the rotten timing of the duke riding past at just the same time as they were returning home. Could she? She chewed on her lip absently as the worry chased itself around in her head.

Seeing the worried faces of the children, Victoria quickly shook herself out of her doldrums. It was her responsibility to take charge, and if she could not reassure the children, she could at least distract them.

"Who would like to play hide and seek?" she asked with forced enthusiasm.

"Me!"

"Me!"

"I do!"

"I will be 'it' first," declared Victoria. As she closed her eyes and slowly counted aloud to ten the little ones scurried around the room stifling their giggles as they searched for a hiding spot. Victoria tried to ignore the sounds they made, grinning wryly and knowing it would be an effort not to find them too quickly. Half the fun for the children was the terror of being found.

With exaggerated concentration she gazed about the room. "Where could they have all gotten to?" she asked out loud. "Is Gwennie under the table?" This question elicited a hastily muffled giggle from the other side of the room.

By the time she had "found" all the children, they were giddy with hilarity. Their happiness dimmed marginally when Victoria announced that it was time to go visit the earl and countess, but the fear did not return to their eyes. For that small fact Victoria was relieved.

Upon entering the countess' drawing room they discovered, much to Victoria's relief, that the earl was not going to be joining them that afternoon. Victoria made every effort to hide her relief, and was thankful for once that the countess was so inattentive.

After the usual awkward half hour of stilted conversation between the children and their mother, Victoria answered the few questions Lady Bartley had in relation to the children's studies and activities. They were just about to leave the room when Victoria forced herself to face the difficult subject weighing on her mind.

"M'lady, I recall that the earl decided I was not to take the children to Hyde Park, nor are we to speak to the Duke of Wychwood, but might I ask if going out of doors at all with the children is forbidden? We have stayed inside these past few days, but it is nearly unbearable for the young ones and me too, I must admit. Do you suppose it would be acceptable if we were to walk around the block on occasion, and perhaps run about in that small parkette at the end of the street?"

"Oh, I should not think there would be anything unacceptable about that. Just see that you do not stray too far from home," Lady Bartley answered rather distractedly, feeling at a decided disadvantage before her beautiful, articulate niece.

"Thank you, my lady. I bid you goodnight." Victoria nearly fled from the room, relief pouring through her. She had not thought to ask permission in advance of taking the children out, but now that it had been granted, she was more certain that the earl would not take her to task for their outing that day. Now that it was all above board she would be able to take them the next day with a clear conscience and no feelings of trepidation.

Gwen had lingered at the door and had heard the exchange between her mother and her aunt. Almost dancing on light feet in her delight, she still looked at her aunt with serious eyes. "It is a relief to be sure, is it not?"

Grinning at her too-knowing cousin, Victoria agreed, "That it is, my dear. Now let us be off. The youngsters are going to have the nursery torn apart before we get there if we do not make haste."

Giggling softly, they dashed to the top of the stairs.

Victoria struggled to keep the children entertained that evening and was deeply grateful for the increasing maturity found in Gwendolyn's help. After supper and some games, she got the last of the children bundled into bed and she finally made her way with relief to her own chamber. Bidding the nursery maid goodnight, Victoria shut the door and allowed the events of the day to wash over her in remembrance.

Looking into the mirror as she took the pins from her hair she silently asked all the questions tumbling around in her mind. What could the duke be thinking, looking for me in the park? What possible reason could he have for pursuing a relationship, however distant, with me? I am no suitable wife for one such as he, but neither could I be anything less as the daughter of an earl. Perhaps he finds some amusement in pestering me. No doubt he has no idea what my uncle is like, so he cannot realize that he is making trouble for me.

Victoria gazed off into the middle distance for a moment, and concluded, Perhaps he has the sensation that he saved my and Daniel's life, and so somehow has a connection or obligation to us. That does seem in keeping with what I know of him. I really do not know him at all, but he seems to be the type to hang much importance on chivalry and honour.

With a heartfelt sigh, Victoria tried to force her mind away from the trouble sure to be stirred up should the duke's attempt to be a presence in her life continue. All the same, a delightfully warm sensation formed in the pit of her belly at the thought of him actually caring about her future. It had seemed that since the death of her parents no one had cared much for her. Of course, the children loved her and the servants were kind, but it was not the same as the attentions of someone in a position to do something to aid her—someone who could give heed to her needs, wants, or desires. While the proud duke seemed not to be giving much heed to her feelings about his intrusion into her life, he had expressed concern over her future well-being, and it had felt genuine to her.

She took that thought to her pillow, warmed and comforted, and was not at all surprised when the handsome man, Bryghton Alcott, Duke of Wychwood, held center stage in her dreams for another night.

Chapter Twelve

After the duchess had finally finished her chronicling of the anticipated guest list, she swirled into action and swept from the room, claiming she needed to confer once more with the housekeeper and cook. In her wake, there was a short silence amongst her three doting offspring while they considered all she had said. Alanna was the first to break the silence with a tinkle of laughter.

"Well, my dear brothers, it is apparent I am not the only one she is anxious to marry off. The guests this evening are an interesting mélange of eligible mates for each of us. We can say one thing for the duchess, if nothing else—she is certainly not boring. And this dinner party of hers shan't be boring either. Even if we cannot find a suitable marriage partner, we shall not lack for good conversation."

"And she is delightedly bourgeois in her lack of nobility," commented Bryghton.

"True, but she is remarkably greedy despite the state of our own coffers," Drake observed. "I believe not a single guest could claim an income of less than ten thousand."

Bryghton teased, "That is no doubt for your benefit, for as the younger brother, your pockets are decidedly more to let than mine."

Drake tried for an expression of nonchalance, but could not maintain it as he remarked with a dour face, "Especially of late."

Immediately contrite, the duke hastened to lighten the mood. "How cruel would it be if we were to each select a likely candidate and let our mother think her ploy is working?"

They grinned at the thought before Alanna sobered and pointed out, "Decidedly cruel if we were to raise unwanted hopes in someone, especially in your case, my lord the duke."

He had to concede her point. "Was there no one on the list who might not want to be wed to a duke? Someone quite comfortable with their own state of affairs that I could enjoy a light-hearted flirtation with for the evening without raising expectations in anyone but the duchess?"

"No," answered Drake rather baldly. "Our mother is no fool."

With a resigned sigh, Bryghton had to acknowledge their mother's expertise in the art of attempted matchmaking. "Well, at least, as Alanna said, we shan't be bored this evening."

Drake laughed. "And, too, Mother's cook is remarkably skilled."

A commotion could be heard at the door, and the three siblings rose in good humour and unity to greet their mother's guests. It would seem everyone was arriving at once. Within a short space of time the evening was under way.

Despite the siblings' jesting, not every guest was on the Marriage Mart, so Bryghton eased into the evening's entertainment by striking up a conversation with the gregarious Dowager Countess of Chorley. Despite being nearly seventy, she loved to dress in the latest stare of fashion and it amused the duke to have to avoid the ridiculously large feather she had protruding from her elaborate hairstyle.

"How are things at Chorley Park, my lady?" he inquired politely.

"Oh, things there are quite lovely, thank you for asking, your grace. That irresponsible son of mine has managed not to burn it down for another year, so that is a blessing to be sure. The only sensible thing he ever did in his life was to marry himself a good woman. Pamela is a wonderful addition to the Chorley family. Not only did she have the sense to have three strapping boys so there is no concern for the succession, but she has the organizational skills of an army general. She has taken over many of the duties that my dearly departed husband cared for but that my rapscallion of a son cannot trouble himself about."

Bryghton, unsure of how to reply, made a noncommittal sound of acknowledgement. The lady needed no prompting to continue.

"You cannot get him out of his workshop for the life of him. Always experimenting, he is. Nothing has come of it yet, and the boy is nearing his fiftieth birthday. Would you not say it is time for him to put such things aside and see to the estates?"

Bryghton was dismayed to realize that the dowager countess appeared to want him to comment. Feeling slightly harried, he came up with what he thought was a reasonable answer. "It would seem that he has seen to his estates. Did you not say Lady Chorley is seeing to things in quite an exceptional way? And of course, if you are still in residence, your expertise no doubt goes a long way to adding to her success. It seems to me that Chorley Park is in excellent hands." He accompanied this with a charming smile and waited for her response.

The dowager countess stared at him for a moment before barking with laughter. "You certainly are a clever one, aren't you, Wychwood? You are, of course, perfectly correct. Between us, Pamela and I do an excellent job of running the estates. But I still think he should at least pay some attention."

"You are no doubt correct, my lady," he answered. "Have they come up for the Season?"

"No, the indolent rat could not tear himself away, and poor Pamela does not think it seemly to come without him, especially not while the children are still in school. It might actually be a shame they did not have a daughter. At least then Pamela would have a good excuse to come to Town. Surely she would have to provide a daughter with a Season." Lady Chorley must have realized that this really was not the type of conversation she should be having with the young duke. Giving her head a slight shake that sent her feather bobbing around haphazardly, she changed the subject.

"What about you, Duke? Are you looking forward to the Season? Should we be expecting any exciting developments amongst your family this year?"

Bryghton grinned at her in good humour. "Did my mother put you up to asking that?"

His companion chortled. "It is every mother's desire to have her offspring happily married off. Then her job is finally done. Your poor mama has you, the duke, still on her hands. Surely it is a worry for the dear lady. Especially with your father gone and you already having the title, she no doubt feels it her responsibility to secure the succession."

"Mayhap you are right, my lady. However, I feel I must point out the fact that I am merely thirty. Surely I am nowhere near the grave. There is plenty of time for me to concern myself with filling my nursery," the duke protested mildly.

"That would be more true if you were still the heir. Now that your father has passed on, there needs to be another heir."

Bryghton realized there was a sliver of truth to this statement, and he offered a benign smile. "Well, you had best get a good seat, m'lady, as it would appear this year the Season is going to be a good show."

This prompted another delighted chortle from Lady Chorley before she advised him, "You had best get on with the show then, my boy. What are you doing talking to an old bird like me? Go get yourself one of those lovely young misses your mama has invited for you to inspect."

Bryghton could not contain his grin over the elderly lady's choice of words. She was right—it was as though his mother was trotting out a group of young ladies and misses for him and Drake to look over. And lords for Alanna, of course. But that was what the Marriage Mart and the Season were all about—those doing the inspecting and everyone else watching the show. Gritting his teeth over the ridiculousness of it all, Bryghton turned to survey the crowd that had grown considerably while he had chatted with Lady Chorley.

The Duchess of Wychwood had outdone herself. There was a wide variety of guests from varying levels of high Society milling about the duchess' receiving room and the rumble of polite conversation was at sufficient volume to assure the hostess that everyone was engaged. The duchess had clearly given a great deal of thought to this evening, choosing intelligent, articulate ladies and gentlemen as her guests, knowing that her children would not be interested in anything less. Even if her own offspring did not find mates this evening, there were many potential matches amongst the well-born crowd, and the duchess would be able to proudly claim some responsibility for whatever unions might follow.

Despite the interesting choices for conversation before him, however, Bryghton could not prevent himself from wishing rather wistfully that the lovely Lady Victoria Bartley were present. He could just imagine the sparkle of amusement in her eye if she were to see Lady Chorley's bobbing headdress.

With a soft sigh and a rueful shake of his head the duke fixed a congenial smile onto his handsome face and turned to survey the gathered throng once more. His eye was quickly caught by a buxom woman wearing a daringly cut gown in a hue to match the necklace of large matching rubies that hung heavily around her neck. She was laughing graciously at something her companion was saying and the duke could not help smiling in response. Despite her rather homely face and figure, her openness seemed to invite one to enjoy her presence. He stepped forward to make their acquaintance.

"Good evening, I am Alcott, and welcome to my mother's home," he introduced himself with a perfect blend of formality and familiarity.

"Of course, your grace, we know who you are," the lady answered before blushing over stating the obvious. She quickly recovered, introducing herself and her companion. "I am Miss Melinda Lambert and this is my brother, Robert, the Baron of Shelton. This is our first Season, although as you can see we are not the usual age for making one's debut."

"I am pleased to make your acquaintance. Is this your first time in London?" he asked politely.

The brother and sister smiled amusedly. Robert maintained his silence but his sister answered in her tinkling melodic voice. "Lud, your grace, we are well out of the schoolroom. We have made the journey up to your fair city a time or two. We just have not come to join the social whirl until now." Melinda glanced at her brother and continued. "To be honest, your grace, my brother has decided he ought to go into politics, so he needs to make some connections, meet people, and all that. And he decided he might also need a hostess for certain endeavours, so I have joined him in this adventure."

The duke tried to keep his astonishment from showing. In his experience, politicians could hardly be kept quiet. This young man had yet to open his mouth. Bryghton searched his mind for something to say. "Shelton, you said? Is that in the north?"

Melinda let out a tinkling laugh once more, smiling indulgently at the duke. "Your grace, we are in London. Nearly everything is north of here. I would say that is cheating."

Delighted by her teasing, Bryghton joined her in a brief laugh but regarded her steadily with an upward quirk to his eyebrow. He was not applying the full power of his aristocracy, but Melinda, unused to the haughty ways of the ton, quaked at his stare. Blushing to her roots, she launched into speech, "Yes, m'lord, it is north. It took us two days of travelling all day to get here, which I would say is probably fairly average." Regaining her equilibrium and her cheek, she asked the duke, "Did you have to travel far to come up to Town, your grace?"

"Not terribly," he answered uninformatively, his eyes dancing with amusement. "I must say, Miss Lambert, I think you are going to have a very successful Season. Lord Shelton, I wish you good fortune in your chosen career. We shall no doubt meet again throughout the coming weeks." With that he excused himself and moved on to speak with others.

Seeing Drake not far away, the duke joined him for a moment. "How are you enjoying our mother's efforts thus far, young cub?" he teased.

Drake gave a mock shudder. "I must say, it would seem the ladies are rather aggressive in their attentions. I do not have the cloak of impenetrable importance that you seem to be able to don whenever someone becomes a bit de trop. Such a useful skill that seems to have come with the title."

Bryghton looked at his brother assessingly. "Are you saying you are getting too much attention from the ladies?" he demanded, sarcasm dripping.

Drake blushed like a schoolgirl. "You see, it is that exact tone that can suppress pretention in a heartbeat. Where did you learn to talk like that?"

"I have no idea what you are blathering about," Bryghton replied with boredom now colouring his every note but amusement evident in the glint in his eyes.

Drake gave up his protests, realizing that his brother was in on the joke. Looking back at their mother's guests, Drake gave a careless shrug. "I am actually having a rather enjoyable time thus far, in answer to your original question. Everyone here seems to be very amusing and easy-going. It shall be an interesting evening."

"Indeed," said the duke. "Shall we return to the fray?"

While his brother was speaking, Drake had been looking about his mother's receiving room when his eyes landed upon a most unwelcome sight. Bryghton was perplexed to see his brother's face flush with bright colour before becoming pasty white.

"What ails you, cub?" he demanded, his voice no longer displaying boredom, but an urgent sense of concern as he too scanned the crowd searchingly.

"Dalton is here," Drake croaked through his suddenly dry lips as he made an effort to recover his composure.

The duke's face darkened slightly at this news but he maintained a brilliantly inscrutable façade. "Have no fears, cub. Dalton may be many things we should not express in our mother's receiving room, but he is a gentleman. He will not shame you. Really, how could he? As I have told you innumerable times, you have naught of which to be ashamed. Now buck up and go delight the ladies."

Drake threw his brother a rather harried look but did as he was told, plastering a seemingly unconcerned look onto his face and turning back to rejoin the social whirl. He failed to notice the hard look that had settled upon Bryghton's own features as he turned to go in search of Lord Anthony Dalton.

"Dalton, how surprising to see you amongst my mother's assembled guests," Alcott began in silky tones, his inscrutable face hiding his anger well.

"Wychwood. It was a pleasure to receive her invitation," he replied noncommittally, his eyes alert for any threat from the duke.

Bryghton smiled without pleasure as he perceived the other man's discomfort. He admonished the other man in an undertone, "Have no fear, Dalton. I am not about to cause a scene to discomfit the duchess."

The other man relaxed imperceptibly at the logic of this but did not turn away, continuing to eye the duke uneasily. Alcott felt his irritation with the other man increase. "For heaven's sake, my lord, pull yourself together. I am appalled at your gall to enter this house, but if you stay away from Drake you shan't have anything to worry about from me. We can meet to discuss anything we need to air out at another, more appropriate time."

Lord Dalton visibly put the steel back into his backbone, raising his chin to a haughtier level and quirking a supercilious eyebrow to the Duke. "Indeed, Wychwood. We could meet any time you wish."

The duke stared at his mother's guest coldly, wondering if he had just uttered a veiled threat. Bryghton decided he did not much care if it was. He answered in a hard tone, "It would be a pleasure."

The two noblemen stared coldly at one another for the length of another heartbeat. Dalton was the first to blink. Without fully backing down, he bowed slightly to the duke and said, "Until we meet again, your grace." He then turned and waved to someone on the other side of the room and walked away, leaving Bryghton feeling the tinny taste of dissatisfaction in his mouth. He maintained his façade of pleasantness, and was relieved when it was finally announced that dinner would be served.

Offering his elbow to his mother, he escorted her to her elegant and perfectly arranged dining room. Bryghton was taken aback by his mother's piercing look as they stopped at her chair. "Is everything all right between you and Drake?" she asked in a low tone, not to be overheard by any of the guests.

"Of course, your grace, why do you ask?"

"The two of you seemed to be in a rather intense conversation not long before dinner was announced," she answered, awaiting his response.

The duke managed a negligent shrug before answering her in all honesty. "Drake and I are better than ever. There is naught to worry your beautiful head about, my dear mother. Now enjoy your guests."

The duchess continued to eye him askance, causing her firstborn to laugh good naturedly.

"I promise, your grace," he vowed, solemnly placing his hand over his heart. "I adore my little brother and there is nothing amiss between us."

His mother looked unconvinced for a moment, searching his eyes seriously, but then she smiled and took the seat he was holding for her. "Well, then, since that is settled, let us eat." She dimpled at her son.

There was a contented buzz of conversation as the assembled guests enjoyed the duchess' hospitality and the skills of her well-trained kitchen staff.

Bryghton took his seat at the foot of his mother's table, admiring her elegance at its head. He glanced around at the assembled guests and was appalled to see that Alanna had been seated next to Lord Dalton and was busily striking up a flirtation with the handsome viscount. He was dismayed to see that Drake had also noticed the turn of events and was glaring hotly at the pair. Bryghton could not blame him for the sentiment, but wished his brother could better control his thoughts and reactions.

Just before the steam began to pour from his ears, Drake glanced around the assembled diners and saw his brother looking his way. Accurately interpreting the pointed look the duke was discreetly shooting him, the young lord blushed mildly and pulled himself together, turning hastily to the lady sitting on his left so he could no longer see his sister flirting with one of his enemies. He had no idea what she was talking about, but having been trained by the Duchess of Wychwood he had no problem going through the appropriate motions of polite Society.

Bryghton, watching from his end of the table as his little brother gathered the shreds of his composure and displayed a maturity he had yet to witness, could not suppress the grin of pride that briefly creased his face. His eyes strayed to the head of the table and briefly caught those of his mother. He was surprised at the knowing smile on the duchess' face and just barely managed to hide his astonishment as she winked at him. He covered his shocked grin by turning to converse with his dinner companions.

The courses were passed and the evening flew by. The duchess stood to lead the ladies out and Bryghton was left to preside over a somewhat abbreviated session of port drinking. It seemed that all the men were of similar mind, and wished to join the ladies again as soon as possible. There was very little conversation as the gentlemen broodingly stared into the bottom of their port glasses, seemingly finding more consolation from their depths than in the few stilted words from their fellow gentlemen. Bryghton was relieved that Drake continued to steadfastly ignore Lord Dalton and the viscount too confined himself to a few words to the gentleman on his left. Gazing down the length of his mother's dining table, the duke stood as the last man placed his glass on the table with a satisfied thump. The rest of the gentlemen hastened to follow his lead, not waiting for another round to be poured.

The duchess looked up with a charming smile as the gentlemen filed in to rejoin the ladies. She dearly loved to entertain but she was not sad over the prospect that her guests would soon be departing. It was obvious that her sons had things they needed to discuss and she wondered fleetingly if they would ever confide in her. Eyeing her youngest son with some misgiving as he stalked towards his sister, she wondered if she would again have to create a diversion.

"I need a word with you," Drake said through his clenched teeth while keeping a tight smile affixed to his face.

Alanna could feel her eyebrows inching towards her hairline over her brother's unusual tone. "You can have all the words you would like, my dear Drakey," she said, smiling.

He was not in the mood to allow her to cajole him, and he increased his efforts to keep his feelings off his face, momentarily distracted by wonder at Alcott's ability to always appear implacable. Drake was able to keep his anger under control, and taking Alanna's elbow, he steered her away from the crowd for a degree of privacy.

"What did you think you were doing flirting with Dalton?" he demanded.

Alanna's own quick temper was ignited by his low but fierce tone. "Whatever do you mean, Drake? I am in Town for the Season. It is my job to flirt with all eligible partis."

"He is not an eligible parti." Drake was proud of his firm and controlled tones.

Alanna was decidedly not. It might be one thing for the duke to try to tell her what to do, as he was the head of the family, but there was no way she was going to tolerate this behaviour from Drake. It would not do to cause a scene in her mother's drawing room, however, so she made an effort to keep her voice down.

"How can you say that? He is a guest in our mother's home, he is a viscount, and from what I can see he is well respected by others, even those here for our mother's dinner. What do you have against him?"

"It does not matter why. You just have to accept that he is dead to our family."

"You are being ridiculous, Drake. He is not dead. He is right there living and breathing. In fact," she said, being unable to resist taunting her brother for his inexplicable behaviour, "he is doing a remarkably handsome job of it."

"If you will not listen to me, ask Bryghton." Drake fell back on his best defense, knowing he was about to lose his control if he did not quickly end the conversation.

"I do not feel the need to discuss Lord Anthony Dalton with Bryghton. There is nothing to say. We were seated next to each other at the table. We talked. There is no reason for you to be so worked up over it." Both of the younger Alcotts were so caught up in their argument they failed to notice their brother approach.

"I trust you children are enjoying your evening." Bryghton could not help smiling over their guilty faces as they turned to him in surprise.

"Drake is being a toad, if you must know," Alanna said coldly, trying to regain the composure she had allowed to slip.

"Was this conversation absolutely necessary while our mother's guests are milling about, cub?" Bryghton asked. Judging by Bryghton's face, any onlookers would think this conversation was perfectly cordial. The duke's ability to keep his face completely impassive while his voice dripped with disdain was a thing to marvel at.

Drake did not have that ability and his angry disgust was plain to see. Luckily, his back was to the crowd and he kept his voice down as he explained himself to the duke. "She was flirting with Dalton, Bryght, what else was I supposed to do? I could not stand by and watch calmly."

"Actually, you could have, but that is a conversation for another day. Surely you realize our sister is not a chit fresh from the schoolroom. You really could have waited until later to discuss this." The duke carried on before his brother could interject. "Now, why do you not go help our mother entertain our guests, or better yet, go find someone to flirt with yourself. You know that will bring delight to the duchess' heart."

Bryghton had to bite his lip to keep from grinning at the disgruntled look his younger brother shot him before he went off to do as he was told. The duke doubted Drake would be able to strike up a flirtation in his current mood, but he looked on with pride as the younger man did approach a young lady and began speaking to her.

"Drake said Dalton is ineligible for me and I was not to flirt with him." Alanna's angry huff brought Bryghton's attention back to her.

"That was a rather bold statement for him to make. Did he say why he felt that way?"

Alanna needed to exert strong effort not to roll her eyes at her brother's dry tone. "No, he did not. Instead of explaining himself, he told me to ask you about it."

"He must have been truly desperate if that was the only explanation he could come up with," Bryghton smiled at his sister's chagrin. "You really should talk this over with Drake later. Now is hardly the time for it. I overheard you telling Drake that it is your job to be flirting with all the eligible gentlemen. You were right, so why are you not doing that?"

"Because Drake dragged me over to this corner to demand that I not speak to the viscount," she reminded him as her patience slowly drained away.

"I met someone recently that you might know, a young lady." Bryghton gave up trying to get her to let it go and decided to try distraction instead.

"Lady Victoria, the earl of Pickering's niece. Did you know her when you went to finishing school for that year?"

This brought his sister's full attention. Bryghton never asked anyone about ladies, especially not his little sister. Alanna realized he might be trying to distract her away from talking about Lord Dalton, but there was something about his tone of voice when he mentioned Lady Victoria that caught her attention.

"I know whom you are speaking of, but I do not think I have ever made her acquaintance. She is at least one or two years younger than me, so if we had been at school at the same time she would no doubt have been beneath my notice." Her voice carried notes of snobbishness but her brother could see the twinkle in her eye that belied her words.

"Are little girls as beastly as boys?"

"Mayhap worse, Alcott, I will admit."

"And our mother thinks I should be setting up my nursery?" he asked, amazement colouring his tones.

"Are you thinking to set it up with Lady Victoria?" asked Alanna incredulously.

"Good heavens, how did you jump to that conclusion?"

Alanna's shrug was uninformative. "It seemed that was where you were heading when you asked if I knew her."

"You distracted me. No, I am not thinking of my nursery at this time," Bryghton struggled to keep his voice even as he remembered watching Alfred play with little Daniel. Seeing his sister's speculative look he quickly marshalled his thoughts. "I merely asked because I thought you might know her. Alfred and I met her recently and it struck me that she might be in need of a friend."

Bryghton, irritated by the grin on his sister's face, decided to end the conversation. "It is of no matter. Shall we mingle?" He remained stoic as he heard her amused giggle following him. Alanna's gaze followed him, her head tilted in what everyone knew to be her thinking pose. If Bryghton had seen it he would have been wary, but instead he strolled away as nonchalantly as possible.

"Are you having a good time, dear?" the duchess asked him.

Bryghton could not help grinning at his mother's tone of concern. "You should walk the boards at the theatre, your grace."

The innocent look on her face did not quite reach her eyes but she batted her eyelashes nonetheless. "I have no idea what you are speaking about, my dear."

"You would have us all believe you know nothing but the latest fashions and gossip, but you are fully cognizant of all that is going on, are you not?" Despite his best efforts, he could not quite keep the incredulity from his voice.

"I pray you do not sound so surprised, your grace." The duchess kept her usual, pleasant smile pinned to her sweet lips but she allowed her voice to harden. "Do you think the duchy ran itself between the time your father died and you graduated from school? Now, be a good boy and go make Miss Symmington's evening by telling her how ravishing she looks. We can discuss all the strange things you have been keeping from your poor mama of late on the morrow."

Bryghton felt his chin starting to drop in shock but managed to clamp his lips together just before they fell open. His mother walked away calmly and he would have sworn he heard her whistling. She glanced back and again allowed her eyelid to dip into a wink.

Shaking his head with amazed admiration, Bryghton watched her stroll gracefully through the mingling guests before he turned to do as his mother had bade him, and approached Miss Symmington for a brief, pleasant conversation.

Before long the assembled guests began to take their leave of the duchess in order to move on to other engagements for the rest of the evening. The four Alcotts stood in the foyer and waved off the last of the duchess' guests before returning to the withdrawing room.

"Thank you, children, for all being here and helping me entertain my guests. I think everyone had a good time, don't you?"

"You, my lady mother, are a lovely hostess and everyone had a smashingly good time, including me," Alanna grinned in delight. "Now shall we ring for the carriage? We should be at the Roxborough ball by now."

"I am certain the butler has already seen to it, as the entire household is aware of your eagerness to practice your dance steps. Now run upstairs and have your maid run a comb through your curls. Somehow you have managed to disarray your hairstyle. Whatever could you have been doing to accomplish that during dinner?" There was no answer to be had as Alanna dashed from the room before her mother had even finished speaking, which perhaps was answer enough.

Turning to her sons, the duchess said with a fond smile, "That girl has yet to comprehend the word slow."

"'Tis true, Mother, but you can comfort yourself with the fact that she does hasten gracefully."

The duchess could not resist chuckling at the duke's comment.

"Shall you two be joining us at the Roxborough ball? I am certain they should welcome you even if you did not reply to their invitation."

Drake and Bryghton looked at each other with consternation, neither wanting to disappoint their mother but both dreading the prospect of such a crush as the ball promised to be.

"I am promised elsewhere this evening, m'lady," answered Bryghton, striving for a measured tone of regret despite not feeling the least regretful to miss the event.

The duchess did not appear to be discomfited in the least. "It is just as well. I will have enough trouble keeping an eye on Alanna, and I should not wish to worry about the two of you on top of it all." She trilled a happy giggle over their bemused expressions as she swept from the room. The clatter of the carriage being pulled to the front door was heard just as Alanna skipped down the stairs from her rooms.

"Shall we go, my darling daughter?"

"Yes, please."

The two Alcott gentlemen stood in the drawing room as the two ladies departed. There was a moment of silence before Bryghton burst out laughing. Drake was unsure what the mirth was about, and his brother shook his head and elaborated.

"That mother of ours is far more knowing than she lets on."

Drake's eyes rounded in surprise. "I find it hard to believe that you are just noticing. I have learned in my life that nothing gets past her. I had thought the same was true of you, but now I am not so sure. How did you not realize that she knows everything?"

Bryghton shrugged rather negligently. "I suppose she does such a good job of being frivolous. She bamboozled me along with the rest of Society into believing that all that's going on inside her pretty head are thoughts of fashion and her next entertainment. I wonder why she hides it?"

"Makes her much more effective, I would think."

"Astute observation, cub." Bryghton remained in thought for a moment before turning his own astute gaze upon his younger brother. "Now why don't you tell me what you were thinking when you confronted our sister during our mother's party."

Drake blushed hotly under his brother's piercing eyes and began a rather disjointed explanation of his intentions.

Chapter Thirteen

Alanna smiled in satisfaction as she stood at the top of the grand staircase leading into the Duke of Roxborough's ballroom. The room below her was a flowing sea of bright colours and twinkling lights as the candlelight glanced off the jewels of all the well-born ladies swarming about the more drably attired gentlemen. Despite how she had jested with her brothers earlier, she loved the Season with all its complexities, especially at the beginning. She knew by the time it was wrapping up she would be looking forward to heading back to their estate, but for now she was anticipating the thrills that were in store over the coming weeks.

Picking up her skirts, she gracefully glided down the stairs as quickly as the crowds and her elaborate dress would allow. Acknowledging her mother's admonition not to stray too far from view with a slight inclination of her head, her eyes began their task of scanning the crowds. Just before she reached the bottom of the stairs, her eyes finally alighted on whom she was searching for. With a slight wave to her mother as the duchess turned to the side of the room where other matrons were gathering, Alanna braved the gathered mass and struck out to intersect with Alfred, Lord Lynster, her brother's best friend.

"Lady Alanna, what a delight to see you here this evening," Alfred greeted politely. "I was not sure if any of you Alcotts would be attending this evening, as the duke had told me your mother was entertaining tonight."

"It was merely a dinner party. Everyone has left for other events, so here we are." Alanna contemplated how best to proceed. She began with the usual niceties. "How have you been, my lord? Are you enjoying the beginnings of the Season?"

Alfred could not help grinning. "I do not think gentlemen enjoy it nearly as much as ladies seem to do, but I am having a fine enough time, thank you for asking, my lady. My aunt and sister just arrived in town, so that has been a pleasure thus far. I do not have separate lodgings as your brother does, so I may not be feeling that way later as my house becomes overrun with their guests," he concluded drolly.

Alanna smiled distractedly at his dry attempt at humour, preoccupied by her own thoughts. "How lovely," she replied without thought. Giving up her attempts at trying for a subtle approach, she decided to get straight to her point.

"My lord, do you know Lady Victoria Bartley?"

Alfred blinked at the abrupt turn of the conversation before glancing around to see if Alanna had been overheard. No one was yet taking any notice of them, but he made an attempt to guide the conversation and his friend's sister away from any unwanted attention.

"As a matter of fact, I have made her acquaintance. Could I fetch you a glass of lemonade, my lady? I find it is a trifle close in these rooms now that the crowds have gotten so large."

"Do not try to fob me off, my lord. I would dearly like to have a conversation with you," Alanna said in a low but definite voice.

With a resigned sigh, Alfred extended his elbow to her. "Then shall we take a stroll about the room? It would not do to appear to be in a heated debate over something as inconsequential as a mere acquaintance."

"Thank you, m'lord, that would be delightful," she answered, playful now that she had gotten her way. Alanna was careful to smile at her acquaintances as they slowly inched their way through the room and allowed a few moments to pass before returning to her subject of choice.

"I apologize for putting you on the spot, my lord. It is just that my curiosity is near to killing me. Bryghton mentioned the lady to me this evening in an attempt to divert me from a different subject and now I find that I must know what the story is behind his encountering her."

Alfred admired her honesty and lack of artifice while also feeling profound relief that his own little sister was not as smart as the duke's. It did not do to underestimate an intelligent woman, and he was amazed that Bryghton had evidently forgotten this universal truth. His own curiosity was now enflamed. "What was the subject he was trying to divert you from that was so engrossing he made the drastic step of asking about a lady?"

Alanna grinned, delighted that the baron caught onto the same train of thought. "That is a subject for some other lengthy discussion. I will not allow you to use the same tactic in reverse, my lord. Suffice it to say that he and Drake did not want me associating with Lord Anthony Dalton."

"Ah, I see," replied Alfred, comprehension dawning. "So what did you wish to discuss?" he asked.

"I know Bryght was just trying to distract me, but you should have heard his voice. There was a note in his tone that I have never heard from him before. I think he has feelings for this lady, feelings he may not even be aware of himself. And I want to help."

"Are you about to try your hand at matchmaking, Lady Alanna? Do you not think the duchess is doing enough of that for your entire family?"

Alanna offered an uninformative shrug while thinking for a moment. "I do not wish to rush him into an unwanted relationship, but you must admit he has to marry someday. It might as well be before he's old and grey."

Alfred suppressed his mirth to a low chuckle before drily replying, "I know you are a fair bit younger than him, but you do realize he is not that old, don't you?"

She again lifted her shoulder in a lopsided shrug the baron was starting to find rather appealing. "He just has not appeared truly interested in a lady before. And I think it is time we expanded our family. Neither Drake nor I are ready to do it, but somebody has to. The house of Wychwood is a rather small little lot. It would be quite lovely to have a large family. It is too late to do it naturally, with cousins and aunts and uncles, so we must do it through marriages and children."

"Well, if that is how you feel you ought to set your sights on some other lady for the duke. Lady Victoria is an orphan living with a rather nasty uncle. She does have five young cousins who seem to be quite lovely, but they cannot quite offset the negativity of the Earl of Pickering."

Alanna fell silent while she contemplated this piece of information. Again she offered the same shrug. "Young cousins might be fun," she grinned. "If you know about them, you must have met them, am I right? So have you seen my brother around this lady? Am I right in thinking there was more to his conversation than merely trying to divert me?"

Alfred debated how much to reveal to his friend's sister. Obviously he could not tell her about their feud with the earl and he was still unsure of the wisdom of pursuing even a mere acquaintance with the lady given that feud, but he could also not argue with the truth of her words that there did appear to be sparks between the duke and Lady Victoria. And he too wanted to see his friend happily attached. Everyone knows a duke has to wed. It would be perfectly lovely if it could be to someone with whom he could find happiness. That decided, he smiled at Alanna.

"Yes, I have met the lady, and have seen your brother with her. You know how the duke is. He can so easily hide his thoughts from others, but yes, I did think there might be some warmer feelings from him towards her. But, m'lady, I must warn you, there are complications in the situation that may not be surmountable."

Alanna tilted her head in question, absorbed in the baron's words. "What kind of complications?"

"For one thing, and it is a major roadblock, she does not go about in Society."

"Why ever not? She is the daughter of an earl, and I would think an heiress besides. Is she ill?"

"Not ill, nor deformed in any way," Alfred said, laughing. "But she has the misfortune to have been left to the guardianship of an uncle who appears to think only of himself. He does not seem to concern herself overly about her future and is quite content to allow her to expend her energies looking after his children."

Alanna gazed at him with eyes full of surprised dismay, and he could see that her intelligent mind was wrestling with the questions of this situation.

"Are there no other relatives that could take an interest in her affairs? I do not at the moment recall her entire family tree, but surely there must be some other aunts somewhere who should be able to arrange for her to enter and take her proper place in Society."

"I would imagine there are, but none of them have yet to take an interest. She is not yet terribly old and she has been tucked away in schools for many years. It is not an excuse, but her relatives may have forgotten about her."

Alanna felt her jaw drop open inelegantly at this statement. "How could anyone forget about their relatives?"

"Do you really expect me to believe that you regularly contemplate your family tree and wonder what you could be doing to make life easier for every aunt, uncle, or cousin?" Alfred asked in an effort to help her see reason.

"No, but that is because I am well aware that they are all taken care of." Alanna heard the defensiveness in her tone and fell silent for a moment. "That is rather terrible, I must say. Well, that decides it then—clearly we must do something. Even if she does not wish to be the next Duchess of Wychwood, she is still the daughter of an earl and has the right to take her place amongst her peers."

Alfred was full of admiration at her zeal for this project. "What would you suggest we do, my lady?"

"I am not yet perfectly sure. First you must introduce me to her. Once I have met her I will decide how we must proceed."

"I fear I am not perfectly sure of the wisdom of this course, my lady. Nor am I sure that your brother would approve."

"Do not be a ninny, my lord, I beg you," she chided. "Neither of us has to answer to the duke for our actions," she declared with near honesty.

"I would hate to call you a liar, m'lady, but you must know that is not completely true. As the Duke of Wychwood, he is the head of your family, and as my dearest friend, while I do not answer to him, I do feel a hesitation to do something that would be contrary to any plans he might have."

"Well, then, never mind about matchmaking. There is a travesty to justice taking place with a young lady of the realm. Is it not our aristocratic responsibility to ensure she has the opportunity to join Society? It really has nothing to do with my brother at all."

Alfred grinned at this feminine logic and waited for her to continue.

"So how did you two meet her? And do you think there is any way that we could arrange for me to meet her? If her uncle is so nasty, perhaps it would not do for me to show up on her doorstep demanding entrance."

The baron sobered quickly at her words, realizing how the duke would feel about his young sister associating with the Earl of Pickering. "Absolutely not, my lady. It would not do at all for you to simply show up."

Alanna bristled at his tone. "Well, I do not see why not. There is nothing unacceptable about the daughter of the Duchess of Wychwood calling on the daughter of the Earl of Pickering."

Realizing he may have overstepped and pushed her to rebel out of spite, he quickly sought to placate her. "That is not at all what I was trying to imply, Lady Alanna. The problem is that you might cause problems for Lady Victoria. There is no knowing what her uncle will do. He does not particularly wish for her to have friends, you see."

Somewhat mollified, Alanna acknowledged that she really knew nothing of the situation. "Well then, what do you suggest?"

"Bryght and I met her in the park while she was out with the youngsters in her care. I would suggest that you and I go for a ride and see if we might run into them."

Alanna grinned with delight. "What a smashing idea, my lord. What time should I be ready?"

Alfred was glad that he had been able to maintain a degree of control over this awkward situation, but he wondered if he was under obligation to inform his friend about this turn of events, and if so, how he would react. Alfred struggled momentarily with these thoughts and so did not answer her right away.

"Are you wishing now I had stayed out of it and regretting your offer, my lord?" Alanna asked, biting her lip in indecision.

Alfred laughed. "I must admit, I do rather wish you had stayed out of it. But no, I do not regret my offer of help. If you must know, I was wondering what Bryght would think were he to find out what we have in mind."

Alanna lifted her shoulder in her signature shrug. "I do not see how it is any of his nevermind what efforts we make to rescue a young lady from her life of servitude. He would no doubt applaud our efforts were he to take any interest, which I am sure he is much too busy to do."

Alfred didn't quite believe her despite her airy confidence, but he allowed it to pass. "Would four o'clock be suitable for you? I think that was approximately the time we encountered them in the past."

"That would be perfectly lovely. Thank you, my lord," said Alanna, trying to suppress her grin of triumphant delight.

The baron shook his head with a touch of chagrin before bidding her adieu and moving on lest they draw unwanted attention to their prolonged conversation.

Alanna turned back to the crowded ballroom, surprised by the press of people all around. During their conversation she had been oblivious to the crowds around them. Despite her previous anticipation for this social event, she was now impatient for it to be over so she could get on with her plans to rescue the young noblewoman from her current fate.

Displaying a practiced smile, Alanna accepted the next gentleman that came to claim her hand for a dance and wiled away the rest of the night. No one watching her would ever suspect that she was not enjoying herself to the utmost, or that her mind was busily planning for the next day.

Chapter Fourteen

"But why can't we go to the big park anymore, Aunt 'Toria? It was ever so much better than that tiny little place you have been taking us to all week," Vanessa whined.

Victoria winced at her cousin's words. Crouching down to look her in the eye, Victoria held onto her patience by a thread as she replied. "I know the bigger park seems more exciting, little one, but your father has said he does not wish us to go there. Perhaps when Daniel is bigger we can go. He did not explain his reasons to me, and we just have to do as he said."

The little girl looked as though she was going to argue, so Victoria cut her off quickly with a reminder. "Would you not agree that the little park is much better than staying home all day? I myself am getting quite tired of being inside the house, but if you prefer it, I will see if one of the maids could keep you company."

"No Aunt 'Toria! I promise I would ever so much rather go with you to the park. And you are right, any park will do if only we can get out of the schoolroom."

Victoria hid her smile, relieved that her ploy had worked. Not fully understanding her uncle's reasons, it was difficult to explain to the children why they could not go to the lovely big park they had enjoyed so much. But she had not lied to the little girl. At this point, it was true that anywhere outside would do.

Victoria was getting increasingly tired of playing the role of governess, no matter how much she loved her young cousins. She wasn't even getting paid, but no amount of money would really be enough to compensate for the huge task, she mused, and wondered how real governesses managed. Realizing that in all reality she was a real governess, Victoria fell into a brown study of worry as she went through the motions of getting the children ready for their outing.

I keep telling myself that I am not truly the children's governess, but what else am I? A governess is someone who must earn their way since they have no other options. What options do I have? My uncle is not paying me for my services, and I have nowhere to go. I am actually worse off than a real governess! I ought to have as open and honest a conversation as possible with the earl and establish what my position really is and what my future holds. Surely my parents left some sort of provision for my future.

Thus resolved, Victoria managed to pull her thoughts out of the dark clouds and return her attention to the children. As she reminded herself, This difficult position is not the children's fault. Even if their father has not provided them with someone more qualified, I must do the best I can for them.

"Is everything all right with you, Aunt Victoria?" Gwendolyn asked, maturity sitting strangely on the shoulders of the nine-year-old girl.

"Everything is fine, Gwennie, I am just a bit dull today from not getting enough sleep last night. It is nothing a brisk walk to the park will not cure. Shall we be off?"

The group stepped out as always, the four young children being herded along by Victoria and one of the upstairs maids. Everett was busy with his tutor, as usual. Victoria tried not to think sourly of the unfairness of the tutor only having to watch over one adolescent boy while she had to look out for four children of such varying ages. But she loved the darlings, so she shoved away her resentment. As anticipated, the fresh air and sunshine soon brushed the cobwebs from her mind, and she was her usual sunny self by the time they reached the small parkette.

Little Daniel was so delighted about managing to hold onto his ball for the entire walk, he immediately set to playing with it. His three sisters quickly fell in with his plans and Victoria stood to the side watching fondly over their energetic play.

Meanwhile, a few streets away, a frustrated Lord Alfred was escorting a deeply disappointed Lady Alanna out of Hyde Park in his smartly turned out phaeton. Alanna had lost all delight in the sporting equipage when it did not succeed in carrying her on her appointed errand. They had circled the park twice in an effort to find the elusive Lady Victoria, but to no avail.

"What are we going to do, my lord? How am I supposed to help the lady if I cannot find her?" Alanna nearly wailed in her distress.

"Never fear, my lady, this is only the first day of our quest. Mayhap she shall be here tomorrow," answered the baron in an attempt to soothe his companion.

"I cannot continue to ride out with you every day. My mother, your aunt, and Society will expect an announcement if we make such a display of ourselves."

Alfred started in dismay at this pointed reminder, feeling the heat of a blush rising up his neck. "I apologize, m'lady, I never gave any thought to that complication. No one pays any attention to how often I am in the company of your brother; I plumb forgot that the same cannot be said of spending time with a lovely young lady."

Alanna smiled distractedly at his compliment, wondering again if she should just go to the earl's house and ask to speak to Lady Victoria. Alfred's next words pulled her from her thoughts.

"There is one other possibility," he mused, taken aback as Alanna turned with energetic eagerness at his words.

"What possibility? Do you know somewhere else we might look?"

Laughing over her enthusiasm, Alfred canted his head in an inquisitive angle. Alanna blushed brightly. "I do not wish to wait, m'lord. I am eager to get on with our project."

"I understand, my lady. But I pray you do not get your hopes up overly. I was just remembering that the last time your brother and I encountered Lady Victoria, when she told us very briefly the troubles she was having with her uncle, she and the children were returning home from the opposite direction of Hyde Park. And if memory serves correctly, there is a tiny little park at the end of their street. Perhaps they might be taking the air there."

Clapping her hands with delight, Alanna bounced beside him on the seat, causing the horses to toss their heads in protest. "Sorry," she said sheepishly before impatiently prompting, "Well, let us make haste, my lord. It would be terrible if we missed her."

Laughing with delight over her contradictions, the baron did as he was instructed, directing his horses towards the nearest exit from the park and heading towards the fashionable neighbourhood where the Earl of Pickering lived. They rode in silence for a few minutes while his companion looked about curiously.

"You do not put on an air of boredom like the other ladies of fashion," he remarked.

Alanna grinned and shrugged. "Oh, I can be bored with the best of them, but I see no need to act so nonsensically with you, my lord. You have known me since I was in the schoolroom. Surely you would see through any airs I would put on."

Alfred felt his admiration for the lady growing, and he had to remind himself that this was his best friend's little sister, and there was a strong need to tread carefully. He was distracted from his thoughts by her urgent whisper.

"Is that her, my lord? The young lady over there watching the four youngsters?"

Following her discreetly pointed finger, Alfred was surprised to see they had arrived at their destination. "How ever did you know?"

"You told me all about her, you ninny, it was easy to figure out. Now hurry and stop the horses, I must go and make her acquaintance."

Without another word and before he had brought the team to a complete stop, she was out of the carriage and hurrying across the street. Alfred had his hands full with his spirited mounts and was unable to stop her. Castigating himself for not having the foresight to make a plan, all he could do was watch as Alanna dashed across the street, narrowly avoiding being run down by a hackney driver. Throwing the reins to his tiger, Alfred climbed out of his phaeton and too crossed the street at a much more sedate pace.

As soon as Alanna made it safely across the street, her pace began to slow. She almost halted completely, as it began to dawn on her that it might be a trifle awkward to run up to a stranger and announce, "I am here to save you."

She dithered on the sidewalk long enough for Alfred to catch up to her. "Is anything amiss, my lady?" he asked with concern.

He admired her pinkened cheeks as she admitted her embarrassment. "I have absolutely no idea what to say now that we have found her." Alfred's eyebrows rose in expression of his surprise. He never thought it would be possible for this particular young lady to be at a loss for words.

"Come along. I shall introduce you and you can take it from there."

Alanna held back a moment longer. "What if I make matters worse for her, my lord? I came on this errand thinking I knew just the thing for this lady I have never even met. But I truly know nothing of her circumstances. What if my impulsiveness causes her distress?"

Smiling over her attack of conscience, Alfred took her arm in a gesture of comfort. "I do not think an offer of friendship coming from you would cause anyone distress. For that is truly what you are here to do, is it not? You wish to offer Lady Victoria Bartley your friendship. And friends help one another. That is how I understand our errand. Is that not how you understand it?"

Her sunny grin returned as reward for his efforts. "Of course, my lord. What are we doing dithering here on the sidewalk? Let us make haste."

With those bracing words, Alfred was dragged along into the park. Amazingly, the occupants of the park had not noticed them until then, so they were unaware that they had been pursued to this spot.

The children noticed them first. "It's m'lord Fred, Aunt 'Toria! The duke's friend. Are we allowed to talk to him?" Daniel had begun with great enthusiasm but then dwindled down to confusion on his last words.

Surprised, Victoria turned to watch the handsome couple approaching, looking beyond them to see if the duke had accompanied them. Hiding her disappointment that they were alone, she smiled in welcome and question.

"Good day, my lord. What a pleasure to see you. What brings you to this neighbourhood?"

Not about to admit the entire truth, Alfred bowed over her hand politely before introducing his companion. "I was out taking the air with my friend, Lady Alanna. When we saw you with your delightful youngsters we thought we would stop to say hello."

It was true that Victoria was not used to Town ways, but even she thought this sounded a trifle odd. However, she was well-bred enough not to show her dubiousness as Alfred performed the introductions.

"Lady Alanna, please allow me to introduce you to Lady Victoria. And these young ladies are Gwendolyn, Felicia, and Vanessa, and that handsome fellow is their little brother Daniel."

Alanna was delighted at the children's reactions to having the baron introduce them like adults. They appeared to be deeply gratified that he even remembered their names. Alanna followed the baron's lead and gravely shook each child's hand in greeting.

"It is a pleasure to make your acquaintance."

Victoria was proud of the children's lovely manners and gratified at the attention they were receiving from the other adults. She was troubled, however, by what problems could arise from once again encountering the baron. And while it had not been stated, she was fairly certain the young lady was none other than the Duke of Wychwood's sister. This situation was becoming highly uncomfortable.

"Lady Victoria Bartley," Alanna was saying, drawing Victoria's attention away from her troubled thoughts. "You are some connection of the Earl of Pickering, are you not?"

At Victoria's affirmative nod, Alanna continued. "I do believe we may have been at school together." When Alanna saw Victoria's eyebrows rise in question she hastened to add, "Oh, not in the same class, of course. I am, I think, a year or two ahead of you, but perhaps we were there at the same time."

Victoria could not resist the jest. "You are correct, although I can hardly credit you acknowledging it, my lady, as the girls in the upper classes would never admit to knowing us younger girls."

Alanna dimpled prettily at the younger woman's tease. "You are correct. I do believe little girls can be absolute beasts. But we are no longer in school, so the stigma of acknowledging you surely will not attach itself to me."

Victoria could not help laughing as Alanna covered her mouth in regret when she realized the little girls had been listening with wide eyes. "I apologize profusely, ladies. I am certain you are not beasts. No doubt you are veritable angels. I should have said some girls can be beastly."

Gwendolyn answered the noble lady with a shrug reminiscent of Victoria's. "Do not trouble yourself to apologize, m'lady." With a darkening glance at her little sisters she continued, "I believe you are correct that all little girls have a beastly tendency."

Everyone laughed and the ice was truly broken. Alfred drew the children away to engage in a quick game of chase-the-ball while the ladies took a seat a little ways away.

Alanna decided to get straight to the point. "I do not believe I have seen you at any of the functions I have attended thus far during the Season. Surely the ton is not so large that we could be avoiding each other so completely." Proud of herself for her turn of phrase that inquired without inquiring, Alanna sat back to see how the conversation would unfold.

Victoria looked at her new acquaintance with doubt, convinced she must have been sent by the duke, but unsure why he would do such a thing. She resolved to be cautious. "I can assure you I have not been avoiding anyone deliberately, my lady. But I do not attend Society events, as I am not 'out.'"

Alanna feigned disbelief. "Not 'out?' Why ever not? Are you not an earl's daughter?"

Victoria's smile was rather wan as she answered. "I am, but it is a trifle complicated, my lady. I should not wish to bore you with the mundane details of my life."

Alanna grinned as she looked at Alfred playing energetically with the children. "Well, it would appear that my escort is thoroughly distracted and may remain so for some time. Feel free to share your story with me. I can assure you I will not be bored."

Victoria struggled with how to answer but decided to ask some questions of her own. "Why are you asking me about myself, my lady? I must admit I find it difficult to believe what the baron said about the two of you just happening by. When I first met Lord Lynster I also made the acquaintance of the Duke of Wychwood. Am I correct in assuming he is your brother?"

Alanna blinked at Victoria for a moment before admitting, "Yes, he is."

"Well, my lady, I am certain I mentioned to your brother that I do not go about in Society. Is there a reason for your family's interest in my affairs?"

Taken aback by the younger woman's astute questioning, Alanna struggled to formulate an answer, but then decided on full honesty, or at least a portion of it. "My brother does not know I am here, and I must admit I am unsure how he would react were he to know. I do know he met you, and in my curiosity I questioned Alfred about you. He did tell me you do not go about Society. I apologize for our subterfuge. I was trying not to embarrass you. But I tell you freely, I think it is a travesty that you do not. It is your rightful place. How shall you meet an acceptable husband if you do not take your place in Society?"

"Is that a lady's only fate? To find an acceptable husband?"

Alanna grinned. "I shall not debate the issues of women's rights today, m'lady, although I am certain there are many sides to that particular issue. The fact is, as women, our futures do depend to a rather large degree upon the men in our lives. And they are quite necessary if one wants to have children of your own instead of the responsibility of someone else's."

Victoria laughed quietly at this, and had to agree. She waited for Alanna to continue.

"When Alfred told me that you were caring for your young cousins and not going into Society I felt the need to stick my nose into your affairs. I know, it is no doubt highly ill-bred of me, but here I am. I apologize if it causes you offense, but in my defence I felt a need to stand up for you even though we have never met. And you were right—I do not truly remember you from school. As you said, beastly girls that we were."

Although this admission should have made Victoria less than comfortable, the other lady's honesty put her at ease, and she smiled kindly at her companion. She again waited patiently for Alanna to continue.

"I must say, my lady, you are remarkably self-contained. You keep sitting there silently, smiling in all the appropriate places so I know you are listening, but your silence keeps making me feel the need to talk." Alanna laughed self-deprecatingly. "One thing you will need to learn if you are to go about the ton is that silence is unacceptable."

This finally prompted Victoria to speak. "Why ever would silence be unacceptable, m'lady? In my position I find that I adore silence. I almost never experience it with four or five children about, so I cherish the few times that it creeps up upon me."

"I can see why that might be the case for you, but of course, no one else that I know of amongst the ton is caring for five children. For the most part, the fashionable ton abhors boredom."

Victoria dimpled at this and replied, "Well, if more of the ton would care for their own children there would be far less boredom to be concerned with."

Alanna smiled in return, enjoying the joke, but then sobered. "But that is the problem with your situation, my lady. These are not your children."

Victoria's face took on a serious cast, and Alanna felt sorry to have stated the bald facts. However, there was nothing she could do to take back her words, and they were no less than the truth. She found herself more determined than ever to help her new friend.

"I apologize, m'lady, for being so forthright. But I must tell you, I am determined that you and I shall be friends."

Victoria eyed her askance, unsure of how to take the other lady's declaration. "I think I should say thank you, as I am sure it would be quite lovely to have a friend, but I am unsure what you think to do about that friendship. I truly do not have the circumstances to be a good friend to you, Lady Alanna."

"Never you mind about me. I would like to be a good friend to you. Besides, seeing how loyal you are to your relatives, I am sure you would be a perfectly lovely kind of friend to have." Alanna paused and regarded Victoria quite seriously for a moment before continuing. "Now that we have determined that we shall be friends, there is no need for us to stand on ceremony. You must call me Alanna and I shall call you Victoria. Or perhaps even 'Toria.' I must say, I thought it absolutely darling when your little cousin called you that."

Victoria smiled. "Daniel is a darling."

"So, my dear 'Toria, you must tell me why you are the children's governess and thus far too busy to come around with me making calls or attending balls."

Victoria blinked in surprise. "Well, you certainly are putting away all ceremony, are you not?"

Alanna had the grace to blush, but did not take back her words, merely regarding the other woman steadily and awaiting an answer.

Victoria looked over Alanna's shoulder into the distance, as though searching there for the answer to the slippery question. "I cannot in all honestly say exactly how it happened. When I was finally completed school I had nowhere to go except to my uncle, who has been my guardian since my parents died seven years ago. I had used to stay with them during my summer vacations from school. During the shorter vacations I would remain at the school for the most part, but for the summer the earl would send for me. During the summers, I would often play in the nursery with the babies as they were such fun and I did not have much else to do. So during that final summer I was much in the nursery and just started doing more and more with the children. The governess they had was really rather useless and lazy, and the children needed so much attention. I did not really have anything else to do so I filled in the gaps. Then the governess left. I am still not certain if she was asked to leave or if she quit, but the earl asked me to take over her duties until another suitable candidate could be found. That was two months ago." She fell silent with a small, rather helpless shrug, hoping Alanna would have something to add. When she remained silent Victoria continued with brisker tones.

"Just recently, though, my uncle did repeat his promise of hiring someone so that I could have a little free time, so I am hopeful that I will have a little bit of peace and quiet."

"It is not peace and quiet you need, Victoria! You are young and beautiful. You should be having a grand time. Maybe even loud, rambunctious diversions. Shopping and dancing and laughing until your cheeks and feet are sore."

"Do you really dance until your feet are sore?" she asked wonderingly.

"Nearly every night during the Season," Alanna answered with a delighted grin. "And I have occasionally danced a hole right through my slippers."

Victoria laughed with delight. "Oh, that does sound like such fun. How I would love to have a night like that."

"And so you shall. Now let me look at you."

Victoria was taken aback, as the duke's sister proceeded to catalogue her strengths and weaknesses. "You have a perfect figure and your hair is very pretty, although not styled at all, really 'Toria you must do something with that hair. You could be absolutely ravishing with the right gown and hairstyle. It would appear you have been out of doors without your parasol as well, I see a dusting of freckles across the bridge of your nose. On you it is rather fetching, but the sticklers will no doubt comment when they are looking for something to criticize. And your frock, well, I am sure you would not want to wear your best while drudging about the park with the children, but we shall have to see about your wardrobe."

Victoria blinked in disbelief before regaining her backbone. "Now see here, Alanna. If the members of the ton are going to pick me to pieces I do not think I wish to meet any of them. While you and your brother and the baron have all been lovely, I am not certain going about in Society is what I wish to do with any spare time I might be able to acquire. And I do not think it would be diverting in the least to attend a ball where everyone will be examining me in such detail."

Alanna heaved a sigh of dismay. "Oh no, I am truly sorry. I did not mean to cause offense or alarm. It is true that there are certain members of the ton who are not always the kindest, but I assure you they are in the minority and the marvellous time we shall have will more than make up for any discomfort. Besides, if you are dressed and coifed in the best way, there will be no cause for anyone to make any negative remarks."

"But how can I be dressed and coifed in the best way, Alanna? I am a governess. I do not even know what my financial affairs truly are even if I wanted to buy some appropriate gowns." It was now her turn to sigh in dismay. "I do not think your idea can come to fruition, my lady. It does not matter that my father was an earl. I am a governess, and as such I need to get the children home for their supper."

Alanna grabbed her hand as Victoria got up to leave. "No, please, my dear Victoria, do not rush off. We surely can come up with a strategy to arrange it all right and tight. I promise I did not mean to offend you in any way. And I truly do wish to offer my assistance in any way possible. In fact, when I was examining you I meant to say that I have the impression we are the same size, so you could easily wear some of my gowns. Since we have different colouring it would probably not be remarked upon at all. Or we could alter some of my gowns to better suit you and no one would be the wiser."

Victoria slowly sat back down but remained on the edge of the bench as though poised for flight and regarded Alanna with a steady gaze. "Why would you want to do this for me? You do not know me and you owe me nothing."

Alanna shrugged helplessly. "I cannot explain it, I just want to. It just seems wrong to me that you should be relegated to the role of an upstairs servant when you should be out with the rest of your peers. I feel as though I cannot enjoy my own Season as I should if I do not do something to help you have one as well."

Victoria smiled. "Do you realize that makes you sound a trifle odd?"

Alanna laughed. "Mayhap, but that does not bother me a jot. Now I know you need to get the children home, but please, say you will let me help you at least a little and we can both go our separate ways and think about our options. Let us meet up here again on the morrow and plan it all out."

Victoria was no longer smiling, but she gave a small nod. "I cannot make any promises, but I will think on the matter. If you are here tomorrow I will not give you the cut direct."

Alanna burst into laughter. "Oh, my dear, you shall take. I can just see how the ton will love you. You will be a hit to be sure."

Victoria looked unconvinced as she bade her new friend adieu and went to collect the children. Seeing how they had run the poor baron ragged, her stern expression gave way to a sweet smile. "My lord, I do believe your valet will have your hide for the state you have allowed yourself to get in to. How ever shall you escort Lady Alanna home looking like that?"

The baron summoned a look of haughty dismissal, which strongly reminded Victoria of the duke. "Never you mind about the state of my attire. I had a smashing good time with these youngsters and I have plenty of clothes at home. And Alanna is not so high in the instep that she will refuse to ride home with me." As he looked down at his pantaloons his haughty demeanour dissolved and a look of chagrin spread across his face. "And as luck would have it, the particular style of my phaeton means that as long as I remain seated, no one will remark upon my unkempt look."

Having mercy, Victoria forbore to offer any further comment. "Well, I thank you for showing the children such a lovely time. They have been pining for a good romp like that and I, sadly, do not have the strength to keep up with them to the extent that you do. I am in your debt."

Alfred bowed over her hand in farewell. "The pleasure was all mine, my lady. I bid you good day, until we meet again."

He then gravely bent over the grubby hands of the children as they took their leave as well, much to Alanna's delight.

"That was very well done of you, my lord. Those children adore you. I had no idea you were such a hand with the youngsters."

Alfred felt heat creeping up his cheeks once more. "Well, do not spread the word around, I beg you. My reputation will be in shreds."

"Maybe amongst the rakes, but the matrons would love you for it," Alanna teased, laughing as the baron paled visibly.

"My lady, no, please, I beg of you, you must not let on to the matrons of Society that I have an affinity of children."

"Rest easy, my lord. I promise you, I was merely teasing. Your secret is safe with me." She paused for a moment while looking at him speculatively. "Although, I must admit to you it is a rather attractive trait."

Alanna laughed as she watched the fiery blush continue to swiftly rise up Alfred's face. "Come along, m'lord. We must allow the children to get home for their supper and I must carry on about my business."

Victoria, who had been silently watching the byplay, allowed a giggle to pass her lips. "You two had best be on your way." Turning, she collected the children and strode for the entrance of the gate, heading home.

Alanna was charmed by seeing the youngest little girl turn to wave with a sweet, dimply grin. "I cannot recall the name of that child, but she is a delight. I predict she shall break a few hearts several years from now."

"Bite your tongue, my lady. The darling little Lady Vanessa will never do something so crass as break a young man's heart."

Alanna giggled at the baron's insistence. "I apologize profusely, my lord. I meant no offense to the little lady. Now could you please take me home? I need to make my preparations for the evening's entertainments."

Alfred followed her as she swept towards his carriage, admiring her air of assurance. She climbed into his carriage without waiting for his assistance. "So, did you accomplish what you had set out to do this afternoon, my lady?" he asked.

Alanna chewed at her lip in indecision. "Yes and no," she replied slowly, followed by a giggle as she saw the baron's raised eyebrows at her uncharacteristic wishy-washiness. "You did introduce me to Lady Victoria, and for that I am grateful. I am also even more determined to assist her than ever. Unfortunately, I do not as yet have her full cooperation. It would seem that her circumstances are rather more complicated than I realized, despite your attempts at warning me. And she is burdened by a level of pride that will make it difficult for her to accept my help. She is even more like Bryght than I had thought possible. It is no wonder I thought there might be a match brewing there."

Alfred made as if to protest her final words but she interrupted and waved them off. "Oh, never fear, I am not attempting to match make for the duke. I have discovered that I like the lady and would like to be of assistance to her if she will have me. The trouble is she seems reluctant to brave the wilds of the ton and enjoy a Season with me. And there is the added complication that she has not been properly provided for. I offered to share my wardrobe with her, but she did not seem to appreciate the offer overmuch. The most that I accomplished is that she has almost agreed to meet with me tomorrow after she has had some time to think on the matter."

Alfred seemed perplexed. "What do you mean that she almost agreed?"

Alanna sighed. "She would not commit to anything. She said if she was in the park tomorrow and I happen by she would not refuse to speak with me."

It was now Alfred's turn to laugh at her expense. "And in that you found that you had some success?" he asked drily, causing Alanna to colour in response.

She answered defensively, "She did not refuse outright. I do believe that after she has had time to mull it over and I have an evening to think of further arguments, she shall see the wisdom of allowing me to help her go about amongst Society. Surely finding a suitable husband and getting a home of her own has to be better than her current circumstances of being an unpaid governess to her relatives."

"So one would think," Alfred agreed.

Alanna sighed discontentedly. "She seemed rather sure that she did not like my plan, though, my lord. I am uncertain if I shall be able to convince her. Do you think I should consult the duke? You had mentioned that they are friends of a sort. Do you think he could have any bearing on the topic?"

Alfred gazed at her in some surprise before having to turn his attention back to the horses who, having sensed his distraction through the reins were now tossing their heads fretfully. Regaining control swiftly, he turned his attention back to Alanna's question. "I do know that he will not take kindly to what he may perceive as our meddling in his affairs. But I would have to say that I think it best that you do consult him." Alfred paused for a moment in deeper thought before he turned back to her with a grin. "Just make sure you think through your words carefully."

Alanna grinned at him, momentarily setting aside her worries on the subject. "I shall just tell him it was all his idea. He is the one who told me about her, after all."

Alfred grinned back at her. "It is very obvious that you are an Alcott of Wychwood. You are so like your brother."

They passed the rest of the drive back to the duke's townhouse in companionable silence while Alanna planned out what to say to the duke as well as how best to convince Victoria to accept her help.

Pulling up in front of their fashionable address, the baron jumped down from the phaeton and hurried around to help his passenger alight. Watching his friend's pretty little sister elegantly descend from the high perch while chatting cheerfully about her plans, Alfred felt an unfamiliar flutter in the region of his stomach. He frowned in response to the unwelcome feelings.

Alanna caught the fleeting look and stopped in midsentence. "What is it my lord? You do not wish to partner me for the quadrille this evening? I thought it would be the best opportunity for us to talk about my plans without drawing undue attention to ourselves."

Alfred forced himself to grin at her, pushing the uncomfortable thoughts aside. "Of course, I would be happy to partner with you for the dance. Just be sure you mind your steps. It should be disastrous if you were to tread on my toes if you were too wrapped up in your story to pay attention."

Alanna threw back her head and laughed heartily at his taunt, tapping him lightly on the shoulder with her closed parasol. "You are too droll, my lord. I sincerely thank you for your kind assistance with this project. You are a good friend to this family. Until tonight, farewell."

Alfred stood at the bottom of the stairs, watching her ascension with a tight smile on his lips at her use of the word friend. Even after the butler closed the door upon her entry, he continued standing there until he realized he was being a simpleton. Shaking his head to rid himself of his uncharacteristic doldrums, he leapt back in the phaeton and set off towards his own home in a bit of a brown study.

Chapter Fifteen

"Thank you, Walter," Alanna greeted as the butler helped her with her wrap. "Could you please have a footman take a note round to the duke requesting that he stop in to see me?"

"Right away, my lady," the butler answered, gesturing over an ever-attentive footman who hastened off upon the errand. "Would that be all?"

"Please ensure he is brought to me straight away upon his arrival. I shall be in the morning room working on some correspondence. And perhaps have the kitchens send up some sort of refreshment upon his arrival as well. Thank you, Walter."

"Very well, my lady."

Alanna did her best to write some letters but her mind was elsewhere and her heart was not in the project. She got up to pace impatiently as she wondered if the footman had been able to find the duke and whether he would respond to her request for an audience with any degree of haste. When she heard the clatter of an arriving horse pulling up in front of the house she ran to the window and was gratified to see her brother, nattily dressed, climbing swiftly from his favourite mount.

Relieved for the efficiency of her mother's well-trained staff, Alanna forced herself to settle back on the settee as she awaited the duke's arrival.

Bryghton refused the butler's intention of announcing him. "She is expecting me. I shall announce myself." He dismissed the butler.

Closing the door behind him he strode in and stood before his sister. "Well, brat, what do you have to say for yourself? I am here as summoned. What was so urgent that I must drop everything and appear before you at my earliest convenience?"

Grasping her brother's hand and pulling him down beside her on the settee, Alanna apologized. "Oh dear, did the footman make it sound terribly dire? I am sorry if I led you to believe there was some sort of emergency. I did not mean to alarm you. You know how I am when I have an idea. It is such a silly bother that we do not live in the same house when we are in Town."

Sinking down beside her but retaining her hand, Bryghton accepted her apology. "Do not trouble yourself, I did not have any other plans that required my urgent attention. I do believe spending a little time with my sister would be more preferable than whoever might have been my companion at my club, which is where I was heading when the footman found me."

He waited expectantly for Alanna to tell him what was on her mind, but when she just sat there looking at him rather helplessly, he prodded her gently. "You mentioned you had an idea you wished to discuss with me. Do you care to share it now or are you just going to allow it to continue to revolve in your head for a while longer?"

This caused Alanna's tongue to loosen and she allowed a pent up tinkle of laughter to escape her lips before she spoke. "I met your lady today."

Bryghton showed no reaction to this sally, merely raising one eyebrow in question. "My lady? How interesting. I did not realize I had a lady. Would you care to elaborate?"

With another tinkle of laughter, this one leaning on the nervous side, Alanna hurried to add more details. "Remember yesterday, when you were trying to distract me from Drake's ill-thought words about the viscount, you told me about Lady Victoria?"

"I vaguely remember the conversation," he allowed, his face impassive.

"Well, I was intrigued by your story about this young lady who does not go amongst the ton despite being an earl's daughter, so I talked Alfred, Lord Lynster, into taking me to meet her."

Bryghton did not reveal his thoughts about his friend's defection by so much as a flicker of his eyelid. Alanna was momentarily distracted from her tale and complained, "How do you manage to hide your thoughts so well, brother dearest? It is a most annoying trait, I must tell you. I could be telling you about the weather on our estate for all you appear to care."

"What made you think I would care whom you and Lord Lynster choose to encounter in your day?" he asked mildly.

Alanna shrugged rather helplessly, abandoning the complaint and returning to the situation at hand. "Never mind about that. I did think you might care a little bit about Lady Victoria, but it does not matter overmuch whether you do or not. I now find that I care about her, and I think I might be in need of your assistance."

At her brother's silence she paused, but his inclined head prompted her to continue. "As I was saying, Alfred thought she might be at this little park near her house, as she seemed to be avoiding running into you for some reason that I did not fully understand. As it turns out his guess was correct and we found her and her darling cousins there. Alfred played with the children while I spoke with the lady. I took an instant liking to her and tried to talk her into accompanying me to some balls or some such but she did not jump at the idea. She came very near to refusing to even see me again, but I almost got her to agree to meet me at the park again tomorrow so that I can continue to plead my case after I have come up with some better arguments than those that had occurred to me at the time."

Alanna paused for breath and looked at her brother with a touch of uncertainty. She continued, her tone almost pleading. "I must admit when I set out to meet her it was with some idea that she might be of some importance to you, and I was moved by curiosity more than anything else. But now I find that I quite like her, and I feel an obligation to help her despite her reluctance to accept any such help from me."

Bryghton still did not appear to have anything to say, so Alanna continued to explain. "I do not quite understand her situation. It seems that her parents died some time ago and she came under her uncle's guardianship. She spent many years at boarding school, only coming home for the summers. She said that she had gotten in the habit of spending most of her time in the nursery on her vacations from school, as she loved her cousins. So it seemed quite natural when she left school permanently that she would spend some of her time there. It seems that no arrangements have been made for her to have a Season and when the governess quit she did not want to see the children left in the lurch so she stepped in to fill what she thought was to be a temporary need. But it would appear that her uncle has made no move to replace the governess, expecting her to fill that role."

Bryghton finally broke his silence, as his sister appeared to have come to the end of her tale. "I still do not see how you think this involves you or how it necessitated an urgent message to me."

"Well, somehow, I find I am feeling a sense of obligation towards her. There is an injustice being brought upon her and I am moved to try to do something about it. But I hate to admit that I have no idea what I can possibly do to help her if her uncle refuses to allow it. I thought I could take her about Town with me. No one would question her presence at any gathering I went to, as her bearing and manner are completely above reproach. No doubt she does not have anything appropriate to wear, but I offered her full access to my wardrobes. That may not have been the right thing to say, because it was after that that she appeared prepared to give me a set down. I asked you to come because, as much as I would deny saying this, you are smarter than me. And besides that, you know her better than I do. So do you have any ideas?"

Bryghton smiled slightly at his sister's question. He had all sorts of ideas, but he was unsure how many of them he wished to share with his little sister. "The problem with this, Alanna, is that it really is none of our business. We cannot force the lady to enter Society if she does not wish to."

As Alanna made to protest, the duke interrupted. "I know it is hard to imagine that any young lady would prefer the life that it appears she is living. But we do not know the full situation. And she does have the right to refuse our offer of assistance. Now all that being said, I fully understand your desire to be of assistance, and I share that desire in this case. Why do we not plan to go together tomorrow and discuss it with her? Perhaps between the two of us we can convince her to give the ton a chance."

"Really, Bryght, you would come with me?" Alanna asked with some surprise.

"Of course. I would be happy to help you with what I see as a worthy goal. It was kind and generous of you to offer the use of your clothing and it would no doubt be very helpful to her, but you must realize that the poor woman no doubt has her pride. That could be why she began to freeze you out. So when we see her tomorrow you will have to think of a more tactful way of phrasing it when you repeat your offer."

The duke paused, deep in thought for a moment while his sister waited, watching him expectantly. "The problem with me coming with you is that she has been forbidden from seeing me and it could put her and the children in an awkward position with the earl. Do you want my assistance sufficiently to take that risk?"

Alanna now was undecided. Bryghton waited while she stood before him chewing nervously on her lip as she thought the matter through. "What do you think is best, your grace? I will gladly follow your council in this matter, as I have absolutely no idea what is the right choice to make."

"I have good news and bad news on the subject. If the earl finds out about her visit with you yesterday he will have no trouble vouchsafing who you are and will assume we were in cahoots when you went to see her. Should he feel inclined to make trouble for her over it, he will do so whether I accompany you or not."

"I can see why you called it good news and bad news," Alanna grumbled with a disgruntled wrinkle to her nose. "So what you are telling me is whether you come with me or not, I may have already caused her trouble, so you might as well come with me, is that correct?"

Bryghton gave her a sheepish grin. "In a nutshell, little sister."

"In that case, I will be happy to have your company for a ride to the park tomorrow afternoon. Will you be prepared to know what to say to her, do you think?"

"Of course. Have you ever known me to be at a loss for words?"

Alanna could not prevent her grin. "I have not, I must admit. Very well, my lord, the duke. I look forward to seeing you at your verbose best on the morrow."

The duke stood and gave his little sister a mocking bow. "Now, do I have your permission to go about my business for the rest of the day?"

"Yes, your grace," Alanna answered formally before bounding up from the settee and giving her brother a warm hug.

Before Bryghton could stride from the room, his sister called out to him. "Are you going to any of the ton gatherings this evening, or will you be holed up in your clubs all night?"

"I see no need to attend any of those senseless affairs. Why ever would you think I would set foot in one if I do not need to? I only go when our mother demands it of me," he said drolly.

"But if you are going to help me with Lady Victoria you should start showing your face around now if you do not want it to be remarked upon and have the gossips' tongues set on fire with the tale."

The duke paused and looked at his sister with a face of disbelief. "You are not the silliest chit ever, are you? That is a sound piece of advice, however awful it shall be to follow." He paused for a moment while contemplating with displeasure the prospect of entering the social whirl. "Which invitations have you accepted for this evening? Perhaps I could accompany you somewhere and then leave after showing my face for a little while. No one will think anything is amiss about escorting my sister. In fact, it is no doubt my duty to be keeping an eye on your whereabouts." This brought another thought to the older brother's mind. "Now that I think on it, why are you so unoccupied that you must stick your nose into my affairs and that of the lady Victoria?"

After laughing uproariously at the duke's question, his sister composed herself enough to reply. "Your grace, really, every lady of the ton has developed this skill even more sharply than have I. It is a form of art to be able to plan parties, gad about to the shops, attend all the best parties each evening, and still keep all the various tidbits of gossip straight. Truly, that is the whole purpose of the Season, is it not?"

Bryghton could not suppress the shudder of distaste that shivered up his spine. "Then why do you do it?" he asked dubiously.

With an uninformative shrug Alanna answered, "It is the way of our world, my dear brother. And it is terribly interesting, I must say, especially now that I am not in my first Season. When I made my debut people made more of an effort to shelter me from much of the gossip. Now it would appear that there are no such restraints. I must admit to you that I find many of the tales spread about to be so outlandish as to be out of the realm of possibility to be true. But it is beyond entertaining to hear the stories being bandied about at times. Some people have exceedingly active imaginations."

Bryghton was glad to see that his sister, while having developed a distasteful appetite for salacious gossip, had not lost her innocent view of the world. "So are you going to tell me where you are going this evening, or not?" his impatience began to shine through.

With a start Alanna remembered his earlier question. "My apologies, Bryghton, my dear. Mother and I are promised to the musicale that Miss Melinda Lambert is hosting this evening. You remember her from the duchess' dinner, don't you?"

"Oh, no, Alanna, I could not bear a musical evening. Perhaps I shall have to postpone my foray into ton events for another evening."

With a giggle, Alanna shook her head at the duke. "That is not the only thing we will be doing this evening. I fully understand why you might not wish to attend, although I must say I am looking forward to it. The baron and his sister seemed to be a most interesting pair. I cannot wait to see whom they have assembled to entertain their guests."

After Bryghton continued to shake his head in denial of any interest in attending, his sister carried on with her explanation of her plans for the evening. "After the musicale we have promised to attend a ball at the Earl and Countess of Pembroke's home. It shall be a terrible crush but it would be an excellent place for you to accompany me. We would be making a late appearance, so there would be plenty of people to remark upon your attendance at my side, which would be just the thing for our designs."

With another rueful shake of his head the duke agreed to his sister's plan. "Shall I collect you from Miss Lambert's home and have my carriage deliver us to the Pembroke's ball?" he offered graciously.

"That would be lovely, thank you. Remember that Mother will be with me, so we should have an acceptable explanation as to why you are suddenly accompanying me about town."

"Can a duke not go to a few parties without needing to explain himself to his mother?" he demanded with a twinkle in his eye.

"Not with our mother. Besides, you must admit that it is rather out of character and will get her heart all aflutter with plans for your future."

"Well then, let her. That will be our explanation if we must. Start with saying I am watching out for you. If she does not consider that a believable explanation, we will allow her to think I am checking out the new crop of debutantes. She will be so excited that she shall not allow herself to disbelieve."

"I do believe we are most unnatural children, are we not?" Alanna asked.

"She is a duchess, Alanna, and far savvier than we give her credit for. Do not trouble yourself over her thoughts. She can handle whatever situation might arise with aplomb. Now tell me what time to come for you. I must be on my way and finish my own affairs before I ready myself for the evening."

"Midnight should be fine for arriving at the Pembrokes' event. There will be a terrible line-up of carriages, so I think it best if you collect me at half past eleven. It is not unbearably early to leave the musicale, but it will help us avoid the crush of carriages there, at least."

Bryghton shook his head over the foolishness of all aspects of the Season and agreed to his sister's directions. "I bid you adieu until then," he flourished a gallant bow and hastily took his leave lest she drag him back into conversation.

Chapter Sixteen

As ordered by his sister, the duke was dutifully waiting beside his carriage as Alanna and the duchess descended the stairs at half past eleven. Bowing gracefully to his mother, he took over for the footman and handed her up into the carriage.

"It was such a pleasant surprise when Alanna told me you would be escorting us this evening, Bryghton dear. It is too bad Drake has decided to return to the country. It would have been so lovely to go as a foursome. But I could hardly credit it when your sister told me you would be joining us. It is your usual wont to avoid such affairs like the plague," she said with mild question, awaiting an explanation.

A slightly charged silence descended upon the occupants of the carriage as it was set into smooth motion by the well-trained driver as he gave the matching chestnuts their head.

Alanna portrayed a marked interest in the goings on outside the carriage as they went, so the duke was forced to address the question.

With a negligent shrug he smiled benignly to his mother. "I realized that it behooves me to take an interest in my siblings' activities. As the head of the family I find that I have been overly concerned with our financial affairs and all the responsibilities that accompany the dukedom, but I thought it best that I give thought to my sister's future in other ways as well. This is her third Season and she is still single, and I wish to see why."

The duchess turned shrewd, disbelieving eyes upon her firstborn while Alanna choked back a gurgle of laughter. Bryghton merely gazed at them with his eyebrows slightly raised in irony. Despite his mother's obvious derision over his tale, he stuck to it, even managing to meet her eyes while he expertly changed the subject.

"Was the musicale to your liking, Mother?" he asked.

The duchess' lips twitched with what could almost be described as amusement before she answered, matching his bland tone, "It was one of the least annoying musicales I have attended in recent years, so I would think it safe to say it was to my liking. I cannot tell you whatever possessed your sister to accept the invitation, as it is so rare that there is anyone with true talent at these things, but somehow Miss Lambert did manage to find some artists worthy of the title."

Alanna chimed in at this point. "I do not understand why neither of you will admit that a musical evening can be a lovely way to spend one's time," she said plaintively. "And you are correct, Mother, Miss Lambert's efforts truly paid off this evening. I was disappointed that the hour had arrived when I had agreed to meet Bryghton. I would have enjoyed staying even longer."

The duchess allowed a delicate shudder to show itself upon her features. "I do believe in this moment that you are your father's offspring, not mine. That second singer, and I believe I am being generous in calling her such, strained every skill I possess to not make a scene, so horrid was her caterwauling."

Now Alanna could not hold back her amused snort. "For one thing, you have never been tempted to make a scene in all your born days. And for another, I thought her song choice was quite entertaining even if she did not quite possess the vocal range to be able to pull it off successfully. We must give her credit for having the courage to attempt it, especially with such an audience around her."

The duchess had nothing constructive to add to her daughter's comments so she turned the subject. "Let us hope the Pembrokes have not scrimped on the expense of their musicians. I do not think I could bear it if the music is sub-par here after what my ears have been subjected to thus far this evening."

"Bravo, my lady," Bryghton applauded. "I must say this is the closest to waspish that I have ever heard you be."

"I know, my dear. I should probably apologize, but I just cannot stand these musicales that your sister insists we attend upon occasion. Blessedly, I manage to restrain her for the most part but every once in a while she gets one past me and accepts the invitation before I realize what she is about."

Alanna grinned at her mother but answered meekly enough. "Thank you, Mother, for your forbearance this evening. I had a lovely time, and I am only sorry that you did not enjoy it as much as I did." It was now her turn to try to change the topic. With a little bounce on the seat, which brought a slight frown to her mother's brow, Alanna allowed her youthful excitement to shine through. "Do you think the prince might attend this evening? It is rumoured that he enjoys attending events hosted by the Earl of Pembroke and might make an appearance tonight."

"Why would you be interested in his attendance?" the duke asked with mild curiosity.

"Wherever he goes he is accompanied by such an entourage and an aura of excitement. I have yet to attend the same events as him this Season and I have missed the added spice."

"Never you mind getting caught up in the Prince's spice, my dear," reprimanded the duchess with caution. "He may be our future king, but I do not have any aspirations of you being a part of his court."

"Would you have me deny him were he to invite me to dance?" Alanna asked incredulously.

"Of course not. That is why you should ensure you are on the opposite side of the ballroom whenever you find yourself at the same event as him."

Alanna turned rounded eyes upon her mother. "Are you verging on treason, Mother?"

The duchess relaxed back against the cushions of the well-sprung carriage and allowed a tinkle of laughter to escape her lips. "Pray do not be a silly goose, Alanna. I am merely warning a young girl about the dangers that accompany the Season. Ah, we have arrived. Now mind your hem as you step out of the carriage, my dear."

Alanna allowed her eyes to meet her brother's for a moment and he gave her a conspiratorial wink. He whispered in her ear while handing her down to the waiting footman, "Have no fear, I shall contrive not to allow the Regent to behead her."

Still grinning as she thanked the footman and awaited her mother, Alanna tucked her hand into her brother's bent elbow. With his mother on his other arm, the duke escorted both beautiful ladies up into the earl's elegant and large home. Alanna dutifully held her voluminous skirts away from their feet as they ascended the stairs while gazing about with interest at the beautiful décor. It would seem the countess had remodelled her public rooms since the last time they had visited.

Bryghton immediately noted the stir caused by the appearance of most of the Wychwood family at one event. There was a cascading murmur amongst the assembled throng as the trio stood momentarily at the top of the stairs. As there was no one currently trying to ascend, they remained as they were, three abreast, and descended to the crowded ballroom below.

Alanna had been correct, Bryghton acknowledged to himself—his presence was remarked upon much more than he would have anticipated. It was true that he rarely attended such events, but he was taken aback at the extent of others' interest in his being there. It was a good thing he had followed her advice and made an appearance this evening. If they were able to convince Lady Victoria to go about with them a bit during the Season it would be less remarkable if he already were a fixture rather than an oddity.

He could not help thinking that it was going to be a long night as he forced a smile to his face instead of the grimace of discomfort that was threatening to display itself. He was relieved to hear a familiar and welcome voice hailing him as they reached the bottom of the grand staircase.

"I could barely credit my own eyes when I saw you coming down those stairs," Alfred declared drolly, slapping his friend playfully on the arm as the duke waved off his mother who had just spotted someone she wished to speak to. "Two balls in one week? Whatever are you doing here, your grace?"

Bryghton looked at his friend with an inscrutable glare before replying, "I am escorting my beloved little sister to a ton event, and whatever are you doing here?"

Stifling his amused chuckle, Alfred matched the duke's tone. "I, too, am escorting my sister. In my case, it is actually true, as this is

Eloise's first Season and she does not seem to be quite up to snuff. The chit really needs her big brother watching over her, whereas I am quite certain your Alanna has never needed her big brother breathing over her protectively."

"Thank you, my lord," said Alanna, dimpling, and dropping him a quick curtsy.

Assuming a dignified air, Alfred bowed to her as he said, "Merely stating the truth as I see it, my lady."

Bryghton looked sternly down his nose at his dearest friend. "You remind me that I have something of a rather serious nature to discuss with you, my lord."

Catching the warning note in the duke's voice, Alfred's jovial expression was replaced with a more serious mien. "Really, your grace, I would hardly think the ballroom of the Earl of Pembroke is an appropriate place for any serious discussion. Surely we must find some willing ladies to escort to the dance floor." Turning to Alanna, the baron bowed formally and invited her to the dance.

Smiling, Alanna accepted and was swept into the fray.

"I take it you told him about our expedition this afternoon. It is often hard to tell with your brother. Is he truly angered or was that just bluster?"

Alfred did not seem overly worried, but Alanna recognized that he too was often hard to read. "I do not think he is at all angry on the matter, but as you say, it is difficult to tell. You shall have to see for yourself." She grinned at her dance partner, not at all flirtatiously. "But he has agreed to come with me tomorrow to speak with the lady, so he cannot have hated the idea overly, I should think."

"Mayhap not," said Alfred, unconvinced. Changing the subject, he asked solicitously, "How was the musicale you attended?"

Sighing rapturously, Alanna launched into a delighted description of her evening thus far, concluding with the words, "You should have been there—it is just impossible to describe."

Alfred grinned at his partner. "It is hard for me to believe that you are a jaded lady of Society, m'lady. When you rhapsodize so enthusiastically it reminds one of a chit straight from the schoolroom."

The baron chuckled at Alanna's playful swat over this traitorous statement and continued, "Truly, Lady Alanna, I must say the thought of attending such an event sets my hair on end, and I think your description was much more enjoyable to listen to than the evening could have possibly warranted."

Alanna looked at him appraisingly. "Have you been talking to my mother already this evening?"

"No, why? Is she of the same mind?"

"Exactly so! She was questioning my sanity before we even set foot into the baron's home. Now, never mind about that. This number seems to be ending. Now you must take me to see your sister. I can hardly credit that she is out of the schoolroom. I must welcome her to Town."

"Should I not take you back to your brother?" Alfred asked, minding the proprieties.

Alanna looked to where her brother was on the side of the dance floor, seemingly engaged in a conversation while still maintaining an eye on her progress through the room. "He can see me from where he is and can join us if he so wishes."

Alfred met his friend's eye across the room and gave him a helpless shrug and a brief nod. He was relieved when the duke returned his nod with a half-smile of his own. The baron escorted his dance partner from the floor and over to where his aunt and sister were gadding happily.

Standing a bit to the side, Alfred watched with amusement as Lady Alanna exclaimed prettily over his little sister.

"My dearest Miss Lynster, it has been an age since we last saw you. And Lady Sybil, I am delighted to see you again. You really must call upon my mother at your earliest convenience, she will be overjoyed to have a visit with you, to be sure."

Eloise dipped into an elegantly practiced curtsy, making Alanna laugh. "My dear girl, I am far from royalty, you must never dip so low to what really amounts to your competition." This remark caused the inexperienced younger girl to release her pent up nerves in a giggle.

"Lady Alanna, I am very happy to see you again, but you really must call me Eloise."

"Gladly, and you must call me Alanna. Now tell me all about your doings since you came to Town and how you are enjoying your debut thus far."

Alfred felt his eyes beginning to glaze over with boredom as his sister launched into a very detailed description of all the tedious matters connected with her sojourn in the city. Marvelling at Alanna's ability to appear interested in the extensive descriptions, the baron was relieved when he felt a familiar presence at his side.

"My lord duke, what a pleasure to see you," Alfred said, grinning.

"You appeared a little in need of rescue."

"And you have come to enjoy seeing yourself in the light of rescuer of late?" bantered the baron.

"Does not every gentleman wish to see himself in such a way?" He continued in an undertone on to a touchier subject. "Whatever possessed you to take my sister to meet Lady Victoria? I do not want her mixed up in the mess with Drake and Pickering."

Alfred turned a wide-eyed innocent look upon his friend. "Have you ever tried to dissuade her from doing something she wished to do?"

"How did she even know about wishing to do this, I wonder?"

The baron stared at the duke in some surprise. "She told me that you told her all about your meeting. She was filled with romantic ideas about arranging a match between you and the poor noblewoman. Escorting her to meet the lady was the best idea I could come up with when your sister told me her plans of going and knocking on Pickering's door demanding to meet the lost lady."

Bryghton's eyebrows were knitted together in question. "She said I told her about Victoria?"

"It was some sort of distraction technique at your mother's dinner the other evening, she said."

"Ah yes. She was flirting with Drake's nemesis, Dalton, and Drake inelegantly demanded that she cease. When it appeared they were about to launch into an ill-bred scene I stepped in and told her the tale. I never thought it would motivate her to meet the lady for herself. And she wanted to go straight to the earl's house?" he asked, barely suppressing his shudder of disgust.

"In her defense, she knows nothing of the earl's history or reputation. I told her as little as possible but enough to dissuade her from actually going to the house. That is when she demanded to be taken to the park to meet the lady and I complied."

"Well then, I owe you my thanks rather than my censure, do I not?" Alfred managed not to laugh at his friend's disgruntled tone as the duke continued. "Did the chit tell you she has convinced me to return with her on the morrow to lend my voice to her pleas to be allowed to sponsor Lady Victoria in her curtsy to Society?"

"She did mention something of the sort. I admit I am surprised you agreed to it. What of the earl's demand that she not see you?"

"As I told Alanna, her interfering in the lady's affairs could have already caused her trouble. If the earl finds out she met with my sister he will not easily believe I was not behind it. Whether she goes by herself or with me, the result could very well be the same. I would rather be there to attempt to control the situation as best I can."

The two gentlemen paused in thought for a moment before the duke continued. "I admit to you, my friend, while I still want my revenge on the earl, I cannot see a way to use his niece to do it nor can I bring myself to want to use her in such a way. I am uncomfortable with the thought of my sister being in association with the lady, but I cannot bring myself to deny her this. If Alanna wants to bring out Lady Victoria I will do what I can to help her, even though the earl is my enemy."

"I can foresee some interesting dilemmas are in your future."

Bryghton looked over at Alanna, as she seemed to be wrapping up her conversation with the baron's sister. There was a gathering of young men obviously waiting to be introduced to the pretty youngster. Turning back to his friend with a grin, the duke could not resist saying, "You are about to have some dilemmas of your own, my friend."

Following his gaze, Alfred felt his face tighten in dismay. "How have you managed to bear up under three Seasons of this?"

"I leave most of it to the duchess to deal with. She can somehow turn away any unsuitable young men without them even realizing they have been set down. She has remarkable skills in that department. Never fear, your aunt appears to be nearly as skilled as my mother." Seeing the look on his friend's face, the duke grinned. "That is exactly the right look to have. Glower away, it will build your reputation as a terrifying older brother and will suppress any of the less determined. But for now, I will put an end to all the puppies' hopes by claiming her hand for myself."

With those words Bryghton cut through the throng of young men surrounding Alanna and Eloise, and bowed over Eloise's hand. "Miss Eloise, it is a pleasure to see you here this evening."

The duke's attentions caused the young debutante to become all aflutter and, with a stammer, she began to babble nervously. Bryghton had to resist the urge to roll his eyes. He had thought his long standing as a friend of the family would have made Eloise much more prepared to greet him with equanimity. Alfred, who had joined them, did not feel the need to resist rolling his own eyes. He glanced at the duke with a grimace of embarrassment and turned to his young sister.

"Stop making a cake of yourself, Eloise. You have known his lordship most of your life. Just being at your first ball should not make this much of a difference. Pull yourself together."

Eloise blushed to the roots of her hair and was shocked into silence. Bryghton took pity on her, feeling he had witnessed his friend kicking a puppy.

"I was hoping I could ask for your hand in the next dance if you are not already spoken for."

The young debutante, who had looked to be on the verge of bursting into tears, now had a wide grin begin to bloom upon her face. "It would be a pleasure, your grace, and no, I am not promised to anyone for the next dance, thank you."

She was now flushed with pleasure. Alfred barely stifled his growl of disgust over his sister's behaviour. Bryghton decided his friend was being a little too toplofty.

In a low tone that he hoped could not be heard by Miss Eloise, Bryghton admonished the baron. "Mayhap you ought to pull yourself together, my friend. Keep in mind the poor chit was, until recent weeks, still considered a child. She is entitled to her share of squeals until she gets a little ton bronze. Have mercy."

Alfred looked at his friend as though he could not recognize him. "But, Duke, she is a Lynster; she should be able to adjust without pain and seamlessly."

"Ah yes, of course, forgive me for forgetting." His eyes were dancing with merriment, with only a faint hint of sarcasm in his tone. He turned his attention back to Eloise.

"Our dance is about to start. Would you care to walk around the dance floor with me prior to the number commencing, if it is all right with your aunt?"

Eloise managed to keep quiet, but her eyes shone with excitement as she looked eagerly at her aunt.

"Of course, my dear, I know you shall come to no harm with his grace. Mind your manners and be sure to return to my side when your dance ends."

Eloise tucked her little hand into the duke's elbow and skipped along happily at his side. Maintaining her silence, she looked around with wide eyes, basking in the experience of being escorted by such an exalted peer.

"Pay no heed to your brother, he is just doing his big brotherly duties. He needs to keep you from getting too inflated of an opinion of yourself with all the compliments you are no doubt receiving this evening since you are looking so fine," Bryghton said kindly.

Eloise glanced down at her gown, nearly identical to that of all the other young girls making their first curtsy to Society. Wrinkling her nose at the duke, she asked tentatively, "Do you really think so, your grace?"

"Of course," he replied valiantly. "You look quite lovely. I can hardly believe you are the same young lady I have seen growing up whenever I have visited Lord Lynster."

The delightful young chit let out a surprisingly low chuckle. "Oh, your grace, you are a complete hand. Of course I look better than when I was still in the schoolroom. I was covered in spots and had yet to let down my skirts or put up my hair."

"Well, be that as it may, Miss Eloise, you are looking quite fine this evening."

"Thank you, your grace," Eloise said sweetly, a dimple peeking from the edge of her cheek.

"It is my pleasure, to be sure," answered the duke.

"I am not merely thanking you for the compliment, your grace," she said quietly. "I am thanking you for rescuing me from that crowd. No one had even noticed me until your sister came to talk to me. I was unprepared for the attention of that many young men."

"But you can handle the attentions of one duke?" he asked quizzically.

"You do not count, your grace," she answered with a sweet smile.

Intrigued, the duke demanded, "Why not?"

With a slight roll of her eyes, Eloise answered simply. "You would never be interested in pursuing me. You asked me to dance as a favour to my brother, who happens to be your best friend. Or perhaps because our mothers were friends, or any number of possible reasons. But not out of a desire to strike up a flirtation with me. So you are safe."

Bryghton blinked with surprise over the young woman's observation. His reputation as a bit of a rake was not fully deserved nor cultivated on his part, but he had never been described as "safe" before. He was unsure if he enjoyed such a description, but he understood what she had meant. With a wry tilt to his eyebrows, the duke teased, "You, my dear, are wise beyond your years. But I beg you not to tell anyone else you consider me to be a safe companion. It would leave my reputation in shreds."

"I doubt anything I might say could come close to touching your reputation, your grace," she answered seriously before dimpling and continuing, "but your secret is safe with me."

Bryghton had never much enjoyed the company of debutantes, but he found his friend's sister to be an interesting specimen and was surprised when the dance came to an end. He escorted her back to her aunt and bowed over her hand.

She whispered, "I take back my description of you as safe. I failed to appreciate that the result of dancing with a duke would be an exponential increase in potential suitors."

Bryghton had to bite his lip to keep from laughing out loud. With a wiggle of his eyebrows he whispered back, "I am glad to be of service."

"I am undecided if it is a good thing," she murmured before stepping back and dismissing him.

Bryghton turned to Alfred with a grin. "That young miss is going to take the ton by storm," he declared. "It is difficult to fathom that she is just out of the schoolroom. You do not need to be overly concerned about her, in my opinion. She truly seems to have her head on her shoulders."

Alfred cast the duke a dubious expression. "You are not seriously considering yourself to be one of her admirers, are you?"

"I am absolutely an admirer," Bryghton replied. "But most definitely not a suitor. Now tell me what have you done with my sister. Whilst I was engrossed in conversation with yours I took my eyes off my own."

Alfred indicated with a tilt of his head where Alanna could be found on the dance floor. "She was invited to dance by your dear friend, the viscount."

Bryghton's face hardened noticeably at the sight of his sister in the arms of Lord Anthony Dalton. Barely containing a growl, he glowered. "That chit is going to be the death of me."

Chapter Seventeen

Glancing over the shoulder of her dance partner, Alanna stifled a giggle as she saw her brother glowering in her direction. She turned back to address her dance partner with a serene face. "My lord, I must apologize. I have allowed my mind to wander."

Alanna was fascinated by the viscount's attempt to control his amusement. She found his usually rather imposing features to be quite attractive when lightened with mirth.

"I would think I am the one who owes you an apology for not doing a better job of engaging your interest, my lady," he said gravely.

Now Alanna could not contain her gurgle of laughter. "You, my lord, are a complete hand. It makes me wonder why you are not friends with my brother. I would think the two of you should well enjoy each other's company."

The viscount's face returned to its usual impassivity, much to Alanna's disappointment. "Why would you think that, my lady?" he asked politely.

"You put me in mind of him, my lord, and I think the two of you would have much in common," she answered simply.

"We have not had cause to be much in each other's company."

"Why, then, is he glaring in our direction?"

Dalton again allowed his amusement to display itself but forbore to comment, as the dance was coming to an end. "Thank you, my lady, for your charming company. Do I have your leave to call on you sometime?"

"I dare say you are a brave man if you wish to risk the duke's ire," Alanna replied without answering his question.

The viscount recognized her sidestep and bowed his acknowledgement. "No doubt we shall see one another about over the coming weeks."

"No doubt." Alanna dimpled at the viscount before turning to the next gentleman waiting to escort her on the dance floor.

Seeing how the duke was glaring as his sister danced with the viscount, Alfred made an attempt to distract his friend and keep him from making a scene. "You never did tell me what you are doing here. You rarely attend ton parties unless the duchess is hosting them, or there is something political to be gained by it. And do not tell me that fustian about needing to keep an eye on your sister. You did not bother during her first Season, so I strongly doubt you would need to now."

Despite his irritation with his sister and the viscount, Bryghton grinned at Alfred's words. "You did not buy that story?"

"Not for a second."

"It was Alanna's brilliant idea. She has the notion of bringing Lady Victoria about in Society, and has demanded my assistance in her schemes. I agreed. But in order to keep the tongues from wagging at my sudden appearance at the ladies' side, we realized that I need to make an appearance before Lady Victoria does. As Alanna put it, I wish to be a fixture, not a novelty."

"In theory it is a sound idea, however, unless the ladies wait some time before Lady Victoria makes her curtsy you still run the risk of setting tongues wagging," the baron cautioned.

"Mayhap, but as uncomfortable as it was being the centre of so many staring eyes when I first arrived this evening, I am glad I got it over with before I have to also worry about Lady Victoria's reception."

"Why would you take it upon yourself to worry about her, Alcott? Even if she cannot be an instrument for your revenge, she is not anyone for you to be concerned with."

"Of course, my friend," the duke answered noncommittally before turning the subject. "Now, I do believe I have spent sufficient time in the ballroom. Shall we see if they have any tables set up for cards elsewhere, or do you wish to depart and check out some of the clubs?"

Looking aghast, Alfred answered, "I cannot leave my sister. This is her first grand event." Realizing he might be sounding a trifle dotty, he grinned before continuing, "Besides, if you are serious about wanting to make yourself a fixture, you really ought to dance with several more of the debutantes. Then the gossips can declare that you have finally decided to get leg shackled, and all the matrons can smack their lips over the delightful idea of getting their claws into you."

Bryghton chuckled. "I do not wish to raise the hopes of the matchmaking mamas, but you may be right about needing to spend a bit more time in the ballroom. Perhaps I should set my own matchmaking mama's heart aflutter and ask her to introduce me to some eligible ladies."

Alfred chuckled, and warned, "That might be an act of cruelty, Alcott."

"The duchess can handle it, have no fear." On those words, the two friends parted on very different errands, the baron, to stand guard over his little sister, and the duke, to make himself more visible.

Striding through the throng of brightly dressed high Society, the duke made his way to his mother's side. "Are you enjoying yourself, my lady?" he asked solicitously.

"Immensely, my dear, and how are you faring this evening? This is not your usual milieu—are you managing all right?"

Smiling, the duke saw the opening and took it. "I am managing, but perhaps you could use your expertise and introduce me to some likely dance partners."

Bryghton nearly winced under his mother's sharp glance. "Is there something you wish to tell your mother, your grace?" she asked.

"Yes, your grace—I am without a dance partner at the moment." He grinned at her dubious expression. "Now that I think on it, you would be the perfect dance partner for this next number. Would you do me the honour?"

The duchess knew her son was up to something, but she decided to watch and wait, as she could not resist the allure of the dance floor. She followed him into the dance, glad that this particular number would allow them to have some conversation. When the dance brought them together she asked mildly, "What sort of dance partner would you like to meet? Someone to amuse you, or debutantes to set the gossips aflutter?"

Once again surprised at his mother's perception, Bryghton smiled and answered, "How about a few of each?"

Amused, the duchess inclined her head in acknowledgement. "I shall have a lovely list compiled in my mind as soon as this song is done."

And so it went. Bryghton spent the rest of the night dancing with whomever his mother introduced to him. He was impressed with the variety of partners she brought him. It was the perfect combination to make him visible without raising too many hopes. And so it was— he could feel the eyes of the ton watching him, discretely, behind fans or through lowered eyelashes. The gathered throngs had clearly taken note of his presence amongst them. He was grateful that his mother's choices of dance partners were so varied that it was not obvious to anyone if he was searching for a wife, some other sort of companion, or merely amusing himself for an evening.

He found himself grinning like a simpleton, which caused his current dance partner to blink in surprise from the sudden but appealing sight of the Duke of Wychwood's mirth. His smile was swiftly wiped away as the debutante—whose name he could not for the life of him remember—simpered and batted her eyelashes at him, putting him in mind of a matronly bovine he had been fond of as a boy. He quickly schooled his features and prompted her into acceptable conversation.

"Are you enjoying the Season thus far?" Racking his brain, he could not recall if he should be referring to her as "Miss" or "my lady," so he hoped fervently she did not remark upon his lapse.

"Oh your grace, it is perfectly lovely. Everyone has been exceedingly kind and I am finding absolutely everything to be highly diverting."

"Everything, you say," Bryghton mused, trying to keep the sarcasm from his voice. "What in particular has been a favourite, if I might ask?"

"I do believe it has all been my favourite, your grace," she said in such a tone of seriousness that Bryghton could not allow himself to laugh.

She must have caught the wry tightening of his lips, as she herself burst into giggles. "That statement no doubt made me sound like a simpleton, did it not, your grace? My apologies. You must realize that dancing with you has brought on a case of the nervous fidgets so severe that it would appear that any sense I might have possessed has gone clear out of my head."

The young woman's frankness was unexpectedly charming, but Bryghton had very little appreciation for such silliness.

She sobered and continued with more aplomb, redeeming herself somewhat. "To answer your previous question, your grace, I would have to say meeting so many interesting people has been the best part of coming for my first Season. I was even presented at court, which was a truly spectacular experience."

"You enjoyed court?" he asked with surprise.

The young woman blushed. "Well, no, your grace. If you recall I said it was spectacular. Does anyone actually enjoy court?" Bryghton was glad that the question appeared to be rhetorical, as she continued talking. "I found it to be so much work for the five minutes I was actually in the queen's presence. And the clothes one must wear for such an event! Clothes that you can never wear again unless you wish to pursue a career at court, which I have no intention of doing. Thus, while I found it sparkling and diverting, and there were any number of highly interesting people, I would not exactly say that I enjoyed the experience—although I am grateful that my aunt took me to introduce me. Do you enjoy court, your grace?"

"I must tell you, I am one of those highly interesting people whose responsibilities call upon my presence at court on a regular basis. But I can fully understand why you did not enjoy the experience. There is certainly nothing overly comfortable about going there. Just imagine how the queen must feel about it."

The young woman gazed at Bryghton with wide eyes and an arrested expression. "I had never thought of it like that, your grace. You are right. It must be so difficult to have to wear court dress every day. And to have everyone staring at you must be terribly uncomfortable."

"I would imagine so. Of course, our beloved monarch handles it beautifully. But when I am at court and find myself wishing I was elsewhere, I try to think of it from the monarch's perspective, and I am grateful that I do not have to be there overlong or terribly often."

"That is very broad-minded of you, your grace."

Bryghton was not entirely sure if she was being cheeky or if it was a genuine compliment, but either way he found the chit to be amusing. He found himself wondering what Victoria would make of her, and hoped one day he would be able to introduce the two—if he could ever remember the young woman's name.

As the musicians ended the number with a resounding flourish, the duke escorted his partner to the side of the dance floor and was relieved to see his mother, as he had no idea where to take the young woman.

Graciously, Lady Wychwood welcomed the duo back. "Miss Monica, you dance beautifully. Are you having an enjoyable evening? Would you like me to introduce you to some other eligible dance partners?"

Smiling, Monica answered, "Thank you, your grace, I am having a perfectly enjoyable evening. And thank you so much for offering me help in finding dance partners, but I have actually promised Lord Lamport I would dance the next cotillion with him and I do believe that is what the band is striking up, so I had best see about finding him."

"It was a pleasure to make your acquaintance, Miss Monica. No doubt we shall see each other upon occasion throughout the Season. Enjoy your cotillion."

Monica's smile widened as she dipped into a curtsy and took her leave of the duke and his mother.

"That was diverting," said the duchess.

"What was, mother?"

"Watching you try to comprehend the workings of Miss Monica's mind. For the most part you are highly skilled in keeping your face blank at all times, but there were a few moments where your thoughts were peeking through the cracks in your façade. What a delightful child that one is. She will do well as long as her parents help her to find a suitable match. She needs someone who will appreciate her delightful qualities, not try to squash them out of her."

"Are you trying to consider me for the role?" Bryghton asked curiously.

"Not particularly, my dear. Not that I think you would flatten her, but I do not believe you would have the patience to allow her to grow into her potential. I think that lovely young miss should wait another year or two before she marries. You, my darling son, should be getting yourself leg shackled at the earliest possibility, as you are not getting any younger."

The duke chuckled, giving a satirical bow as he said, "I do believe, mother, if I am aging so are you. Are you afraid you will not be around to meet your grandchildren?"

"Not at all. I think you are gaining on me in age. Besides, I cannot believe grandchildren are too far off if you have finally seen the wisdom in entering the Marriage Mart."

"What makes you think I have entered the Marriage Mart?" he asked with some horror.

"You are here, are you not?"

"Why can the two facts not be mutually exclusive?"

"That is not the way our world works, and well you know it. Now I have promised myself I would not tease you for any names, but I shall be keeping my eyes on you. Do tell me if you are in need of any more assistance." With those words, the duchess swept away gracefully, leaving a swirl of perfumed air in her wake and her flummoxed son blinking behind her.

"You look rather comical, Wychwood. Is everything right with you?"

Bryghton turned at the sound of his sister's voice and her teasing words. "Of course, all is right, little chick. Are you having a good night?"

"I do believe I have danced my shoes ragged, which is the epitome of success for a lady during the Season, so I would say yes, I am having a good night. And what of you? You are still here, so you must not have yet been bored to tears."

"No tears on this manly face. In fact, I have been nearly beside myself with amazement over the fact that I have not been bored to the verge of tears. I actually made the tactical decision to enlist the duchess' help in choosing dance partners. She has kept me busy most of the night with a varied array of ladies. It has been most enlightening." The duke paused and surveyed the slightly dwindled crowd milling around them.

He continued. "However, I would say I have had my fill for this evening—or should I say morning at this point? What say you to my escorting you home? I would think your ragged feet could use some time in their bed."

"Yes, and it would not do to be the last ones to leave." Alanna took her brother's arm. "Shall we go collect our mother?"

They made short work of finding the duchess, calling for the carriage, and taking leave of their hosts. A short while later, the duke handed them down in front of their house with a promise to see his sister on the morrow.

As they mounted the stairs to the house, the duchess turned to her daughter with an appraising look.

"Something tells me you and your brother are conspiring something, and I am unsure how worried I should be."

Alanna turned wide and innocent eyes on her mother. "I have no idea what you are speaking of, my dear mother."

"Of course you do," replied the duchess bracingly. "I think it is perfectly lovely that the two of you feel close enough to one another to conspire on something. My only concern is what it could be and whether or not I should involve myself."

Smiling sweetly, Alanna's only reply was, "The less you know the more innocence you can plead."

Her mother conceded with a chuckle and a warning. "Try to keep both your reputations unspotted, would you please. I would be delighted to have a couple of weddings in the family this Season, and clean reputations are important for that particular goal to be achieved."

"Now mother, do not say that, or there could be dire consequences."

Laughing in good humour, the two ladies climbed the stairs to their private quarters and settled in for the night.

Chapter Eighteen

As promised, Bryghton arrived right on time to escort his sister to her meeting with Lady Victoria. After handing her up into his phaeton and climbing in after her, he posed a tricky question.

"Have you decided on which arguments you plan to use to convince the lady to fall in with your plans of launching her into Society?"

Smiling sheepishly, Alanna shook her head. "Not exactly. I was hoping you might have a brilliant plan."

"I think you have to allow the lady to make the choice for herself. She is a grown woman and despite our thoughts and feelings on the subject she should be allowed to make her own decisions. You should reiterate your offer of support and friendship and leave the matter with her. You cannot drag her to parties kicking and screaming behind you. It surely would cause a stir amongst the gossips."

Laughing, Alanna nodded her agreement. "I fear you are correct. There really is nothing I can say to convince her if it is not something she wishes to do. That is sound advice, my darling brother. I think you shall make a perfectly lovely duke one day."

"I am already a duke. Do you not think I am a good one now?" he asked with some incredulity.

Unrepentant, his little sister burst into a fit of the giggles. In good spirits they bantered back and forth as they made their way to the park where they were to meet Lady Victoria.

As the duke handed his sister down, she looked up at him with a rueful smile. "Can you believe I am rather nervous? How remarkably droll."

Bryghton grinned, offering no comment but tucking her hand snugly into his elbow.

Victoria had been feeling anxious all day, and was finding it difficult to keep her attention fully on the children as they played in the parkette. That morning she had asked for an audience with her uncle, and she fought against discouragement as she thought back to the brief conversation.

"Do you have a moment, Uncle?"

His exasperated sigh almost made her back out of the room. "Not really, Victoria. What is it?"

Forcing herself not to be evasive, she was blunt and to the point. "I would like to discuss my future with you, my lord. Will my aunt be arranging a Season for me? Do I have a dowry? What will come of me if I do not marry? I am afraid I am unqualified to be a governess, and I am struggling to manage all four of the younger children."

"I do not have time for this right now, Victoria. There is nothing for you to worry about in regards to your future. We promised your parents to look after you, and we will."

This comment contained no warmth, and no comfort. She swallowed her disappointment and nodded, keeping her attention on him, hoping he had more to say.

"My wife has no complaints about your care of the children, so I doubt you are insufficiently qualified, but we have hired someone to help. She should be starting in the next day or two."

"That's a relief, Uncle. While I love the children, I would very much appreciate a little time for myself."

"That sounds selfish to me, girl, but don't worry, the woman seems capable enough, and you should be able to take some time for yourself to do whatever it is you want. And we are still looking for a governess, so do not trouble yourself about that. Now if there is nothing else, I need to get back to my work."

Heat had flooded her over his words. Victoria did not think she was being selfish to want help with the children and some time to herself. Their own mother didn't spend time with them. Simmering inwardly, she bobbed a small curtsy and left her uncle to his occupation.

She was aware of the carriage's arrival as soon as it pulled up outside the park, as she had been anxiously anticipating Alanna's appearance. Feeling the blood drain away from her cheeks at the realization that the lady had brought her brother, Victoria wondered absently if she should find somewhere to sit so she would not become faint.

The children noticed the new arrivals, stopping their game to run over to their cousin. Daniel declared the obvious, "It's the duke!" before shoving his thumb into his mouth with a worried look at his sisters. The children's concern helped Victoria snap out of her own fidgets and she crouched down to reassure them.

"Do not trouble yourselves, children. You may politely greet our friends and then carry on with your game. We are in a public place and it cannot be helped who we encounter. Perhaps the duke and his sister are merely here to take the air."

Vanessa gave her cousin an incredulous look, stating the obvious. "They are coming to speak with you, Aunt 'Toria. Do you want us to tell them to go away?"

Laughing at the children's desire to protect her, she reassured them once more. "There is no need for that. We shall all be polite. Now mind your manners and say hello, then go ahead and have some playtime before we have to head back to the house."

"It is too bad of the lady not to bring Lord Alfred with her," Felicia was heard saying just as Bryghton and Alanna got within earshot. "He is ever so much fun."

Alanna could barely stifle her laughter as she turned to her brother. "Clearly you have been found wanting, your grace."

Bryghton redeemed himself in the eyes of the children when he stopped and bowed to them politely. "Hello ladies and my lord, Daniel. How are you all doing today?" He gravely shook each child's hand and placed a chaste kiss on the back of Lady Victoria's, not remarking upon the slight tremble in hers but glancing at her pointedly when she would not meet his eyes. He endeavoured to contain a self-satisfied grin over her heightened colour and quickened breath. He turned back to the children.

"My dear friend Lord Alfred could not accompany me today, but he has told me what a good time he has had with you and I was hoping you could show me the game you were playing with him. I must warn you that I may not be as skilled as he is, but I am a duke, so I shall give it my very best effort."

Four wide-eyed little faces gazed at him for a silent moment before Gwendolyn and Daniel burst out in a cheer. "Yay! Very well, Duke, we shall show you just what to do."

Vanessa, always more sober-minded, looked to her guardian for direction. Victoria, hiding her own disbelieving grin, gave her cousin a slight shrug. "Go ahead and show him your game. Dukes are allowed to play once in a while too, it would seem."

Alanna did not bother to hide her skeptical look from her brother. "Ensure you do not break any bones, your grace. You will be of no use to me if you are laid up for the rest of the Season."

Bryghton ignored his sister as the children grabbed him by his hands and pulled him over to where they had left their toys. He had to apply his considerable intellect to keep track of the four threads of conversation being strung around him haphazardly.

Smiling their amusement, the two ladies made their way to a nearby bench.

"When he agreed to accompany me I had no idea he was going to be a distraction to the children. That is brilliant of him, but so unexpected."

"Your brother is certainly full of surprises. I must say I was surprised to see him accompanying you today," Victoria commented carefully.

"Will that be a problem for you?" Alanna asked anxiously.

Victoria could only offer a rather helpless shrug. "I cannot say for sure, Lady Alanna. I have far more questions than answers of late."

Both ladies lapsed into silence for a moment, watching as the children were demonstrating to the duke how to play the game to their specifications. In order to amuse the children Bryghton was making exaggeratedly droll errors and the four children were nearly collapsing with gales of laughter.

Victoria turned to Alanna with sad eyes belying the smile upon her lips. "I gave a great deal of thought your offer yesterday. You are right. I absolutely love my darling cousins. Even their big brother Everett can be a dear. But they are not my children and my position in my uncle's household is precarious at best. I do need to make arrangements for my future. I am currently unsure of my financial situation, so I do not know if I could establish an independence if I could no longer live with the earl. Perhaps your suggestion of going about amongst the ton has merit. It will at least avail me of the opportunity to make an informed decision on the matter, at any rate."

Alanna was nodding eagerly in agreement. "That is exactly my thoughts. We do not have to make it a big to-do if you do not wish—you may simply accompany me as I make some morning calls or to a ball or two."

Blushing, Victoria pointed out the largest obstacle. "There is still the issue of what I can wear." She hesitated with an air of indecision before launching into an uncomfortable explanation. "I asked for an audience with my uncle this morning. He was terribly busy so he could not give me very much time. I had several matters I wished to discuss with him about my future, such as whether or not I was to have a Season under their direction and where I stand with a dowry or what arrangements have been made for me whether I marry or not. He brushed aside all of my questions, promising to discuss them with me some other time. He did say, however, that he has arranged for another maid for the nursery, so I am to have more time to myself. He also promised to see about a governess for the children."

"That is wonderful news, Lady Victoria!"

Victoria allowed a small sigh to escape her lips. "It is a little progress, but it is still so nebulous. I am really no further ahead. I do not know if the children will be provided for, and I do not know where I stand for myself."

"If I may be so bold as to ask you a rather personal question, have you decided whose interests you are going to place first if you must choose? Yours or the children's?"

Victoria felt her face flame red at this question and she turned startled eyes to her companion. "Whatever do you mean?"

"If the earl does not hire a governess, will you still come about with me?"

Victoria tore her eyes away from Alanna's searching gaze and watched the duke playing energetically with the four youngsters. A sweet smile formed on her lips. "I would dearly like to give it a try, my lady, and I thank you for the kindness of your offer. I cannot guarantee what the future holds, but I would like to taste this world you are offering me a glimpse of." Victoria trailed off for a moment, gazing off into space, but then refocused her attention on her new friend. "I do fear the earl's reaction if he were to find out, so I think it would be best to contain myself to some understated doings for now, but yes, please, I would look forward to it."

"Excellent. Now we must make some plans. Bryght suggested I should plan some sort of entertainment at our mother's house and you could stay with us as our guest, which would raise no eyebrows. This would allow you to become familiar with some members of the ton in a more comfortable setting than at a stranger's grand event. As well, I would be happy to take you with me as I make calls to introduce you to some of my friends."

Alanna paused before answering the touchier subject. "As to what you could wear, I would be perfectly happy lending you anything from my own closet that you would like to try. Since we are of the same height, everything would fit you, and with our very different colouring I'm sure that no one would notice or remark upon it, as I might have mentioned the other day. If you would prefer, we could even do some alterations to some of my gowns from last Season so that they are more your own. You could keep those ones, as I no longer have any use for them."

Victoria was taken aback by this offer. "Why do you have no use for them? Why did you not make them over for yourself for this Season if they are still serviceable?"

Alanna gazed at her new friend with an arrested expression before bursting into laughter. "Because I am a disgracefully spoilt urchin who has no compunction about spending my brother's seemingly endless wealth. You will be salving my conscience if you take my wasteful gowns off my hands and give them a new life."

Victoria blushed fiercely. "I meant no offense, my lady," she stammered.

"None taken. Now, did we not say we are to be friends? So we must stop 'my lady-ing' each other. Victoria, my dear, please say you will allow me to take you about with me. How soon can we start? When did your uncle say the new maid was to begin working in the nursery so that you might have some free time?"

"I do believe she was to start right away. I would be most comfortable to wait a day or two to ensure the little ones are going to accept her." Victoria trailed off before turning stricken eyes to her new friend. "That is why you asked me whose interests I would put first, is it not? I always put the children first. But in this case, I believe it is the right thing to do. It will not ruin your plans any, will it, if I wait a day or two?"

"Not at all," Alanna answered. "It will take me a few days to plan my party and get the invitations out, anyway. I would like to take you around a bit with me at least a time or two before the party, though, so let us say in two days from now you come to my house in the late morning and we can look through my frocks and gowns and decide which will work for you. That should not take overly long. The next day you can come and accompany me upon my morning calls. And perhaps a se'nnight later you could tell your family you are staying over at a friend's house and we can have my party."

"That seems like a sound plan, my lady—I should say, Alanna."

So intent were both ladies upon their conversation that they had not noticed the approach of the duke. "What is your sound plan?"

Startled, Victoria turned a sweetly blushing face to gaze at the duke, but Alanna was not put off by her brother's presence. "Victoria has agreed to come with me about Town a wee bit and we have figured out a good way to accomplish it."

"Do you care to divulge your ideas to your big brother?"

"As it turns out, I have no need of your help," Alanna answered dismissively.

Victoria could not allow that to pass. "In all honesty, we could never have had this conversation if the children were anywhere nearby. They have the sharpest hearing and would be far too excited about it to keep it to themselves." She turned an impish smile upon the duke. "So you were of some help."

"Thank you for your acknowledgement of my worth, my lady," was Bryghton's reply as he made her an exaggeratedly elegant bow.

Victoria could not resist a fit of the giggles over his antics, but then sat back with a sigh as she gained control over her mirth. Squeezing Alanna's hand with gratitude, Victoria smiled a trifle sadly. "It has been much too long since I have laughed like that. Thank you for the lovely visit. And thank you for your efforts on my behalf, however puzzling I find your attentions. I appreciate it regardless. And I shall look forward to our meeting two days hence. But now, I surely must take my leave of you both and see that the children are returned home at an appropriate time." She stood to leave and took a few steps away before turning back abruptly.

"I shall do my very best to meet you as we have arranged. But if something should arise to detain me, I cannot be certain if I would even be able to get a message to you. It would be unforgivably rude of me should I not show up without sending my regrets, but I must warn you that there is a possibility that that could be the outcome. I apologize in advance if that should become the case."

Alanna laughed light-heartedly, springing up from the bench and embracing her new friend. "You, my dear lady, worry far too much. Do not borrow trouble. If you stand me up, I am forewarned of the possibility and will not hold it against you. I will do my best to re-establish contact, and we shall cross that bridge if we come to it."

Victoria grinned, dropped a quick curtsy to encompass both her noble visitors, and hurried away to collect the children.

Alanna was still smiling when she turned to her brother and observed the arrested expression upon his usually impassive face as he watched the lovely lady stride away. Alanna's smile turned into a grin, as she could not resist teasing her brother.

"What happened to you, brother dear? You look completely flummoxed. Are you afraid the Earl of Pickering will be coming after us in retribution for this adventure?"

Blinking himself out of his reverie, the duke turned to his sister in puzzlement. "Whatever are you yammering on about, Alanna? Why would you think I could be afraid of the likes of the Earl of Pickering?" His frosty tones brought astonishment to his sister.

"Gracious, Alcott, you sound positively fierce on the subject. Did I strike a nerve, perhaps?"

Bryghton forced his thoughts into order as he gazed at his sister, his face once more inscrutable. With a pleasant, if somewhat tight smile, he held up a hand to stem the tide of his sister's ill-timed teasing.

"Perhaps you are right, little sister dear. I am experiencing a bevy of mixed emotions on the subject of the earl. On the one hand I have absolutely no fear of the man towards myself. There is naught he could do to harm me or mine. However, I would not entrust the man with my enemies, let alone a friend, and certainly not a sweet, innocent, inexperienced, young woman like Lady Victoria. I will admit to you I have some trepidation over what will become of her from this adventure of ours."

"Are you taking responsibility for things then, your grace? You call it "our" adventure."

Bryghton shrugged nonchalantly. "You did say it was my words that set you on this course in the first place. I must take at least some responsibility, would you not agree?"

"I think you have a level of interest in our lady to which you will not admit, perhaps not even to yourself," Alanna speculated.

Bryghton would not acknowledge any truthfulness in his sister's words, saying dismissively, "You, my dear girl, have an overly active imagination."

Seeing she was about to argue the subject further, he curtailed further discussion by rising from the seat beside her and reaching for her hand. "Now, my little lady, what say you we make our own way home? Our presence here is no longer required. I dare say we are soon to become a spectacle if we do not vacate the premises."

Alanna allowed herself to be tugged to her feet, smiling at her brother's droll words, and allowing the duke to divert the conversation away from his unadmitted feelings for their new protégé. "Very well. You are correct, it would be best if I returned home shortly, as I have much to do in order to prepare for this evening's activities."

As the duke handed her back up into his phaeton she made pleasant conversation. "What are your plans for the rest of the day?"

"I have places I need to be this evening and people I must see," he answered with a teasing twinkle in his eye, as his sister swatted him playfully over his intentional lack of information. "And mayhap I shall look in on whichever entertainments you are attending."

"But you were not included in my invitations for this evening," Alanna protested.

The duke turned an incredulous expression upon his sister. "Do you truly believe I would be turned away by any of the potential hostesses?"

Alanna could feel her eyebrows arching towards her hairline, so surprised was she at her brother's haughtiness. "Until I heard you use those words I would have said no, but I have a suspicion now that no one would want you around if you were to be sounding like that."

Delighted, Bryghton could not resist tweaking his sister's distastefully wrinkled nose. "I shall make an effort to curb my haughtiness for your benefit, little chick. I apologize if I offended you by my seeming expectation of a welcome wherever I go. But truly you must admit that most hostesses would be happy to have an unattached duke attending their gatherings."

"Mayhap," replied his sister, unconvinced, "but I am sure you are supposed to at the very least feign a lack of knowledge on the subject. It is surely not done to acknowledge such a ridiculous state of affairs."

"Again, I apologize, my dear. Truly, I was merely funning. If you think it best, I will sit at home this evening and twiddle my thumbs, contemplating my obvious lack of couth."

This finally moved his sister to relent as she erupted into a delightful gurgle of laughter. "Now that is a mental picture I shall carry with me for some time. But no, Duke, one cannot leave you languishing at home. You may accompany me on my rounds this evening. No doubt you are quite right that the ladies will be absolutely delighted by your presence. We must not disappoint them with the news that you are repenting of your arrogance. That is just not done, to be sure."

Chuckling with good humour, the duke arrived at his destination, pulling his carriage to a standstill and helping his sister to debark. Alanna was climbing the stairs to the door being held open by an attentive servant when she glanced back over her shoulder and noticed Bryghton was not following her.

"Are you not coming home with me?" she asked in some surprise, having greatly enjoyed the afternoon spent with her brother.

"Not right now, little chick. I have things I must attend to before I join you in the social whirl this evening. I shall meet up with you somewhere along the way tonight. You shall be perfectly fine with the duchess," he concluded soothingly as his sister stuck out her lower lip to sulk her disappointment.

Alanna shrugged herself out of her brief dispirit. "It would seem you are spoiling me, your grace. I could become used to the attentions of my big brother. Very well, have a lovely evening. I shall see you when I see you." With that she turned back, swept up the stairs, and entered the large house without a backward glance.

Chapter Nineteen

Bryghton sat in his phaeton staring absently at the door of his mother's house after it closed behind his sister. He supposed idly that it was his house, as he had inherited it from his father at the same time he had come into his title, but he could only ever think of it as his mother's. He was quite happy to have his own smaller but much more comfortable townhouse not far away on Charles Street. His mother was rather horrified that he chose to maintain his own residence, but it would turn out to be a blessing if he ever did decide to marry, as his mother was obviously eager for him to do. Where would he put a wife otherwise, he wondered as he deftly turned his carriage in the narrow street, setting off back towards St James Street, hoping to catch up with Alfred at White's.

He was in luck. As soon as he stepped through the front door of his club he was hailed by a number of gentlemen, and, briefly acknowledging their greetings, he made his way straight to where his friend was sitting savouring his brandy.

"Alcott, my good man, where have you taken yourself off to all day? I have not seen hide nor hair of you since you demanded my sister partner you in the waltz."

"I can assure you I returned Eloise to your aunt Sybil just as soon as the dance was concluded," Bryghton protested in mock defense.

Laughing, the baron persisted, "Yes, but where have you been?"

"I am surprised you did not notice me, Freddy. I spent most of the night on the dance floor with various partners that I allowed the duchess to pick out for me. When I had danced with one too many vacuous debutantes I escorted my mother and sister home. You had informed me that you needed to remain in attendance overseeing your little sister, so I did not bother to invite you to accompany us."

Alfred nodded. "Let me tell you, Bryght, I would have bolted with you if you had offered, so it is no doubt a good thing that you didn't. Eloise is a sweetheart, but she is not the brightest of ladies, if you know what I mean. We were practically the last to leave the ball! This Season just might be the death of me." The shudder he displayed was only half in jest.

Bryghton grinned and continued his explanation. "What I have been doing with my afternoon is why I wished to speak with you. My sister has managed to convince Lady Victoria to accompany her about a little during this Season and I wanted to enlist your help in keeping the two of them out of trouble and away from the earl. I feel responsible for this blasted situation, as it was my ill-thought words that sent Alanna on a search for the lady in question."

"Of course, Alcott. I quite like the lady anyway, so I would be happy to be of assistance to her if at all possible. What, though, did you have in mind?" he asked, with a touch of hesitation.

"Oh man up, my lord, you should not sound so weakwilled about it. It is not as though I am going to ask you to do anything havey-cavey. I merely meant that you should go out of your way to make her feel welcomed and comfortable at whatever occasion you might happen to encounter her."

"Well, of course, I would do that anyway. But are you expecting there to be some sort of trouble from her uncle?"

"The Earl of Pickering does not go about amongst Society—no doubt he is not welcome in most places—so I am not overly concerned that my sister and Lady Victoria shall run into him face to face. But he does have some friends who might make it their business to make her uncomfortable. And then there is the fact that despite being an earl's daughter, she will not have a proper sponsor, and being a rather attractive young lady she might attract some catty behaviour from some of the other ladies."

Alfred nodded in agreement. "Have you had any luck finding out about the lady's affairs? What did your secretary find? Are you concerned about fortune hunters being after her?"

Bryghton sighed. "As you were probably quite aware, women in fact have no rights. As a single woman, she is a little better off than a married one with regards to being able to inherit. In her particular case, it is, as expected, that she doesn't actually inherit until she turns twenty-five or gets married. And the way it was set up, if she is not married she will never gain full control over her own funds even after turning twenty-five. That might be part of why Pickering doesn't set her up with a Season. As long as she remains unmarried, he is guardian over her fortune."

"So Pickering will have all the more reason to prevent her from associating with you or anyone of the ton. Do you think it wise, then, for Alanna to be embarking on this adventure? Could you not dissuade her?" Alfred questioned, worry showing in his tone.

"Really, Alfred? You ask me this now? You were the one who could not dissuade her from even meeting the lady. Now that she has, Alanna has decided that it is her mission in life to ensure Lady Victoria has been given a chance to mingle amongst the ton. She will not rest until she has seen to it and we shall all be borne along in her wake. I thought Lady Victoria was made of sterner stuff, but she has fallen to my sister's persuasions. So there is naught we can do but go along and do our best to smooth the way for her."

"As you said, her uncle doesn't go to ton events. Perhaps all will be well in that quarter." He paused in thought and remembered what else the duke had said. "Do you really think the other young ladies could give her trouble? She is such a lovely young lady I have a hard time imagining anyone could be unkind to her."

"You have a sister—I am surprised you even have to ask. If you ask me, women are considerably worse than men in their behaviour towards one another. For example, Alanna cannot be friends with Miss Sophie Beckett because Sophie's mother and our mother had some sort of squabble when they were making their debut."

Alfred was so nonplussed by this information, thinking about his own sweet and innocent sister, that he felt the need for fortification. After draining the last of his brandy he hailed a passing footman to bring him another. Turning back to Bryghton, he asked what was uppermost in his mind. "What is Alanna planning to do with Lady Victoria? Is she going to take her in and sponsor her Season?"

"No, no, nothing like that. She is going to have Victoria accompany her about somewhat, such as on morning calls or walks in the park. Alanna is also planning to host some sort of a dance or soirée next week, I believe, so you had best make sure that you and Eloise are free to attend. I cannot imagine your sweet little sister participating in the sorts of dramas I will expect from some of the ladies."

"I should think not, she is a Lynster after all," said Alfred rather huffily.

Both men paused, their eyes met, and they burst into loud guffaws of laughter, causing some of the other club members to turn and glare. Bryghton regained control of his mirth but almost lost it again when he realized he actually had to wipe tears from the corners of his eyes as a result of his hearty laughter.

"We sound like a couple of doting fathers worrying about our darling daughters' first Seasons. What have we come to, my friend?" asked the duke drolly.

Wiping his own eyes rather ungraciously with the sleeve of his coat, the baron continued to chuckle for another moment before he too shook his head and answered truthfully. "I have no idea how it happened, but it would seem we have left our carefree bachelor days behind us. Mayhap your mother was right, and it is time we thought about setting up our own establishments and taking wives for ourselves."

"Do you really think so? If sisters and their friends are this much trouble, just think what kind of a circus a wife would cause."

Alfred gazed at his friend thoughtfully for a moment before his face became creased with a playful grin and he waggled his eyebrows suggestively. "They may be a passel of trouble, but they can be an awful lot of fun to have around, too."

Bryghton's jaw dropped open in shock, and he choked on more laughter. "Are you suggesting you might be considering getting yourself leg shackled, my lord?"

"I do believe I would, your grace," Alfred answered gravely. A grin broke over his face and he shrugged. "Really, we are both going to have to one day, so we might as well face the challenge head on and start looking for the least annoying female we can find."

"I do believe you have an idea, but my advice would be not to let the ladies hear you say what your criterion is. I do not think even the most level-minded female would take too kindly to receiving a proposal of marriage because you thought she was the least annoying choice."

Bryghton cleared his throat and ordered his face into a serious expression. "Now shall we return to the matter at hand? Unless, of course, you are considering Lady Victoria to be a candidate for a future bride?"

"Not at all, Duke. I should not like to get my family mixed up with the likes of Pickering. She is a nice enough young lady and I will be happy to assist her, but she does not fall into the category of least annoying. Her uncle is plenty annoying if you ask me."

"True enough, Alfred, my good man. But we must consider her marriageable material, as that would seem to be Alanna's intentions in launching her. She is convinced it is highly inappropriate for the lady to be governess to her cousins, and Alanna has decided Lady Victoria must find a husband."

Alfred sat back in his chair and drained his brandy once more. "I have clearly not had enough of this very fine brandy. I was thinking your sister was merely interested in having company for the Season or that she was considering the lady as a hobby. I did not realize the extent of her ambitions." The baron sat gazing off into space for a moment before turning back to face Bryghton with his face schooled into serious lines. "But it is not a terrible idea. She is really a beautiful young lady and connected to the earl. It should not be all that difficult for your sister to get her married off."

"It would seem, though, that my sister wants to find a love match for the lady. She will not be content with merely finding the lady an acceptable home. She wants to provide for her happiness."

"That's right kindly of her, would you not say?"

Bryghton smiled. "Of course it's kind, but it is also complicated. I will keep you informed of my sister's plans."

"Well, thank you for the information. I did wonder what your sister was going to manage to accomplish in that quarter."

The two gentlemen sat in companionable silence for a few moments, each lost in their own thoughts. Alfred contemplated with admiration what a merry adventure Alanna was setting up for herself and her friend for the coming weeks. She was a charming lady; there was no doubt about it. He felt his pulse quicken as his mind dwelt on her. A wave of guilt swamped him over such thoughts about his friend's sister. He shook his head, hoping he wasn't blushing like a schoolgirl. Bryghton, seeming not to notice, roused himself from his own thoughts and got up from the table.

"Where are you off to now?" Alfred asked with feigned curiosity.

"I thought I would stick my head into a few of the ton gatherings this evening. Alanna and the duchess are attending a ball at Viscount Chorley's tonight. I figured Lady Chorley would not turn me away even though she did not invite me. Actually, it is entirely possible she did invite me but my secretary discards all such correspondence upon my orders. I should probably try to remember to tell him that I will need to attend a few of those things now."

"Eloise and my aunt have accepted Chorley's invitation as well, so I will most likely see you there."

"Possibly, although my sister has informed me it is likely to be a terrible crush."

"With your shiny golden head I should be able to pick you out of the crowd. Fair thee well, my friend. And see you later."

Bryghton shook his head amusedly and took his leave. As he made his way out of the club, he was again hailed by many of the assembled noblemen. It was slow progress, stopping at nearly every table to shake hands and exchange greetings, but before too long he was out on the street in front of the club, glad that he had left his tiger to walk the horses.

"Thank you, Ernie. I had not planned on being inside for quite that long. It was good that you kept them walking. These two would no doubt be in high fidgets by now if you had not."

"I know me horses, me lord. You need never be afeared when they're in my hands," boasted the young tiger as he clambered up to his perch behind the duke and they took off at a brisk pace, heading back towards the duke's rooms in Albany.

That night, the duke showed up at Chorney's ball, one of the last guests to be received by the viscount and his wife. Bowing elegantly over Lady Chorney's hand and placing a kiss flirtatiously upon her wrist, Bryghton had on his most winsome smile as he charmed the couple. "My sister told me she would be attending your ball this evening and I offered to come with her. She informed me that I had not been included in her invitation, so I was of two minds on the subject. Is it terribly maladroit of me to attend without having received an invitation? If I promise to dance with at least two wallflowers and three debutantes will you allow me entrée?"

The viscount watched the young duke's antics with a baleful eye but his wife laughed with delight. "Fie on you, your grace, of course you are always welcome in our home. The only maladroit thing you have done is point out how remiss I was in not sending you an invitation in the first place. Had the gossip gotten around to me by the time I issued my invitations that you were out this Season you can be sure that you would have received one. As it is, the knowledge only reached my ears this afternoon that you had been seen dancing at the Pembroke ball last night. You can be sure that your front hall will be positively littered with invitations by tomorrow."

Bryghton suppressed a shudder at the viscountess' words, maintaining his charming smile, although now lacking some of the luster. The viscount, always observant, saw the duke's reaction and brightened considerably. It was obvious to Lord Chorney that, while the young duke clearly had some sort of agenda, he was not overly eager to be entering the social whirl of the ton, nor did he have inappropriate eyes for the viscountess. Taking mercy on him, the viscount interrupted his wife's enthusiastic welcome of the duke.

"Come along Wychwood, I do believe I have served sufficient time standing here welcoming my wife's guests and I now deserve some sort of libation as a reward for my good behaviour. You must come with me and fortify yourself for the night's ordeals."

"Robert, are you trying to imply that attending my party is going to be an ordeal for his lordship?" his wife asked, equal parts horror and humour in her tone.

Bryghton stepped in to save the viscount, grateful for his welcome. "No doubt your dear husband remembers the trepidation with which he faced events such as these prior to having you in his life to smooth the way for him socially. He is merely expressing empathy for the situation I am in as a poor unmarried duke. Surely you understand, my lady."

"Get along with you, the both of you. Of course I understand. Now do not forget your promises to my unpartnered guests, your grace, no matter how good my husband's port might be."

Winking, Bryghton said, "I could never forget my word, my lady—particularly not to such a charming lady as yourself."

"Come along you scamp, and quit flirting with my wife," growled Lord Chorney as he took the duke off to his library for the promised drink.

As they entered the distinctly masculine room, Chorney commented conversationally. "This is probably the only room in which we can have a moment's peace tonight. My lady wife has thrown the doors wide upon the entire house but she had the good grace to leave me one place to escape to if I needs must." He poured the brandy, remarking, "You can be sure nothing she's serving tonight will be as good as this." Realizing the insult to his wife's hospitality, he hastily continued, "Not to imply that she would be serving anything inferior to our guests—it is just that one does not serve brandy at events such as these."

"Of course, I understand fully," answered Bryghton. "I have been to plenty such events and know exactly what you mean. I'm grateful for your hospitality in offering me some of the good stuff before I throw myself to the wolves."

The viscount grinned at his younger guest. "Looking to get yourself a duchess this Season, my boy? No doubt it is about time for you."

Bryghton held onto his good humour by an effort of will, gritting his teeth against complaints about why everyone was in such an eager hurry to marry him off. "I am merely checking out the lay of the land, my lord, and casting a brotherly eye upon my sister's actions. I am as yet undecided on the subject of my own duchess, but my good friend's sister is making her debut this year and this is my sister's third Season, so it did seem to me that there was an obligation for me to make an appearance."

Lord Chorney did not buy Bryghton's story for a moment, but was intuitive enough to realize it was not as simple as the duke searching for a wife either. He allowed the subject to drop. Taking a last sip from his glass he banged it down on his desk with an enthusiasm he did not quite feel, and smiled at his guest. "Shall we enter the fray, then, your grace, if you are finished?"

Bryghton too downed his glass, as though hoping it would smooth the way for the ordeal he was about to face. He wondered again why he was feeling the need to enter the social world of the ton in order to smooth the way for Lady Victoria—his enemy's niece, of all people. Realizing his smile was starting to feel more like a snarl, he cleared his throat and followed his host from the room.

The fates must have been smiling fondly upon the duke that night as he entered the crowded ballroom. With relief, he realized Lord Lynster, his little sister, and his aunt were not more than ten feet away from him. His grin was genuine, as he realized he could relieve himself of at least one debutante commitment by taking little Eloise to the dance floor.

Eloise accepted his offer, and he led her to the dance floor.

"Are you having a good time here tonight at Lady Chorney's ball, Miss Eloise?" he asked.

"I am having a perfectly lovely time, thank you, your grace. It is particularly exciting, as Lady Alanna has assured me that it shall be a veritable squeeze. I will admit to you I have been dearly wishing to know how it feels to be in attendance upon such an occasion."

"You have? That leads me to believe you have particularly odd tastes. Why ever would you wish to be present when a hostess' rooms are overflowing their capacity? It can become decidedly unpleasant, I can assure you."

"Well, I can understand why you would say that, as it has become dreadfully close, besides the various odours," the pretty young debutante wrinkled her nose delicately at this statement. "But, your grace, it will no doubt be remarked upon in the newspaper tomorrow and how exciting will it be to know we were there? And when we make morning calls tomorrow, if we happen upon anyone who was not in attendance we can feel so important, but we will, of course, try to sound blasé, as we admit with just the perfect tone of ennui that 'but of course we were at Lady Chorney's party.'"

The duke chuckled. "You are not nearly as innocent and naive as you would have others believe, are you, Miss Lynster?"

"Perhaps not as much as my older brother would wish to believe, at any rate," she agreed with sage aplomb.

"What do you look forward to during your Season, besides attending a crush, if I may be so bold as to ask?"

Eloise grinned and allowed a deep sigh of contentment to pass her lips. "It is hard to say what I look forward to most, your grace. I wish to experience everything I have ever heard about. Your sister is such a generous correspondent and has been kind enough to stay in touch with me. Her letters while she was in London for the Season were always the most exciting, full of her adventures and whom she had seen. I would like to do everything she has told me about."

The young woman paused for a moment, as though contemplating all the possibilities before her. She turned back to the duke, and said confidentially, "She once told me about going to see a balloon ascension. That sounded delightful. It would be so exciting to watch the balloon go up and away out of sight. But do you know, I think it would be even more exciting to be in the basket and watching the ground drop away. You would feel just like a bird, would you not, your grace? I wonder if they would allow ladies as passengers. Have you any idea who one should ask about such a thing, your grace?"

Bryghton was struck nearly speechless by the question. "You are a strange little wench, aren't you, Miss Lynster?"

"Not at all, your grace. Surely many people would wish to try such a ride. Is that not why the things were invented?"

"Well, I cannot fault your logic, Miss, but you are the first of your gender that I have ever heard of wishing to try it."

"Perhaps the ladies you know just did not think to tell you of their wish. You are not an inventor, so they may think you have no knowledge of the subject and therefore cannot help them to attain their desire. I, on the other hand, have known you forever and know how delightfully resourceful you can be, so I thought perhaps you might be a good one to ask. You could, no doubt, at least steer me in the right direction." She paused for a moment while casting him a scrutinizing look. "I have faith that you can at least be trusted not to ring a peel over me even if you do not share in my aspirations. And you will be good enough not to tell Alfred."

The duke grinned. "So you do realize that this particular adventure could meet with some censure."

"I do believe that any adventure could meet with some censure. No doubt it would not be an adventure if it did not."

"I now understand why my good friend seems to have suddenly turned into a hovering nursemaid," Bryghton said with a note of wonder in his tone. "I am wholeheartedly glad that you are not my responsibility."

Eloise's innocent stare began to border on a glare. Bryghton allowed another chuckle at her expense. "Oh, do not get yourself ruffled up, little chick. I will not out you to your brother if I have your word you will not try to stow away on the next balloon you come across. In fact, I will promise to escort you to an ascension if you will do your best not to have too many censorious adventures."

"I knew you could be counted upon, your grace. I will do my very best to stay out of trouble."

"Now come along, it sounds as though the band is winding down and I should be escorting you back to your aunt."

"Thank you for dancing with me, your grace. Thanks to you, no doubt my importance has climbed in rank and there will be any number of young men waiting to ask for my hand for the next dance. Is it not just so perfectly exciting?"

"I am glad to be of service," Bryghton answered wryly, never having given much thought to such social power he might wield.

Bryghton was relieved to have the chit off his hands. He was feeling rather trepidatious about the rest of the dances he had committed himself to, but thankfully they turned out to be of the harmless variety that he had expected Eloise to be. It was somewhat mind numbingly boring to dance with missish young debutantes, but there was no more talk of wishing to have adventures. The duke went back to stand beside his friend as soon as he had acquitted himself of his promise.

"Where have you been, Wychwood? I have barely seen you for most of the night."

"I have been on the dance floor, which is where one should expect to be when one is at a ball, would you not agree?"

Alfred merely grinned at his friend's apparent ill humour. "Has the social round become too much for you already, your grace? The Season is still young. You do not need to retire to your estate for a repairing lease just yet, do you?"

"Why are you enjoying my discomfort so much? I, at least, do not have responsibility for one such as your sister."

"What did the chit do now?" Alfred asked suspiciously.

Bryghton belatedly remembered his promise not to tell the baron of his sister's wish for adventure, so he had to think quickly to cover up his misstep. "Oh, it was nothing she did, it is just that I realized while dancing with her and some other young debutantes, that while I feel a sense of responsibility towards Alanna, having our mother here to watch over her makes a world of difference for me. As well, since this is her third Season, she is, no doubt, much more up to snuff than the younger ladies would be, and I do not have to fear that she will unknowingly venture where she ought not."

"Mayhap not, although, I would think there would be a different set of problems that would accompany an unmarried lady that has been out for a few years. She may become bored of the usual entertainments and begin to search for adventure. Or she may become desperate to marry and decide she ought to accept any offer that may come along."

Bryghton stared at his friend with some dismay. "Has Alanna said anything of that nature to you?"

Alfred grinned at his friend's discomfort. "Now you understand how I have been feeling."

"Have mercy, Freddy, misery should not love company." The duke shook his head in some disgust over the state of affairs they found themselves in. "Now tell me. Do you need to stand guard for the entire night or could we perhaps vacate the premises and go in search of some less genteel adventures of our own?"

Alfred looked out onto the dance floor where Eloise enthusiastically and almost elegantly gliding around in the company of a young man he was not perfectly familiar with. "You have danced with her, Wychwood, what do you think?"

Bryghton laughed. "I think I will have to find someone else to make merry with tonight."

"Sadly, I think you are right."

The two gentlemen took their leave of one another, going their separate ways. Bryghton, feeling restless, went to various locales he had previously enjoyed but found his heart was just not in it this night. Giving up in frustration, he made his way home and found himself in bed at an unfashionably early hour.

"Here I am practically keeping country hours," he said sourly to his valet as he was helped out of his coat. "What has become of me? I will be tied to some silly young chit's apron strings before I know it at the rate I am going."

"I have a hard time envisioning that, your grace," answered the staunch valet.

Bryghton grinned. "Thank you, Timothy. I appreciate your faith in me."

"Not at all, your grace," he answered, stifling his own grin with an effort of will. "Will you be requiring my services at a particular time on the morrow, your grace?"

"With the ridiculously early hour at which I am going to bed I will no doubt be rising earlier than usual, Timothy, but unfortunately it is impossible for me to say whether I will be able to sleep soundly or not. I have no appointments scheduled for which I need to be prepared, so let us just say that I shall ring for you when I have need of your services."

"Very well, your grace. Then I will bid you a good night."

"I hope it is, Timothy. Thank you for your kind wishes. I bid you a good night as well." With that the duke dismissed his servant and climbed into the high bed for a restless night.

Chapter Twenty

True to his prediction, Bryghton awoke at what he would have previously considered an ungodly hour of the morning, as he usually did not rise before noon while in the city. Despite his restless night, he swung down from the tall bedside with a surprising amount of energy in his step. He felt ready for whatever the Season could throw at him that day.

Surprising his secretary with his arrival in the library, that young man hid his shock behind a stack of papers. Bryghton set to work and accomplished a remarkable amount before his restlessness got the better of him and he could stand to sit no longer. Bidding his secretary a good day, he rang for his phaeton and matched bays to be brought round.

Pulling up in front of his mother's house, he jumped down and tossed the reins to his tiger, promising the young servant he would return momentarily.

"Good afternoon, Walter," Bryghton greeted the butler as he opened the door. "Is my sister available?"

"Welcome home, your grace. I shall see about her ladyship. Would you like to have a seat in the morning room while you wait?"

"Would it be an imposition for you if I wait here? I left my cattle with my tiger standing on the street and I do not wish to be here for over long. I stopped in to see if Alanna has any commitments for the afternoon or if she would like to go for a drive in the park."

A footman, having heard the duke's request for his sister, had already set off to fetch her. Alanna was at the top of the stairs when

Bryghton said this last bit. She squealed and dashed indecorously down the grand staircase.

"Oh, would I ever, Bryght, thank you for the lovely invitation. But I am not ready to go riding just at this moment. Could you perhaps wait for me for a few minutes?"

Impatiently, Bryghton replied without thought. "You look perfectly fine to me, just grab a wrap or some such and let us be on your way."

"Do not be a noddy, Bryghton. Surely you realize the hour. I cannot just go for a drive at this time of the day and have no concern for my appearance," she said with a level of horror.

"Oh, very well, but make haste. How quickly can you be ready?"

"I will make haste, have no fear. I will be in your carriage in no more than ten minutes," she called over her shoulder as she ran lightly back up the stairs.

"That will be the day," the duke said rather drily to the butler as he made for the door. "I had best go out and walk the horses. You will have a footman come out with her to hand her up into my phaeton, will you not, Walter?"

"Of course, your grace. Enjoy your drive."

Alanna was almost true to her word; within a quarter of an hour she was bouncing down the front stairs with a footman hurrying to keep pace with her in order to help her into the duke's high-perch phaeton.

Clapping her hands as she settled herself, Alanna almost crowed to her brother. "How delightful that you brought this particular carriage. How did you know that I was nearly dying with my wish to go for a drive this afternoon and I had made no such arrangements?"

"Do you not know that dukes are nearly omniscient?" Bryghton asked drolly.

"Oh, fie on you, but never mind your tomfoolery, I am just delighted that you stopped by to collect me. One would think you are coming to enjoy my company, your grace."

"I always enjoy the company of my family, little chick—what a strange statement to make." The duke looked at his sister questioningly.

⸰ "Oh, Bryghton, my dear, do not get yourself in a bunch. I know you love your family and perform every duty required of you with almost no reluctance. It is just that you have never been one to seek out my company, particularly during the Season—not even when it was my first." Seeing his arrested expression she hastened to add, "It is not that I am complaining. Sometimes I am of the mind that a big brother can be un peu de trop. And I have been blessed with two of them," she concluded with mock horror.

Bryghton still did not appear mollified. "You do not truly think that I do not enjoy your company, do you, Alanna?"

"It is not that, Bryght. It is just as I said, you have never been in the habit of seeking me out, and now this is the second day in a row that you have taken me for a drive. And this time it was entirely at your own initiative, not because I asked it of you."

Bryghton was silent for a moment as he digested his sister's words and contemplated his own feelings. "The funny thing about you and Drake is that you seem to be vastly improving with age. I used to like you because you are my family. Now I find that I just like you."

Alanna looked at her brother with tears beginning to shimmer in her eyes. "That is quite the nicest thing anyone has said to me."

"Is it really? Then I can quite see why you have yet to accept any offers for your hand," Bryghton teased. "Now tell me, how did you enjoy your evening's entertainments last night, and what do you have planned for this evening?"

"Mama and I had been invited for supper at the Chorneys' before the ball so it was a rather relaxing evening, although the ballroom did become rather crowded by the end. I saw you a few times through the crowds and was happy to see that you had managed to get in despite your lack of an invitation. You seemed rather busy dancing with any number of girls throughout the evening."

Bryghton had the grace to blush at his sister's words and admitted, "I made a promise to Lady Chorney, as I invited myself into her evening, that I would dance with a certain number of debutantes and wallflowers."

Alanna burst into laughter at these words. "Why ever did you make such a promise?"

Bryghton shrugged sheepishly. "When you questioned whether or not I would be granted admittance I grew worried about my reception. I thought any hostess would be happy to have someone willing to seek out those who might not be enjoying themselves."

"Clearly your strategy worked."

"Rather well, yes. I must tell you, some of those girls who do not get asked to dance are rather interesting. I do not know what is going on in the upper works of some of the young gentlemen of the ton these days. I quite enjoyed meeting Miss Smythe and Miss Quinn. I cannot even tell you why they were not as busy as you or Eloise were upon the dance floor."

Alanna looked amazed at her brother's words but refrained from much comment aside from a quick warning. "Do make sure you are not raising unfounded hopes in any poor girl's mind. The attentions of a duke, no matter how innocent or well intentioned, could turn the head of even a sensible young woman."

"I was under the impression that there was safety in numbers. Is that not why we devised the plan of me going about Town in advance of your having Lady Victoria tag along with you, so that it is not remarked upon if I am in your company or ask her to dance? I trust I am not making a cake of myself for no reason."

"Oh Bryghton," said Alanna, laughing lightly. "You are not making a cake of yourself by being so kind as to dance with a few girls. And you are correct, the reasoning is sound that if you dance with several girls it will be less remarkable than if you dance with only one or two. But our plan was with the gossips in mind, not the individual girls. I am merely warning you to have a care with their feelings, especially the wallflowers."

"I do believe this entire Season business is a ridiculous plot to drive us all quite mad," declared the duke.

"You may be right, Alcott, but I do not know who would benefit if that were the case."

"Why, the dress-makers and all the rest of the trades people who make their living off the ridiculous rituals."

"Well, they do need to make their living, do they not? Not everyone can be titled landowners like yourself."

"Careful, my dear, we are getting mighty close to philosophizing. Shall we return to the carefully artless chatter of social gossip? You were going to tell me what your plans are for this evening."

"You are getting much too good at these things, my dear brother. If you are not careful you will gain the reputation of being a dandy rather than the rake that you are currently known as," teased Alanna.

Bryghton threw his sister a disgruntled look and made as though to pull over to the side of the road. "You could get out here if you would like, my dear."

"Oh, do not be such a noddy. If you really wish to know, Mama and I are going to the theatre this evening. I have heard many raving about how wonderful Mr. Kean is in his role and I absolutely must see it for myself." Alanna paused for a moment before turning to the duke. "If you would like, you could likely join us. There is usually room for at least one more in any box. We would only have to ask a footman to fetch a chair if there were not one free."

"Thank you, little chick, but I cannot say I enjoy the theatre. One can so rarely hear the performance over the chatter of the crowds. It makes one wonder why anyone bothers to attend."

"Why, to see and be seen, why else?"

"Perhaps I shall stop in during the intermission and visit your box in order to be seen but not have to put up with the actual performance," mused Bryghton.

"You are hilarious, Duke, but that would no doubt serve your purpose quite well. You can be visible without having to bear up under the burden of enjoying the theatre. It would seem you do not care for the other half of being seen, the seeing part."

"Not particularly," he answered with simple honesty. "Now here we are at the park. Shall we drive around or do you wish to go for a stroll? I have my tiger with me, so he can watch the horses if you wish to get down for a bit."

"My, you are being accommodating, aren't you?" she asked with a light laugh. "All right, if it is up to me, I say we take one pass around the perimeter and then we take a little walk when we get back here. I would like to see where you fished Victoria and Daniel out of the river."

Bryghton laughed. "So much has happened since then, it is hard to believe that was barely over a se'nnight ago."

They drove in companionable silence for a time, pausing to greet various acquaintances as they drove slowly around the park. When they got back to the agreed-upon location, the duke pulled up and ordered his tiger to take the horses head. After helping Alanna down he instructed the young servant to walk the horses and allow them to cool down. "We shall be back in about thirty minutes."

"Very good, m'lord."

As they strolled towards the river, Alanna kept up a pleasant flow of chatter, sharing tidbits of gossip about the various people they had already encountered that day.

"How do you keep track of all that silly information?" Bryghton asked.

"Well, I do not consider most of it to be silly. I truly do care about many of those people, and I think it is important to know about them. It is much like how you know every last detail about each horse in your multiple stables."

"But I have to know about the horses in order to properly manage their care."

"Is that not what you have stable masters for?"

"But it is my responsibility to know about it, too. I care about my cattle," Bryghton answered somewhat defensively, still not seeing her point.

"And I care about people. Just as you need to know about your horses in order to make sure they are properly looked after, I need to know about people in order to properly care about them. For example, Lady Pemberton's sister had a bad fall recently. They were estranged but the accident has helped to heal the rift between them. Knowing those various pieces of gossip means I will only ask very general questions but I will express my sympathy for her sister's pain."

"You would make a good wife for a politician," Bryghton remarked with dawning wonder.

"Thank you, I think," answered Alanna dubiously.

"I never realized some people gossip out of a genuine interest in people. I thought it was always motivated by a desire to one-up others."

"Sometimes it probably is, but there are many good people who have an interest in their fellows and wish to know what is going on with everyone. It is no doubt only those who do not have enough going on in their own lives who take an unhealthy interest in that of others."

They had finally reached the edge of the Serpentine.

"Have a care near the edge of the water, little chick. I am not in the mood to fish anyone out today," the duke teased.

"I do not think it is your mood that is in question, you just have no wish to have another pair of Hessians damaged."

"That is true, nor do I wish to hear my valet's recriminations on the subject."

"Have no fear, I will stay back a healthy distance. But do show me where they were when you found them."

"Did you hear the entire tale from Alfred? How we were too far away when Daniel fell in and how fearful we were when we saw the lady jump in after him? I am not ashamed to admit to you that my heart was in my throat as I ran towards the edge. Of course, when I peered over the bank, there she was standing in the water with that monkey of a little boy clinging to her as though she were a tree he was climbing. If I had not been so beside myself it would have been quite funny."

"No doubt no one saw any humour in the situation at the time."

"No, and I compounded matters by yelling at her for the foolishness of jumping into the water without help around."

"What would you have expected her to do?" asked Alanna, incredulous.

"Clearly I was not thinking, I was merely reacting, which was the entire point. Neither had she been thinking when she jumped in— she was motivated by something other than logic. It all ended well. Everyone survived to tell their tale."

"It is rather an amazing thing that she has consented to remain friendly with you," said Alanna.

"Well, I really can be quite charming when I put my mind to it."

"There you go again displaying your limitless humility," she teased.

Not deigning to reply, the duke merely rolled his eyes at his sister and offered her his elbow. "Shall we stroll back to the carriage so I can get you home in time to make your preparations?"

"Very well, your grace," she answered with mock dignity, accepting his proffered arm and heading back in the direction they had come.

There was companionable silence between the two siblings for a time before Alanna broke it. "You will have a care for her feelings, will you not?" she asked worriedly.

"What ever are you on about now? I am beginning to wonder about your opinion of me as you keep asking such questions."

"Lady Victoria," Alanna persisted. "You will have a care about her, will you not? You just finished telling me a few minutes ago about how charming you can be."

"You know I was merely funning, Alanna," Bryghton defended.

"I know, Alcott, but the fact is that it is true. You do not even realize how your smooth talk can affect silly young girls. I know, I know," she interrupted as he made to protest. "Lady Victoria is not a silly young girl, but she is inexperienced, and as I have undertaken to take her under my wing, I feel a responsibility to ensure she does not get hurt in the process. I do not want you charming her," she concluded sternly.

Bryghton looked at his sister with a haughtily quirked eyebrow and a steady stare while he pondered her words, his steps slowing to prolong their journey so as not to be overheard by anyone.

"I do not think I will allow you to dictate my actions, little chick, but I will promise you to do my best not to hurt any of the ladies I encounter this Season. I do believe you already extracted this promise from me, but I will reiterate it now. It applies equally to all the ladies and misses I encounter. Will that satisfy you?"

With a sniff and a shrug, Alanna answered, "Just barely."

This was too much for the serious duke who burst into laughter. "You are a complete hand, my lady. Now come along and quit your sermonizing, you are far too young for it."

Alanna decided she would have to be satisfied with her brother's incomplete promises and shrugged herself out of her temporary ill humour, resuming her sunny chatter as they returned to the carriage and while the duke drove her back to the elegant townhouse in Mayfair.

The footmen were watching for Alanna's return and one came hurrying down the steps as Bryghton pulled his team to a stop in front of the house. He did not bother getting down, allowing the servant to assist his passenger to alight.

"It was interesting, my dear, I will give you that," he told her as way of farewell.

Alanna grinned up at her brother. "Thank you for taking me for a drive, your grace. Will you still stop by our box at the theatre this evening?"

"Perhaps," was all he would allow, causing her to cast him a disgruntled look before she accepted the footman's escort up the steps.

That evening, much to the duchess' and her daughter's delight, the duke did grace them with his presence during the intermission of the theatre show.

"My dear son, how delightful that you could join us," said the duchess, smiling.

"Thank you, your grace. Are you enjoying the performance thus far?" Bryghton asked.

"Not as much as I had hoped, but I had been led to believe that this production was going to be beyond anything I had previously witnessed, so I had higher than usual expectations."

"Well then, that is where you went wrong." He laughed and turned to his sister.

"And you, little chick, are you enjoying yourself?"

"Immensely," she replied with a grin.

His mother reclaimed his attention. "Are you here with a party of your own?"

"Not exactly," was his uninformative response, causing his mother to lift her eyebrow in inquiry but she forbore to comment.

"Did you wish to join our party for the rest of the performance? You know everyone here, do you not?"

Bryghton ignored her first question, looking around at her assembled guests, greeting everyone in turn before returning to his mother. "You have assembled quite a pleasant group for yourself this evening. I bid you goodnight. I have to speak with Alanna for a moment."

Taking his sister a little towards the front of the box where they were less likely to be overheard, he leaned closer and asked in an undertone, "Do you think I have been here long enough to qualify as having been seen?"

Alanna's laughter rang out in the crowded theatre, causing many heads to turn in their direction. Clamping a hand over her mouth to stifle her mirth, her colour rose slightly but her eyes continued to twinkle. "You barely just got here, Bryghton," she protested. "Although, now that my laughter has drawn everyone's attention I suppose you have been. Was that your intention?" she asked suspiciously.

"Not at all," he drawled before bending over her hand and fluttering a kiss a breath away from her skin.

She pulled her hand out of his light clasp and swatted at his arm playfully. "Get on with you, your grace. Do not practice your airs on your sister. Do say you will join us for the rest of the performance. The reports I had heard were quite accurate. Mr. Kean is doing a marvellous job of entertaining us tonight."

"Thank you, my dear, for the generous invitation, but I really should be getting on my way. Enjoy yourself tonight, and have a care not to lead our friend astray on the morrow," he countered, imitating his sister's ill-placed concerns for Lady Victoria.

Alanna caught his inference and smiled her acknowledgement. "Good night, Duke. I shall see you around, I am sure."

With a wink and a wave, the duke exited the box and quickly took his leave of the theatre before he could be ensnared in further conversations. He was looking forward to meeting up with Lord Lynster and enjoying a rousing night of games of chance. It was a rare night that Alfred was not hovering over his sister, and Bryghton was looking forward to the evening with his friend.

Chapter Twenty-One

Alanna was pacing impatiently in the morning room early the next day when her mother strolled in to join her.

"You are going to wear a path in the rug if you keep running to the window whenever you hear a carriage in the street. You do realize she will no doubt be arriving by foot, do you not?"

With a start Alanna stared at her mother in surprise.

Smiling, her grace chided, "I am not a duchess for nothing, my dear. Have you still not learned that I know everything?"

Alanna continued to gaze at her mother with her mouth agape, prompting her mother's teasing words.

"Do shut your mouth, Alanna, or else you shall be catching flies. It is most unseemly."

Alanna shut her mouth with an audible snap and asked hesitantly, "But you do not have any objections, do you?"

"Not at all. If I had you would have heard about it before now, have no fear. I think Lady Victoria is a lovely young woman and I think it rather despicable that she has not been sponsored before now. There is some sort of issue between her uncle and your brother, of which I do not have all the details. I just hope it does not cause you or her any discomfort. It is a shame that you can only have her accompany you and not sponsor her completely. Do you think perhaps we should suggest it?"

Alanna blinked a trifle owlishly at her mother's words. "I absolutely think we should suggest it. I did not before now, as I am not fully aware of her circumstances, nor was I sure if you would agree."

"Of course I would agree. She could come and stay with us as our guest for the Season if she would like."

"Thank you, mother, perhaps you could speak to her on the subject when she is here later this morning. In case you do not know, I should tell you that she is not fully informed on the subject of her own circumstances, or at least she was not the last time I spoke to her. She was not even sure if she would be able to come today."

"Have no fear, I am sure she will show up. I knew her mother," was the duchess' soothing if cryptic answer. "In fact, that sounds like the door knocker right now."

Marvelling at her mother's near omniscience, Alanna turned towards the door as the butler admitted her guest.

"Lady Victoria Bartley to see you my lady," Walter intoned as he ushered the young lady in.

The duchess graciously welcomed her daughter's friend. "Come in, my lady, and welcome to our home. It is a pleasure to make your acquaintance. I knew your mother when we were girls. I am very sorry for your loss."

Taken aback by the warmth of the duchess' welcome, Victoria had to fight back the prickle of tears. She dropped into a polite curtsy. "Thank you for your kindness, my lady; it was a long time ago."

"True, but I am sure you continue to feel the loss." The duchess carefully changed the subject to spare their guest's feelings. "Now tell me, are you in a hurry or do you have time for a few refreshments before you two girls retire to Alanna's room to giggle over fashions?"

"I am delighted to say that I have several hours to while away this morning, so a little refreshment would be lovely, thank you."

"Then please, have a seat and tell me all about yourself."

Victoria, conscious of her far less fashionable attire, was initially uncomfortable in the presence of the two ladies but Alanna quickly settled her nerves with her beaming smile and beckoning wave to have her sit beside her on the settee.

"So is the new nursery maid up to your standards?" Alanna asked with a tease in her voice.

Victoria blushed and looked at the duchess, wondering how the highborn lady would feel having a governess in her morning room. The duchess smiled graciously and said, "Rest easy, my dear, I know all about it and I look forward to having you in our company this spring."

Turning back to answer Alanna's question, Victoria said with a small smile, "She actually seems to be quite competent and the children have taken to her rather nicely. She is not qualified to do much with their lessons, but my uncle has assured me that he will see about finding them a governess at his earliest convenience."

There was a brief lull in the conversation as the housekeeper brought in a tray of goodies and a pot of tea. Victoria accepted a delicate cup of piping hot tea before continuing her tale.

"I actually spoke with the earl last night for a few moments to again try to ascertain the extent of my circumstances. I again asked him whether or not he thought his wife would be in a position to sponsor me for the Season. He seemed strangely alarmed by the question and could not answer me very clearly. He then turned the question around on me and wanted to know why I was showing an interest in such things. I simply told him again that I had to give thought to my future now that I was finished school and I wanted to know where I stood. He told me he had an appointment he must get to and he would speak to me more on the subject some other time."

Victoria heaved a soft sigh and continued. "I am no further ahead in my knowledge and I am not all that confident that he will be any more forthcoming in the future."

"Well, never mind about him," said the duchess dismissively. "Alanna and I would be delighted if you would join us for the Season as our guest. You could even come and stay here in our house and share in all of Alanna's activities over the coming weeks. It would be such a lovely diversion for us to have you with us."

Blushing with equal parts embarrassment and pleasure, Victoria was at a loss for words, merely stammering out, "Oh, no, I could not impose in such a way."

"It would be no imposition, I assure you," answered the duchess as Alanna was quickly saying, "Not at all, we would love to have you."

The duchess continued, "If I understand correctly, Alanna has already promised you the use of her wardrobe from last Season. I assure you that is no imposition whatsoever. If you do not make use of her gowns they will most likely go to waste, as no one else in the household would have any need of them and the fabrics are not ones that can be used for household maintenance."

Looking a little dazed, Victoria laughed weakly, "No I would imagine they could not." She paused for a moment, slightly discomfited by the eager gazes of the duchess and Alanna. She cleared her throat delicately and continued in stronger tones.

"I am not completely confident about the propriety of leaving my uncle's house to come to stay with you for the Season. And to be perfectly honest with you, if I were unsuccessful in my search for a potential mate, I am uncertain what would happen to me. My uncle has been quite clear that I was not to associate with your son, the duke," Victoria said while feeling a hot blush creeping up her cheeks. "If I were to stay with you it would no doubt be nearly impossible to avoid him completely. I am unsure of the consequences if I so defied my uncle."

"Oh dear," said the duchess. "I was unaware that the situation was as bad as that." She paused for a moment in thought. "There are several thoughts I have about what you just said. First of all, I do not see anything inappropriate about you coming to stay with us if we are going to sponsor your Season. It would seem that your aunt is not feeling up to the task. It is the usual thing for a young lady to stay with whomever is bringing them out. Another thing I think I should point out to you, and I apologize in advance if it seems indelicate to be discussing such a vulgar thing as finances, but the house in which you and your family are living is actually yours, if I understand correctly."

"Well, yes, I do realize that to a certain extent, or rather it is supposed to become mine upon my twenty-fifth birthday. But since I have no funds I am clearly not the one keeping it up, so it really is just a technicality. Upon my parents' death everything they owned went to the new earl."

The duchess' look was bordering on pitying, much to Victoria's dismay, and the duchess answered in a soft, kind voice. "I believe you are misinformed, my dear. I have it on rather good authority that your parents provided very well for you in the event of such a tragedy as their deaths. Any unentailed property was to go to you, as well as whatever income was generated by said properties. Your uncle was to act as your guardian and look after the properties for you until such time as you marry or reach your majority."

Victoria sat in silence, trying to absorb this information. "Do you know which properties we are speaking of?" she asked in a small voice.

"Not offhand, my lady, although I could easily get that information for you." The duchess made as though to ring for a footman.

"I do not need it right now, thank you, Your Grace."

"One I do know of is the London house in which you are residing. Your father and his father never saw the need to entail it in any way, as it was a luxury and has no property so it was easy enough to arrange for it to go to you. I do not fully understand all the factors that go into property inheritance and all that, but I do know that your uncle cannot put you out of that house, as it is legally yours to do with as you please. The Earl and Countess of Pickering are living there as your guests, not the other way around."

There was another stretch of silence as the younger women gazed at one another with rather dazed expressions. Alanna was the first to break the silence with a little bounce in her seat and a clap of her hands.

"Well, is that not just the most lucky thing you have heard today?" she asked, grinning.

Victoria could not help but grin in return. "Yes, it is lovely good news, to be sure." She turned back to the duchess. "Thank you ever so much for this information. I am unsure of how I will use it. I will have to think on the matter some more. For the time being, I believe it would be best if I stick to the plan Alanna and I devised. I have been living very quietly up until now and I am not confident in the support of my family. I would rather just have a little taste of the Season before I decide if I would like to dive in head first."

The duchess inclined her head gracefully. "Perhaps that is wise. The offer remains open to you whenever you choose to accept it."

She took a last sip of her tea and rose elegantly to her feet. "I have a few things to attend to so I will leave you two girls to your own devices. I believe the maids have been shaking out the gowns and have them displayed in one of the spare rooms above stairs. Ask one of the footmen to direct you when you are ready."

Victoria scrambled to her feet and dipped into a perfectly executed curtsy. As her grace left the room, Victoria turned to Alanna with a nonplussed look. She gazed rather blankly at her friend for a moment before bursting into a fit of giggles, in which Alanna soon joined.

"Are all duchesses like that, or just her?" Victoria asked, before realizing how her words could have sounded. Turning beet red from her neck to her hairline she hastily stammered out an apology. "I mean no disrespect to your mother, my lady. I merely was referring to how in control your mother is and how she knew so much and how she does not appear familiar with taking no for an answer."

Alanna was almost falling over on the settee from the force of her giggles. Gasping for breath she managed to interrupt Victoria. "Please, stop, I took no offense. I completely knew what you meant." Regaining a modicum of control, she continued. "To answer your question, I do believe all the duchesses of my mother's generation are the same or worse, not that there are that many, but you should see the dukes! They are far worse than my mama. She, at least, manages to couch it in such pleasant terms that you do not feel all that managed. Bryghton is still growing into his powers, but he does not have Mama's skill of making you think something was all your idea when really she was behind it the whole time."

Victoria gazed rather wistfully towards the door through which the duchess had exited. "I do not think countesses are like that at all. My aunt certainly is not, and I do not think my mama was either. My aunt does not seem to have a thought of her own that was not put there by my uncle. It seems terribly sad to me. My mother was such a kind, sweet woman. She managed the household quite well and of course saw to the needs of the tenants in the village, but she did not concern herself with anything beyond the scope of her duties and her family." Turning back to Alanna with a wicked grin, she said, "I think it must be glorious to be a duchess! No one would ever tell your mother what to do, and I have a hard time imagining her ever being undecided about her own future."

Alanna rose from her place on the settee and linked arms with her friend, pulling her towards the door as she went. "Well then, my lady, if you wish to be a duchess, we had best see to having you meet an eligible duke."

With matching giggles the girls left the room.

Some time later, after examining all the gowns and discussing various alterations that could be easily executed to make the gowns suitable for the present Season and to best suit Victoria, the two girls sat down with a sigh of relief.

"Gracious, Alanna, I have never seen such a collection of beautiful gowns. I am still having a difficult time fathoming why you did not just make some of these alterations for yourself instead of buying a whole new set of gowns for this Season. I know you tried to gammon me with the tale that you are spoiled, but I do not believe that for a moment."

Alanna offered an unconcerned shrug. "I love to shop and my brother never quibbles at my spending. And, to be honest, I was bored of those dresses and wanted new ones. I thought it would bring me more success in finding a match this Season."

"Is it so hard to find a suitable match?" Victoria asked curiously.

"It does not seem so for other girls. Many become engaged within weeks of the start of their first Season. I was quite determined to enjoy at least one entire Season without even thinking of accepting any proposals. I was quite proud of the number I racked up. My brother said there were six different gentlemen who applied to him to pay me their respects. Thankfully he refused them all on my behalf, as I would have been highly uncomfortable to face them myself. I was young and silly and just wanted to enjoy myself. It all felt like a diverting game. I did not give a great deal of thought to the seriousness behind it. Nor did I think of anyone's feelings being involved."

Alanna gave a little self-deprecating laugh before continuing. "In my own defense, I do not believe any of those gentlemen had their feelings engaged overmuch. They thought I would make an acceptable wife, and no doubt most thought my dowry would make a lovely addition to their own circumstances. Last year, for my second Season, I was much more serious about it, but no one really struck my fancy as someone I would care to see at the breakfast table for the rest of my life. I also caught a rather nasty illness and had to repair to our country estate to recover, so I missed a great deal of the Season. This year I think I shall have to settle on someone or I will face the prospect of being on the shelf, and then no one will consider me an eligible parti. I can assure you, I have no interest in being the maiden aunt to my brother's children or the dutiful daughter to my mother, the duchess, for the rest of my days. She is perfectly lovely, but I do not want to be second in command. I wish to run my own household."

"It would seem you have given this matter a great deal of thought."

"Of course, have not you? Is that not why you are here?"

"Well, I suppose so. Although, I have not had multiple Seasons to ponder the matter, nor do I contemplate having that luxury. I must decide rather quickly whether there are any suitable matches for me to be had." She paused, and added quietly, "If I am unable to find a match, there is always the convent."

"Heavens! You can't be serious, Victoria?" asked Alanna, horrified.

"Well, I must consider my options in the event my plan to marry comes to nothing," Victoria answered pragmatically.

"My dear, with my help it shall never come to that! Now, tell me what you are looking for, and perhaps I can narrow down the choices for you and make sure I introduce you to all the appropriate people."

"Don't you need to be looking about for your own match?" Victoria asked.

With a shrug Alanna replied, "I have already met everyone. I just need to get to know a few people better to make up my mind."

Victoria laughed. "Well, I did say I wish to be a duchess. There cannot be that many single dukes sitting around."

Alanna wrinkled her nose. "Well, there are the Royal Dukes. And they are actually all rather desperate for a suitable wife, but I would not recommend any of them to you as a possible husband. I do not wish to sound disrespectful to the king's sons, but every single one of them has several illegitimate children, and they are all old."

Victoria gave a little mock shudder. "Every single one of them? But how could that be?" She blushed and hastily added, "Do not bother to answer that, I beg you. I do declare I shall have to gain control over my tongue before I accompany you anywhere. I am quite convinced that the gossiping biddies you have told me about will shame me right out of the first place you take me to and neither of us will be able to show our faces again."

Alanna laughed at her friend's dramatics. "Have no fear, my dear, you shall be declared an original and everyone will love you. Now you must tell me how soon you can join me as I make my morning calls."

"Well, I think I should be able to get a couple of these gowns ready within a few days," Victoria began before Alanna's gasp of dismay stopped her. "What have I said now?" she asked.

"You are not going to do the alterations, you silly gabby. My lady's maid will do them. She is very good at it and since I shop so much she almost never has to do it for me."

"Oh no, I could not put her to so much trouble," Victoria protested.

"First of all, how do you propose to get the gowns in question to your house, especially if you wish to keep it a secret from your uncle? And then you would have to get them back to my house in order to get ready here, again in secret. I assure you, it is no problem at all for Sally to do the work, and it will be much simpler for all of us."

"I do see your point, Lady Alanna, and I thank you sincerely. When I agreed to this scheme I never thought about all the subterfuge that would be required."

"Do tell me you are not having second thoughts," cried Alanna.

"No, I am not," said Victoria. "I have set my mind to give this a try and I mean to do so. I just feel a trifle hesitant over how complicated it is turning out to be."

"It could be less complicated if you just moved in here with me for the Season," reminded Alanna with a wheedling tone.

"Oh, get on with you," said Victoria dismissively. "Very well then, I will leave the work in Sally's capable hands, with my deepest gratitude."

"Excellent decision!" replied Alanna with a grin. "And I believe my capable Sally could have a few of these gowns ready by the morrow. Some of them need very little done to make them suitable for you so you could even have a selection to choose from."

"Do you have calls planned for tomorrow?" Victoria asked, surprised.

"Oh, but of course, my mama and I make calls almost every day, except when we are at home ourselves to receive calls, like we will be this afternoon."

"Very well, what time should I be here?" Victoria asked, summoning such a look of bravery that Alanna set into another fit of giggles.

"Oh Victoria, I am so happy that I have made your acquaintance. It shall be so pleasant to have a partner to share the rigours of the Season with." Alanna flung her arms around Victoria and gave her a quick squeeze.

After the two girls made their plans for the next day, Victoria took her leave, surprised that only a couple hours had passed. It seemed to her that her life had altered course that morning, and she was feeling trepidations and shivers of excitement as she contemplated all that lay before her. She walked home in a haze of daydreams and worries.

"Aunt 'Toria! Where have you been?" demanded Vanessa plaintively. "Stupid Susan does not know any of our games. You should have been here."

"Vanessa, my dear, we do not call anyone 'stupid' for any reason. And why did you not just teach Susan how to play our games? I am quite certain she would have enjoyed learning them and playing with you. Do you not remember that I told you I will not be with you children as much, since I have some things I need to take care of for myself?"

"But I have decided that I do not want you to go," declared the little girl. "You must stay here with us forever and ever."

Victoria suppressed her wince over her little cousin's unintentionally prophetic words. Forcing a smile to her suddenly rigid face, she bent down and gave the little girl a warm hug.

"I shall love you forever, my little one, so there's no need to worry. I cannot stay with you forever and ever. One day you will grow up and leave home yourself and then where will I be?"

"I don't think that is at all the same thing, Aunt 'Toria," the youngster said pugnaciously.

"Perhaps not, Vanessa," said the harried "aunt" before turning to greet the other children who were clamouring for her attention.

Daniel, the youngest and least familiar with Victoria ever not being a part of his life, wanted to be picked up and cuddled, which she promptly did. Hugging the little boy close, she was swamped with feelings. While she was desirous of establishing a life for herself, she had very mixed emotions about the necessity of leaving the children behind in order to do so.

"Felicia, my dear, did you have a nice morning?" she asked cajolingly, hoping the middle child's anxiety to please would help the children through this adjustment period.

"It was fine, Aunt 'Toria," she replied with a shrug. "Daniel and Nessie cried a lot, but Gwennie and I were all right. I think you should stay here with us from now on, though."

Victoria was surprised by the most biddable child's defection, but she did not allow this to deter her. She did her best to ignore the children's demands that she never again leave their side, changing the subject to ask if they would like to go to the parkette.

"Yes, yes, how lovely," they all clamoured with more enthusiasm than the outing warranted.

"Perhaps Susan and Mary would like to accompany us," Victoria suggested, to the children's dismay.

"No, Aunt 'Toria, just you and us," Vanessa insisted.

"I think it would be far more enjoyable if we all go, and would you not agree that it would be best if they know where all the best places are in case I am not here some other time?"

This may have not been the best thing to say, as it reminded the children that she had not vowed never to leave their sides again.

After an unpleasant session of whining, the group finally got on its way with the nursery maids included, much to Victoria's relief.

Once they were in the park, the children seemed to be happy to play with the young maids as their beloved cousin looked on. Victoria was deeply grateful the maids had come along, as she was unusually tired from her morning's activities.

Who knew trying on gowns could be such hard work, she mused to herself as she stifled another yawn. On the other hand, it could be the restless night I spent while worrying about my decision. Whatever the case, I must shake it off and manage to get through the rest of the day until the children's bedtime. Judging by their reaction to my absence, there is likely no way they will allow me to retire early.

With those thoughts in mind, Victoria got up from the bench and went to join the youngsters in a rigorous game of chase.

After the game, the children seemed much more at peace with the maids, Vanessa even going so far as to hold Susan's hand as they walked back to the house. The rest of the evening was rather uneventful as the children were bathed and put to bed. With relief, Victoria sought her bed as soon as the last of the children were tucked in.

Her dreams were a little restless, but they were happy ones filled with beautiful gowns, welcoming hostesses, and perhaps a handsome duke.

Chapter Twenty-Two

"You must tell me something," Victoria stated with a laugh in her tone, sitting as still as possible while Alanna's lady's maid put the final touches on her hairstyle.

"Anything, my dear friend, although I am having second thoughts about having you accompany me. You are looking positively ravishing and shall quite put me in the shade. I do not think it well planned of me to have one such as you accompany me about the Season if I am serious about finding a husband this year."

"Oh, get on with your foolishness," said Victoria dismissively before continuing with her question. "Why are they called morning calls if we are going to be arriving upon people's steps well after noon?"

"Do you know, I have absolutely no idea? Perhaps it has something to do with the fact that most of the ladies we will visit will receive us in their morning room. Or perhaps in previous generations they made the calls in the morning and slothful creatures that we are have pushed it back to the afternoon because we cannot drag ourselves out of bed before noon after dancing until the wee hours the night before. Does it really matter why?"

"Not terribly, no, I am just curious. There are so many traditions connected with the Season that I have no knowledge of and are seeming a wee bit strange to my unaccustomed ears," Victoria said. "Are there any rules you think I should know about?"

"If you were making calls by yourself you would have to confine yourself to anyone you already knew, which would be rather difficult as you do not yet know anyone. As well, you have to confine yourself to calling upon your social equals or inferiors unless they have already called upon you. You also should have cards made up." Alanna had started in a tone as though reciting long-memorized lessons, but the final words were tinged with worry. "Oh Victoria, it completely slipped my mind. I never thought of the need for cards. Well, hopefully it will matter little today. While we are out we can stop by the stationer's shop I frequent and have some ordered for you."

Victoria blushed upon hearing these words. "Oh dear, yet another thing I do not have properly. And I have no pin money with me, so I cannot order anything."

"Do not be silly. I shall have it added to my account and Bryghton will look after it."

Victoria's blush darkened. "The duke cannot be expected to look after my bills, Alanna. I shall see to my own expenses. According to your mother, I should be in a position to do so."

Alanna, not wishing to quibble over such fripperies, merely shrugged. "It is a rather urgent matter, so why do we not place the order today and you can either set up an account for yourself or if the bill needs to be forwarded to Bryght you can pay him back when you have sorted things out?" She huffed a little breath before continuing.

"Now, I was telling you what you need to know for today before I so rudely interrupted myself. We cannot stay at any one place more than half an hour. We therefore must not discuss anything of import that would require a lengthy conversation. That is why it is almost always the latest gossip which is discussed."

"So why do we make these calls then, I am forced to ask?"

"It is just what one does. And it can be rather interesting, to be sure. During the Season everyone takes turns being at home to visitors, so while you are making your calls you could run into any number of interesting people in the morning room of whomever you are seeing. And really, one must keep informed of all the latest gossip anyway. And of course, if someone calls on you, you have to call on them." Alanna paused for a moment, looking at her guest, and they both burst into giggles.

"You are correct, my friend, it is terribly silly, but it is what the ton does during the Season. At home, in the country, morning calls are usually much less structured and are usually made with a purpose in mind, such as to issue an invitation or to check on a neighbour if you have heard they are sick or some such. During the Season it really serves no purpose except to keep us occupied socially. But have no fear, I am certain you shall enjoy it immensely."

"It will certainly be better than trying to help Felicia with her arithmetic," Victoria answered with a smile and a shrug. "The poor girl has absolutely no head for numbers and feels there is no need for her to work on it. It can make for a frustrating afternoon. A few minutes of gossip should be entertainment compared to that."

Victoria giggled at Alanna's owlish expression.

"What do you tell Felicia as an explanation as to why she should make an effort with her numbers? I have to tell you that I am with her—I could never understand why I should bother. It is not as though I shall be a banker."

"Of course not, but if you are to be mistress of your own home you must understand enough of the basics to ensure that you are not being taken advantage of at the shops or by tradespeople."

"But that is what Bryght's secretary is for." Her incredulity caused Victoria to succumb to another fit of giggles.

"Not everyone has a duke's secretary at their service. Did you not pay attention to anything they taught us at the Young Lady's Academy? Remember Miss Cuthbert used to often talk about a mistress' need to keep a watch over the trades. I always thought she was excessively suspicious, but I have to agree that ladies do need to know at least the basics." Victoria gave Alanna a shrewd look before continuing. "As you pointed out, there are a limited number of dukes available to us. I know my aunt, who is an earl's wife, does not have access to a secretary. It is true that the earl's secretary looks after many of the household accounts, but my aunt has to keep track of the kitchen accounts as well as ensuring the servants receive their pay. It is not that difficult, but it is important."

"My, you sound quite fired up on the subject."

Victoria smiled self-deprecatingly, "When you have a shortage of funds you realize the importance of holding on to what you do have.

Now come along, enough about arithmetic. You must tell me what some of the latest on dits are or I will have nothing to discuss while we are making our calls."

With a grin, Alanna launched into a detailed list of all the latest stories that might be discussed that afternoon. Victoria found it hard to believe that anyone would wish to pass their time discussing such things, but decided to reserve judgement until she saw for herself.

"I can see that this holds very little interest for you," Alanna observed, laughing. "That is fine. It would be good if you can produce that exact look of polite boredom upon demand. It would not do for you to appear eager or excited about the goings on of the Season."

"Are you being serious or are you funning me?" Victoria asked suspiciously.

"I am perfectly serious. Only the very young debutantes find everything exciting. Now we both look absolutely lovely so it is time for us to get on our way. Come along my dear, and do try to contain your grin."

Victoria saw the twinkle in her friend's eye and realized she was being teased. Giving her head a shake, she obediently followed Alanna from the room.

Sitting in the morning room of Lady Coupland, the Viscount of Sheridan's wife, Victoria had to school her features into the look of polite interest Alanna had taught her. It was a struggle not to look around in vulgar curiosity. Alanna had insisted that vulgarity was the most unforgivable sin one could commit amongst the ton. While Victoria was still unsure all that could be considered vulgar, she was quite certain that gazing about the room with her mouth agape in amazement would be on the list. But it was a battle to keep her eyes on their hostess' face as Lady Coupland recited some monotonous story about who had attended her rout the night before.

"It was too bad of you not to have been here, Lady Alanna, and you too Lady Victoria, although of course I did not know you, but I would have been delighted to have you attend had we been introduced earlier."

"Of course, my lady, thank you for your kindness in saying so," Victoria managed to answer politely. She experienced a profound sense of relief when she saw Alanna getting to her feet. Victoria quickly but gracefully joined her.

"Thank you so much for your pleasant hospitality, Lady Coupland," Alanna was saying.

"It was a pleasure to see you," the lady answered, "do call again soon."

Both girls curtsied politely and the footman escorted them to the door.

As soon as they were safely upon the sidewalk Victoria turned to Alanna. "Why did you not warn me about that room?"

Alanna burst into a gale of laughter. "I just had to see your face when you took in all that splendour."

"That was not very well done of you, Alanna. What would you have done if I had gasped with my shock over seeing so much gilt all in one place?"

"I would have declared you a vulgar mushroom of whom I have no acquaintance. Now come along, we have no time for lectures now, we must hurry to reach Miss Lambert's house. She always has the most interesting guests."

"Is there anything I ought to know about Miss Lambert before we get there?" Victoria wisely thought to ask.

"Her morning room is perfectly lovely, have no fear. I must say, Victoria, you could have a career upon the stage if you do not find being a governess to your liking. The way you managed to wipe the look of amazement from your face was truly awe-inspiring. I had no idea you had such self-control. I am impressed. I do believe Lady Coupland was disappointed. I think she decorated in just that way to inspire reactions."

"That strikes me as rather odd."

"The ton is a rather odd assortment of individuals," Alanna replied airily. "Now as for Miss Lambert, she is quite lovely. I met her not overly long ago. Her brother has political ambitions, so they are in Town trying to make connections. Apparently I am useful due to my relationship with Bryght. They manage not to be vulgar about it and they are amusing. You shall see for yourself. They are just around this corner."

The two girls walked along briskly.

"I was surprised when you mentioned we would walk. I thought ladies of the ton did not dare set their feet upon the ground and must take carriages wherever they go," said Victoria.

"Do not mention it when we are visiting, because you are quite correct. But it is rather silly considering that these people are all my neighbours and it would take so much longer to get around by carriage with all the traffic. If we were going much further I would be sure to take a carriage, as I do not wish to wear myself out for this evening, but I figured we surely could manage a few blocks. You are not getting tired, are you?"

Victoria laughed, "Not at all. This is decidedly more restful than my usual day."

"Are you missing the children? You would normally be at a park right about now, would you not?"

Victoria was surprised by her friend's perceptive question. The Lady Alanna gave the impression of being somewhat empty-headed and unconcerned about things other than her attire, the latest gossip, and her upcoming entertainments. But Victoria could see intelligence shining through Alanna's eyes as she gazed steadily at Victoria and awaited her reply.

Victoria surprised herself with her answer. "I do not actually miss the children overmuch. I know they are in good hands and I will see them when I return home. They were not pleased with me yesterday when I returned home, but I am confident that today will be better. It is time for all of us to realize that I am not truly a governess, and that I need to get on with my proper life."

There was a momentary silence while the girls walked on steadily. Alanna waited patiently for her friend to continue.

"I will freely admit to you that I am terrified about the future. Ever since my parents died I have done everything in my power to ensure my place in my uncle's home was secure. But I realize now that that should not need to be secured. As my uncle and guardian, my place in his life should have been already assured. I dearly hope I am not jeopardizing my relationship with the children, but I do need to secure a new arrangement for my future."

"Good for you. Now come along, we have arrived at our final stop and I am quite certain you will enjoy this call."

They had arrived in front of a tall townhouse that was a bit smaller than the house they had just visited. It was much smaller than Victoria's own home and positively tiny compared to that of the Alcotts'. But it looked inviting, and Victoria found herself smiling at the prospect of entering it.

The butler admitted them to the proportionately small foyer and asked them to be seated as he checked to see if Miss Lambert was receiving.

Victoria wiggled her eyebrows comically at Alanna as they heard a gale of laughter issuing from the room as the butler opened the morning room door. It was obvious the lady of the house was home and had guests, but, of course, protocol said the butler must check to see if the new arrivals would be welcomed.

They did not have to wait long. As the butler returned to fetch them, Miss Lambert herself hastened from the room in his wake.

"Lady Alanna, what a pleasure to see you, and you have brought a friend with you, how delightful."

Victoria worked hard to contain the grin that wanted to spread across her face over their hostess' enthusiastic welcome. She dipped into a polite curtsy as Miss Lambert stepped forward to meet her.

Alanna performed the introductions. "Lady Victoria, I would like to present to you my friend, Miss Melinda Lambert, and Miss Lambert, this is my dear friend Lady Victoria Bartley."

"It is my pleasure to meet you Lady Victoria, and thank you for coming to call on us this afternoon. Please come into the morning room. There are already a few guests you may already know, but there is room for more despite our cramped quarters here." Miss Melinda smiled knowingly, recognizing that her guests would be unfamiliar with such tight spaces.

Victoria was again presented with the necessity not to gape like a cit. This time it was not the hostess' decor, which was absolutely lovely, but the other guests assembled in her drawing room that were the source of her curiosity.

Lady Cordes, Viscountess of Asquith, and her lovely daughter Eileen, were seated and talking quietly with a handsome young man when Miss Lambert interrupted to introduce the new arrivals.

"Lady Alanna, I am sure you are familiar with everyone present, but Lady Victoria, please allow me to introduce my other guests."

Victoria was made uncomfortable to be on the receiving end of so many curious stares, but she steeled her spine and dipped into a curtsy of the perfect depth to indicate her politeness but also her position in Society. Lady Cordes acknowledged the introduction with an inclination of her head while her young daughter stood to dip into a curtsy of her own. The two gentlemen in the room stood to be presented as well.

"Mr. Dylan Mead does some sort of work within the House of Lords for his uncle the Earl of Wessex—I admit to you I do not fully understand it. And Mr. Benjamin Appleton is his associate."

"It is pleasant to meet you both," answered Victoria, unsure of the proper protocol in this exact situation. Alanna thankfully stepped in and assisted.

"Lady Victoria is visiting me for a bit this Season and we are having such a lovely time together. We are thinking of doing a spot of shopping later, but I just had to stop in to see if you were at home, Miss Melinda."

Lady Eileen broke her silence upon these words. "Oh, Lady Victoria, if you are still visiting, then you absolutely must accompany Lady Alanna when she comes to my ball this week. I could have an invitation sent around to include you."

"That is very kind of you, Lady Eileen, thank you. I would be delighted to attend," Victoria answered graciously, smothering her smile over the knowledge that Alanna had been planning to bring her to that very ball even without the proper invitation. Victoria shot a shrewd glance at her friend, wondering if she had known the Cordes ladies would be visiting at this time. Alanna liked to lament how the duke and duchess seemed to know everything, but Victoria realized it was a family trait.

Just as Alanna and Victoria were getting settled into their seats the other occupants got to their feet with varying levels of reluctance. Lady Cordes appeared to be dragging her daughter away, who looked as though she would be happy to stay for the rest of the afternoon. The two gentlemen followed shortly in their wake.

"Your timing was perfect, Lady Alanna. You got to briefly meet my other guests but now we can have a little visit in peace. Is not Mr. Mead the most deliciously handsome gentleman you have ever met? It is such a tragedy that he is merely a mister."

"I suppose there could be worse tragedies," Victoria answered pragmatically.

"Perhaps, but it does limit his options. And his brother, the earl's heir, is nearly as ugly as a troll," continued Melinda.

"It would seem to be cosmic justice, do you not think?" asked Alanna. "The true tragedy would be if the younger son got neither blessing. This would seem to be more of an equalizing."

"I can see your point. It is a good thing that women are not allowed into the House of Lords. I would vote yes to anything Mr. Mead presented without even thinking about it. I am quite certain that is not the proper way of politics," Melinda concluded with a giggle.

"Are Mr. Mead and Mr. Appleton working with your brother on anything in particular?" Alanna asked.

"Oh, Lady Alanna, it is kind of you to take an interest, but I am not kept fully informed on their doings. My job is to play the hostess role, not to trouble my head with the politics."

Victoria maintained a polite smile while wondering absently what Alanna saw in this particular friend. She seemed as empty-headed as Alanna at times presented herself to be. This thought brought Victoria up short and she sharpened her gaze upon their hostess as she searched for any sign that she too was putting on an act.

"Of course not," Alanna was saying sweetly. "Did you enjoy your visit to the gallery last week?"

"It was a trifle boring, as I did not understand much of the proceedings, but it did make my appreciation for my brother's efforts grow considerably."

Melinda's response was uninformative on the one hand, but on the other it helped Victoria to understand they were not discussing a gallery of art but rather the visitors' area in Parliament.

Alanna allowed the subject to drop and the trio discussed some tidbit of gossip, which Melinda embellished with the details she had gleaned from some of her visitors that day. Finally, Alanna got to her feet, indicating that the prescribed time had ended. Melinda protested their departure.

"Oh no, my lady, there is no need for you to leave. No one else is here so there is no need to stand upon ceremony. I would be delighted to have your company a while longer."

"That is generously kind of you, Miss Lambert, and thank you for the invitation, but we really must be on our way. I was not stretching the truth when I said that Lady Victoria and I have some purchases to make and we really must make haste."

"Thank you for a lovely visit," Victoria murmured as she took her leave behind Alanna. She managed to be noncommittal when their hostess mentioned her desire to return the call upon Victoria, as she had not given thought to that particular possibility. Maintaining her composure until they regained the street, she quickly turned to Alanna.

"I gave absolutely no thought to the fact that people feel the need to return the calls you make. What shall I do, Alanna? I have not broached the subject again with my uncle and have never discussed it with my aunt. If people call at my home I do not know if I could receive them."

"I do not see why you could not. It is your house after all. Surely there is nothing untoward in you receiving visitors. But if it would put your mind at ease, we could have my address put upon your cards."

"But if my aunt and uncle found out about that I would think it would be an even greater insult to them than my going about without informing them. No, if you think I need cards, I will put my own name and address upon them and face the consequences when they come upon me. The earl and countess will have to find out what I am up to at some point anyway."

Alanna clapped her hands in applause. "Good for you. You must stand up for yourself and face things head on. Now come along, you shall simply adore the stationer's shop."

They walked along briskly towards the shops, each lost in their own thoughts. Victoria broke the silence momentarily.

"I must ask you, why does everyone hide what they are?"

"Whatever do you mean?"

"Please do not think this question is impertinent, or else forgive me if it is, but both you and Melinda act as though you were rather empty-headed when you are both obviously intelligent young women. Why would you do such a thing?"

Alanna laughed with delight. "Well clearly you are not so stupid yourself, as you have found me out. It is all part of the game that makes up the Season. Most men do not find particularly intelligent women to be attractive. And other women may find it threatening. If you let it be known that you are not 'empty-headed,' as you called it, you run the risk of being considered a bluestocking or even bookish. That just would not do."

"So you just pretend to be fascinated with gossip and shopping and such?"

"Oh no, not at all. I adore gossip and shopping and all the other fripperies that go along with coming to London for the Season. It is just that those are not the only things I enjoy."

"It all seems rather complicated. I do not know if I wish to be a party to so much dissemblance."

"You shall see. It can be highly diverting. Think of it as a game."

"But Alanna, what happens when some man who thinks you are just a pretty simpleton asks you to be his wife and you say yes? I do not think it would be a game I would wish to play for the rest of my days. And if you do not play it, there will be quite the surprise for both parties after the vows have been exchanged."

Alanna again laughed over her friend's earnestness. "Being a pretty simpleton merely catches their eye, but any man worthy of having me will not want to keep me that way. He would have to truly know me before I said yes. That too is part of the game."

Victoria heaved a rather weary sigh. "I am beginning to have my doubts about entering the ton. No one is as he or she seems and you have to be on your toes at all times."

"But did you not enjoy yourself this afternoon?"

"I did, more than I thought I would, to be honest with you," Victoria admitted with some surprise.

"You see, the game is not so bad. Wait until the Cordes' ball. Then you will see how very diverting it can be. Now here we are at the stationer's. Let us make our selection and be on our way."

"Yes, I should no doubt be getting home soon enough."

A short time later the girls exited the shop and made their way briskly back to Alanna's beautiful Mayfair home. As they were ascending the front stairs they were hailed from the street.

"I wish you good day, ladies," Bryghton greeted them with a jaunty grin.

Victoria was facing away from him but had recognized his voice instantly. She was amazed at her own reaction—feeling anxious and excited all at once, she was frozen for a moment as she pondered what to do. Alanna broke the spell as she turned to greet her brother.

"Bryght, how perfectly delightful to see you! Are you arriving or departing? We were just about to have a little refreshment before Victoria has to go home, would you care to join us?"

Victoria felt as though she were on tenterhooks awaiting the duke's reply. Nervous anticipation to spend time with him warred with an anxious knowledge of her uncle's disproval, for which she still did not understand the source.

The interminable-seeming wait ended as Bryghton climbed down from his phaeton and replied to his sister's invitation.

"Why thank you, little chick. I would be quite happy to pass a few minutes with you ladies and hear how your afternoon has been thus far."

Victoria finally forced herself to look at the duke, hoping she had on the appropriate look of polite boredom that Alanna had described, but when she saw Bryghton's dimpled grin she worried that her face betrayed just how appealing she found the sight of it.

The duke's face was a picture of studied impassivity as he took in the sight of Lady Victoria. Even the most searching gaze could not discern if he were fascinated or bored to tears. Victoria attempted to imitate his stoic gaze.

Bryghton could not believe the transformation from governess to lady of Society that had overtaken Lady Victoria. In his mind he had thought of her as just Victoria, almost as a friend. Now, standing calmly before him in her perfectly altered clothes, she was the impeccable Society belle. One would never imagine that such a short time ago she had been standing in the Serpentine holding a dripping little boy and glaring at him so fiercely. While she had then invited his attention, he now felt uncharacteristically nervous to speak to this beautiful young woman.

Fortunately for them both, Alanna was blissfully unaware of the tensions gripping her two companions and she chattered enthusiastically about their afternoon.

"And Bryght, you will just love the cards Victoria ordered. They put me in mind of yours. It would seem that the two of you share the same tastes."

"I look forward to seeing them," Bryghton answered in a polite murmur as the butler welcomed them and ushered them into the morning room.

"I will see that tea is served, my lady," Walter intoned before bowing himself out of the room.

"Lady Victoria, what did you think of your first foray into the ton?" the duke asked curiously.

"It was interesting."

"Interesting?" he asked with mock horror.

"Yes, interesting. I thought it would be somewhat boring after Alanna explained all the rules to me and gave me a quick lesson in what would likely be discussed. But, although everyone seems to make such effort to be the same, their own uniqueness still shines through and I find the silliness of 'the game' as Alanna calls it to be quite amusing."

"Which parts amused you today?" Bryghton prompted.

"The best example was when we were received by Lady Coupland in that ghastly gilt-encrusted chamber she passes off as a morning room. Alanna did not warn me as she wished to tickle her twisted sense of humour by awaiting my reaction. Hearing her explanation was in itself a source of amusement."

Bryghton held onto his silence, enjoying her confidences and hoping there were more to come. Victoria continued with a slightly guilty face.

"I probably should not be saying such things to you, but I am trusting your discretion not to tell tales. I should no doubt be grateful for the lady's graciousness in receiving me even though we had not been introduced. And she truly seemed an amiable sort. It was just that room! Have you seen it for yourself, your grace?"

Grinning, the duke answered, "I have, in fact. Lord Coupland is an old acquaintance of mine, we actually went to school together, and he asked me to come by and see it. He was hoping I would be able to say that it was lovely. He gave his new wife carte blanche to do with the room as she saw fit. He was of the opinion that she had impeccable tastes, so he thought no ill would come of it."

"Alanna is of the opinion that the lady secretly enjoys observing her guests' reactions and it is some sort of test of character for her."

"That is quite possible. The lady does seem to be a keen observer of people."

"I wonder what she gathered from my reaction," Victoria mused.

Alanna had been silently observing her brother and her friend during this exchange but finally broke her silence. "Victoria, you were magnificent. You barely flickered an eyelash and your mouth did not so much as quiver. You could almost match Bryghton for how contained you were. It was quite a surprise to me, as you are so often very expressive in your reactions."

Victoria laughed in real amusement. "But, my dear, you had been quite clear on the need to display polite boredom. I was prepared to be fascinated, as everything today would be new to me, so it was not overly difficult for me to hide my reaction. Although I freely admit that that room was not at all what I had expected from the handsomeness of the front of the house."

"It would seem her ladyship's remodelling was curtailed after the one room," Bryghton relied drily, which produced laughter all around.

The conversation was briefly interrupted as the butler wheeled in the tea service. Alanna poured and passed the tea around before resuming her seat.

Victoria sipped and sighed with contentment. "This has been such a lovely day, Alanna. Thank you so much for your kindness in my behalf. I truly appreciate it." With regret she put her tea down and rose to her feet. "I really should be getting on my way."

Alanna looked up at her with regret. "Must you leave already? You have not even tried Cook's lovely cake."

"It does look delicious, but I know the children will be asking for me by now and I want to ease them into this transition. I would prefer they not run complaining to their parents that I have abandoned them. And I truly do not wish for the poor dears to feel as though I have left them completely. So, yes, I really must."

"Very well," Alanna allowed with reluctance before she thought of one more thing. "Did you wish to wear those things home with you or were you planning to leave them here?"

Victoria felt the fiery blush climbing her cheeks and could not keep her eyes from straying to the duke's at this reminder of her straightened circumstances. Feeling suddenly like a fraud, she could no longer face him and headed for the door without answering Alanna's question.

Bryghton, already on his feet in respect when she stood, made as though to go after her. Alanna leapt to her feet, waved him away, and went after her friend.

"Victoria, wait. I apologize for my gauche question."

Victoria's fiery blush had given way to pallor, but she bravely faced the duke's sister with humour. "I could crush you with an icy stare or accuse you of being a vulgar mushroom."

Alanna grinned, "But you will not do such a thing because your heart is too soft. Now come along up to my room and fetch your things. You are more than welcome to wear those clothes home, they are yours after all, but if you do not wish for your aunt and uncle to ask questions, you might as well change out of them and leave them here for next time." Alanna allowed a pause before asking contritely, "There will be a next time, right? I have not given you a disgust of the whole venture, have I?"

Impulsively, Victoria threw her arms around her friend in a warm embrace. "Do not be a mutton-head! Of course I shall be back. You cannot be rid of me so easily."

The two girls linked arms and hurried up the stairs. A few minutes later, Walter allowed the much less finely dressed Lady

Victoria out the front door and watched as Alanna slowly returned to the drawing room.

"Well you rather made a mull of that, did you not?" Alanna's brother did not mince his words as he took her to task as soon as she appeared.

"I have no idea what you are talking about, your grace," she prevaricated, but without success.

"Yes you do, and do not bother 'your grace-ing' me now. Why did you not warn her about what to expect at Lady Coupland's? Are you trying to make her an outcast before she even really makes a debut?" Bryghton demanded angrily.

Alanna's own temper fired up at this. "Do not ring a peel over me. You do not know what you are talking about. I would never try to set Victoria up to fail. She is my friend. And I resent you even suggesting such a thing."

Bryghton was not mollified by her words. "Well then, why did you not prepare her?"

"Because I have enough confidence in her ability to handle herself beautifully in whatever situation she might find herself. I do not think she needs to be coddled. She is a beautiful, young, well-bred woman who has every right to enter Society and be welcomed by the ton. She will be welcomed and embraced by Society with or without my involvement. She did not need a warning from me. She is bang up to the mark on everything. And you are a clunch."

"She is a green girl and you are a hoyden."

"You are acting like a chaw-bacon."

"What is going on in here?" the Duchess of Wychwood demanded from the doorway.

She received no reply, as the two other occupants glared at one another, their insults traded for silence.

"You look like a couple of children. Do I need to turn you both over my knee in order to gain some cooperation from you?" the duchess asked in deceptively sweet tones.

This rejoinder brought laughter to Alanna who could never hold onto her anger even when fully justified. "No, mama, you do not need to turn me over your knee. I know I was no doubt behaving like a shrew, but I could not help myself. Bryghton was being insufferable."

The duke did not deign to make a reply to his sister but did step forward and place a welcoming kiss on his mother's cheek.

The duchess took a seat and beckoned for her children to do the same. "Is this tea fresh?" she asked, attempting to break the ice forming in the room.

Alanna leapt back to her feet, offering to pour. "It is fairly fresh, and very good."

"I see there are three cups already used. Whom did I miss?"

"Victoria was here but had to hurry away," Alanna answered without elaborating.

"Poor girl," replied the duchess. "Did she reconsider coming to stay here with us, do you think?"

"Did you make her such an offer?" Bryghton asked with surprise.

"Of course. She seems lovely, and it would be quite a simple thing for us. I knew her mother, it would be easy enough to explain the relationship, and there would be no awkwardness with her accompanying us anywhere. But the poor dear does not wish to upset her relations. I think she fears what would become of her if they were to cast her out in anger for her association with us."

Bryghton looked away and would not meet his mother's eye after that statement.

The perceptive mother rightly surmised that Victoria had been the subject of her children's argument and continued her questions. "Did the two of you have a good afternoon making calls?"

"It was quite lovely," Alanna's replied, still uninformative.

The duchess continued probing. "Do you think Lady Victoria enjoyed the experience?"

"I believe so, but she does not prattle on about such things, so it is sometimes difficult to tell what she is thinking." Alanna huffed. "And Bryght has made me worry that I put her in an awkward position. I got angry at him because he may be right."

Bryghton could not keep the surprise he felt from being written on his face, which made his sister laugh with renewed delight. "Yes, Bryght, I will admit it—as annoying as it is, you may be correct. I did not think it was unkind not to warn her. I thought it would be diverting. And it was, but I suppose if I were a true friend I would not seek amusement at my friend's expense."

"You have now lost me in this discussion, my dear," the duchess gently complained.

With a little laugh, Alanna explained, "Victoria and I called on Lady Coupland. I did not tell her anything about what she would see when we got there. Bryght thinks I should have in case she was not able to contain her reaction. I told him I trusted she would maintain her composure under any circumstances. I was right that she handled it beautifully, but he was right that I should have told her. But mama, it was so droll to see her eyes widen ever so slightly while keeping that pleasant half smile upon her face that makes one wonder what she is thinking. She seemed like an expert at handling the ton."

Her grace shifted her eyes between her son and her daughter, assessing both of their countenances. Alanna's was by far the easiest to decipher. Bryghton, on the other hand, was steadfastly keeping his thoughts to himself. The doting mother had a few questions for her firstborn.

"If it had been Eloise accompanying Alanna this afternoon, would you have expected a similar warning to be given?"

Bryghton offered a negligent shrug. "Probably not," he replied somewhat grudgingly.

"Why not? She is even younger than Victoria, and therefore her reactions could be even less restrained."

"But she has been making calls since she was in the schoolroom," Bryghton answered impatiently.

"So do you think it is a mistake for us to introduce Lady Victoria to the ton? Do you think she is beneath us?"

"Of course not," Bryghton replied, with a touch of horror colouring his tones. "She is a lovely young woman who deserves the best in life. The ton does not deserve her, not the other way around. I simply didn't want to see her embarrassed by any situation she might face while in Alanna's company."

His last bit of explanation seemed a bit weak to his mother, but she allowed the subject to drop, leaving time for his own words, and what they had revealed, to sink into his thoughts. Hoping Alanna had not caught on, she expertly turned the subject.

"Alanna my dear, do not refine upon it too much. I can see your brother's point about Victoria's inexperience, but you are right in realizing the dear girl will instinctively handle herself well. Even though her aunt has not taken her about, Victoria was well trained from infancy by a dear woman. Neither of you have anything to fear on her behalf. Now tell me, what do you and Victoria have planned for the future?"

"We are planning to make some more calls on the morrow so that she will know a few people when she attends my ball at the end of the week. By the by, your grace, have you consulted with the housekeeper about all the plans?"

"It is all well in hand, have no fear on that score. The responses have been pouring in; I think you will be quite happy with the turn out. It has been quite some time since we have had such a grand entertainment here. I think the staff are excited about it."

Getting restless, the duke stood to take his leave. "I will leave you two ladies to sort out the details. I wish you a good day."

Bryghton bowed over his sister's hand with an elegant flourish. "No hard feelings, little chick?" he asked.

"Of course not," Alanna said loyally. "You might be a clunch, but I love you anyway."

The duke was still grinning as he stooped to kiss his mother's cheek. "You are a good boy," she said fondly, if somewhat inaccurately, causing his grin to broaden.

Chapter Twenty-Three

The next few days flew by as Victoria continued trying to fulfill her duties as governess while accompanying Alanna on calls and helping with the last-minute preparations for the ball. The earl had still not produced a governess to replace her but thankfully seemed unconcerned about her activities. The children had finally accepted the new nursery maid and did not lament Victoria's absences overly, much to her relief.

Victoria had accepted Alanna's invitation to stay over for a couple of nights in connection with the ball and she was relieved when her aunt and uncle did not ask too many questions when she told them she would be absent.

"Good afternoon, Walter," Victoria greeted as the butler opened the door to her.

"Good afternoon, Lady Victoria, it is a pleasure to see you again. Let me take that bag from you, it looks to be too heavy for you to be lugging around."

Victoria laughed easily. "I am not nearly as fragile as I might look, Walter, but thank you. I will admit that after carrying it from home I do not mind setting it down now."

"I understand you will be staying with us for a while."

"Yes, for a couple of nights. It will be that much easier to help Alanna and the duchess with all the preparations for tomorrow night. And then, of course, if we dance until dawn I cannot walk home after that," she said with an eager grin.

"I will have a footman deliver your things to your room, then, my lady."

"Thank you. I believe Lady Alanna is expecting me."

"That she is, my lady. I will take you to her now."

After a short walk from the foyer, Walter announced formally, "Lady Victoria to see you, my lady."

"Welcome, welcome," Alanna jumped up from her seat and ran to greet her friend. "I was just reviewing our guest list and ensuring we have enough of everything for the numbers. I am so glad you are here now. I am heartily bored of being inside for so long. Would you mind terribly if we went for a brief stroll?"

Victoria did not remind her aristocratic friend that she had just walked here, and instead smiled kindly and murmured, "Not at all. It is a lovely day and you will no doubt enjoy some fresh air."

"You are already dressed for walking. Give me a few minutes and I will be changed and ready."

With those words Alanna left her guest alone in the morning room. Victoria paced to the front windows and was rewarded with the sight of the duke pulling up in his fancy carriage with the matching bays. Flustered, Victoria did not know what to do with herself. Should I run after Alanna and allow the duke to cool his heels on his own? she asked herself rather frantically before shaking her head in denial of that necessity. Do not be a silly gudgeon. No doubt he is here to see his mother and he will not be concerned about your presence in the slightest. With that bracing thought, she turned back to the window to entertain herself with the passing traffic.

Bryghton denied Walter the need to escort him. "No need, my good man. No doubt my sister is in the morning room like always. I will just see myself in." The duke strode purposefully into the room, pulling himself up short when he saw that it was occupied only by Victoria with her face to the window.

"Hullo, my lady, I did not expect to see you here."

Victoria started at his words. "Oh, your grace, you startled me. I saw you pull up and thought you must be here to see your mother. Alanna and I are about to go for a stroll and she had to run up to her room to change her attire."

"How fortuitous for my timing," he grinned, causing Victoria's heart to flutter, much to her dismay. "I swung by to see if Alanna wished to accompany me for a drive. We could join our forces and drive to the park for a walk if you would like."

Victoria smiled shyly, and hesitated before replying, "I am uncertain what exactly Alanna has planned for the rest of our day. I just arrived a few moments ago."

"Have you been for a ride in Hyde Park at the fashionable hour?" Bryghton asked curiously.

"No, your grace. I have watched from afar, I will admit, while there with the children."

"Well, I am sure it is bound to be a much different experience. I promise we will stay far from the Serpentine."

They smiled at each other rather intimately at the shared remembrance. Alanna walked into the room at that moment, interrupting the unsettling moment, much to Victoria's relief and Bryghton's uncertainty.

"Bryght, what a delightful surprise, I did not think to see you until my ball tomorrow."

"I thought you might need a breath of fresh air and stopped by to invite you for a ride. Lady Victoria told me you planned to take a walk. Would the two of you like to accompany me to the Park?"

"What a perfectly delightful suggestion," Alanna said, quick to accept. "It is the exact right time of the day for Victoria to be seen by virtually everyone, so there will be an opportunity to introduce her around or at least show her off so people will be expecting her tomorrow. It will ensure the success of my party." Alanna was gleeful until she turned to Victoria with a look of dismay. "I apologize, my lady. I should ask you if you wish to go. I do not mean to use you as bait to ensure the success of my ball, I assure you."

Victoria gurgled with laughter. "Have no fear, I do not feel like bait. I have always wanted to know how it would feel to be one of the pretty people riding around the park. Certainly let us go. It is just as well that his lordship has offered to drive us. It would not do for you to overtire yourself the day before the ball."

Alanna laughed. "But what about overtiring you?"

Victoria dismissed this concern with a negligent wave of her hand. "I rarely tire. Nothing the ton does could be as tiring as chasing after Daniel."

Bryghton looked at her pointedly at this reminder of her usual life, and wondered if she was having second thoughts about venturing into Society. "Are you sure you are up for this adventure?" he asked gently.

"Absolutely," she replied. "Lead on, your grace."

With an ironic bow, the duke led the girls out to his carriage and impatiently waiting horses. "I will apologize in advance for my cattle. These two have been cooped up in the stables for too long and are anxious to be put through their paces."

"Do not hold them back on my account, your grace," answered Victoria with a shiver of anticipation. "Although I am unsure if the traffic will allow you to do much more than a walk."

The duke grinned arrogantly as he anticipated demonstrating his skills with the ribbons. "You had best hold on, ladies, as we will certainly be going faster than a walking pace."

He put the beasts in motion and was surprised by the giggle of pure delight that erupted from the usually very contained Victoria.

"What beautiful goers they are, to be sure," Victoria said, and added shyly, "You handle the reins with considerable skill."

Bryghton grinned widely while throwing his little sister a quick wink. "Clearly our friend is more experienced than we had thought, little chick."

Victoria coloured at his teasing. "I may not have gotten about much in Society but I have observed much as I have gone about Town with the children."

"Quit teasing her, Bryght," Alanna admonished. She reminded Victoria, "Now wipe that delighted grin off your face. Remember, you must look politely bored. We are almost there."

Victoria allowed another peal of laughter to escape her lips but dutifully schooled her features into what she hoped was the appropriate expression.

Bryghton watched in amazement as she went from looking like a mischievous schoolgirl to a blasé member of Society. He uttered a low whistle of approval. "One would think you were an old hand at this, my lady."

Victoria lifted one shoulder in a negligent shrug. "Mayhap I am, your grace," she said in an offhand tone before meeting his eyes. He grinned at seeing the sparkle of laughter in her eyes, much in contradiction to the expression on her face. She reprimanded him, "Do not grin at me, Duke, you will quite ruin my effect. It took a ridiculous amount of practice to manage this exact look and I shall not be able to hold onto it with you smiling so at me. Now I pray you do not take it amiss, but I shall not be able to look at you for the rest of our time in the park, for I am certain an idiotic grin will break over my face if I do."

Bryghton was delighted by her honesty. He fiercely hoped the thoughts coursing through his mind were not written upon his own face as he met his sister's probing gaze.

Alanna searched her brother's face trying to read his reactions to Lady Victoria. She would have sworn the duke was showing unprecedented attention to her, but she was unsure of his reasons. She could feel her frustration rising at his impassivity, but she could not help grinning when he once again flicked her a wink as they entered the park and he brought the horses to a trot to ease into the slow-moving traffic as the fashionable world took the time to show themselves off to one another.

After a few minutes passed in silence, Victoria finally broke it. "Alanna, my dear friend, I do declare that my face is about to crack from this impossible expression. Do say we can stop a moment and take a little stroll away from the probing eyes, as I really must smile and gaze about with real curiosity."

"Oh Victoria, I am truly sorry," Alanna was instantly contrite. "I did not mean to say you cannot smile at all. We should be conversing and you could react as naturally as you wish to whatever we discuss. But perhaps your suggestion is better. We did say we wished to stroll after all."

At those words Victoria turned a brilliant smile upon her two companions and Bryghton and Alanna could not help responding in kind. "This is the most amusement I have had in ages. Do some of these people not realize how ridiculous they look? That last lady with dogs in her carriage looked quite like her furry friends. And the other lady with the purple plumes sticking out of her headdress, I am quite certain she did not think how they would look when in motion."

Alanna giggled at Victoria's words, unaware of her brother's intent expression as he gazed at the earl's niece.

Pulling his horses to a standstill and helping the ladies out of the carriage, Bryghton fought his growing attraction to the young lady as he reminded himself just whom she was related to. He remembered, somewhat ruefully, that he had meant to use her as a means for revenge against the earl, but he knew now that would be impossible. With rising frustration he wondered at his feelings for Lady Victoria and what he could make of their connection. With a shake of his head, he shoved the concerns to the back of his mind and found a conveniently placed tree to tie his horses. Turning back to his companions, he offered each an elbow.

Strolling along in silence, the duke enjoyed listening to the two girls banter and chatter with one another. He momentarily lost himself in thought as Alanna was hailed by a passing acquaintance. He was pulled from his reverie by a soft voice.

"Is everything all right with you, your grace? You have become strangely quiet," Victoria asked in an undertone. "Or are we talking too much to allow you any room for comment?"

"Naught is amiss, my lady," Bryghton answered. "I am merely enjoying the pleasure of having two such lovely ladies on my arms. It is not every day I have the honour of escorting my sister and her friend."

Victoria, with an effort of will, kept her smile in place at this reminder that she was merely his sister's friend. She had started to think that she could count the duke as her friend too, but she realized, with a wistful, though silent, sigh, that that was a foolish thought. Forcing her mind to the practicalities of her situation, she turned her attention to contemplating the various men they had encountered.

"Now it is you who has turned quiet, my lady, is aught amiss with you?" Bryghton turned her words back on her with a smile.

She did not return the smile, but answered him seriously, "I am contemplating the potential suitors your sister has so far introduced me to. I am not sure if any of them would well suit with me, but I promised myself I would be open minded and think through all my options."

Bryghton blinked in surprise at her honest reply. He had known this was one of the main reasons she had considered his sister's presumptuous insistence on introducing her to the ton, but he had not seriously considered the possibility of her marrying one of his friends. With effort he maintained his stoic manner and as blandly as possible asked her about her options.

"Do you as yet have any favourite potentials?"

"Not really, your grace. It is far more difficult than I had thought. These are real people with whom I would be spending the rest of my life. It is a rather daunting situation. I know ladies do it every Season, but they usually have the backing of family and supporters who will vouch for both parties. I am in a unique situation for this venture."

"Are you wishing you had someone to vouch for you?" he asked, his voice husky from concern.

"I am actually more concerned about wishing I had someone I deeply trusted who could vouch for potential mates. It seems to me that it is a far more consequential thing for the lady than for the gentleman when a marriage bargain is struck, and I fear that your sister, despite how very kind she is, is not in a position to advise me seriously." Victoria shot a look of concern his way lest he think she was insulting his sister.

"Alanna is a green girl despite her protestations otherwise, and I would never entrust her with my own future, so I can understand your concerns. Would you consider my assistance?"

Victoria blushed to the roots of her hair and stammered out a reply in her discomfort. "Your grace, I have no wish to burden you with my meagre concerns. I deeply appreciate your offer but I would hate to impose on you in such a way."

"It is no imposition, my lady. I feel a sense of responsibility for your situation, as it is through me that Alanna became acquainted with you and dragged you into your current dilemma."

Victoria's blush deepened, causing Bryghton to be concerned for her health. "Are you sure you are all right, my lady?"

Victoria held onto her smile with sheer force of will. She would rather live under a bridge than discuss specific potential suitors with the duke but did not feel it prudent to tell him so to his face. "I appreciate your offer, your grace. If I find myself in too much of a quandary I may take you up on it." She managed to blurt out the lie without choking on it.

"What are you two discussing so seriously?" Alanna interrupted, much to Victoria's delight and Bryghton's dismay.

"Nothing of import," Victoria dismissed airily, hurrying to Alanna's side and urging her to continue their stroll.

A short time later, Alanna decided it best that they return home and imperiously demanded that the duke comply.

With a wry bow, Bryghton answered, "I am, as always, yours to command."

"Oh, fie on you, Duke, do not get all starchy with me. You know my mind is preoccupied with our plans for tomorrow. And I have a surprise for Victoria this evening and we really must get home to prepare."

Victoria turned to Alanna with a face full of delight and wonder, bringing a fond smile to the duke's own face.

"What kind of a surprise?" Victoria asked, her eyes shining.

"You will have to wait and see," Alanna teased.

"You truly must give me a hint before I expire of my curiosity," Victoria insisted as they hurried to Bryghton's carriage.

"A hint?" Alanna asked provocatively. "You shall have to change into evening attire," was the only hint she would allow.

"Well, that is of no help," said Victoria, laughing. "If I understand it correctly, you change into evening attire nearly every night of the week."

Alanna shrugged with a glint of mischief in her eyes and refused to make any further comment. Bryghton found the girls' interaction to be amusing and engaging, enjoying their company more than he ever would have expected.

They drove quickly out of the park and towards the duchess' townhouse. Victoria was the first out of the carriage and hurried up the steps with barely a glance back for the duke. Unperturbed, Bryghton caught his sister's arm before she was able to descend.

"You are not going to lead her into trouble tonight, are you? Could I be included in your plans to keep an eye on the two of you?" he asked her in a low tone.

Alanna let out a peal of laughter. "I am not about to lead her astray, Bryghton, my dear. But of course, you are welcome to join us." She lowered her voice still further in order for Victoria not to overhear. "Mama and I are escorting Victoria to the theatre tonight. Since she always wants to get home at an early hour when she spends time with me I have been unable to take her thus far, but since she will be sleeping over we are free to stay out as late as we would like."

Her impish grin brought a growl to her brother's throat. "Mind you do not stay out later than is seemly."

Alanna rolled her eyes at her brother's imperiousness. "You are turning into a wet nurse, Bryghton. Nothing unseemly will be taking place. We shall be in the company of the duchess. Now let me go, I must make haste."

"What time should I come by to collect the three of you?"

"Why do you not just meet us there? We are attending a dinner party before the theatre and I cannot finagle an invitation for you at this late hour," she replied rather harshly as she yanked her arm from his grasp and turned to the stairs.

"Behave yourself, little chick," Bryghton called out after her, laughing as she turned to glare at him.

"That man is impossible," she grumbled half-heartedly to Walter as he held the door for her. "But one cannot help being fond of the lout."

"Welcome home, my lady," Walter replied with a formal bow and a fond smile.

"Where has Lady Victoria gone off to?" Alanna asked, surprised not to see her awaiting her in the foyer.

"I believe she has gone up to your room. The last I saw her she was climbing the stairs and mumbling something about evening attire."

Alanna grinned. "I did not tell her what we have planned for the evening, merely telling her she must dress in evening attire. It is to be a wonderful surprise which she shall love once she gets over her distress of not knowing what she is getting into." Alanna glanced towards the stairs and grinned anew. "I had best get upstairs and help her decide what to wear."

"Walter tells me you were grumbling to yourself," Alanna teased as she entered the room.

With a guilty blush, Victoria admitted, "I confess that I find it disconcerting to try to plan for something when I do not know what it is."

"Now quit worrying and pacing. If the duchess were to see you she would call the both of us to task. Let us go above stairs and see which gowns are prepared for your use and which you would most like to wear this evening. We might as well start our preparations now. Would you like the maids to draw you a bath?"

Delighted by the offered luxury, Victoria gave up on her concerns and agreed to Alanna's plans. It did not take them long to select which gown Victoria would wear for the evening, and a short while later Victoria was happily settling into the steaming tub and contemplating the possible excursions for the evening.

When one of the maids returned to help her out of the tub, holding a large warmed towel for her to step into, Victoria sighed with delight. She was still grinning as she strolled into Alanna's room.

"What do you look so happy about?" Alanna asked with a matching grin.

"I have decided that I could get used to living in the lap of luxury, so my list of potential suitors must include only the gentlemen who can support sufficient staff for there to be a maid to pass me a warmed towel whenever I choose to take a bath."

"You do not usually have your towels warmed?" Alanna asked with some dismay.

Victoria laughed over her friend's innocence. "Alanna, my dear, I usually have to fill my own bathtub and make all the other preparations."

"But your uncle surely has sufficient staff to meet your needs." Alanna's tone was coloured with disbelief.

"True, but the governess does not in general have the use of the maids for herself," Victoria reminded gently. "I pray you, do not trouble yourself on this matter, my friend. All is well. I am wholeheartedly enjoying your and your mother's hospitality."

Alanna forced a smile back to her face, but concern for her friend buzzed at the back of her mind like a small bug that would not let her be. The two girls continued to giggle and gab their way through their preparations, but Alanna slipped out of the room while her lady's maid was arranging Victoria's hair.

Scratching on the door, Alanna entered upon hearing her mother's, "Come hither."

"Alanna, my darling, you look lovely, as always. You are ready faster than usual, which is a surprise, since I thought you two girls would take forever."

"Victoria does not take too long to do anything," Alanna explained. Her amused smile gave way to a worried frown as she continued, "I wanted to hurry so I could speak to you before we go."

"What is troubling you, my child?"

"Victoria's circumstances. I feel that she is being mistreated in her home. Surely there must be something we can do about it. This afternoon she was so happy about having the maids help her with her bath. Should this not be something that she takes for granted? That house she lives in is hers. So surely those must be her servants. She should be able to command them as she wishes. Not be one of them herself."

"I understand your concern and I share it, but I am unsure if there is much we can do aside from what we are doing, introducing her to Society and hopefully a suitable gentleman who will take control of the situation for her." The duchess paused in thought for a moment and continued in an altered tone of voice. "I do hope, though, that you are not using Victoria and your matchmaking efforts on her behalf to get away with not thinking about making a match for yourself."

Alanna flashed a rather guilty look at her mother, but protested nonetheless. "On the contrary, Mother. It is so much more diverting to have someone to share the experience with. It is interesting to discuss the pros and cons of various gentlemen with her. She has an interesting perspective, and I am enjoying seeing the Season through her eyes. And we make an excellent team to find a match for each other."

"Very well, my dear. Now tell me, is it still a surprise from Victoria, what we have planned for this evening?"

Alanna did a little dance of glee. "It is. I can hardly credit it. I have never been able to keep a secret in my life."

The duchess could not resist smiling in amusement over her daughter's delight. "Now run along and finish getting ready, we should be leaving shortly. And try not to worry overmuch about Victoria's situation. Between the three of us, we shall be able to ensure that both of you are arranged for securely and happily."

Impulsively, Alanna threw her arms around her mother and gave her a quick, warm squeeze before skipping to the door. She turned, blew her mother a kiss and ran from the room.

Upon returning to her own bedchamber she blew a low whistle when she caught sight of her friend. "Lady Victoria, I do believe you shall break a few hearts."

"That does not sound very nice, but I am quite sure you meant it as a compliment, so I will say thank you." She suited her words with a curtsy. "Where have you been? You must hurry and get ready."

"I was just confirming with the duchess if all was in readiness," Alanna dismissed as she headed towards the maid who was waiting with her gown. "I must say, Sally did wonders with your hair. That style perfectly suits you."

Victoria could not resist preening in front of the mirror. "I apologize if this sounds terribly immodest, but I would have to agree with you. I swear I do not even recognize myself."

The two girls shared a giggle.

"You look right lovely, m'lady," complimented the maid as she arranged Alanna's skirts. "The two of you are goin' to be right popular this night."

"Thank you, Sally, that is a very sweet thing to say," answered Victoria.

"I ain't turnin' you up sweet, it's the truth I'm tellin' you."

Alanna hugged her favourite maid. "We appreciate your words, Sally, thank you. You have worked your magic over both of us."

Victoria grinned at the two but then returned to seriousness. "I have no idea where we are going, but I do believe we had best be on our way."

"I cannot decide if I think you are handling this well or not," Alanna said. "You have not thrown an ill-bred fit, but you have certainly brought the subject up often enough to demonstrate your dislike for surprises."

Victoria could not help the guilty look that crept over her face at Alanna's words. "I am truly sorry, Alanna. I do not wish to make you regret all you have done for me. You must realize that I have had very few good surprises in my life, so I am rather distrustful of the unknown."

"You want to be in control, just like everyone else. It is completely natural, and I fully understand. But I promise you this is going to be a perfectly lovely surprise and you will enjoy yourself wholeheartedly. And you are quite correct; it is definitely time we were on our way. Come along."

In fine spirits and in good humour the two girls joined the duchess in the foyer.

"The carriage is awaiting you, your grace and my ladies," Walter announced.

"Thank you, Walter."

Chattering like magpies, the two young girls kept the duchess amused as the party made their way through the streets. It was not yet late, so the traffic was not overly heavy and they quickly arrived at their destination.

Victoria had to force her chin not to unhinge itself as she gazed at the elegant façade of the house they were about to enter. "We are to visit the Earl of Sommerton? How deliciously extraordinary. Are you certain they are expecting me to be accompanying you or shall I throw out their numbers?"

"Rest tranquil, little one. You worry overly," admonished the duchess. "Of course they know we are a party of three, and you will be warmly welcomed. Come along, children."

Victoria felt a trifle ashamed, realizing she had inadvertently insulted the duchess by her nervous question. Resolving to give neither herself nor the duchess any further cause for shame that night, she set her chin at a firm angle and followed the other two ladies up the stairs.

They were soon shown into a large, elegantly furnished receiving room which was already half full with milling guests. Victoria whispered, "No gilt showing in this lovely room." Alanna managed not to guffaw in reaction to the private joke.

The earl and his daughter stepped forward to greet the newly arrived guests.

"Welcome, your grace and Lady Alanna, we are pleased you could join us this evening. And it is a great pleasure that you could accompany them, Lady Victoria," the earl said, welcoming them and announcing their presence at the same time.

Victoria dipped into an elegant curtsy that managed to show respect to their host as well as the whole room.

The earl continued in conversation with the duchess as Alanna introduced Victoria to the earl's daughter. "This is Odelia. She and I made our debut the same year. And her father is despairing of her making a match just as much as mama is of me. So we are soul sisters in our suffering."

Victoria grinned at Alanna's wry humour and looked curiously at the other young lady. "Do you share Alanna's misgivings about marriage?"

"Not at all, my lady, I am just too busy having fun. I know I will have to settle down soon, but I am afraid that as soon as I marry I will be expected to start a family and I might have to miss the Season. My aunt has assured me that it is all worth it, but while I am enjoying my little baby cousins I do not yet wish to have one of those creatures of my own."

Victoria could not relate to the girl's sentiment, as she thought having children would be the most delightful thing in the world, but she did not wish to dampen the new friendship so she quelled her tongue. Alanna, knowing her quite well, winked discreetly, helping her keep the prescribed politely bored expression in place.

Looking around at the mingling group, Victoria was curious about who her fellow guests were and wondered about the social etiquette involved in making introductions. She quietly drew

Alanna's attention to the dilemma during a pause in her lively conversation with Odelia.

"Alanna, my dear," Victoria discreetly murmured, "I do not know anyone present. In this particular situation, do I wait for you to introduce me or do I mingle and meet people for myself?"

"I will introduce you to a few people, and when we are seated for dinner, you can introduce yourself to your neighbours. Or you could go join the duchess and she will introduce you to whomever she is speaking, but, no, you cannot go about meeting people for yourself, unfortunately."

The two ladies shared an amused look before turning back to Odelia, who was regarding them curiously. To smooth over the awkward moment, Victoria asked, "Did you just arrive in London recently, my lady, or have you been in residence for a while?"

"My father is an avid Parliamentarian, so we were in residence early so he could be prepared for the opening sessions," Odelia answered with a roll of her eyes. "I do not really mind coming up to London early, as I do love to shop, but it is a bit strange being in Town when it is virtually empty."

Victoria stifled a giggle over the girl's description of London as being empty. Of course, she was referring to the aristocratic population, but Victoria was well aware that there was a sizeable percentage of London's residents who did not have the luxury of more than one home.

"What about you, Lady Victoria? Have you just arrived?" Odelia was asking.

"No, my uncle had much to attend to, so we too have been in residence for a long time," Victoria answered.

"But I have not seen you at any of the ton parties. Why have we not yet met?"

"I have been otherwise occupied thus far this Season," Victoria answered truthfully but uninformatively.

Alanna stepped in to deftly change the subject. "Odelia, my dear, as always, I adore spending time with you, but we must not monopolize you as you are hostess this evening. We shall mingle while we allow you to return to your guests."

Odelia, distracted by the arrival of some new guests, did not notice she was being dismissed. "Of course, thank you, my friend. I trust you will enjoy your evening."

Turning back to the crowd to survey who else was in attendance, Alanna murmured, "Come along, green girl, I shall introduce you about."

With a twinkle in her eye, Victoria followed in her wake. The two girls made polite, inane conversation with a few different people as even more guests continued to arrive. Dinner would be served momentarily, and Victoria was beginning to very much look forward to it. She was turning away from the current conversation when she, with a shock, met face to face with someone she knew.

"Oh, my lord, fancy meeting you here," she stammered out.

"Victoria?" Lord Dalton asked, with acute surprise.

Victoria covered her nervousness by turning to Alanna. "Lady Alanna, are you familiar with Lord Anthony Dalton?"

"I am, but I must admit to being surprised that you are," Alanna answered before wishing she could bite off her tongue for her thoughtless speech.

Victoria blushed slightly but maintained her composure. "Lord Dalton is my uncle's nephew through marriage, so although he is not truly a relative of mine we are fairly well acquainted. His mother is the sister of Lady Pickering."

"Oh yes, I had quite forgotten. Clearly I need to brush up on my reading of Debrett's," Alanna said, laughing to cover her faux pas, and hoping to allay a scene as she could see the viscount was eyeing Victoria with curiosity.

"Is my aunt here with you?" Lord Dalton asked, looking around.

"No, I am in the company of Lady Alanna and the Duchess of Wychwood," Victoria answered, unconsciously raising her chin with determined pride.

The viscount, never having paid much attention to the young woman living with his relatives, was vaguely curious about this turn of events and if it had anything to do with the feud between Pickering and Wychwood. He was about to probe deeper, but they were interrupted by dinner being announced.

The two girls stepped away after curtsying to him in farewell. Exchanging chagrined expressions, they accepted the elbows of gentlemen offering to escort them to the dining room.

Sitting down at the beautifully set table, Victoria distractedly wondered if she would be able to eat a single bite as the butterflies in her stomach were fluttering vigorously. Glancing down the table, she saw the duchess sitting next to their host, the earl. As though sensing her momentary distress, the duchess turned her head in her direction, met her eyes directly and gave her a little nod of approval. It was all the encouragement Victoria needed. She wiped the worry from her mind, placed a slight smile upon her lips, and turned to meet her dinner companions.

Surprised to see that on her right was someone she had already met, she greeted Mr. Dylan Mead. After a moment of discussion with him she turned to make the acquaintance of the gentleman on her left. Robert Lambert, the baron of Shelton, quickly launched into a conversation about his political ambitions. Victoria soon realized she was in for an evening of political conversation, as both gentlemen worked in the House of Lords. She hoped the two young men would not be too terribly uninteresting.

Fortunately for Victoria, both young men were clearly passionate on the topic of politics, so although she did not share their interests it was entertaining to hear them expound on their chosen subjects.

The soup that was served to begin the meal smelled heavenly, and Victoria was pleasantly surprised to feel her appetite return in full force as she listened politely in turn to each of her companions. Fortunately they both had plenty to say and were pleased by her periodic nods and murmurs of assent, so she was able to allow her mind to drift a little as she discreetly glanced around the table to observe the other guests in various conversations.

Victoria found the people of the ton to be endlessly fascinating as they engaged in social banter and followed all the many unwritten rules of their Society. Her attention was dragged back to the gentlemen beside her as she realized one had asked her a question.

Blushing rosily, she stammered, "I apologize my lord, my mind has become quite occupied with this lovely brisquet. Could you please repeat your question?"

Smiling condescendingly over the lady's apparent empty headedness, the baron repeated his question slowly. "I asked if you had heard anything about the voting in Parliament over the union with Ireland. But I dare say you would not understand what it is about."

Victoria was shocked over the obvious insult to her intellect but realized that the ridiculous young man found a lack of intellect to be an appealing quality in a woman. Stifling her natural reaction, she smiled sweetly and answered his question, endeavouring to keep her amusement to herself. "Yes, my lord, I have heard a little about it, but it would be best if you explain it to me."

It was all the encouragement the young baron needed, and he launched into an eloquent soliloquy on the benefits to the two nations to join their parliaments. "The Honourable Mr. William Pitt is quite convinced that this union will strengthen the connection between our two countries as well as being advantageous economically, particularly for the Irish, you see. And of course, it will make it easier to grant concessions to the Catholics that reside in England if Ireland is unified with us," he concluded.

"Oh, I see," Victoria answered feebly, not quite following all of the baron's logic. She was further distracted by Mr. Mead interrupting in order to disagree heartily with the baron's arguments.

"That is such a bunch of foolishness," Mr. Mead declared hotly. "England is Anglican and we cannot be making concessions to the Irish Catholics. Besides the fact that the government has clearly purchased all the votes necessary to make it pass, I cannot see how this effort is going to have any success!"

"Why is that, sir?" Victoria asked curiously.

"Clearly the Irish will not be happy about losing their independence. You mark my words, this is not going to end well," Dylan insisted.

Victoria was about to comment but the baron cut her off.

"Do not listen to him, my lady," Lord Lambert said dismissively, "The Irish cannot help but be happy about this Union, you shall see. It will be so much to their benefit. They simply did not have the foresight needed to see how beneficial it will be, that is why financial persuasion was required to secure the votes."

Victoria was relieved to be spared the need to comment as the servants had returned to remove the tablecloth and spread out the dessert course. She struggled to think of an innocuous topic of conversation with which to conclude the meal.

As the jellies and nuts were served to her she turned to the baron and asked, "Since you are so busy in the House, how do you find time to attend events such as these?"

"Oh my lady, one must make time. My lord, the earl, is a very important member of the House of Lords so if he invites one to his home, one must never decline such an invitation."

It was an effort not to giggle over this supercilious comment and Victoria was happy when Mr. Mead interjected on her other side.

"Taking a break from the rigours of politics is a refreshing change. Having the pleasure of the company of such lovely ladies as yourself makes us remember why we do what we do every day. We have to make this country be the best it can be for the benefit of our ladies."

Victoria blinked rapidly, unsure how to respond to the young man's clumsy efforts at flirtation. She smiled pleasantly. "No doubt all the ladies appreciate your efforts, Mr. Mead. It is important work, running the country smoothly."

When Odelia stood to indicate it was time for the ladies to depart, leaving the gentlemen to their port, Victoria did not hesitate in the least to get to her feet, but she did turn to each of her companions to thank them sweetly for keeping her entertained throughout the dinner.

"It was a pleasure meeting you, Lord Lambert, and seeing you again, Mr. Mead. No doubt we will meet again. I wish you a pleasant evening."

She made her escape before either of them could launch into further speech, and caught up with Alanna in the hallway. "Oh my dear goodness, Alanna, that was the most hilarious evening! Those two gentlemen I was sitting between were clearly on opposite sides of the political spectrum. Etiquette dictated that they could not argue over me so they had to each tell me their opposing thoughts on various matters. It was an interesting combination of entertaining and exhausting. But the most amusing part was when the baron kept assuming that I could not possibly understand whatever he was talking about and so would launch into a long-winded explanation. I, of course, could not explain to him that it was not that I had not understood whatever he had said, but rather that in my boredom of his excess of words I had allowed my mind to wander."

"Oh dear, I am sorry you did not enjoy it," Alanna began to apologize.

"Oh, that is not the case at all. It was highly diverting. My uncle is not overly involved in politics as far as I am aware, so it was true that I did not know everything they were discussing, but it was fairly interesting for the most part. The only problem was that I was more fascinated by watching everyone else, so I could not keep my attention focused if they blathered on for too long."

"Well, that is good then. And our evening is not nearly over yet! You shall have plenty of time to indulge your desire in observing the ton. Come along, my dear."

With those cryptic words Alanna lead the way to the morning room where the duchess was taking her leave of Odelia and the other ladies.

Victoria dipped into a dignified curtsy as she took her leave of the gathered women.

"It was a pleasure to meet you, Lady Victoria. I must call upon you soon. When are you at home?" Odelia asked, surprised to see the apparent consternation her question elicited.

"Oh that is so kind of you, my lady," Victoria stammered. Regaining her composure quickly, she rallied, "I do not have a regular at-home day, as I have just begun dipping my toe into the activities involved during the Season. Lady Alanna has been kind enough to allow me to accompany her as she makes her rounds, so perhaps it would be best if you called on her, as I would be more likely to be there than at my own home." Victoria was rather proud of herself at how she had managed to recover but she dared not meet Alanna's eyes lest she burst into a nervous fit of giggles.

Odelia did not appear to find anything strange in Victoria's explanation and merely repeated her pleasure at having had the trio as their guests that evening. The duchess shepherded the two younger girls from the room and the three descended to their carriage in silence.

As soon as the door was shut upon them, Alanna and Victoria's eyes met and the two allowed gales of laughter to flow. Even the duchess could not resist smiling over their hilarity.

"What are you two giggling so merrily about?" she asked, sending the two younger ladies into another fit of giggles.

Victoria finally regained sufficient composure to reply, "It really is not all that funny, my lady. I do believe it is an excess of nervous energy that is causing us to laugh so much. Lady Odelia asked if she could call on me. I am quite certain the expression on my face when I made an attempt to reply was not one that is perfectly acceptable socially. I think I pulled it off fairly well, but Alanna and I are finding it ridiculous in hindsight."

"Oh Victoria, the look on your face was hilarious! You managed to wipe it off remarkably quickly but for a split of a second you looked equal parts terrified and mortified. I must tell you how impressed I am with your ability to regain your composure. I do not think Odelia will even remember the momentary look of panic on your face, nor remark upon your response. It sounded reasonable and should not cause you any problems," Alanna assured.

"Do you think it would be terribly awkward if someone were to call by your house and ask for you?" the duchess asked with concern.

"I would certainly not be dressed in the first stare of fashion, for one thing," said Victoria while she contemplated how best to answer the question. "And some awkward questions might be asked. But, no, I do not think it would be a terrible situation, just a trifle embarrassing for me to be caught out in my role as governess by someone I had been socializing with."

The duchess nodded in agreement with Victoria's explanation but had a reasonable argument of her own to offer. "Keep in mind, if someone were to call when you are not feeling prepared for company you can always have the butler tell the new arrival that you are not at home to company. It is not unacceptable, and would not be considered rude. Your guest would merely leave their card and expect a return visit when you are in a position to do so. There is no need for you to panic if someone asks to call on you. You can merely smile graciously and say how lovely it would be to see them again."

Victoria felt her face warm. "You are absolutely right, my lady. I rather made a muck of that, did I not? I hope you are correct, Alanna, in thinking that Lady Odelia did not remark upon my questionable response."

"No harm was done, my dear, have no fear," the duchess assured her. "Now put that from your mind. We are about to have a lovely night."

Victoria could feel that the carriage was coming to a stop and looked from the nearest window to see where they were. She was on the side of the carriage facing away from their destination, it would seem, as she could see very little from her window. She eagerly peered out the door as it was opened by an attentive footman.

"The theatre!" she gasped with excitement as she squeezed Alanna's hand. "How delightful! Thank you ever so much!"

The footman handed the ladies down and Victoria looked around in amazement. "Everything looks so very different here at night with the lights blazing and so many beautifully dressed people milling about."

"Good evening, ladies."

Victoria felt the hairs on the back of her neck stand up at hearing the duke's voice behind her. She was relieved that the duchess and Alanna were replying to his greeting, as she felt momentarily struck dumb. She absently wondered if she would be able to handle the excitement of the theatre coupled with being in the duke's presence at the same time.

"You seem to be a world away," Bryghton was saying to her.

Victoria cleared her throat, hoping speech had not completely deserted her. "I am merely revelling in the anticipation of the treat before me this evening," she replied and then grinned, delighted that she had managed to sound so composed.

Bryghton, unaware of her thoughts, assumed her grin was caused by her delight at visiting the theatre, and admired once more her beauty and sunny disposition despite her past misfortunes. He returned her grin with one of his own.

Victoria had to catch her breath at the sight. The duke so often maintained a serious expression, or one that was akin to boredom. It was rare that he allowed a full smile to grace his face, and Victoria had to blink in order to restore her focus after being so bedazzled. She forced her attention to return to the ladies.

Hoping her voice sounded normal, Victoria turned to Alanna and asked, "Do we have much time before the performance begins? Should we make our way to wherever we will be sitting, or is there time for you to show me around?"

"There is not sufficient time, this evening, my dear, I am sorry to tell you," the duchess interjected before Alanna could reply. "We would have to come well in advance if you wanted to be shown around. The halls would be far too crowded at this point for the two of you to be traipsing about by yourself. Come along, we shall get ourselves seated and you can look around from there."

Victoria tried to hide her disappointment but she must not have done a complete job of it, since Bryghton took her arm and quietly promised, "Do not trouble your mind, my dear. I shall make sure to give you the full tour next time."

Victoria smiled at his kindness but wondered if there truly would be a next time. Her face must have again betrayed her thoughts, as the duke squeezed her elbow reassuringly and whispered, "I will make sure there is a next time." She felt a thrill shimmy up her back and she almost grinned anew.

After the quartet reached their box, the rest of Victoria's night passed in a pleasant blur. If she had been later asked, she would not have been able to tell which production they had seen. She would only be able to tell how much she enjoyed it. She was dazzled by the glow of the myriad candles flashing upon the jewels of all the well-born guests enjoying the spectacle as they divided their attention between the drama on the stage as well as that going on in the surrounding boxes as the social scene unfolded.

Victoria smiled in all the right places and responded to any questions or comments that came her way, but her mind was certainly not fully engaged. She was not lost in fantasies or daydreams; she was merely glowing, basking in a level of happiness and contentment that she had not experienced for many years.

As the duke escorted the ladies back to their carriage he caught himself casting sidelong glances at Victoria, wondering if something was wrong, as she was even more quiet than usual. "Is anything amiss, my lady?" he asked her quietly, trying not to draw the attention of his mother and sister who were busily discussing the merits of the play.

Victoria turned to him with a sunny smile. "Everything is perfect, your grace, thank you for asking. This evening has been glorious. I feel somewhat like Cendrillon from Charles Perrault's tale. Your mother and sister are the fairy godmothers who have turned my rags into this beautiful gown, and I have had a wonderful time."

"And well you deserve it, as you are as lovely and gracious as Cendrillon in that tale."

Victoria felt the blush heating her cheeks. "Your grace, that is not what I meant at all."

Bryghton offered a negligent shrug. "Nonetheless, it is the truth. Now tell me, will you save me at least one dance tomorrow?"

She cast her lashes downward and made an effort at coquettishness. "Perhaps," she simpered before bursting into laughter. "I cannot play the proper debutante."

"Do not be anything but yourself and you will have the ton at your feet," the duke vowed quietly just before they rejoined the duchess and Alanna, once more robbing Victoria of her voice.

Victoria could feel the duchess' searching gaze upon her but she was relieved when Alanna was the one to pepper her with questions.

"So did you love the theatre? What was your favourite part?"

With a laugh, Victoria answered as best she could. "I did love it, thank you ever so much for taking me. You were quite correct when you said I would be able to indulge my enjoyment of people watching. It seemed to me that more people were looking around than were looking at the spectacle on the stage."

"I told you that the entire premise of the Season is to see and be seen, did I not?"

"That you did, my dear friend. I loved looking around at everyone and all the beautiful details of the theatre, but it did strike me as exceedingly rude to not be looking at the stage. Those actors were so skilled. The story they presented was so believable that I felt as though I was transported to another place and time. They must have had to work very hard to learn all their words and movements, and then so many could not be bothered to even pay them any attention."

The duchess could not prevent herself from interjecting. "Oh, my dear, you are showing yourself to be a green girl now. The ton does not care about the feelings of those who are being paid to entertain."

Victoria was not completely certain if the duchess was including herself in that assessment, so she contained her response to a quiet, "But they are people too."

Alanna had not really been paying attention to the direction of the conversation, still thinking about the drama they had watched. "I must say, I wonder why every single one of Mr. Shakespeare's works are so dark and dreary. Did the man not believe in a happy ending?"

"I suppose they would not be classified as dramas if they had a happy ending," mused Victoria before interjecting, "but I do believe you are forgetting Twelfth Night. It has a lovely, happy ending."

Her grace joined the discussion. "And he did write many comedies. What about A Midsummer Night's Dream?"

"That does not have a happy ending, Mother," objected Alanna. "Demetrius decides he does not love Hermia and everyone thinks it was all a dream."

"Perhaps it does not have a fairy tale ending, my dear, but you know life rarely does," her mother reminded gently.

"Well, I do not have to entertain myself with real life, do I, Mother? The sad bits about life are going to be there for me whether I like it or not. I do not need to be confronted by them while at the theatre."

Victoria stepped in to soothe her friend's ruffled feathers. "Never mind about Mr. Shakespeare. No doubt the sixteenth century was rather grim. But my first theatre experience was perfectly lovely, and I thank you wholeheartedly for taking me. Now tell me, what do we have left to accomplish before your ball tomorrow? Is there anything I could be doing to help with the preparations?"

"Not tonight, silly," teased Alanna, allowing her attention to be diverted. "Nearly everything is in readiness. My mother's staff is terribly efficient. But no doubt the housekeeper would appreciate a couple pairs of extra hands on the morrow before we barricade ourselves in my room to get ready."

"You girls must make an effort to get a good sleep tonight and do not be in a hurry to get out of bed in the morning. You will be dancing all night and will have to remain in attendance until the last of the ladies has departed, so you want to be well rested so you do not begin to droop halfway through the night," the duchess advised.

Victoria bounced a little in her seat across from the duchess, bringing a fond smile to the lady's face. "You really are excited about this, are you not?"

"I cannot help it, your grace. Going about making calls with Alanna is all well and good, but to attend a ball during the Season at which half the ton will be in attendance is almost more than I can fathom," she replied with a wide smile which dimmed a trifle as she continued. "My mother used to tell me about her own Season when I was a little girl. It sounded so glamorous and exciting. Not at all like the life we had on our country estate. She would tell me that a lady's Season is not real life but a playtime before her real life begins. So I feel as though perhaps my real life will begin soon."

A look of concern flashed across the duchess' face as she wondered what to make of the girl's words.

"Oh my lady, please do not allow my whimsical words to cause you alarm. It is merely the silliness a mother says to her young daughter when she thinks she will be around forever to guide and direct her. My mother had every expectation of accompanying me on my journey through the playtime and on into the rest of life. It shall be perhaps a touch bittersweet tomorrow."

The Duchess of Wychwood leaned across the carriage in a rare display of affection and clasped Victoria's hand warmly. "I cannot take your mother's place, but please know I will be happy to accompany you and provide any guidance you might need."

Victoria tried valiantly to prevent her lips from wobbling as she smiled at the duchess' kind words. "Thank you, your grace. I am sure I will need some direction, to be sure."

Alanna chimed in at this, linking her arm with Victoria's affectionately. "You do not need a single word of direction, my dear. Your manners are perfectly lovely, you always maintain your composure, and you never say the wrong thing. If I did not like you quite so much, I would not want to have you for a friend, as you show up all my hoydenish ways."

These words brought laughter to everyone and the serious moment passed as they returned to discussing the theatrical production and the dinner party they had attended. As they were handed down from the carriage and began to climb the stairs, Victoria was surprised by a huge yawn she could not contain.

"You see, girls, you really should be in your beds getting your beauty sleep in preparation for the exertions tomorrow. Now get yourselves off to Alanna's room and tucked in as speedily as possible. I will not be leaving my rooms until at least noon, so please do not disturb me before then."

The duchess dismissed the girls with these haughty words but with a warm twinkle in her eye shining clearly for Victoria to see as she shook her hand in farewell.

Chapter Twenty-Four

Victoria was quiet as she and Alanna climbed the stairs to their room. Alanna eyed her friend perceptively, and asked in a quiet voice, "Does being with my mother make you miss your own?"

Victoria nodded a little dully before perking up and explaining. "Your mother is lovely. Not as lovely as mine was, of course," she said with a teasing smile, "but her motherliness at times reminds me of the lack in my life. My uncle's wife has never really even felt like my aunt, let alone taking a motherly role in my life."

Victoria paused for a moment but then quickly continued when she realized how self-pitying she might have sounded. "I do not mean to complain. I am quite well aware that my situation in life could have been ever so much worse. I have been well provided for, for the most part. I suppose it is quite natural to miss one's parents when they are no longer here, especially when they are taken from you when you are so young." She again paused before tilting her lips in a teasing smile. "You need not fear that I shall turn into a watering pot at the ball if your mother is kind to me. I shall keep myself quite contained."

"You always do—it never even crossed my mind to be concerned that you would not. Now hurry up and get into your night-rail, I want to giggle and gab a little longer before we drift off to sleep."

The two girls hastened to shed their finery with the help of the ever-attentive maids. Victoria absently marvelled over how delightful it was to have the ready assistance of servants. Dismissing the intrusive thought, she jumped onto the high bed and snuggled down into the warm, thick covers.

Alanna chattered about the handsome lords she had seen at the theatre and talked to at the dinner party, and slowly Victoria felt her heavy eyes drift closed.

Blinking herself awake, Victoria was confused to see bright sunshine flooding the room.

"Good morning, sleepyhead," Alanna greeted with a giggle.

"Morning?" Victoria croaked before giggling herself and sitting up in the comfortable bed. "I am so sorry, Alanna. I must have fallen asleep while you were talking about Lord Smythe—how terribly rude."

"Pay it no mind, my dear. You must have been very tired. But the day is now well along and I am becoming rather hungry. If you get up now we can go and break our fast together."

Victoria threw back the covers, dangled her legs over the side and looked about. "I must tell you, I am particularly famished myself."

Victoria was surprised by how fast the time flew despite how little they did that day. In her usual hectic days of caring for the children she was never surprised to feel as though she had blinked and the day was over, but she had always thought that if only she had nothing to do the minutes would not whizz by with such breakneck speed. Perhaps it was the excitement, she mused to herself as she watched the skilled hands of the maid tending to her hair. Or perhaps it is the dread, she pondered, that just like the Cendrillon she compared herself to, it would all disappear at the stroke of midnight.

"Why the deep sigh?" Alanna asked from the other side of the room. "You are not worrying your head over silly trifles again, are you?"

Victoria blushed at being caught out. "Perhaps a little."

"Well, I tell you to stop it at once," Alanna insisted in a pseudo-fierce voice. "You absolutely must enjoy yourself this evening."

"I have every intention of wringing every last drop of enjoyment there is to be had out of this evening, have no fear. I am certain that once we step foot into the ballroom there will be no place in my mind for worries."

"Now that is the correct attitude," beamed Alanna as she finished preening before the looking glass. She turned back to Victoria. "Now if you are ready, we should go and present ourselves to the duchess."

"Thank you so much, Sally. Your handiwork has turned this duckling into a swan," Victoria marvelled.

The maid blushed with pleasure but demurred. "You was never a duckling, m'lady. You jest wasn't having any need for such stylin' 'til now."

With a grin, Victoria followed Alanna from the room.

Several hours later, Victoria found herself standing on the sidelines of the dance floor for the first time that evening, momentarily separated from either Alanna or the duchess. Watching the dancers taking their turns she lost herself in thought as she remembered the duchess' words just before they began welcoming the guests.

"Victoria, my dear, I wonder if I might broach a rather delicate subject with you," the duchess had asked almost hesitantly.

"Of course, your grace. I would hope you do not stand on ceremony with me," Victoria had smiled.

"I wanted to warn you to guard your heart this evening. We are not hiding your identity in any way, so many will assume that, as the daughter of an earl, you might be a considerable heiress."

Victoria had made as if to protest but the duchess had cut her off.

"I understand you do not have the information as to the size of your inheritance so I have not felt in a position to put any word around about your situation. You may be a grand heiress or you may not. The fact is, some unsavoury characters will assume that you are, and may pursue you in the hopes of gaining control of whatever funds you may have. I merely wish to put the bug in your ear to be on your guard that not everyone who pursues you this evening will be doing so out of the purest motives."

Victoria had blinked blankly at the duchess for a moment, at a loss for words. She forced a light laugh. "Well, I am happy to hear you think some gentlemen will pursue me this evening, even if I have to question their motives. I would hate to be a complete wallflower at my first ball."

"I have absolutely no doubt that you will be the farthest thing from a wallflower," the duchess had replied kindly.

Victoria could feel the duchess' watchful eyes searching hers for her true reaction to her words. Victoria did not wish to reveal the hurt she was feeling, so with another light laugh she turned away with the words, "I do believe I hear your knocker, your grace. We had best join Alanna and help her with welcoming her guests."

The duchess had allowed her escape.

Victoria's melancholy thoughts were interrupted by an incredulous voice calling her name.

"Lady Victoria?" Lord Dalton asked.

"My lord," Victoria answered, dipping into a polite curtsy despite her inward wish to groan and run away.

"I must say, this is the very last place I would ever expect to see you."

"Why do you say that, my lord? I was in the company of Lady Alanna and the Duchess of Wychwood when we saw each other last night. It should not be such a surprise to see me present tonight." She added a charming smile in an effort not to appear confrontational.

The viscount ignored her statement. "Does the earl know where you are?"

Victoria raised her chin slightly. "I do not wish to be rude, my lord, but I do not see how it is any business of yours where I might spend my evenings."

"It may not be my business, but I am quite certain the earl would consider it to be his," Lord Dalton replied.

"I am no longer a schoolgirl, Lord Dalton, and I can make decisions for myself. My uncle knows I am spending a few days visiting my friends. I am a guest of the Duchess of Wychwood this evening, which is perfectly aboveboard."

"But I understood that the earl had forbidden you to have any contact with the Duke of Wychwood."

Victoria blushed with equal parts embarrassment and anger. "Do my aunt and uncle really discuss my personal affairs with you?" she demanded in a low voice.

Before he could reply, Bryghton, who had noticed the exchange, appeared at her side.

"Dalton, once again I find myself surprised to see you in my house."

The viscount fixed a cool glare upon the duke. "I was under the impression this is your mother's house."

"It is mine. She and my sister merely live here," the duke answered haughtily. "And Lady Victoria is their guest. I will not have her accosted by the likes of you."

"I too am a guest of your sister. Do you wish to see the invitation she sent me?" Dalton asked derisively.

Bryghton did not allow himself to be diverted. "That is neither here nor there. I will not allow you to make Lady Victoria uncomfortable. I would like you to leave."

Victoria, seeing that the situation was in danger of getting out of control, put her hand on Bryghton's arm. "Your grace, all is well. His lordship was merely asking after my relatives. Please pay it no mind."

Victoria blushed as the viscount looked pointedly at her hand resting on the duke's arm, but she merely lifted her chin in defiance of the rather sardonic look on his face. "Your grace, was this not to be our dance," she asked rather boldly of Bryghton.

Bryghton did not indicate by so much as the flicker of an eyelash that he had not, in fact, arranged for a cotillion with her, merely nodding curtly to the viscount and offering Victoria his bent elbow.

"I could have sworn you had promised me the next waltz, not a cotillion. I would rather that so much more," he stated in a low growl in her ear, his face remaining impassive as they neared the dance floor.

Victoria blushed with a combination of delight and embarrassment over her forwardness. She stumbled over an apology. "I—your grace, I am so very sorry. I wanted to get out of that awkward situation with the viscount and did not know any other way that would not be ill bred or cause a scene, which I would rather die than let happen at your sister's ball."

"I was merely jesting with you, ma petite. I pray you, do not trouble yourself over it. Although, I will reserve the right to claim that waltz you promised me a little later."

Victoria felt the colour return to her cheeks but this time it was with unadulterated pleasure. She was at a loss for words, which was just as well, as the dance took them away from one another for the time being. By the time they returned to each other she had herself well in hand once more, reminding herself that she was not to get any ideas in her head and to guard her heart as the duchess had admonished her. She knew the duke would not be interested in her imagined inheritance, but nonetheless she ought not to get inflated ideas as to his kindness to her. She pulled her thoughts sharply into order, realizing that even they were rambling. She fixed a sunny smile upon her face, hoping the duke would not wonder at her strangeness.

"Are you certain all is right with you?" he asked, looking concerned.

"Of course, what could possibly be wrong? Your sister has done a marvellous job of planning this ball. I must say I am remarkably impressed with how quickly she managed to pull it all together. I would have thought an entertainment of this size would take many weeks to arrange."

"She and my mother love to entertain, so they get a lot of practice," he said, smiling. "And since they now have a reputation for successful events, their invitations are given priority by their invited guests."

"That must be so lovely."

"I am certain you will make a marvellous hostess one day," the duke answered in an attempt to cheer her up, and as he said the words he knew them to be true.

"Why would you say that? I have no experience in anything resembling putting on an event such as this," she said with an expansive gesture to encompass the beautifully decorated ballroom, the teeming crowd of people, the delectable food, and the small orchestra tucked into the corner.

"You may not have planned a ball as yet, but I do know you are a highly organized person. And I firmly believe that anyone who can keep four or five youngsters in order can handle anything a ton party could possibly throw at them."

"But we met during a display of just how unsuccessful I can be at keeping the children in order," she reminded him with chagrin.

"I do not recall that in the least. As I remember it you had everything under control. You were keeping an eye on the girls even as Daniel was climbing you as though you were a tree. If Alfred and I had not happened along you would have been just fine, as you had told me."

Victoria allowed herself to glance up at him through her lashes and was startled by the degree of warmth shining in his gaze. She felt a flutter in her midsection that was not unpleasant. Her smile was tremulous as she returned his gaze.

As the last strains of the cotillion floated on the air, their moment of unity was interrupted by the duchess greeting them. "You two looked quite lovely paired up for the cotillion, but Victoria you must come along, I have a young gentleman I think you would particularly enjoy dancing with."

The duke shot his mother an inscrutable look and she smiled serenely back at him. Victoria could not help the small tinkle of laughter that escaped her lips. "The two of you could work for the government in matters of subterfuge. Neither of you ever reveal your thoughts by so much as a flicker of your eyes. I am undecided if I wish for this skill or not, but I must say it is a challenge to observe."

The duchess smiled warmly at Victoria. "That is quite all right, my dear. If you become a duchess I shall teach you everything I know."

This brought a slight blush to Victoria's cheeks and stole her last thought as she trailed along in the duchess' wake.

The rest of the ball flew by in a whirl of activity for Victoria as she was handed from partner to partner. There was a brief moment out of time while she danced the waltz with Bryghton and it felt to her as though time was standing still. They exchanged few words but Victoria felt a oneness with the duke she had never felt before and a sense of peace pervaded her heart. But then as he handed her off to her next dance partner she wondered absently if it had been all in her imagination.

As the dance floor began to thin, the wilting ladies and fading gentlemen took their leave of the duchess, her daughter, and Lady Victoria. Bryghton too had taken his leave some time earlier. Despite the thrills she had experienced on the dance floor in the duke's arms and the lovely time she had had dancing with other young gentlemen, her run-in with the viscount had removed some of the shine of Victoria's evening. She tried to push melancholy thoughts from her mind, but with the duchess' warning about some gentlemen's motives still ringing in her ears, coupled with worries over the problems she may face if the viscount tattled on her to her uncle, her mind was not resting easy.

Despite her troubled thoughts, Victoria pasted a cheery smile on her face for her friend as Alanna bounced towards her. "Was that not the best evening you have had in an age?" she asked with a wide grin.

Sidestepping the question, Victoria returned her friend's grin. "I would certainly call this a success. You are a lovely hostess. It looked as if everyone was having a grand time. And it would seem like you did too. Are you happy with how everything turned out?"

"Immensely," Alanna replied with a smug grin. "I expect there will be several gentlemen calling 'round to see my mama about asking for my hand. And yours too. I wonder if they will present themselves to the duchess or will they track down the earl. That is a conundrum we did not foresee. Since you are not being sponsored by the countess there will be some confusion." Alanna wrinkled her nose in slight distress.

"Do not trouble yourself on the matter. I am not convinced there will be any applicants for my hand, but if any gentlemen truly want to marry me they will be able to determine whom they should speak to. And I would hope they would ask for my thoughts on the matter as well."

Alanna's furrowed brow cleared and she was once again grinning happily. "I saw you taking a turn on the dance floor with the Earl of Compton. Was he not just the most divine dance partner? I hope you did not set your heart upon him because I have a mind to set my cap for him."

"He is all yours, my dear. I agree with you about his dance skills, but I cannot remember a single word we exchanged, so I do not think my heart was at all engaged by our encounter."

Alanna gazed at her friend with an arrested expression. "That is exactly the problem, is it not? I too want my heart to be engaged. That is why it has taken me three Seasons. I do not want to make a brilliant match. I want to find someone I can foresee enjoying time with for the rest of my life."

She let out a disconsolate sigh and Victoria gave her a quick, tight hug. "Never fear, he is out there and it will be all the more worth it for the wait. Never settle, my friend. You deserve to find a happily ever after."

Alanna smiled brilliantly at her friend and was about to pursue the conversation further when her mother returned to the ballroom. "What are you girls still doing in here? You should be seeking your beds. The sun will be rising shortly."

Victoria smiled. "I do believe our lovely lady here will be requiring some warm milk or perhaps something a bit stronger to help her nod off tonight. She appears far too excited about her successful party to be able to fall asleep any time soon."

The duchess returned her smile fondly. "You may be right, but I have a suspicion that as soon as she is out of her gown and into her nightclothes she will be singing a different tune. This type of excitement precedes a crash—mark my words, we will not see her rise before noon. What about you, young lady?" the duchess asked as she led the way up to the family's private quarters. "Are you not overexcited from the thrills of your first ball?"

"Not overmuch, your grace. I believe I danced quite enough to wear off the edge of the excitement and I shall sleep like a kitten until the morning is well advanced," Victoria replied as honestly as possible as she climbed the stairs and entered Alanna's room.

The duchess' prediction was accurate. Both girls fell into a deep sleep as soon as their heads hit their pillows. Just before she drifted off, Victoria had fleetingly wondered if her worries would keep her awake. As she blinked herself awake much later in the morning she was glad to see that her worries had left her alone for the night, but disappointed to see they were there waiting for her as soon as she opened her eyes.

With a sigh she rolled out of the comfort of the warm bed and readied herself to face the day. She would be returning to her own home that day and she really should make haste. The children, whom she was ashamed to realize she had barely given thought to, would no doubt be anxiously awaiting her return. Hopefully if she timed it right she would be able to avoid facing the earl until she had been well ensconced in her return home. It was actually fortuitous timing, Victoria consoled herself, because tonight was the evening the earl was hosting a dinner party of his own, so she and the children would not be expected to visit the countess' receiving room this afternoon.

After a hasty breakfast and a reluctant farewell from Alanna, Victoria made her way to her own street. Steeling her nerves, she grasped her small satchel firmly and climbed the stairs to the front door. The butler must have been watching because the door was thrown open before she reached the top.

"Welcome home, my lady," Maxwell intoned gravely. He paused for a moment as a footman stepped forward to take her bag. "The household has been so astir over his lordship's plans for this evening that I do not think your absence has been overly remarked upon, my lady. Although I dare say the children will be overjoyed to see you."

Victoria was relieved by this news, and not at all surprised that the wise old butler was aware she was keeping secrets. "Thank you Maxwell," she answered with sincere gratitude. "I had best get up there and see how they are faring."

The day passed in a blur of activity. While the children did not mind their new nursemaid, Victoria was most definitely their favourite and they kept her busy at every moment, wanting to play all their usual games. She had trouble getting them settled to any lessons that day and was nearly worn to a frazzle by the time she had them all tucked into their beds. Her late night of dancing the previous evening coupled with the activities of the day had her longing to curl up and sleep for two days at least, she thought as she grinned at herself in her small mirror and began taking the pins out of her hair.

Wistfully she recalled Gwendolyn's words from earlier.

"Your hair looks so pretty that way, Aunty. I've never seen it like that before."

"The friend I was visiting had a maid who was very good with styling hair and she was kind enough to show me a few things," Victoria had answered.

"Perhaps we need a maid like that," Gwendolyn replied gravely.

"I am certain you shall one day, my sweet. Or perhaps your mama will share her maid with you when you are old enough to put your hair up."

"That will be so much fun!"

"Yes it will," Victoria had agreed, thinking of how much she had enjoyed her time at Wychwood House.

Victoria shook her head. "Stop your wool-gathering and get yourself to bed," she admonished her reflection just as there was a sound at her door.

A sigh of disappointment escaped her lips as she approached the door, thinking it must be one of the children having trouble falling asleep.

Victoria was surprised to see Mrs. Marks on the other side of the door when she answered the quiet knock.

"I'm sorry to be disturbing you, my lady, but you really must hurry. There's something you need to hear," the aging housekeeper said in quiet but urgent tones.

"What is it, Mrs. Marks? I was just preparing for bed and am really quite tired, can this not wait until tomorrow?"

"No, m'lady, it can't wait, you must come now. Hurry!"

Victoria had not yet changed into her night-rail but her hair was half taken down, so she simply tied it back with a ribbon and hurried after the housekeeper who was walking briskly towards the servants' staircase.

"I apologize for bringing you this way, m'lady, but it is for the best, you'll see in a few minutes," was all Mrs. Marks had to say until they reached the bottom of the stairs. "You had best be as quiet as possible," she admonished as she lead the way.

Victoria's astonishment reached new levels as the housekeeper opened the door to the closet next to her office and pulled Victoria in after her. There was a small candle burning, shielded in such a way that light did not show under the door but they could see a little bit in the cramped space. She made to protest the housekeeper's strange behaviour when she heard her uncle's raised voice saying her name. Victoria gazed at Mrs. Marks with wide, worried eyes, her mouth open on a silent gasp as she listened to what the earl had to say.

"What am I going to do about Wychwood's prying? Ever since his flat of a brother accused me of being a sharp he has been digging into every aspect of my life that he can gain access to. Now he's sniffing around my bird-witted niece, you tell me."

"I would hardly call Lady Victoria bird-witted, my lord," replied a vaguely familiar voice Victoria could not quite place.

"That is neither here nor there," replied the earl angrily. "The issue is that the demmed duke is going to make me real trouble if I do not find a way to either get rid of him or silence him."

Victoria had to clamp a hand over her mouth to prevent a gasp of horror over the earl's thinly veiled threats.

The calmer voice in the next room endeavoured to soothe. "What is the problem if he wants to waste his time digging into your business? I trust there is naught you need to worry overmuch about. Surely it is no doubt irksome having his men lurking about, but he will eventually realize it is all fustian nonsense and he will cease his harassment."

There was a short silence. Victoria and Mrs. Marks strained to listen. The unidentified voice continued with a much-altered tone. "It is all nonsense, is it not, my lord? Surely there is no truth to his claims that you have been fleecing innocents, including your own niece."

Victoria could barely recognize her uncle's voice, as his tone was a strange blend of belligerence and whining. "I was nearly on the rocks and the demmed hussy is overflowing with funds. She has no need for all that money and she'll never even know about it. Besides, my brother never should have left his affairs the way that he did. It isn't right that she got everything and I got nothing."

"I would hardly call the earldom nothing," the visitor answered drily. "With good management you could have done very well with the properties you received."

"Did you expect me to work like a commoner?" Pickering demanded, his horror clearly evident.

"Employing some economy and carefully overseeing one's steward is hardly turning oneself into a labourer," came the reasonable argument. "But that is hardly the point here, is it. What are you going to do about the duke's interference? Can you put the blunt back into her ladyship's accounts? Surely, as her guardian, you are expected to dip into her funds for legitimate reasons such as the maintenance of her many properties and whatever myriad expenses young ladies incur."

"I haven't a sixpence of my own to scratch with at the moment," the earl admitted with terrible reluctance. "We must find some other way to silence him, and keep him away from the girl."

There was the scrape of a chair as the guest evidently rose and the voice drew nearer. "There is no 'we' in this my lord. I cannot stomach the thought of you robbing your niece and I will not be a party to it. My involvement was solely on the grounds that I believed Wychwood was telling Banbury stories. You are on your own with this."

"But we are family, Dalton. It is your duty to stand behind me."

"Lady Victoria is your family, too. Are you standing behind her?"

There was stunned silence in the broom closet as Victoria realized the voice was none other than Lady Bartley's nephew, the viscount, Anthony Dalton. She did not trust the man, but was gratified that he had at least stood up for her. Mrs. Marks and Victoria both held their breath while there was the tread of heavy steps in the hall outside their door as the viscount made to leave and the earl hurried after him. The women could no longer hear their conversation but Victoria had heard quite enough as it was. They waited in silence for some time until they were quite sure the earl was not returning to his library.

Victoria gazed at the housekeeper in dismay. "Thank you for making sure I heard this, although it was highly questionable behaviour, and I am uncertain what to do with this information."

"My lady, there is nothing questionable about making sure you are informed. I know you have been worrying yourself about your circumstances and your future of late. I had my suspicions about his lordship but I did not realize the extent of his perfidy. When I overheard them talking I just knew you had to hear it too."

Squeezing the faithful servant's hand gratefully, Victoria's smile was sad. "It is a relief to know my parents provided well for me, but I am left feeling more alone than ever over my uncle's betrayal. I pray you, Mrs. Marks, please do not mention what we have heard to anyone. I will have to ponder over this and figure out what to do."

The housekeeper reacted with horror. "Of course I would never breathe a word about your private business. You can rely on me."

"I know I can, forgive me, my mind is all a muddle over this."

"That's all right, dearie. Now you just wait a minute while I make sure the way is clear and then you get yourself off to your bed. You will need your rest in order to have your wits about you."

Victoria crept back to her room and climbed into bed, but it was a long while before she was able to find slumber that night.

Chapter Twenty-Five

The young servant could not quite meet Victoria's eye as she stepped over the threshold of the nursery when the footman came to speak to her. Victoria felt her stomach turn over as her nerves tightened. She had always been very comfortable with the servants in this house; it was not a good sign if one would not make eye contact.

"Good morning, Joseph. What can I do for you?"

"Good morning, my lady. I am sorry to disturb the children's studies, but his lordship is waiting to speak with you in his library."

Victoria felt a wave of nausea and briefly saw spots before her eyes. Taking a deep, fortifying breath she smiled a little wanly at the footman and answered, "I did not know we had an appointment."

"I don't think it is an arranged meeting, my lady. It seems quite urgent, though, so you had best make haste." The young servant blushed hotly for overstepping the bounds, but it was obvious he was more nervous about angering the earl than offending the governess.

"I will just take a moment to check my appearance, as the children and I have been playing this morning."

"If you think that's best, m'lady," Joseph replied with uncertainty.

"I do," Victoria answered firmly. She was feeling decidedly unprepared to face her uncle after what she had overheard the night prior. It felt as though it had just been a bad dream.

When she reached her room she took a moment to comb her hair and pinch her cheeks in an effort to restore some colour. She smiled bracingly at her reflection, hoping to banish the sense of dread that seemed to permeate her. Deciding it was pointless to prolong the inevitable, Victoria placed a brave smile upon her lips and forced her reluctant limbs to carry her from the room.

She descended to the foyer, and allowed the butler to escort her to her uncle's library and announce her despite the silliness of the formality considering he was expecting her.

"Come in, Victoria, come in," the earl welcomed her in an uncharacteristically warm voice. "Did you enjoy your stay with your friends?"

"I did, thank you for asking," Victoria replied politely, her brow knit with questions.

"You look like a curious little cat right now," Lord Bartley commented.

Victoria knew he was trying for a teasing tone but it came off as snide to her ears. She smiled politely. "Joseph mentioned you wished to see me."

"Well, my dear, it has come to my attention that you have disregarded my request that you avoid all contact with the Duke of Wychwood. I understand you were at a ball at his mother's house the night before last." He paused for her reaction but she maintained her silence, waiting to see what else he had to say. "I did not know you had undertaken a Season for yourself and I am unsure how you came to be at such an event, but do you not recall my telling you that neither you nor the children were to be in the company of the duke?"

"I do recall that conversation."

"And yet evidently you felt comfortable to dance with him?" The earl was clearly trying to contain his anger but was doing a poor job of it.

"I obeyed your edict about the children's association with the duke, but I felt that as an adult I am in a position to choose my friends for myself," Victoria answered as calmly as possible.

"Do you really think the Duke of Wychwood cares about being friends with you?" her uncle almost sneered before he regained his composure. "My dear niece, I am merely trying to protect you. What I did not tell you originally is that the duke has a vendetta against me.

He is determined to bring me down, and I am afraid that he has decided that he can get to me through you. That is the only reason he is pursuing any sort of friendship with you."

Her heart seized for a moment, on both these awful words and the realization of how shallow her uncle's feelings were towards her. All she had ever wanted was to feel as though she belonged, but the coldness with which he was treating her made her see that she would never truly belong here in this household.

Victoria gazed at her uncle coolly for a moment. "Are you saying that you do not think I am worthy of being known by someone such as a duke?"

"Of course you are not. You are a green girl, just out of the schoolroom, who has been a governess for the past many months. What do you know about going about in Society?" he asked incredulously.

Her uncle's words stung, and brought to her mind the duchess' warning that most men would only be interested in her for her dowry. But what of the duke? He may not have been after her money, but if it was true that the duke had a vendetta against her uncle, perhaps his attentions to her were not innocent. She quaked inwardly at the thought that it seemed no one was to be trusted.

With a small sigh, Victoria rose gracefully to her feet and strode for the door, fighting the tears that threatened. "When my father entrusted me to your care I am quite certain he would have expected you to ensure I was prepared to enter Society. But I thank you for pointing out your opinion of me and of the duke. I need to be alone now. I am going for a walk." With those words she swept from the room, ignoring his demand that she return.

She barely paused to grab the wrap the footman hastily held out for her as she ran out the front door. Disregarding the tears trickling down her cheeks, Victoria stalked towards the parkette at the end of the street, and was relieved to find it empty.

Victoria sat down on a bench and made a concerted effort to sort out her tumultuous emotions. After a few moments she regained her feet and began to pace. She dashed the tears from her cheeks impatiently and resolved to shed no more.

The duchess says most gentlemen will pursue me for any money I may have, she thought, and now my uncle says the duke is only being my friend in some strange effort to seek revenge on him. And my own uncle seems to care nothing for me, only wanting whatever monies my father left for me in his care. Will no one ever want me for just me?

She stopped pacing to stare off into the middle distance. I refuse to believe that Alanna's friendship was merely feigned. Surely I am not such a poor judge of character as that. But what my uncle said is true. I am just a green girl. What could I possibly know about the ways of Society? What could I have to offer anyone in friendship? It may have seemed as though Wychwood was my friend, but perhaps it really was all just a ruse to get something he wanted.

She continued her perambulations around the small green space but they were growing less intense as she reasoned. Of course, the earl himself is not pure in his intentions towards me, so I mustn't be gullible about his words. Why should I believe that what he says is true? She felt her lower lip quiver, but she was proud of herself that she had stemmed the flow of her tears. "If I could somehow confirm if there is any truth to my uncle's words," she said aloud.

Her words trailed off as she glanced up in her pacing and muttering to see a familiar face passing by. Lord Lynster! Her eyes widening, she hastened towards the fence surrounding the park and waved her arm to catch his attention.

"Halloo, my lord," she called, blushing a little over her hoydenish action.

"Good day, Lady Victoria, it is a surprise to see you about today. I would think you would still be resting. Most ladies of the ton do not leave their bedrooms until midday," he said, grinning.

Victoria blinked, surprised at the reminder that so recently she had been one of those ladies. Already it seemed so long ago. She returned the baron's grin with a small smile, and addressed him in a soft but determined voice. "I would quite like to ask you a question, but it is on a rather delicate subject."

Alfred stepped closer to the fence so as to not be overheard, but he graciously replied, "You may ask me anything."

"Is the Duke of Wychwood in some sort of a feud with my uncle, the Earl of Pickering?" she asked baldly.

Alfred blushed hotly and he stammered out a reply. "Well, my lady, that is to say, a feud might be stating it rather harshly, but…" he trailed off as Victoria held up her hand.

"That is enough, my lord, I did not wish to make you uncomfortable. I was merely inquiring into something the earl told me this morning. I must return home. I wish you a good day." With that, Victoria turned on her heel and stalked back towards her house, her mind whirling steadily as she went. She made her way down the street towards what she could no longer refer to as home, and as she drew closer Victoria felt as though her hair was going to catch fire from just how angry she was becoming. It seemed to her that everyone she had encountered had some sort of ulterior motive. Even the children, she thought with despair. Once they had adjusted to the new nursery maid, they hadn't even missed her all that much. Victoria set her shoulders and lifted her chin. She was not going to allow anyone else to try to use her to their own advantage any more. It was time for her to take action and resolve her own affairs rather than simply waiting to see what would happen. Thus resolved, she climbed the stairs to the house.

As the door was opened to her she asked calmly, "Joseph, is the earl still at home?"

"Yes, my lady, he has not yet left the house. I believe he is still in his library."

"Thank you. I will announce myself," she replied as she strode with determined purpose down the hall.

"I have returned to discuss a few things with you, my lord," Victoria stated emphatically as she stepped into the room and closed the door firmly behind herself.

The earl looked up warily, rising to his feet and gesturing towards one of the chairs in front of his desk. "Please have a seat. I apologize if my words earlier injured you in some way."

"Thank you, my lord," she accepted before continuing firmly, "I have decided I cannot be a governess. I would like to see my father's will. I am quite certain he and my mother would have made arrangements for me to be provided for financially."

Lord Bartley's face paled at her words and he attempted to stammer out a reply. "Well, my dear niece, of course you do not need to be a governess. I thought you enjoyed spending time with the children."

"I adore your children, but I need to have a life of my own. If it seems my life is not to contain children of my own, I need to find some sort of purpose for myself. Perhaps I ought to join a convent. So I need to know where I stand financially in order to know what sort of dowry I have to offer."

"Join a convent?" the earl asked rather weakly, before he braced himself. "That might be a good idea. You could no doubt do much good amongst the sisters."

Victoria blinked with her surprise before staring coldly at her uncle, marvelling how delighted he seemed at the prospect of being rid of her. "So, my lord, could I please see my father's will?"

"It is not such an easy thing to produce, my dear. It is with the lawyers, I am sure."

"Well, then, could you please send a note round to summon them and the necessary papers?"

"Now that I think on it, perhaps they are filed on the estate. The solicitor there would probably have it, as your parents were not spending overmuch time in Town," evaded the earl.

Victoria rose elegantly to her feet. "That is just as well, as I wish to retire from London. I will travel to Pickering and see them for myself. Thank you for your time."

"But Victoria, you cannot go jaunting off about the country by yourself," he protested weakly.

"Why not? I am not fit for Society. No one will even notice me, I am certain."

"But it is not seemly."

"Are you forbidding it, my lord? I absolutely must have some resolution about my fate. I no longer wish to reside in the city. I need to make my plans."

The earl looked at his niece and saw his brother's determination shining in her eyes and he paled anew. "Very well, but please give me a couple of days to arrange my affairs and I will then accompany you."

Victoria looked her uncle squarely in the face. "I do not fully trust your promises, my lord, as you have regularly promised to provide a proper governess for the children and to my knowledge that has not yet happened. However, I will wait two days. I will be leaving for Pickering on the third day hence. If you are not ready, I will go alone." With those words she swept from the room, leaving her uncle to sink shakily to his seat.

Victoria, still full of fiery purpose, hurried to her room, wishing to begin her preparations for leaving. Her mind was full of conflicting thoughts. She reflected fondly on the good times she had spent with Alanna, but she wondered if she had been privy to the duke's plots. With determination she sat to compose a note.

My dear Lady Alanna,

I regret to inform you that I will not be coming 'round to visit you in the future. I have discovered I do not have a taste for London life and am repairing to our country estate to contemplate my future. I am thinking of joining a convent that is not far from my uncle's country seat.

Despite finding out about the duke's schemes, I do not hold you responsible for any role you may have played. I enjoyed every minute of my time spent with you, and I hope you will remember me as fondly as I will you.

Sincerely,

Victoria Bartley

Signing the letter with a flourish, Victoria reached to ring for a servant before reminding herself that they did not answer summonses from the governess' room. With a slight sigh she went back downstairs to ask the footman to see that her note be delivered.

Chapter Twenty-Six

A lanna stared at the words, stunned into silence momentarily before she turned on her heel and dashed up the stairs, calling for her maid.

"Hurry, Sally, I must dress. I need to find my brother."

"But, m'lady, you can't go knocking on his door, not at this hour anyhow," the maid protested.

"This is an emergency, Sally. You may accompany me if you would like in order to maintain the proprieties, but he is my brother, and there should be nothing questionable about my going to see him."

"But it's his bachelor establishment, m'lady," she again protested.

"Make haste, Sally. You are being ridiculously foolish," she declared with a huff. "We can even bring a footman. Now come along."

Despite the maid's protests, Alanna was ready in record time and the two made their way downstairs. "Walter, please summon a footman to accompany me. I must leave on an errand."

"Very well, my lady," the well-trained butler answered, despite seeing the worried look on the face of the lady's maid.

Within a few minutes the trio was on its way. The duke's townhouse was not terribly far away and with the pace Alanna set they arrived there rapidly. Sally was out of breath but the young footman was ready to follow Alanna's orders.

"Please go and inquire of the duke if he could spare me a moment on an urgent matter."

The footman disappeared through the door, leaving Alanna alone with her maid who was worriedly wringing her hands. "Oh, Sally, do not fret. I assure you I will not be ruined by visiting my brother." Thankfully the footman returned within moments.

"His lordship is at home and says you and your maid may come up."

Sally moaned warningly but dutifully followed her mistress as she entered the building.

"To what do I owe this strange honour," Bryghton asked in good spirits as his sister stepped through the door.

"Victoria has run off and says she plans to enter the convent," Alanna declared without preamble, waving her note in the air as punctuation.

The duke grabbed it from her hand to read her words for himself. His face darkened in anger. "What does she think I am scheming?" he asked. "What happened since the ball?"

"Nothing happened. She seemed rather subdued when we woke up the next day, but I thought it was just fatigue from our late night. Just before breakfast she decided that she needed to return home with haste, so after eating quickly, she set off to return to her own house. She mentioned something about the earl having a dinner party and she needed to keep the children occupied. I have not seen her since. Something must have happened when she got home, because nothing we discussed would lead to this. What sort of scheme could she suspect you of? And why would it send her to a convent?"

"The viscount must have tattled to the earl that he saw her at your ball," Bryghton answered dully.

"By why would that be such a terrible thing?" Alanna persisted.

"There is no love lost between the earl and me."

There was a knock at the door. The duke's butler opened it to reveal Alfred standing there. Sally began to wring her hands some more.

Alfred looked uncomfortable to see Alanna there. "I need to speak with you rather urgently, your grace," he said, with a significant look at Alanna.

"Does it have anything to do with Lady Victoria?" Alanna demanded.

The baron's look of discomfort increased exponentially but he refused to look at her. "I need to speak with you."

At this point Bryghton's mouth had turned to sawdust and he could barely croak out his words. "Go ahead, Alfred. If it is about Lady Victoria, please tell us both, as Alanna has already received word from her."

With a sheepish glance towards Alanna, Alfred launched into speech. "I was walking near her house, on my way to Gentleman Jack's, when she called out to me from that little park where she sometimes takes the children. She seemed rather upset but she wanted to ask me a question. She asked me if you and her uncle are involved in a feud. I must tell you, I did not know where to look, I was that flummoxed by her question. I started stammering out an answer of sorts but she stopped me as though she had already come to some sort of conclusion and left with barely a by your leave. I carried on to my appointment, relieved that she did not make me discuss the matter further. But as I was going a round in the ring I realized that perhaps she had it all wrong and I thought to myself that I ought to let you handle it, so I made my way here."

"Thank you, Alfred, you did just the right thing. I will look after it from here. Alanna, you should go home if you do not have other calls to make this afternoon. I will bring Victoria back to you. Alfred, I am sorry to cancel on our plans for the afternoon, but this is an important matter I must see to."

"Of course, Alcott, you need to sort this thing out."

"But how are you going to make it right, Bryghton?" Alanna cried. "She sounds quite determined to have nothing more to do with Society. I do not see how you will prevail upon her to return to stay with me."

"Trust me, little chick, I will do my very best to straighten this out for everyone," the duke answered as he called for his carriage to be brought around from the mews. "Will you be all right getting home on your own, or should I drop you off on my way?"

Sally began to urge her mistress to leave with her brother but Alanna put a stop to the woman's pleadings. "We will be just fine going home the way we came. I am well escorted. You go look after my friend."

Bryghton kissed his sister hastily on the cheek and dashed from the room. Alanna grinned at Alfred as he gazed at her blushingly.

"I, er…" he began hesitantly.

Alanna's grin widened but she took mercy on him. "Yes, you are quite correct, we should be on our way. Do you wish to walk with me or do you think I will be well enough cared for by my other two escorts?"

"I would be happy to see you home," the baron replied, returning her grin.

They exited the house and strolled along in silence for a few moments while Alanna's servants trailed behind.

"Do you think Bryghton will be able to straighten this out?"

Alfred was caught by the troubled look upon his companion's brow. "I am certain that he will. He can be quite formidable when he sets his mind to something. I have no doubt that he will have Victoria comfortably settled in your morning room before the sun sets."

Alanna dimpled at the baron's words, slipping her hand into the crook of his elbow. "Do you think he loves her, my lord?" she asked wistfully.

"Despite his usual ability to hide his feelings, it really is impossible for him to hide it, wouldn't you say?" Alfred was puzzled over Alanna's sigh. "Are you disappointed, my lady?"

"Not at all!" was her staunch reply. "I love my brother and I would be delighted to have Victoria as my sister. She would be a wonderful duchess and I am sure the two of them would have many beautiful babies." She paused a moment before continuing softly, "I will admit to you, but you must not bandy my words about, I am feeling somewhat envious at the moment."

Alfred searched Alanna's face, striving to discern her thoughts. Matching her soft tone, he probed, "What are you envious of, my lady? The beautiful babies they are to have?"

Alanna giggled. "That too," she admitted. "Do you not think it would be lovely to have several little Daniels running around underfoot?"

"I wholeheartedly agree." Alfred waited for her to continue.

"But I have been waiting for three Seasons!" she almost wailed. "And I am still unwed."

"What are you waiting for?" the baron asked quietly, holding his breath for her answer.

"Victoria said it best after my ball when I was asking her about one of the gentlemen she had danced with. She said her heart had not been engaged. That is exactly what I am looking for."

"How will you know when you find it?"

Alanna had been gazing steadily ahead during this exchange but she finally stopped and turned to face the baron. His breath caught as he took in her luminous face. She offered a helpless shrug, but the baron's thoughts must have been revealed on his face because her breath hitched slightly and she gazed at him with widening eyes.

Alfred felt his pulse speed to an almost unhealthy rhythm. He took his courage between both hands and plunged into speech. "The reason I ask is because I find that my heart is most definitely engaged by you and I have the sinking suspicion that my future will not be complete without you in it. Would you be willing to do me the honour of being my baroness and sharing your children with me?"

Alanna stared at her brother's best friend, torn between disbelief and elation. Her heart thundered in her ears as it suddenly became clear why she had been unable to settle on any one gentleman in her previous Seasons. What she had been searching for had been right in front of her all along; she had just been too blinded by familiarity to see it.

Alanna gazed at Alfred, seeing all the precious moments she had shared with the baron over the years. She realized how very important the man before her had become to her. After a few moments she realized time had passed and the poor man was looking at her with the colour slowly draining from his face. He was beginning to fidget and looked as though he was about to do something horrible like retract his words in an effort to put them both at ease.

Alanna shook herself to her senses, remembered what his words had been, and burst out in delighted laughter. "I do believe the honour would be mine."

Much to Alanna's delight, the baron had forgotten that they were strolling along a public street in Mayfair because he whooped with joy, clasped her to his chest and twirled her around in a circle. Their mingled laughter was soon muffled as they sealed their agreement with a sweet kiss. Alanna would never be sure how long it would have taken her new betrothed to realize how very public they were because they were quickly brought to task by Sally's very loud, very obvious coughing.

Blushing fiercely, Alanna grabbed the baron's hand and strode off towards home. "I do believe there will be many interesting conversations taking place at Wychwood House this day."

Chapter Twenty-Seven

Victoria was in her room, gathering her few things, when she heard the commotion at the front of the house.

"I wish to speak with Lady Victoria," she could hear what sounded like the duke demanding.

"She is not at home to visitors, your grace," the butler was insisting.

"Well, then, I want to speak with the earl," the duke answered imperiously.

Victoria eased her way down part of the stairs, making sure to remain out of sight of anyone in the foyer. A moment later the earl entered the scene.

"What is the meaning of this?" he demanded of the duke.

"I understand you have told your niece of our disagreement and this has somehow given her a disgust of Society and the wish to leave Town. I would like an opportunity to try to dissuade her from doing so."

"What business is it of yours what my niece chooses to do with her time?" the earl blustered.

"I would like to make it my business," the duke answered, gazing at the earl coldly. "Could you please have her called so I can speak with her? It would seem she has come to the conclusion that I have been associating with her out of some scheme against you and I wish to disabuse her of that notion."

"Lady Victoria does not wish to be disturbed," the earl insisted.

Bryghton took a deep steadying breath before continuing to plead his case. "My lord, you and I have had our serious differences in the past. I am willing to overlook them if you will just allow me a few moments of your niece's time."

"There is nothing you need to say to her," the earl continued, belligerent.

"Actually, there are very important things I need to say to her," Bryghton insisted, holding onto his temper by a thread.

"Such as?" prompted the earl snidely.

"I would like to request that she consider becoming the next Duchess of Wychwood," the duke stated boldly, unaware of the gasp from above as he continued. "I do not need whatever wealth of hers you may have squandered, so you need have no fear of me. If you will allow me to see her and plead my case, I will call off my agents from digging into your questionable business dealings."

Victoria's heart had climbed into her throat. She couldn't quite believe her ears. Had the duke really said what she thought she had heard? She knew she ought not trust the man with her heart, but she suddenly realized it was too late for that. Victoria dashed down the stairs. "You do not need the earl's permission to speak with me, your grace. I would be happy to hear what you have to say."

Bryghton could feel the splash of heat across his face as he realized Victoria had overheard his words. As his gaze became ensnared with hers his heart swelled within his chest, as he realized she'd heard his declaration and wanted to hear him out. From that moment on, nothing the nefarious earl could say would deflate his joy.

The earl was near to apoplexy. "If you speak with this man you are no longer welcome in this house, young lady."

"That might be a difficult thing for you to insist upon, my lord, as I do believe this house belongs to the young lady. But that is perfectly fine, as my mother is waiting to make her welcome in her home. Come along, my lady," the duke said, offering his elbow to Victoria.

"I had just finished packing a small bag. If you would give me a moment, I would like to bring a few small paintings of my parents."

"Of course, you may take all the time you would like." The duke smiled fondly at her as she dashed up the stairs.

Turning back to the fuming earl, Bryghton's smile disappeared. "It would seem the lady has relieved me of the need to keep my earlier promise. I still do not care about her money, but if you bar her from this house or restrict her from visiting with your children, I can assure you that I will use all of my considerable power to ruin you. But since I plan to make her my duchess, we shall be family, and I see no need to have a ruckus. If you play nicely, so will I."

The earl remained struck mute and Victoria was returning down the stairs so Bryghton said no more. He took the satchel from her hand, gave her his elbow, and they exited the house together.

The two lapsed into a strangely peaceful, companionable silence as the duke drove her to his mother's house. He glanced over from time to time, surprised to see a pleasant smile upon her face as she gazed about her as though she was seeing her surroundings for the first time. As they pulled up before the duchess' house, though, she grasped his arm in some urgency.

"Are you quite certain the duchess is going to accept this arrangement?" she asked nervously.

Bryghton put his hand over hers where it lay on his arm. "Hush now, it will all be all right, I promise you. I am absolutely certain that she will welcome you eagerly. And my sister is probably at a window right now awaiting your arrival. It was she who told me of the misunderstanding."

Victoria was about to answer with a rather shamefaced look but he interrupted her before she could say anything. "Let us not discuss it right now, but rather wait until we can be comfortable in the morning room."

She did as he suggested and followed him meekly into the lovely large house that she had so recently exited. The duke's mother and sister were both waiting for them when the butler opened the door. Alanna rushed to clasp her friend in a warm embrace.

"I am so glad you are here. I was so worried when I got your note. It is so good that Bryghton was able to bring you here. Will you be able to stay for a while?"

Despite Victoria's efforts to remain impassive, her roiling emotions must have been displayed, for the duchess quickly hushed Alanna. "Do not trouble her with your nagging just now. Let us all adjourn to the morning room and have a cup of tea and we can sort it all out there."

The housekeeper had been waiting with the tea and it was wheeled in as soon as they were seated. Victoria sipped the familiar brew, grateful for the distraction. She was feeling much better prepared to face whatever questions everyone might have.

The duchess had been watching her son closely and after just a few sips of her tea she stood. "Alanna, my darling, I believe there is something I must show you in the ballroom. If you would be so kind as to accompany me, we can leave Alcott to entertain Victoria for a few minutes."

Alanna looked confused but rose and headed for the door. The duchess stopped before Victoria on her way out of the room and whispered in her ear. "Allow my son to say his piece, but do not feel obligated to go along with anything he might suggest. Whatever you decide to do, you may make your home with us as long as you would like."

It was exactly the right thing to say but it brought tears to Victoria's eyes, as the one thing she wanted most in life was to have a home and feel welcomed in it. She smiled waveringly as the other ladies left the room, leaving the door ajar.

Victoria looked at Bryghton nervously but he too seemed to be at a momentary loss for words. She took her courage in both hands and broached the awkward subject.

"Are you really in a feud with the earl?" she asked in a quiet voice but looking him bravely in the eyes.

"I was, but it had nothing to do with you. He is not the most honest businessman. My brother got caught in one of his elaborate schemes and lost a fair bit of money. We suspected that there was dishonesty involved and I have been looking into his business dealings trying to prove that he has defrauded others."

"Were you trying to use me to hurt him?"

"No. I must admit when I learned of your existence it did cross my mind to try to get information out of you, but as soon as I met you I knew you could not be used in such a way, as you are too pure to have been involved in anything nefarious."

"So then why did you seek me out, and why have you been so kind to me, dancing with me and escorting me places?" she asked. "The duchess warned me that men would be interested in my money and the earl said no one would be interested in me, as I am not up to snuff."

"Your uncle is a simpleton and would not know a lovely lady if she bopped him on the head," the duke declared with feeling, although keeping his language appropriate to his audience. "As for the duchess' words, it is a fact that there are many unscrupulous characters amongst the ton who would wish to marry an heiress, and if she were as lovely as you that would just be the icing on the cake. Perhaps my mother mistook your sweet nature as being overly persuadable and thought you would not be able to discern false motives. But I can tell you truthfully that I am not interested in your potential inheritance, nor do I consider you unacceptable socially. Quite to the contrary, I think you would make the perfect duchess."

Victoria's eyes shimmered with unshed tears of joy as Bryghton stood and pulled her to her feet. "I never thought I would feel this way about anyone, but I find you are quite necessary to my happiness. Please say you will be my wife."

One tear escaped her control as she nodded her agreement and he crushed her in his arms in a display of suppressed emotion. He held her gaze as his head descended towards hers. Her heart turned over with love and joy and her lips parted as her eyes closed. Their first, sweet kiss was followed quickly by deeper, longer ones which left Victoria feeling drugged with delight.

Several moments later, as they heard the duchess approaching, Victoria smiled happily at her betrothed. "I feel just like Cendrillon all over again."

"Well, just like her we are going to live happily ever after."

The End

Have you read Book One of
the Ladies of Mayfair series?

The Governess' Debut

**The governess must charm both the spoiled
child and the haughty earl.**

Orphaned and destitute, gently born Felicia Scott must find
a way to keep a roof over her head. No longer able to enter
the Marriage Mart, but also not of the servant class, the only
option is to find a position as governess.

After his spoiled, seven year old daughter has sent off three
governesses in the 18 months since her mother died, the
Earl of Standish doubts the young, inexperienced Miss Scott
could possible manage the position. Since he's desperate and
she comes so highly recommended, the earl agrees to give
her a chance. Much to everyone's amazement, the beautiful,
young governess succeeds where the others had failed. The
entire household benefits from the calm, including the jaded
earl.

How does he overcome his arrogance to see his governess'
true value?

Available on Amazon

The Duke Conspiracy

Anything is possible with a spying debutante, a duke, and a conspiracy.

Miss Rosamund Smythe is finding the Marriage Mart a dead bore. She'd much rather continue working for her father as a spy than endure another minute of the Season. But things take an interesting turn when she overhears details of a plot against her childhood friend and first love. A family feud drove them apart years ago, but he still holds a special place in her heart, and she won't let anyone hurt him—not now, not ever.

Alexander Milton, the new Duke of Wrentham, has always longed for a simple life. His tumultuous childhood taught him to appreciate peace and quiet above all else. Rose is the antithesis of everything he wants in a proper wife, but her beauty, intelligence, and loyalty call to him. And spending time with her to unravel the plot against him makes him wonder if the simple life he craves might be entirely overrated. Maybe he really does need a little adventure in his life.

But it soon becomes clear that a nefarious conspiracy is afoot—one that puts not only Alex's freedom in danger, but Rose's life. Can they overcome all that stands between them? Or will their second chance at love be snuffed out before it can even truly begin?

About the Author

Wendy May Andrews has been in love with the written word since she learned to read at the age of five. She has been writing for almost as long but it took her some time before she was willing to share her stories with anyone other than her mother.

Wendy can be found with her nose in a book in a cozy corner of downtown Toronto. She is happily married to her own real-life hero, who is also her best friend and favourite travel companion. Being a firm believer that every life experience contributes to the writing process, Wendy is off planning her next trip.

She loves to hear from her readers and can be found at her website, on twitter, Instagram or Facebook.

Website & Blog: http://wendymayandrews.com

Twitter: https://twitter.com/WendyMayAndrews

Facebook: https://www.facebook.com/WendyMayAndrews

Instagram: https://www.instagram.com/WendyMayAndrews

Made in the USA
Coppell, TX
27 January 2022

72433343R00166